# DOROTHY KOOMSON

# EVERY SMILE YOU FAKE

REVIEW

First published in 2024 by Headline Review
An imprint of HEADLINE PUBLISHING GROUP

First published in paperback in 2024 by Headline Review
An imprint of HEADLINE PUBLISHING GROUP

2

Cataloguing in Publication Data is available from the British Library

ISBN 978 1 4722 9814 0

Typeset in Times LT Std 10.25/15pt by Jouve (UK), Milton Keynes

Printed and bound in Great Britain by Clays Ltd, Elcograf S.p.A.

MIX
Paper | Supporting
responsible forestry
FSC® C104740

Headline's policy is to use papers that are natural, renewable and recyclable
products and made from wood grown in well-managed forests and other
controlled sources. The logging and manufacturing processes are expected
to conform to the environmental regulations of the country of origin.

HEADLINE PUBLISHING GROUP
An Hachette UK Company
Carmelite House
50 Victoria Embankment
London EC4Y 0DZ

www.headline.co.uk
www.hachette.co.uk

For everyone who knows how to sometimes fake it to smile

# Prologue

*Please take care of my baby.*

*You're the only one I can trust with him.*

*His name is Arie.*

*I don't want to do this, but I have to.*

*So please don't try to find me.*

*You'll put him in danger.*

*I'll be in touch as soon as I can. X*

# Part 1

# Kez

## 16 May, Shoreham

'This isn't so much a question as an observation,' he says.

We're in Smithdowne Community Centre, a large community centre-cum-library space near Shoreham on the south coast, and this man stands among the 100-strong audience of book lovers, holding the microphone, as he prepares to hold forth.

Every time. Every. Single. Time. There is a someone – usually a man – who will stand up and say this very thing.

This evening began a couple of hours ago at eight p.m. The audience had settled down in their padded blue fold-down seats, and mic'd-up local Sussex crime fiction author Remi Hayford strode out onto the stage and sat down in the blue bucket chair at the centre of the three chairs, ready to talk about her latest book.

Next came the interviewer, Lucy Tumanow-West, an experienced journalist whose work had been in pretty much every national and local publication. She strode onto the stage and went for the furthest seat, next to Remi.

And then came me, radio mic black box in hand because I did not have pockets large enough for it, walking almost apologetically onto the stage to take my seat on the other side of Remi.

Lucy, the interviewer, had gone quickly through her housekeeping – in case of a fire, etc., etc. – and then had asked Remi to introduce herself and the newest book.

'*The Last Dancer At Brightfell Hall* is kind of a locked-room mystery set on a crumbling Sussex estate where the inhabitants hate themselves almost as much as they hate each other,' Remi had begun. 'Something happens that brings members of the wider family together at the estate and pretty soon they are all trying to bump each other off for profit, revenge and/or fun.' As Remi laid out more of the plot the audience lapped it up, hanging on her every word until everyone was rapt, on the edge of their seat, gagging to hear more. It was at this point Lucy turned to me and asked me to introduce myself.

After Remi had whipped everyone up, I knew what I said would barely register at first. But 'My name is Kez Lanyon,' I'd dutifully replied, speaking slightly to Lucy but mainly aiming my words at the audience. My voice came out as clear as Remi's and Lucy's but not as confident. They were used to doing this, I was not. 'I'm a psychotherapist and profiler,' I continued. 'I usually work with companies to give them insight into the dynamics of their staff relationships and how they can improve company culture across their organisation. I used to do a lot of private practice therapy work with individuals, couples and sometimes families, and I have occasionally helped the police as well as working in prisons and other institutions, but I mainly stick with profiling for companies and organisations nowadays.

'Profilers and psychologists like me often help writers when it comes to researching the criminal mind – although not all psychopaths and sociopaths are criminals, many of them become fully functioning members of government . . . I mean, society.' That had caused a few titters and had eased us into the conversation.

It'd been a pleasant evening and the audience seemed to enjoy themselves as Remi did most of the talking and I provided any additional information. And then Lucy had thrown the floor open for questions.

So far I have done seven events with Remi, and I've found that most people are nice, fascinated and have genuine curiosity when they ask a question. But there is always one. Always one that has 'an observation more than a question'.

And tonight it is this man.

This man who holds the microphone in his left hand like it is a chicken he is trying to choke, while his right hand is up and ready to gesticulate his verbalised 'observation'.

I can feel Remi cringe and then internally sigh beside me. Because every time someone has not so much a question but an observation, *every* time someone starts to speak in that way, she knows it's going to go something like this: 'I'm sure your story is very nice and all, but you have to admit it is a bit far-fetched even for fiction, because I'm not sure they'd let someone as unstable as your character be in charge of a serial killer case. It's fiction, but to be taken seriously, you have to at least allow your story to fall within the bounds of reality, and, with all due respect, I'm not sure it does, does it?'

When none of us on the stage reacts, he continues: 'What, I suppose, I take issue with is this assertion that you can "profile" people based on nothing more than their briefly observed behaviour. You make a lot of how your story is based in reality and psychological profiling, how we can all work out other people's motivations and their "sins" just by talking to them for a few minutes, seconds you said, seconds, wasn't it?' He's pointing at me, talking to me now. 'I suppose my question is that . . . no, no, not question, observation . . . is that saying stuff like that can be dangerous. It can give people ideas. We all

7

know this is all a pseudo-science, at best, so I think you should be a little more careful about pushing this stuff.

'It's all well and good making up your nice little stories, and I expect you find some comfort in it, but you should be careful about parading what she says,' pointing at me again, 'as anything other than a fantasy that you write down in those books of yours.

'Don't get me wrong, don't get me wrong, this is all said with the greatest of respect, I couldn't do what you do, it would be too unbearably trivial, but just be careful, in case you and your hobby harm women, hold them back by giving them unrealistic ideas and expectations.'

Remi has written six books so far. Every one of them has been created while she juggles a full-time job and children and a wife. Writing books is not a hobby, it is her second job; the small amount of money she makes from it is what keeps her family afloat some years. And this man has dismissed all that. With his kindly delivered words, mendaciously dressed up in 'all due respect', he has trashed the importance of her work as well as the significance of her life.

We've had this type of 'observation' before, but not this bad.

I joined Remi on her *Last Dancer At Brightfell Hall* tour at the very last minute. Usually Remi works with a criminal psychologist and she was down to take part in these events with her but then said expert had broken her arm. It wasn't so much the arm-breaking that had caused the problem – it was the afterwards. *After* she'd fallen in the street, *after* she'd broken her arm, *after* she'd somehow managed to get seen and sorted in record time – she went home earlier than expected and discovered that her husband's idea of 'working from home' involved screwing their neighbour in their eldest child's bed.

*'How the hell he got away with it for so long, I'll never know,'* Remi

had said when she rang to manipulate me into stepping in. *'And ewww, for his child's bed when other beds are available.'*

Remi and I met years ago during the time I was heavily pregnant and would take my stepson, Moe, who was nine, to Hove Park so he could have a run around and play football. I'd seen Remi a few times, a friendly face who regularly said hello among the blur of trying to keep myself going, and then one day, when I just couldn't peel myself off the bench where I'd practically collapsed, she came over and started playing football with Moe. We were friends for life after that.

I truly valued our friendship, which was why I'd told her more than once when she'd asked for advice, that I wasn't going to give it to her. As far as I was concerned, our relationship was too precious to sully by letting our occupations collide. But the moment I'd answered the phone and she'd started to recount the tale of what had happened to her expert, I knew I'd end up doing it. Of course I would. How could I say no when she was so desperate?

'Do you understand what I'm telling you?' the man with the observation and not a question asks. 'There isn't anything necessarily bad in what you're doing, but it can be dangerous if you carry on unchecked.'

*'There's always one,'* Remi had explained to me on the train home from Birmingham after our first joint event, which had been sold out. *'There's always one person who wants to make you feel small and dismiss your work as trivial.'* I'd been to her book events before as a regular punter and I'd seen it happen, but it's a whole new ball game when you're the one sitting on the other side of the microphone. When it's you the person with the reasonable voice and the passive-aggressive hand gestures is trying to diminish.

This guy is a bit worse than the others, though. There is something deeper, more targeted and personal in his aggression. I look to the woman sitting beside him. Her gaze is trained fixedly on the parquet floor, her mouth is a set line, her shoulders are hunched as she tries to make herself small, invisible. This man is not just getting at Remi and me, he is trying to put his wife back in her place.

'Do you understand what I'm saying?' he repeats to the silence that has followed his tirade. People in the audience, readers who have shown up for a talk by a local-ish author and to hear the stories behind the books, are looking embarrassed for him. He doesn't realise that. He is so lacking in self-awareness that he thinks the silence is everyone being awed by his brilliance, being impressed with his very public take-down of two people who'd clearly got above themselves, while he simultaneously reminds his wife that anything that matters to her is pointless, meaningless.

He waits to see if any of us are going to argue with him, and the triumph on his face is almost too much to bear.

This book is personal to Remi. Into the framework of the story, the scaffolding of the plot, the structure of the characters, she has woven pieces of herself, elements of her life. Her story is there on the pages of this book; her life and heart are on display in a way that they haven't been before. It has taken her years to be able to open up like this, to show the hurt, to hint at the healing that is going on, to examine for herself how far she has come. That is why she needed an expert with her – she needed a shield. She needed someone for the audience to focus on so they would not see that this story of a dancer, damaged and hurt, who finally stands up to her past so she can create a better future, is all about what Remi has been through, what she has come through, what she is moving on from.

And this man, this 'person' has decided to trash that.

Remi is not going to respond. It's the best way, in these situations, to pretend it's not happening, to not allow yourself to be publicly dragged into the muck he's spreading, but her silence doesn't mean she isn't hurting.

'Well, erm, thank you for that,' states Ameena, one of the events managers who was in charge of funnelling the questions from the floor, moving to take back the microphone. She has a rictus smile on her face, her body is tense. I wonder how many times she's had to throw an apologetic look at a stage guest, while smiling at the person who has just insulted or, in this case, hurt said guest.

I stand, scooping up the black radio mic box as I come to my full height. At the same time, I feel rather than see Remi's smile freeze on her face. She knows what's coming and she's . . . well, she's a hair-breadth away from shouting to the man, 'Save yourself! You can still save yourself if you take it all back! Say sorry and save yourself!'

'I do understand what you're saying,' I tell him, my voice more confident now. 'What I think you're saying is that a little knowledge can be a dangerous thing. For example, with the minuscule amount of knowledge that I have, I can't completely work out if you were fourteen or fifteen when you first tried your sister's hair conditioner.'

Everyone falls silent and Ameena has frozen mid-reach for the microphone.

'I'm joking, I'm joking,' I say. 'It was, of course, your mother's really expensive, special conditioner that you used almost all of and it was your sister that you let take the blame for it.'

The man becomes rigid, petrified at what I've just said. I'm right, of course, and he has no idea how I know.

'I just can't work out how many times, exactly, your sister got slapped about it while you pretended to know nothing.'

The man's sallow, scooped-in cheeks start to colour, the red rising up from inside his collar.

'I'm guessing your wife knows it's you that uses her conditioner now?'

A few titters escape from the mouths of the mostly silent audience, and he whips his head around to glare at them to shut up because there is nothing funny about this.

He's right, there is nothing funny about this.

'I think your status as most favoured child in your family has created a sense of entitlement in you that has continued into adult life but has never been adopted by anyone outside of your households. I mean, your job is boring and *everyone* else seems to get the promotions before you, and yes, even those pesky women and brown people and, gasp, *brown women*.

'Your children have never excelled at anything, so you avoid all conversations about offspring achievements because you can't even bring yourself to be proud of them for trying or simply being who they are.

'You're the butt of your friends' jokes but can't understand why because you think you're the life and soul of the party. I'll give you a hint why – it's cos no one likes you. And I'm pretty sure no one will ever say you're the first to put your hand in your pocket to get a round in cos you always "mysteriously" disappear when it's your turn at the bar.

'You truly believe the world is out to get you, which is how you explain why you've never amounted to anything. The reality is, mate, the world doesn't even know you exist.

'But, I think the most important thing I've learnt about you here tonight is this: I would not be saying any of this to you if you'd just sat there and let your wife enjoy her books in peace. You came here tonight because your wife read Remi's latest book, loved it and was probably so excited to talk to her book group about it that she made the mistake of mentioning how much she loved it to you.

'How dare she, eh? How dare she decide on what she does and doesn't like. So you read it, and were *outraged* to find it was full of empowered women who don't need relationships or men to live their best life. And that's your worst nightmare, isn't it? The idea that women could survive without you. So when your wife booked to come hear Remi speak, you decided to come put that writer in her place so you could put your wife in her place. Job done, I suppose.'

His face is a rock-solid mask of horror. No one is meant to know *any* of that, let alone all of that about him. And if somehow someone does find that out about him, they're not supposed to say it out loud.

I pause . . .

One beat . . .

Two beats.

I smile the biggest smile; giggle the girliest of giggles.

'How did I do?' I say, softening my expression, opening my hands, raising my shoulders in cringing surrender. 'I mean, what I do is a pseudo-science right? I'm probably way off base, aren't I? Go on, you can tell me what I got wrong. I can take it.'

My smile becomes a wide grin, and the people in the room almost collectively let out their breaths. No one was sure what to make of what I was saying, if the words were jibes or truths, if they were moments of insight or seconds of me being a bitch. Now my smile, my laugh, my self-deprecating body language and words have put them at ease. 'I was way, way off base, I bet, yeah? Because no one could be like that, live like that, could they? At least, not in real life.'

*'You just couldn't leave it, could you?'* Remi will most likely say to me at some point. *'You just can't stop yourself reading someone for filth and then smiling afterwards. Leaving it is an option, you know.'*

*'Not for me it's not,'* I'll have to reply. *'It's really, really not.'*

13

# Brandee

**BrandeeH**

**@Brandee2ees | Joyn Inn Video | Status: All Joyn Inn |**

*\* February 2020 \**

Hi there! Thanks for dropping by my Joyn Inn page. Haha! I've just got why it's called Joyn Inn – cos they want people to join in! Honestly, I was today years old when I realised that's why private videos are called Joyn Only Me, public ones are called All Joyn Inn and ones for select people are called You Joyn Me. Oh wow! I have only just got that after being on this app for like ten years! Haha! Don't scroll away, I'm not completely ditzy, I promise.

All right, so. About me. I'm Brandee, two ees. You might already know my name and my face though cos my mum is kinda famous. I'm not going to link her in this cos we aren't in the best place right now.

Please don't you snitch link either. I'm sure she'll find this video soon enough.

She became famous for her parenting blog, that became a series of videos and posts on various social media sites. She's a parenting expert and has a spot on a couple of radio shows, a magazine column. She's got over a quarter of a million Joyners. Oh wow! Just got that, too.

But I'm twenty, I live in Brighton and I started this channel cos I need a voice. I need a way to set the record straight when The Mothership does her thing.

My favourite things in the world are spending time with my BF, reading, drawing and learning. Weird, I know, but also really true.

I feel we're going to get to know each other a lot better over the next while, so I'm not going to say too much now. Let me know in the comments who you are and what your interests are. And also what sort of things you'd like to see from me.

And please DON'T SNITCH LINK MY MOTHER.

Peace In.

# Kez

**16 May, Shoreham**

Remi hugs me at the glass front doors to the Smithdowne Community Centre, when her shiny silver taxi pulls up. The driver clicks on his meter as I fold my arms around my friend. The bookseller, Carolynn, from Brighton told us that she'd sold all the books and had to take people's names and addresses for back orders – a first, apparently – so Remi is happy.

While I was watching Remi sign books, chat and have her photo taken with her fans, a few people had come up to me saying, 'do me, do me'. I had dutifully 'done them' and none of them had been taxing. I hadn't gone anywhere near as deep as I did with the other man, but they walked away satisfied that they were 'doable' but also enough of an enigma, enough of an individual, that I didn't get everything right.

It's complicated to explain to people that it is their individuality that makes them profileable. If they were like everyone else, then I would have serious problems working out what made them tick. Like that man, I could tell from the way he had styled his salt-and-pepper hair that he had spent years going to hairdressers instead of barbers, and years trying to find the right products to make it glossy, shiny and manageable. He had been at that a long time, so likely started young. When he was younger, men spending so much time on their looks and hair was frowned upon unless it was to use Brylcreem or the like. His hair obsession had started when he was young and it was a secret, and his contempt for women would have allowed him to let someone else take the blame for using his mother's products.

His reaction to what I originally said about his sister had shown me that I was right about him, that I had been right about allowing someone to take the blame for him. This would have grown as he grew, this would have become more entrenched – his sense of entitlement, his refusal to accept responsibility, the idea that his children not excelling reflected badly on him, the fact that he was a thoroughly unpleasant person. It was all there because he wasn't like everyone else, because he was unique enough to stand up and try to tell off Remi and me.

Explaining to people that being unique makes them more profileable is difficult because it is counterintuitive and hard to make understandable. So I let people think that their uniqueness, their individuality makes them difficult to decipher, when it's actually the opposite.

'I'll see you soon,' Remi says, as we loosen from the hug.

'Yes, I'll see you soon. This was an interesting event to end on.'

'I can't stop thinking about that guy's face,' she says in a low voice. 'I thought he was going to rush the stage and pass out and spontaneously combust all at the same time.'

'Yeah, I think I might have gone a bit too far,' I reply. I do regret it when I – as Remi says, 'read people for filth then smile'. I don't like to hurt people, and I do sometimes wish I had the capacity to not respond when people did bad things.

'No, you didn't,' Remi reassures. 'Didn't go far enough as far as I'm concerned. He was *so* unpleasant. He came here with the sole intention of hurting me and now he's the walking wounded. No one asked him to come here. Talk about bringing it on yourself.'

The man and his wife had left the moment everyone stood up. I felt bad for his wife – she'd probably come to get her book signed, maybe have a chat with the author, and her husband had ruined that for her.

Remi hooks her face mask into place before she climbs into the back of her taxi heading home to Haywards Heath, and I take my keys out of my bag and start down the road to go to the back of the centre to the car park. I should have nipped out earlier to move my car to the front of the centre, but I had been so caught up in talking to people, that I'd forgotten. Now Ameena and her staff have gone so I can't go through the centre to the car park, I have to go on the road.

When I pulled up, it'd still been light and I hadn't realised quite how many streetlights weren't working in this area, nor how desolate it can feel around here. Shoreham is nice, and this area is nice, but at this time, it's taken on a menacing atmosphere. The sprinkles of broken glass and litter that have collected at the base of concrete bollards, and scrappy bits of grassy areas make me feel like I'm walking in a dystopian landscape that a series of movies will be made about that will become cult classics. And it'll start with a woman walking to her car late at night before she's surrounded by a group of ne'er-do-wells on bikes.

*It's a good thing you're not overdramatic or anything like that,* I tell myself as I turn the corner to the car park. I stop for a moment and my heart sinks as I'm reminded exactly where I parked.

*And it's a good thing I'm not parked right at the other end of this*

*empty car park so I have to walk all that way on my own, in the dark,
with my overdramatic sense of fear weighing me down,* I add.

This is the type of night that is more menacing than dark. It's the
type of night where bad things lurk, where stories are changed, lives
are ended. Rational or irrational, it's the type of night that makes me
frightened.

I've been in more than one life-threatening situation, I know that it
rarely starts like this, but my heart is already beating faster, my breath
is becoming shallow, my skin is clammy. I start to move across the car
park, wishing to be in my car as soon as humanly possible.

I sense it before I hear or see it – movement to the side of me, someone stepping out of the shadows, intentionally coming at me. Someone
in the night, coming to get me, to change this part of my story or even
end it.

'I want a word with you!' he hisses as I move back and sideways to
avoid a blow that I thought was coming.

The voice is familiar even behind the threat. It's him. The man I
humiliated earlier. And I'm guessing, he wants more than a word with
me. I suspect, he wants several words with me. And probably more
than words, now I see how his hands are clenched in fists.

I didn't notice before how large his hands are. Nor how generally
huge he is. When I was on the raised platform, he didn't seem so big. I
might have assessed him differently if I'd known, properly, how tall,
rangy, big-limbed, large-handed he truly is. He is *massive*-handed. He
could do a lot of damage with those hands.

I wouldn't have said anything different to him, I would have just
logged in my mind that he was a physical bully as well as a mental and
emotional one.

'You've got a lot to say in front of an audience, haven't you?' he snarls.

The terror suddenly grips like a vice, clenching my heart, my stomach, my chest. Danger radiates from him like a neon sign. He is going to do me real harm.

'Now it's just you and me, say it again. To. My. Face.'

His wife is two steps behind him, embarrassed and terrified at the same time. This isn't the first time she's been in this situation, I can tell. Had I known the true size of him, I would have realised that he would not slink away, tail between his legs, to rant at his wife, ban her from book club and throw out all of Remi's books. If I had known he was a physical bully as well, I would have expected him to wait for me in the car park.

'Say it to my face,' he threatens, coming even closer. 'If you think you're so clever, say it to my face. Right now.'

I've been trained to defuse a situation, I know what will stop this thing from escalating. How well-delivered words, suppliant body language, considered facial expressions, can take the heat out of the moment, can calm everything down so everyone walks away with their dignity intact and their bodies undamaged.

I know how.

I know I should.

But nah.

*Screw him.*

'Which part?' I say, my tone cool. You can only hear the wisps of the worry gripping me inside, the fear fighting with my defiance, if you know me. This man does not know me. He does not know that I can be pretty much petrified, but absolutely able to confront him in the space he has created.

He leans down into my face, his snarl taking over his whole face, pulling his lips back to show his teeth, narrowing his eyes, scrunching his nose and forehead. His wife steps forward because she knows he's going to hit me. She knows, and she's going to try to intervene. She's going to grab at him, shout at him to stop, she's going to scream at me to run. None of it will do any good. If he crosses that line and hits me, nothing will do any good.

Which is why I say, 'Seriously, which part would you like me to repeat? I said a lot of things, which part do you want me to say again?' I am throwing more fuel on the fire of his anger but I don't care.

Honestly, *screw this horrible man*.

I have my keys hooked between my forefinger and middle finger – a weapon ready to be used, I have sensible shoes on that will allow me to run to my car, my safe haven at the first opportunity. But, no matter how scared I am, I'm not running.

He tries to make himself seem physically bigger by lowering his head even closer to mine. The orangey light from the car park casts odd shadows on his face, and adds an extra layer of menace to the air.

I have been here before.

I have been in a place where I have had to choose: stand my ground or run and hide. Fight or flight.

And I chose this, I will always choose this.

I see hesitation flit across this man's eyebrows, the place where involuntary expressions take place. He's uncertain suddenly.

We're all profilers, we can all work out people with minimal information. It takes a while to be able to verbalise a person's personality within minutes of interacting or observing them. But we can all do it. We all *do* do it.

This man is profiling me as he tries to intimidate me and this is what he sees: a late-forties Black woman with shiny black twists smattered with threads of grey, and a spongey body and smallish stature and smart mouth.

He sees a woman whose dark eyes have stared into oblivion. He sees a woman who has stared death in the face and has walked away.

He sees a woman who is probably traumatised, who probably relives those moments over and over, but she is still here.

And most importantly, he sees that she is not backing down.

He doesn't know all this on a conscious level, he knows it by instinct, which is how most of us profile other people. He knows this because his usual tactic of using his size to loom over someone and intimidate them isn't working. Usually, he just balls up those fists, he moves in a threatening way and people capitulate. They shrink away. They concede ground. Rarely does he have to follow through.

With me, he realises, he will have to.

And he really doesn't want to do that. He's not so angry that he could get himself into trouble with the law on a Tuesday night in May.

The realisation makes him hesitate, his anger wavers, his features are suddenly showing his uncertainty.

'Let's never speak of this again,' I state and step back away from him before I walk away.

*Don't look back. Don't look back*, I tell myself as I stride on shaky legs towards my car. I am still trembling. Yes, I've been in dangerous, life-ending situations before, but that has only made me more scared. More aware of how close it's possible to come to not surviving.

*What if you'd read him wrong?* I admonish myself as my breathing in my ears ramps up to hurricane levels, and my heart canters in my chest. *What if he wasn't actually a coward who hides behind his size and loud voice? What if all your profiling and psychological training hadn't been enough, hadn't given you enough information, and you hadn't properly understood him? You could be lying in a pool of your own blood right now.*

22

Being catastrophically wrong has happened before.

I thought I had a profile down, sorted. I thought I had a handle on everything; knew everything about everything. Looking back, I can see it was arrogance, it was me thinking it was possible to know everything about everyone.

And someone died as a result of that.

Someone died because I got it all wrong.

My hands are quivering so much, my fear is so loud in my head, I can barely press the unlock button on my car keys. I try the handle and the door doesn't give. I didn't unlock my car; I've just locked it. That means . . . *Jeez*. That means I didn't even lock my car door before I went into the event. That means my car has been sat out here, open and ready for someone to come steal it. I am a ridiculous person.

Still berating myself in my head, I unlock the car door, throw my bag onto the floor of the front passenger seat and climb in.

Once sitting, I allow my forehead to fall onto the steering wheel. I need to pause for a moment. Recentre myself. Calibrate my body so I can safely drive back.

*There's someone else in the car.*

I can feel it.

I'm not alone in here.

I'm not sure when, but I've stopped checking the back seat before I climb in. I used to do that as standard and now not only have I stopped doing it in general, I didn't even think to do it when I realised my car wasn't locked.

I wait for something to happen, for the person to do something. But nothing. They don't make a move, don't try to grab me.

Without lifting my head, I grope for the door handle, carefully pop the door open, and then slide out.

23

From the safety of being outside of the car, I peer into its now illuminated interior. Then double-take.

Can't be.

*Can't be.*

I quickly open the back door to get a proper look.

Staring back at me is the face of a very young baby.

# Brandee

**BrandeeH**

**@Brandee2ees | Joyn Inn Video | Status: All Joyn Inn |**

*\* June 2020 \**

Hey, hey!! It's your laydee, Brandee. The one with the double ees.

A lot of you ask about this, so let's get into it: my mother. The Mothership. It's no secret that we have issues. Look at her Joyn Inn page and you can see how angry she gets about me.

She's still pee-eed off at me for moving out. She was so mad! It was like something out of a movie. Or *EastEnders*. My mum, if you've met her, you'll know she's always really respectable for the cameras. Nothing outta place, dressed up. But the day my BF's parents took me to get the rest of my stuff, oh she left orbit. Or-*bit*.

She came at his stepmum ready to rip her face off. And my BF's step-mum is all like, 'Go for it.' My dad had to hold my mother back. And my BF's dad straight up stepped in front of his wife to protect her. Not a second thought, he was there, in front of her like a superhero.

25

Don't get me wrong. My dad's a hero too, just in different ways. My BF's dad is one of the people working to clean up the planet. Anyone trying to save our future is pretty cap as far as I'm concerned.

Haven't really seen Mum properly since that day. I've spoken to her mainly on the phone or over Joyn Inn vid call. She starts off OK. All sweet and asking how I am, if I'm eating properly, how I'm getting on at college, what's my love life like.

Thing is, I know it's for her work. But I get sucked in, don't I? I start to think she might actually care. It's the same every time. Then she comes with the 'When you coming home, Brands?' 'We miss you, Brands.' When I don't answer cos I don't like saying 'never', or if I say I can't come now cos of lockdown she loses it.

Screaming, 'I was forty hours in labour with you! I lost my body and my career and sexuality because of you. I'll never be normal again. You owe me.'

I feel bad because she's my mum and she's done so much for me. She's not a bad person. She's just really focused on her work. Yeah, she's done some dodgy stuff, but she's not a bad person. Honestly she's not. Don't send her hate, please. I lived with her, and I don't hate her. She doesn't need it from randoms.

It'll make me feel worse than I already do about our relationship if you all start hating on her. Lots of guilt to work through. Lots.

Ahhh, not the vid I thought I'd be making. May set this to Only Me, will see.

Catch you soon. Peace In.

# Kez

## 16 May, Brighton

> *Please take care of my baby.*
> *You're the only one I can trust with him.*
> *His name is Arie.*
> *I don't want to do this, but I have to.*
> *So please don't try to find me.*
> *You'll put him in danger.*
> *I'll be in touch as soon as I can. x*

When I drive with a baby in the back of my car, I always have my hands tight on the steering wheel, my eyes fixed on the road ahead and my heart in my mouth. Driving with passengers always stresses me out, with children, my anxiety is next level. With an unknown baby, I am barely keeping it together.

I haven't needed to worry very much about driving with children or babies in the back because my children are now eleven and thirteen, and most of the driving with them is done by Jeb. I'd almost called Jeb to come and get me, but realised this wasn't the sort of thing I could tell him on the phone. Best thing would be to get home as soon as possible and tell him in person.

I'd looked around, of course, for the mother. For the person who left this precious being in the back of my car, but I couldn't see her. Even the scary man and his wife had gone, and there were only two other cars parked in that space. I'd gone up to each of them, looked inside, double-checked she wasn't hiding there. I couldn't quite believe that she would have just left her young, young baby in the back of my car and then run off? Surely she would have stuck around to make sure I found him. But no, I couldn't see her, see anyone who might know what was going on. So I had no choice but to head home, ramrod straight in the driver's seat, living through my second dose of adrenaline-fuelled fear in less than an hour.

I know who this little guy's mother is. Apart from him looking how I've always imagined she would look at his age, I would recognise the handwriting on the note anywhere. I've seen it enough over the years that I looked over her homework. And, it would explain what happened to my car keys – they disappeared into the ether after the last time she was in our house, and I'd had to start using the spare set that Jeb usually used. I'd been convinced they'd fallen down the crack in the floorboards or something, but no, she'd obviously magicked them away. For this?

The last time I saw her she *must* have been pregnant, but I had no clue. She'd asked to meet me – just me – in the park near my house. It was November, so we were both bundled up in big coats against the cold – hers was a big black puffa that made her look completely round and faintly ridiculous. Her scarf was wrapped right up her neck. Her woolly hat was jammed down onto her hair, which she'd worn in ten jumbo twists. Now I know why she looked like that – she was trying to hide her pregnancy weight gain from me.

A lot of things are making sense now – she'd seemed tense, on edge. During our time together, we'd talked about all sorts of things but whenever I tried to press her on anything or open up the discussion to go deeper, she pointedly changed the subject.

She'd come back to our house to use the toilet before she left to get the train home, which was probably when she swiped my car keys. In our house she hadn't taken her coat off. She'd also insisted on making her own way to the station, saying she needed the walk. It's all clear now. I'd talked to Jeb about it and he'd brushed it off as just her being her.

I don't know why she didn't tell me she was pregnant. She must have had her reasons, but it stings a little – actually a lot. She's like my child. Why wouldn't she tell me this thing? Why?

Obviously one of the first things I'll do when I get home is call her. But also as obviously, I doubt her phone will be switched on or that she'll answer if it is.

I'm trying not to think about that note but the dread and distress behind those simple words seep into my mind, chilling me all the way through. *You'll put him danger* can only mean that she is in danger.

*Oh Brandee,* I think as I approach our road, *what have you got yourself into?*

# Brandee

**BrandeeH**

**@Brandee2ees | Joyn Inn Video | Status: Joyn Only Me |**

*\* July 2020 \**

Brain dump. Will delete later.

Things are complicated with my Mothership because when she started all of this she had no support. None. She was like this middle-class white woman who'd married this working-class Black man and half her family stopped talking to her. The other half were like always making low-key racist remarks, which got her down.

When I was born, I'm convinced she thought I'd be one of those light-skinned babes with ringletty hair that would be able to pass or would be kind of accepted by the low-key racist family members. That was not me. I'm really dark. My hair is more afro than ringlet. And she couldn't deal.

Part of that is cos down here in Brighton, when I was born, the whole area was really pale. And she couldn't find anyone who was like her online, either.

She told me loads of times how she joined all those forums, the ones that are still around today that mothers find really supportive. And they were for white women with white babies. Occasionally you'd get a question from a Black mother, or white women with mixed children, but mostly they didn't care about anyone except women like them. No shade. No shade at all.

As Mum always says, you have enough to deal with when you have a baby to be worrying about someone else. She decided to try writing a blog. She thought, if I can get one person to respond, then I'll be OK. I'll have a lifeline of someone who'll be able to help me not feel so alone.

She got loads of people responding. People who had mixed kids like her, but also just the ones who didn't see themselves in the forums. And it kind of grew from there. She was like the mother who was scared but admitting it online. People loved that. They loved her.

And when people love you. When people are constantly telling you that you saved their lives, how are you going to ignore that? How are you going to go, no I won't keep posting things about my daughter?

Oh, I get my mother. I understand her really well.

I just kind of wish I wasn't the daughter she was always writing about.

Like I said, private brain dump. Probably delete later.

Peace In.

# Kez

## 16 May, Brighton

'Guess which ultra-sexy woman got a phone call offering her two hundred grand a year for a job today?' Jeb calls from the kitchen when I open the front door.

The thought of me potentially earning a fifth of a million pounds for a government job that is similar to the one I used to have that I didn't apply for and that I've been turning down for over a year has obviously made my husband forget that our children are meant to be asleep. As it is, this job that I was approached about and for which they keep increasing the salary in case I change my mind, is not important right now.

When I don't respond, not even to tell him to keep his voice down like I normally would, my husband pokes his head out of the kitchen door.

He blinks once, blinks twice. He comes into the corridor and puts his head to one side as he stares at me. Over my right shoulder I have hooked a Moschino designer change bag, over the other shoulder I have hooked a Louis Vuitton hold all that has baby clothes, shoes and toys, a blanket and some other things I didn't get a chance to look at properly. Both bags had been on the floor behind the passenger seat. In my hands I hold the car seat with baby Arie. I'd forgotten how much heavier the sturdier car seats could be. I remember spending hours and hours and hours on the internet searching for the safest car seats for Zoey and then for Jonah. It drove Jeb crazy, how obsessive I was with safety, but I had to do the best I could, buy the best we could, to keep our children safe. Eleven years ago this seat that Arie is in was one of the safest. And one of the heaviest.

'Are you holding a baby right now or am I hallucinating?' he asks.

'I am holding a baby,' I say. I sound impressively calm and not at all like I am freaking the hell out, which I am.

'Where did you get the baby, Kez?' he asks, not moving at all to help me. He sounds like I have taken leave of my senses and snatched the baby.

'Could you, like, come and help me?' I ask. 'This baby is small but the car seat is heavy.'

He doesn't move. 'Where did you get the baby, Kez?' he asks again, now openly suspicious.

'From the back seat of my car, Jeb,' I reply, matching his tone.

'The back seat of your car?'

'Yes, someone left him there. Or should I say, *Brandee* left him on the back seat of my car.'

'Brandee? You've seen her?' he asks. This new tone of caution in his voice makes me double-take.

'No,' I say, 'I have not seen her. She left the baby in the back seat of my car and did not stick around.' The muscles in my biceps and forearms are burning from holding this weight for so long.' I go to Jeb, hold out the car seat handle. He reluctantly, I realise, takes it. This is not like him, at all. I dump the bags onto the carpet of our hallway and notice for the ten thousandth time that the beige carpet is coming away from the walls, shrinking because it was badly installed. I hate this carpet with a passion and every time I see it, I'm reminded how much I hate it. That little spike of hatred causes me to sharpen my tone with Jeb, 'What's your problem, Quarshie?'

He frowns. 'What's my problem? You've just told me that you found a baby in the back seat of your car and instead of going to the police, you brought it home.'

'Him. I brought *him* home.'

'That's not normal, Kez.'

'I didn't say it was normal. But she – Brandee – left a note, asking me to look after him. So I brought him home.'

'Did you know she'd had a baby?' Jeb asks.

'No! If I did, I would have told you, wouldn't I?'

'And you didn't speak to her?'

'No. I told you. Can we get out of the corridor, please?'

The under-cupboard lights are on in the kitchen, as is the cooker-hood light, casting the whole place in a warm, orangey glow, with a backdrop of Luther Vandross playing from the Bose stereo. There are two glasses of wine on the table, one that Jeb has been sipping from, the other with condensation on the bowl which means he literally poured it the moment he heard my key in the door. That's the usual routine for when I am out late. I come back, we sit in the kitchen, we talk, we eventually go to bed.

Months ago, Jeb and I went through a rough patch. Niggles turned to irritations, turned to rows. So I suggested we sat down at the end of every day, had a drink – tea was as good as wine – and just had a chat. Not about the kids, the house, not anything other than us. And it worked. We stopped getting as cross with each other, we remembered why we were still together, we saw each other as people with hopes and dreams and things we wanted to talk about. We got the us back that we needed. We still do it, and this is how Jeb has set up the place, waiting for me.

'Keep an eye on him while I go wash my hands,' I tell Jeb.

I have a feeling that it's going to be a while before Jeb and I get to sit down with a glass of wine and have a 'just because' chat.

\*

Jeb is on the floor in the middle of the kitchen, making faces at Arie by the time I return. For such a young baby, he is remarkably quiet. Compliant. He hasn't made a sound and is now silently grinning at Jeb's act.

'He's a gorgeous little boy,' Jeb says.

'I know,' I say, coming to stand beside my husband so I can stare down at the baby too. He waves his hands around, like he's trying to catch motes of dust, or wipe away Jeb from his sight. 'How much wine have you had?'

'A few sips, why?'

'Because he's going to need something to sleep in. You'll have to go over to the twenty-four-hour supermarket at the Marina, see what you can get your hands on. We'll need nappies and other stuff. Bottle steriliser, nappy bags. Other stuff.'

Jeb stands, takes my elbow and gently pulls me a little away from Arie as though he's concerned the infant might possibly understand our conversation. 'So we're just keeping him?'

'Brandee asked me to look after him.'

'Via a note?'

'Yes, via a note.'

'This doesn't feel right,' he replies, finally voicing what his issue is.

'I know. She's in trouble—'

'Well, obviously she's in trouble if she's dumping her baby on us.'

'She's not dumping her baby on us. She's just asked me to look after him.' I take out the note from my coat pocket, hand it to him. 'I mean it when I say she is in trouble. And until I find out what it is, we have to do what she's asked.'

Jeb is older than me by four years and I've known him more than half my life, but haven't been with him that long. It's complicated, but I know him and I know this disquiet is significant. I watch him read the note, his expression closing in on itself.

'What do you think she means by danger?' he asks, folding the note up and handing it back to me.

'I don't know. And with Brandee, I know it could be real danger. It most likely is real danger.'

He says nothing for a while, then: 'Yes, it's most likely real danger. OK, look, I'll head over and get some stuff for him. I guess it can't hurt to be prepared. I told you we shouldn't have got rid of all that stuff. I told you we might need them one day when you eventually changed your mind about baby number three. I told you, didn't I tell you?' Jeb raises his hands. 'Now let me enjoy this moment of being so right I get to say *I told you so.*' He grins at me with the smile that launched a divorce and our current life together.

'Yeah, all right, enjoy this being the only time you'll ever be able to say "I told you so" to me, laughing boy,' I reply. I'm not sure why, but the atmosphere has shifted, Jeb has relaxed all of a sudden and is behaving how he normally does – being charming and pleasant and the man I fell in love with. I don't know what his stress and tension were about, why he reacted like that, but I park it in the back of my brain to examine at another time because there are other things to worry about.

'I'll see if Yasmina from across the road can come over and check

37

him over.' Yasmina is a doctor who is really rather good about people on our street calling on her in an emergency. She and Jeb have a history that makes them both cringe every time they see each other – a few years back, in the middle of the night, Yasmina decided to put her bins out, wearing only her dressing gown. Jeb was on his way back from a night out and had passed her house at the exact same moment two things happened – she bumped her wheelie bin onto the pavement and that bump caused her right breast to pop out of her dressing gown. Slightly drunk and still buzzing from his evening, Jeb had been shocked still by the breast now on display in his face. Yasmina was shocked still by the horror of flashing one of her neighbours and they stood there for long seconds, Jeb staring at her breast, Yasmina staring at Jeb staring at her breast. They'd both come to life at the exact same moment, and while Yasmina had slapped her hand over her exposed breast, Jeb had taken off at a full run, silently screaming until he was inside our house, at which point he covered his mouth with his hands and started screaming out loud until I came to see what had happened. Neither of them have been able to look the other in the eye ever since.

And Jeb always makes sure he is out or leaves when she comes over. 'I'd better get a move on then,' he says and races out of the room.

'It's just you and me, baby,' I say to the infant in the car seat, who has fallen asleep, his plump little lips pursed and his chubby fist beside his face as he makes his way through dreamland.

I pick up my phone and dial Brandee's number.

*'This phone is no longer in service. This phone is no longer in service. This phone is no longer in service. This phone is no longer in service,'* is the response.

Like a lot of things in my life, the thing with Brandee is complicated. And now, it looks as if it's deadly, too.

# Brandee

**BrandeeH**

**@Brandee2ees | Joyn Inn Video | Status: All Joyn Inn |**

*\* January 2021 \**

Hey, hey! It's your laydee, Brandee. That's right, the one with the two ees. Back to give you the content you've been waiting for.

A lot of you are asking me how I met my BF. And it's complicated.

Basically, when I was about ten, I used to go to the park with my mum. She loved the park because she could get lots of footage and she got recognised all the time. All the time. People would come up to chat to her like rah-rah and she would love it. That's how I got kiddie-snatched that time, but that's a story for another time.

So we're in the park and Mum is surrounded by all these mothers as usual and there's this boy and his mum. I didn't know at the time that she was his stepmum but he's playing on his own and his mum is looking done in cos she has a tiny baby in the pram. And I went up to him and asked him if he had a baby sister or baby brother. And he was like, oh, a baby sister. And then he says, 'My—'

39

Actually, let me set this to Joyn Only Me for now so I can come back and edit out the government names. My BF's stepmum is ultra-careful about stuff cos I think she used to work for the government so no names definitely allowed.

## BrandeeH

**@Brandee2ees | Joyn Inn Video | Status: Joyn Only Me |**

**_* January 2021 *_**

All right, so, I'm in the park and I see this kid who's only a little bit darker than me in the park and we get to talking. And I ask him if he has a baby sister or brother and he says, 'Mykez says she's my sister. But she cries all the time unless Mykez brings her to the park.'

I'm like, 'What's a Mykez?'

And he's like, 'She's my Kez.' And he points to his mother.

And I'm like, 'Is her name Mykez? Not Mum?' And then he explains that she's his stepmum and that her name is Kez and that he can't call her "Mum", he can't call her "my stepmum" and he can't just call her Kez cos of the disrespect, so he calls her My Kez and she's cool with that and so are his dad and his mum.

Why was I telling you this again?

Oh yeah, all the while I'm talking to him, My Kez is watching us like a hawk in case, you know, someone takes off with him. When you get to know her you kind of see that she's like dead overprotective. Anyway, so he tells me that he doesn't actually live in Brighton cos he lives with his mum in London and he just spends the holidays and some weekends with his dad. And My Kez.

I didn't meet his dad for ages. Anyways, for a long time I was thinking there was something unusual about My Kez, and I couldn't work it out. Just couldn't work it out. I didn't think she was dodgy, that she would do anything. And then I realised – she wasn't interested in Mum. The Mothership was such a celebrity back then, a minor one but still, she was really well known and everyone always wanted a piece of her. Especially with other mothers and parents of all flavours because she helped so many people feel not so alone. And My Kez, as I called her for years, just wasn't interested.

It was a bit weird. I have to say that. I was just used to everyone being interested in Mum. My Kez started bringing snacks for me when she came to the park and she'd always say to me, 'Go ask your mum if you're allowed to have this.'

And I was like, 'Mum won't care.'

And My Kez would go, 'Go ask her anyway.' Literally Mum didn't care. But I always had to ask.

Where was I? Oh, yeah, I get quite friendly with the little boy, Moe, and it's all cool, but I only ever see him at the park cos he lives in London. And then one day he's there, in my school. In my class. Just like that. He's moved to Brighton.

Urgh, this vid is already too long. I'll have to do another one to explain how he got there. But that's how we met.

Peace In.

# Kez

## 16 May, Brighton

'He looks like a very healthy little boy to me,' Yasmina says. She tickles his bare tummy and he happily squirms, kicking up his chubby legs. 'Very well cared for. And you say someone just gave him to you to look after?'

My neighbour is suspicious, as I would be. From his baby medical record book in the general bag Brandee had left, I'd discovered that Arie is three months old. Born on Valentine's Day.

'Yes. She had to deal with something so she asked if I could look after him. It was so last minute, I thought I'd better get you to check him over. Jeb has gone to get a cot and other things.'

At the mention of his name, red rises to Yasmina's face. It's instinctive and actually pretty wonderful to see. For the first time in an age, Yasmina is feeling something.

'How are you?' I ask her. At my question, she stops playing with Arie and picks up her bag, using the return of her instruments to hide her face.

'I am fine,' she says with a finality that would put most people off.

The past few years have been hard on her. She worked throughout the pandemic, going day after day to the hospital and coming home to collapse in between. To protect her family, they cordoned off part of

43

the house. She had a separate entrance and would use the downstairs shower and toilet, and cook on a plug-in hotplate. We neighbours would drop food over for her and the family, but it never felt like we were doing enough to help. I couldn't officially give her therapy, but I would keep texting her to ask how she was until she allowed me to come and sit in her garden with her, socially distanced, so I could talk at her. Unlike when she had socially distanced contact with her family, she didn't have to pretend to be fine with me. She could just sit and stare into space while I talked and talked at her. After a while, this sitting in the garden while I chatted about everything and nothing, progressed to her leaning forward and crying into her hands. She would cry and cry and I would talk and talk.

Eventually, when we were allowed to be with people again, I would sit in her house with her and she would cry. Or stare into space. Or tell me the names of the people she had seen. So many names, so many souls, so many moments of pain. She was so numb for so long that she could hear Jeb's name, see him, without even a flicker of reaction.

Slowly she stopped needing to talk, slowly she was able to be with her family again, slowly she started to seem better and less haunted. And now, she seems to be getting back to herself again. Slowly. We sometimes go to the seafront and walk so she can cry, but mostly, she doesn't need me any more. Mostly I think she is fine. And now that she's regularly cringing about Jeb, I think other parts of her are healing, too.

'Who did you say asked you to look after the baby, again?' she asks. Classic deflection.

'I didn't,' I reply.

She grins into her bag. 'Fair enough.'

When she's sure I am going to stop trying to find out if she's OK, she lifts her head from her bag. 'Ask me no questions, eh?' she says.

'Something like that,' I state.

'Well, he's a lovely little boy. His little book is up to date and he's had all his injections, his weight is on track and all his reflexes are there. Do call me if you have any problems, but he's absolutely perfect as far as I can see.'

'That's a relief.' I start to dress him, although he seems to take some enjoyment from fighting off the return to his Babygro. I'd forgotten they could be wriggly and uncooperative, even from a tiny age.

'I'll show myself out,' she says.

'I actually think I've forgotten how these work,' I say to her.

'Yeah, rather you than me. He's a beauty and I have never known a more chill baby, but I remember when we got a dog. It was like living with a newborn again – all the wee and the poo and the being up several times a night and the trying to find something they'll eat. Oh and did I mention the poo?'

I have wrestled his arms and a leg into the Babygro, and I am trying to do up the poppers when he lets out a loud, wet squelch that is accompanied by a smell that could only have been dragged up from the depths of hell. I immediately slap my hand over my nose and mouth. I'd forgotten it could smell like this. I whip my head around to look at my friend and neighbour.

Yasmina grimaces, the stench hitting her, too, as she laughs: 'Did I mention about the poo?'

\*

We have a cot, which is on my side of the bed near the window, but Arie is on the bed between Jeb and me. Since he returned from the shop, my husband has been fixated on the little boy. And could barely tear himself away from the infant to go and put up the cot.

'This is why I always wanted a third baby with you,' Jeb says. 'Moments like this when they're asleep and you just watch them all restful. And you think about what's going on in there and all the things they're going to grow up to do.'

'That bit is always the easy bit. It's everything else that goes with it that is hard.'

'Not just hard?' he whispers.

'Not just hard, more relentless. It never stops. And sometimes I couldn't catch up with myself. Are we purposefully avoiding talking about Brandee?'

'I'm still trying to convince myself that we're going to do this, we're going to take him on.'

'It's only temporary,' I say.

'You read her note, she doesn't want you to go looking for her.'

'Do you think Moe's the father?'

'No idea.'

'I don't want to call him and ask him if he's seen her if he's not the father. Did he say what their relationship was like last time you saw him?'

'Not really,' Jeb says distantly. 'He kind of said it was complicated. She did, too.'

'She hinted as much to me.'

'Anyway, don't change the subject. You do realise you can't go off looking for her, don't you?'

'I can't?'

'Well, no, not with this little guy,' he replies, still entranced by the child in front of him. Even in the dark of our bedroom, I can see the goofy look on his face. Earlier, he kept smiling and then making popping faces at him. And Arie was just as entranced by him. He kept giggling when Jeb was playing with him.

'A baby arrives in our lives and suddenly I'm anchored to the house? Is that what you're saying?'

'Give me a break, Kez. How are you going to play detective with a baby?'

'I won't have the baby all the time. I mean, what would you be doing?'

'Working. Sure, I'll take care of him, sure I'll be doing stuff with the little guy, but you'll be the main carer.'

'Sometimes I think the only reason you wanted us to have a third baby was so you'd have an excuse to keep me tied to this house, to keep me grounded and at home. If not barefoot and pregnant, at least here.'

Jeb rips his gaze away from the child between us to glare at me. He's hurt, truly hurt that I would say such a thing. 'And sometimes I think you forget that you've been threatened, harassed, stalked, kidnapped and . . . and . . . *assaulted*. More than once.'

That's the problem with having one of those relationships where you tell the other person everything. They know everything. And they can hold it up to show you any time they want, especially when they have a point to make.

'I am not trying to ground you,' he says. 'I just want you safe. Is there something wrong with that? Every day I fight my instincts to wrap you up in cotton wool and protect you. And yes, I know you think you don't need someone to take care of you. I KNOW you're strong, but I don't want you to be strong all the time. Strong, Black woman stuff is bullshit. You are vulnerable sometimes and the world can be dangerous for you. The world *is* dangerous for you because of what you do and how you do it. And I respect that. But we agreed, you wouldn't take unnecessary risks any more. Not when we have children. And now this little guy.

'You said that guy waited for you in the car park, tonight, he could have hurt you. We know Brandee is in trouble, but she doesn't want you to be involved. She wants you to look after her child.

'And I KNOW you're going to look for her no matter what she says, or what I try to say. But just . . . I just want you to think twice. To think about this guy, about Zoey and Jonah. No matter what you try to tell yourself you have to do, please, just remember there are so many of us who love you, who need you.'

By the time my husband has finished talking, I am not looking at him. I am not gazing at the baby in our bed. I am staring at the door. I am trying to balance what he is saying with the overriding thought in my head: *Brandee needs me too.*

# Brandee

**BrandeeH**

**@Brandee2ees | Joyn Inn Video | Status: Joyn Only Me |**

*\* March 2021 \**

Some of you asked how I ended up living with Moe, well, staying in their house. Start pouring the T, cos I'm gonna be dishing. (Set to private right now, but will edit out government names and post.)

Hey, hey, it's your beautee, Brandee with the two ees. Whatssup? What's happening? As you saw, I'm talking how I ended up living in my BF's house with his 'rentals, Jeb and My Kez. And the littlies, Zo-zo and Joman. Like I say, buckle up, it's quite a story.

Right so, My Kez said from time that I can stay over whenever I like. She said they have an open house for Moe's friends cos she never wants a teen to have nowhere to go. Not sure how Mr Q felt about that, but My Kez was all, we have to make sure Moe knows this is home and he can have any friends he wants over.

So it gets to one night, Moe and me are studying late. Yeah, shut up, we were actually studying. And he says I can crash on the floor. He actually said the bed cos he's a gent like that, but I wanted to sleep on the floor because I have to go out in the night. I don't sleep very well. And I need to go for a quick walk around the house sometimes to calm me down. Yeah, I have anxiety but I don't really talk about it.

So I'm downstairs in the kitchen in the middle of the night and My Kez comes down, and asks what's up. I ask her what's up with her and she says she can't sleep cos . . . I can't actually remember the reason why. Don't suppose it matters. So she asks me what I'm doing and 'Are you doom scrolling?' cos I'm in the dark with my phone in my hand. And I say, 'I'm watching my mother livestream her nervous breakdown about her daughter being out having sex.'

My Kez froze. She was going to fill the kettle but she halted right in the middle of her kitchen floor. Then she went, 'Are you serious?'

And I was like, 'Yeah. She does it all the time. She did one a while back worrying about me auctioning off my virginity. She gets a lot of support. A lot of people ask for more details so they can better advise her.'

'Give me that phone,' My Kez says and virtually throws her kettle aside.

Her face!! She gets the phone and I swear I thought she was going to find a way to climb into the phone to shut my mother up. You've got to understand, this is nothing new to me. My mum does it all the time. The reason why I started posting on my channel was because I needed a way to tell my side of my story.

My Kez turns the sound up just as my mum is going, 'I knew I should have talked to her about the best positions for a woman' and crying and My Kez looked like she was going to throw the phone across the room.

'This is not OK,' she says. 'I want you to know that this is not OK. This is so very, very far from being OK.'

I was like shrugging, cos, as I said, 'It's what she does.'

'That doesn't mean it's OK. I try not to judge, but she is a terrible mother for doing this. She's got your face all over the account and now she's saying stuff like this about you. It's wrong.'

'But I can't stop her, so I try not to get too upset about it. She said if she stops we'll lose our house and we'll never have money for nice things.'

Didn't even know My Kez could look angrier than she already did, but boy oh boy did she get angrier. 'She shouldn't be saying that to you. It's not true. And she shouldn't be lying like that.'

'She said all the money she makes she's putting into an account for me.'

'I'll bet she is,' My Kez says. 'Even if she is, this is not OK. I think I should talk to her.'

Now I couldn't let that happen. Can you imagine? My mum and My Kez? I think my mum has always been a bit someway because My

Kez has never actually cared about her. When we'd invite Moe to my parties, My Kez would wait outside in the car. I mean, my parties were always big because some company or other was paying for it, which obviously meant Mum had to get as many mums there as possible. And My Kez would drop Moe off, tell her that Moe wasn't allowed to be filmed or photographed and then go stay in the car. This made my mum really mad because she needed a bit of colour in her photos and film apart from me and Dad.

My mum kinda thinks My Kez looks down on her for what she does. But I think – well, I know cos she told me – that My Kez looks down on her because she uses me to make money and exposes me to predators.

She didn't tell me the predator bit until I was a lot older. She said there are predators everywhere on the net and we can't do anything about that, but constantly giving them fixes by posting pictures and videos of your children is a really bad thing to do. It gives them a constant hit of their drug and they want more and more until it turns into a real-life thing. Which I know all about since I got kidnapped.

I'll have to tell you about that another time.

But that night, I was all panicking about her speaking to my mum. And she saw that and said, 'I won't say anything,' and I was really relieved.

Then she said she was going to the loo and could I put the kettle on. So I did. And she was gone for ages and then when she came back, she had to reboil the kettle she was gone so long. I asked her where she'd been because my mum's livestream had suddenly ended. Just like that. She was mid crying about not talking to me properly about making the man feel powerful and how to put on a condom when my dad started knocking on the door. She paused the livestream and then came back and shut it off. No explanation or anything.

When I told My Kez that she kind of went, 'Oh, right.'

So I went, 'What did you do?'

And she goes, 'Someone rang your dad and told him that in a WhatsApp group a few people were going to report your mother for talking sux-u-ally about a child online.'

And I went, 'You did that?'

And she went, 'I said someone. Didn't you hear me?'

And I went . . . not a single word came out of my mouth cos what am I going to say to a legend like that?

I've done it again, haven't I? I haven't even got to the point of the story. But you needed to know this backstory though, cos it kind of shows you what my relationship was like with My Kez. She had my back. She always had my back.

Part two coming another time. I'm tired. Hungry.

Peace In.

# Part 2

Part 2

# Kez

## 16 May, Brighton

Once again, sleep is running away from me as fast as it can.

I am motionless, immobile in the bed, and I am trying to will slumber into my body. I am tired. Exhausted. But nothing. I'm tempted to call Moe, see if he's seen Brandee.

I'm also tempted to call Yasmina, ask her for a prescription of sleeping pills. I hate taking them, but I hate not sleeping more. When I don't sleep, I end up in the bathroom or the kitchen, jumping at shiny surfaces, scared of what and who I might see. Terrified it might actually be me looking back instead of the faces of my mistakes, bad choices and horrific decisions.

Jeb doesn't know this about me. He knows pretty much everything else, but he doesn't know I've relied on sleeping pills to get me through the toughest periods of my life. To knock me out so I won't dream, to make me sleep so I won't set my destination for oblivion and try to get there in the quickest way possible.

## June, 1998

'Ooops, sorry,' I said to the party-goers I bumped into as my friend-on-a-mission, Sylvie, dragged me through this house. 'Oops, sorry.'

Her mission was to find herself the man of her dreams, who apparently did exist and lived in Leeds. In Headingly, to be precise, and in this very house to be even more precise. Or maybe it was someone he knew who lived in this house? Or someone who knew someone who knew someone who lived in this house? To be honest, I had no idea. I had come up from London to visit her for the weekend, only to find her in full Sylvie mode – tartan pleated skirt, bright, slash-neck top, the most incredible heels, and beautiful black box braids with blue plaits at the front – going on and on about a party she'd secured us an invite to. Apparently it was the only party worth going to this millennium and 'we are going and don't you dare look like that, Kez, this is the only party anyone will be talking about for the next century and the most gorgeous man in the world will be there and don't you want him to be happy that he's found me let alone me be happy when I'm one of your best friends on Earth'.

She didn't want an honest answer so I'd kept my mouth shut.

*Six hours on a coach for this*, I thought, as she'd gone on and on about this guy that she'd met for all of seven minutes a few weeks ago. He was AMAZING and GORGEOUS and HER FUTURE and everything would fall into place at this party. She had, apparently, spent the last few weeks worming her way into the life of the GOR-GEOUS man's best friend. He'd invited her to this party and now this was her chance.

I didn't bother to ask her when she'd found out about the party, or to ask why she hadn't given me the option of postponing my visit for another weekend, because whilst I knew the answer would be *'cos you're the only person enough of a mug to come to a party where you'll know no one, even though you've been promised a quiet drink at the local pub followed by a pizza and chat in front of the telly'* I didn't want to hear it. Sure, she would have dressed it up differently but it would have meant the same thing and I'd hate myself for being so damn biddable.

I had wanted to talk to Sylvie about the job my masters tutor had been encouraging me to apply for. After college, where I'd met Sylvie, I had worked for a year to scrape together the money for a masters course in applied psychotherapy. I'd known all along that I would have to apply for jobs and save up to do another few courses to qualify as a psychotherapist for real. But my tutor had said she'd heard of this course that basically paid you a good wage while you trained and pretty much guaranteed you a job at the end of it if you passed their assessments. If you didn't, you still had certified qualifications that would help you get another job. My tutor also told me not to mention it to anyone else on our course because she didn't think any of them were right for it. I was torn because the only sticking point was that it was a job working for the government and I was not as OK with the idea of that as others might be. I had thought I could talk it out with Sylvie. But apparently not.

Apparently, my night was to be spent being dragged through the packed, many-roomed house apologising to people for bumping them as we went by.

'Oops, sorry,' I said as we went through the doorway to the second living room.

'Not a problem,' a man said as Sylvie dragged me past him. Except she couldn't drag me past him, this room was particularly full with bodies and she was forced to let go of my hand as she disappeared into the crowd. *How is it possible to get so many people in here?* I wondered as I stayed where I was. Sylvie would come back for me if she

59

couldn't find her man, or she wouldn't if she had found him. Either way, I was staying put.

'You've lost your friend,' the man I had just oopsed said.

'Yeah, she's on a mission,' I replied before I properly looked at him. Then I looked at him and thought . . . well, all thoughts flew out of my head. Never mind Sylvie's GORGEOUS man, this one in front of me was heart-stoppingly good-looking. Apart from anything, he was one of the few other Black in this room, so he – like me – stood out in the crowd. But beyond that, he was just delectable. Tasty.

*I have been single for too long*, I realised. *Way too long*.

'A mission to . . .?' he shouted above the loud music.

'Long story. Boring story,' I said, suddenly hot. Burning hot because the man was staring at me, talking to me. And no one who looked like him usually talked to me. I mean, I did all right, I had my fair share of action and boyfriends, but they were on my level of attractiveness. They were the usual good-looking that I could handle. This man with his smooth dark brown skin, sharp haircut, large brown eyes, broad nose and mouth that went on for ever was way out of my league.

'I have a feeling you would make it interesting,' he said.

'What?' I replied, even though I had heard him perfectly. I was asking him to repeat it because what he said, the way he said it, sounded like he was flirting with me. And I had to be sure.

'Found him! This way!' Sylvie was suddenly shouting in my ear as the man leant in to speak again. Talk about timing! She grabbed my hand, and then dragged me away, through towards the archway that led back round to the kitchen. 'You have to laugh at what I say, make me seem really clever and funny, all right?' she told me as we wove through the crowd, me 'oops, sorrying' my way behind her.

Sylvie didn't actually need me. The guy had been waiting for her to appear, and when she did, he'd practically flattened everyone in his path to get to her. His mate, who she had befriended, told me that he'd been talking about her but was too anxious to actually ask her out. This party had been his chance – if she showed up, he would make a move. Which was great for her . . . but not so much for me. His mate had no interest in talking to me after he expressed his relief and pleasure that the match had been made, so my options were stand and watch her sit on a sofa talking to this guy, or . . . go elsewhere at a party where I knew no one and felt completely out of place.

Across the room, I saw the guy I had been talking to. His large brown eyes were on me, seeming to have been waiting to get my attention. There was no way I was getting back across the room, which was now heaving with gyrating bodies, to speak to him. I would have to go round, through the archway, through the kitchen and work my way back down the corridor to get to him. It was a hassle, but a much better plan than standing here, I realised.

The music morphed from fast R&B to soft rock and the mood and movement of the room shifted. Time to move, Kez, time to get out of here. I looked up to where I was going to be headed and the man was gone. Departed. Great. My waiting to act had allowed him to get away. 'Oops, sorry,' I heard over the music as something splashed across my chest. I looked down and watched as the dark stain spread across my white T-shirt, the liquid dripping down and sticking my top to my breasts, the excess squelching inside my cleavage.

*Great,* I thought. *Just absolutely perfect.*

\*

Most of the doors to the bedrooms upstairs were locked. Smart move. If I had a house party, I would so make sure no one had access to my sleeping area either. The thought of finding out someone had had sex in my bedroom – which, let's face it, happened at most parties – would have me burning everything before arranging a blessing by the local priest. Completely irrational but also totally me.

At the end of the corridor there was a window and beside it was a turning that I don't think most people noticed because it sat flush to the wall. Seeing as I had nothing better to do, I went to investigate and found a door set a little back. When I turned the handle, the door opened outwards and a wave of relief rose through me. I just needed a sit-down – possibly a lie-down – while I worked out how I was going to get Sylvie to leave with me. I'd spotted Handsome Man a few times and he'd smiled at me, grinned actually, across the room. But we constantly had a sea of people separating us and I accepted that someone 'out there' was telling me to mind my business because this man was not for me.

I walked up the carpeted stairs after shutting the bottom door behind me and into the attic room. It was wonderfully spacious and beautifully decorated. It had its own en suite bathroom, there was a large-screen TV on the wall, comfortable-looking cushions on the bed and on the easy chair. A bank of wardrobes and storage. I guessed this was where the person who owned the house lived, and the rest of the people inhabited downstairs. This place was perfect. Perfect. I could take off my top, rinse it out and leave it to dry, while I watched telly. The only blight to my plan was I didn't bring myself any drinks. Or snacks. Both of which would see me very comfortable until I could legitimately drag Sylvie home.

After I used the en suite, I tried to work out what to do. Should I sneak down and get myself a drink? Or should I stop being such an antisocial so-and-so and go join the party, see if I couldn't get to speak to the handsome man after all?

Handsome Man . . . Television and relax?

Television and relax . . . Handsome Man?

Television and relax every time. I just needed a drink or two.

On the steps outside the room, sat Handsome Man, who stood up when I stepped out.

'Ah, so you discovered this place, too,' I said to him.

'I discovered it earlier. I'm staying in there. I'm visiting a friend and that's where I'm sleeping. I forgot to lock the door as I'd been instructed.'

'Oh no, sorry! Didn't realise. I thought . . . well, my friend is off with her guy – mission accomplished on that score – so I was trying to find somewhere to hide until I could leave.'

'It's not your fault, I'm the one who forgot to lock the door. And found it occupied when I came back to rectify my mistake.'

'You should have just come in and turfed me out.'

'I can't be going into a secluded room with a woman on her own – it would terrify her. You. It would terrify you.'

I hadn't met many men who would consider that sort of thing and I was speechless for a moment or two.

'Nice room, isn't it?' he said. 'Luxurious, cosy.'

'Yes. That was why I was going to get a drink, come back and watch some telly until I decided it was time to go.'

'You can still do that,' he said. 'Just lock the door while you're in there and then lock it when you leave. Come find me to give me the key.'

'I can't do that! You don't want me all over your bed.' I honestly didn't mean it like that, and cringed hard the moment after I said it.

'I suppose that would depend on how much you were wearing and what you were doing on my bed,' he said in such a lascivious way, my stomach dipped and lust lit up my body.

He looked at me, obviously waiting for something witty and bright, or sultry and sexy, to come out of my mouth.

But my flirty chat was thus depleted. I was not good at this stuff. I was actively terrible at it, actually. Most of my encounters and boyfriends had come from being asked out for a drink out of the blue or from being lunged at when I – and he – were mildly drunk. 'OK, well, I'll go get a drink, go find my friend, see if she's ready to leave yet,' I said, stepping to move around him. Our bodies brushed up against each other and I wasn't sure how I didn't just grab him and kiss his face off.

'I'll see you later,' he said, with a slight frown.

'Yes, yes you will,' I replied, cringing and mentally kicking myself at the same time as I descended the stairs. *So you couldn't even have said something like 'why don't you find out?'* I berated myself. *Not even, 'why, what would you like me to be wearing?' You don't deserve to have handsome men flirt with you, you really don't.*

I told myself off all the way into the kitchen, pushing through the bodies that were sweatier, clammier, more pungent than before to make it to the make shift bar. I stared at the array of drinks, sitting in spillages and bottle tops and unwrapped foil tops, and realised I did not want to drink a thing. I did not want to be at this party. I did not want to be in this city. I just wanted . . . I just wanted time to think. About the job. About where I wasn't going in life. About nothing and everything and all that lay in between. I did not want to be at a student party that had very few students but was crammed full of people who were – like me – just getting used to life after uni. Who had jobs and bills and responsibilities and places to be five days a week at allotted times.

I was going to leave. Go. I would find a taxi number, I would go back to Sylvie's house. She didn't need me any more. I doubt she'd notice I wasn't there. She hadn't noticed so far and it must have been at least two hours since we'd arrived. I turned to leave and the body behind me didn't move, didn't take part in that unspoken game party-goers played where the slightest touch would have them moving out of the way to let you pass.

'Couldn't find the drink you were looking for?' Handsome Man asked. I could hear him perfectly over the music and voices, the sing-ing and shrieking.

I shook my head, not sure what was going on. If it was coincidence he was here or if he was genuinely pursuing me.

He took me by the elbow, and moved me out of the way of the main throng heading for the bar and into a quieter corner. 'I couldn't help noticing you ran away when I tried flirting with you earlier,' he said, leaning in to my ear. 'You not interested or . . .' He pulled back to have a look at me while he waited for an answer.

'Or I'm not very good at that sort of stuff,' I replied.

'So if I did this . . .' He pushed his lips on mine, kissed me gently but passionately, then moved away, 'you wouldn't object?'

'I wouldn't object at all,' I replied. 'At all.'

*

In the attic room, the moment he had locked the door, I made the first move. I stood on tiptoes and kissed him. He ferociously kissed me back, almost as though he'd been holding back before, and now he was allowed to kiss me, he was going to devour me.

He pushed me against the wall beside the door, his body warm and almost familiar against mine. 'We can just watch TV, you know,' he murmured in between kisses. 'We can just sit and—' I cut him short with a longer kiss because he was being ridiculous. Maybe talking and television would happen after this bit, but I wasn't stopping now. Not when I had never been kissed like this before.

I reached for his flies, unbuttoning the top button as quickly as I could, then unzipping him to free his erection. In response, he reached up under my denim skirt and slipped his fingers inside my knickers. Slowly, teasingly, he ran his forefinger the length of me, pausing to push slightly next to my clitoris. 'You like that?' he asked when I moaned loudly. He ran his finger back and forth again, pausing in the exact same place, causing even more pleasure to escape from my lips. 'Oh you like that.'

I licked my hand and grabbed him tightly before moving my hand slowly and tantalisingly up and down his thick, long shaft. He groaned, then groaned even louder when I teased my thumb over the tip of him. 'You like that?' I whispered.

'What are you doing to me?' he forced out, sounding as though he was in rapture and pain at the same time. I gently swirled my thumb over the tip of him, my touch now so light I was barely making contact, but it increased the intensity and made him cry out, his body buckling violently. I kept going, making his body jerk until he couldn't take any more and snatched my hand away while he looked deep into my eyes. 'What are you doing to me?' he asked again, breathing hard. I returned his look, and for a moment it looked like we were going to rip each other apart.

'Take off your knickers,' he ordered fiercely. My heart thrilled at the forcefulness of his demand. When I didn't move, he lowered his voice. 'I said take them off. *Now.*'

Keeping eye contact, I did as I was told.

Looking at me as though he wanted to possess me, he grabbed my leg and roughly entered me. We both groaned in that moment we were properly together and we both paused, staring at each other as though we couldn't believe this was happening.

He pushed further into me, hard, and I whimpered at the pleasure-coated pain. It was so delicious, so delectable, I could almost taste the feel of him filling me in my mouth. He thrust deeper into me and I whimpered again. He pushed his hands against my bum so he could get closer, and I rocked my hips back and forth, bringing him deeper and deeper, watching his face contort with unchecked desire. 'What are you doing to me,' he groaned. 'What are you doing to me.' All the while our eyes were connected, our breath synchronised, our pleasure threatening to reach its limit and then finding more places to go.

'I'm coming,' he eventually panted, clinging to me. I grabbed his shoulders. 'I'm com—' His words caught in his throat as his body convulsed with his climax, moments later, bliss, like I'd never known it, flooded through me as I orgasmed too.

\*

'So, that was a thing,' I said to him. He sat beside me on the large swing at the end of the garden. After we'd disentangled ourselves, I went to the bathroom to clean myself up, we fixed our clothes and then he suggested we go out to get some air. At the bottom of the garden there was a two-person swing that didn't look too hazardous and we'd sat on it.

'It certainly was,' he replied. He'd lit a cigarette not long after we'd sat down and had been calmly smoking it while we swung in silence.

He offered the cigarette to me, silently asking if I fancied a drag or two.

I shook my head. 'I don't smoke,' I said.

'Neither do I,' he replied. 'Not really. I quit a few years back.'

'And yet . . .?'

'And yet, the method I used to quit tells you to keep one cigarette in a packet with you, to remind you that you've quit, that you've got to the end of another day without smoking. I'm not explaining it properly but I've had this cigarette with me for about three years. First time I've even been tempted to smoke.' He took a long drag on the item in question, but barely held it in before he released a white stream of smoke into the air away from me.

'And you're smoking now because?'

'Because I met this woman, this really cool woman and . . . well, here I am, swinging on a swing and smoking a smoke.'

'That bad, huh?' I replied, embarrassed that being with me had pushed him to restart a deadly habit.

'More like, that good,' he said. '*So* good.' He looked at me, and found me staring at him. I'd been tracing his profile with my eyes, marvelling at how most people in the world had the same combination of features, and yet, the way his genetics had put him together made him so incredibly attractive. *Handsome*. I realised with a start that I still didn't know his name. His face softened when he saw I was intently watching him, his mouth finding an affectionate smile. 'So, *so* good,' he added.

He leant forward and pressed his lips onto mine and I wanted that kiss to last for ever. 'Yeah, you really shouldn't smoke,' I said, when we pulled apart.

He grinned at me, the small action making me weak all over again. 'I'm quitting again after this one.'

'And are you going to ask for my number, call me?' I asked. I had to know. I wasn't very good at waiting for things to play out, or trying to decipher what things meant in these situations. I could read people quite well, but not in situations like this. Not when I desperately wanted to become involved with them. Then, I was completely clueless and the only way to know something was to ask.

My question caused Handsome Man to look away, to reposition his body so he could stare at the house and not at me. In the house, party lights were flashing in a couple of rooms, music spilling out from every possible crevice. Party-goers milled around the back door, smoking cigarettes and dope, others drank and told outlandish stories, others still vomited into the bushes before staggering back into the house to presumably load themselves up again. Where we were at the end of the garden was quite secluded, too far for drunk/doped-up people to venture on a whim. Which was why, I presumed, he had led me there. Privacy. Seclusion. And now, silence.

'OK, silence. Silence, I'm guessing, means: "no, I am not going to call you".' I sighed, desolately. I thought he liked me. He certainly fucked like he did. And he'd just told me I was cool, and that the sex had been so good it'd made him smoke again. But he clearly didn't want to call. *This* was why I needed to ask outright in these situations – I had clearly got it all wrong. I had misread everything. He didn't like me enough to move it beyond the bounds of this party; to anything more than fucking me and smoking next to me.

*At least I know*, I told myself, the disappointment rising like a high wave inside me. *At least I know now and I'm not going to be sitting around waiting for a call that's never going to come.*

'It's not that,' he said, staring at the glowing end of his cigarette. 'I don't even live up here. I'm just out . . . well, I'm just up visiting friends. I'm not from Leeds.'

'I'm up visiting a friend, too,' I said. 'I went to college up here, but now I live in London.'

He could suddenly face me again, delight dancing on his features. 'Me, too. Went home to London after the degree was done. Weird that we never saw each other. But I am older than you, I guess. That's mad that we have this connection.'

'Yeah, mad, and yet, I'm sensing you're still not going to call.'

'I am,' he said suddenly and decisively. He was staring right at me when he said that. 'I am going to call you. I just don't know when. I have a lot going on right now.'

'Does that lot going on include a girlfriend?' I asked. He stared at me, his silence almost brutal in how it was making me feel. I didn't regret fucking him – who could regret that amount of pleasure? – but I did know that it wasn't going to do my ego or self-esteem any good to keep getting sucked into this slipstream of thinking I was somehow special to him to then have him push me out with silence and deflection.

'It does not include a girlfriend,' he replied. 'I do not have a girlfriend.'

'But you have a lot going on right now?'

'Yes,' he replied. He dropped his cigarette butt on the ground, slipped forward to crush and extinguish it underfoot before sliding back onto the swing. He wrapped his hand around mine in a warm, sweet gesture of connection. I stared at his hand for a few moments, willing myself not to get too comfortable with this or attached to him, not when I knew in the next moment he would be pulling away and literally leaving me swinging.

He placed his other hand on my face, stroked his thumb across my cheek, then leant in and pushed his lips against mine again. This time there was no hesitation, he was firm against my mouth, almost urgent as he kissed me, his tongue slipping into my mouth again as though he wanted to possess me. This kiss was like the kiss earlier that led to you know what. But different, too, familiar and longing. Like we had been doing this for a while and each time we kissed it brought us closer together. When he eventually pulled back from the kiss, he rested his forehead on mine, his nose on mine, too. 'Give me your number,' he murmured. 'I will call you when I can.'

'Honestly?'

'Yes, yes. I will call you.'

## 16 May, Brighton

There's no point being in bed, listening to Jeb and Arie gently snore their way through dreamland. I have made sure that Arie is on his back in his cot and now I am outside the bathroom, playing the 'Shall I? Shan't I?' game. It might not happen tonight. I might not break down. I might be safe tonight.

*August, 2007*

'Your husband couldn't join you today, Hella?' I asked the nervous woman in front of me. 'If I may call you Hella?'

Her hands were wringing themselves together, her whole body was poised to flee. But she also looked *determined*, like she was going to do this thing; she was going to begin the journey of sorting out her marriage no matter what.

'He could, I mean, he can, he's just parking. I told him we'd need to leave earlier to find a parking spot because we don't know this area. But it would be fine, apparently, I was worrying unnecessarily, apparently. It was not fine. So now he's out there driving around and around trying to find somewhere.'

OK, she was in a bad place. Not quite I-want-to-stick-a-fork-in-his-hand-because-he's-breathing-too-much territory, but not far off. I don't write that down in my notepad because it will freak her out but they are in a worse place than either of them realises. She resents him, he dismisses her.

'You were quite vague on your form?' I said.

'I didn't want to be unfair to him and I didn't want you to prejudge us before you met us in case you decided that you couldn't help us. There aren't that many Black therapists who do couples that have space for us.'

'I wouldn't make any judgements until I'd met you. And even then, I don't make judgements, I try to assess the situation and work out the best way forward. The forms are really only a way to give me a broad overview of your situation so you don't spend the fifty minutes having to recount everything.'

'I thought it was an hour?'

*Yeah, a lot of people think that*, I replied in my head. 'It's actually fifty minutes of contact time and then I have ten minutes of writing up my notes. So, it is an hour that I spend with you. I need to write my notes up straight away so I can make sure the next time we speak I have all the information to hand. If I left it till the end of the day, I'd probably forget who had said what.'

'And you probably have to recalibrate yourself between sessions,' she said insightfully. I liked this woman, she was a good person. You could tell that from the way she sat, the way she held herself, the fact she thought of me at all when she was this stressed. She was also incredibly beautiful. Her dark brown skin glowed with the health of someone who took their self-care seriously, her glossy black hair was tied in a loose bun at the nape of her neck and she was make-up-less except for her manicured, sea-blue nails.

She was the type of woman – person – who made me feel better about leaving my last job in disgrace then setting up as a therapist. I was doing good here, a lot more than I was doing in that place.

There was a short sharp knock at the door, and the person on the other side didn't wait for me to call 'come in' before they opened it.

'This'll be my husband, Jeb,' she said just as the door swung open.

*Jeb?* I thought. *Jeb?!*

Handsome Man from the party where Sylvie met her husband all those years ago had been called Jeb. He told me that hours after we'd had sex while he walked me back to Sylvie's place. I hadn't met anyone with that name before that night nor since then because he didn't call. Of course he didn't.

Surely it couldn't be. Surely it couldn't.

It was.

I fixed my face before Hella, his wife, noticed my complete horror, but he did a double-take when he saw me, and stopped in the doorway. She glared at him. 'Are you coming in or what?' she snapped, her patience clearly depleted. They were in a bad place all right. Imagine how much worse it was going to get if she found out who I was.

While he settled in the comfy yellow seat next to his wife and opposite me, I scrabbled around, trying to remember what I was meant to be doing. I should recuse myself, of course, but I couldn't do that right now. The damage it would do to her would be immeasurable.

'I, erm, well, it's good to meet you, Mr Quarshie. Your wife was just about to explain the reason why you're both here so we can see if we can work together.'

'I told her that she was the only Black therapist I could find that dealt with couples who had space, so I want this to work out.'

He didn't say anything, just nodded. He was looking at her, so, I presumed, he wouldn't have to look at me.

'So . . .' I began.

'He cheated on me!' she declared. From the way her body sagged in relief, her face fell in release, she'd obviously been wanting to say that for a long time. The words had been there in her chest, in her throat for years, probably, and now they were out. Now she was free.

'Recently?' I asked, trying not to glare at him.

'No. Years ago. The week before our wedding. A week! He went to Leeds for his stag do with his best friend, ended up shagging some skank at a house party.'

*Am I that skank or is she some other unsuspecting woman who was stupid enough to think she was special? Even when he didn't call she thought she was special and had spent years staying away from other men just in case he did decide to call.*

'When did you find out?' I asked gently.

'Right away,' she replied. 'He came back that Sunday night, sat me down while I was cooking him his favourite meal because I'd felt guilty about flirting with a waiter on my hen weekend. Then he just told me he'd met this woman, the skank, and fucked her. Unprotected. Who does that? Who meets a random at a party and lets him stick his thing in her without protection?'

Me, apparently.

'Hasn't she heard of sexually transmitted diseases? She could have given him anything. He could have given her anything. He could have got her pregnant. Can you imagine that? He goes on his stag do and comes back a baby daddy.'

'How did that make you feel?' I asked dutifully.

She dropped the rightful rage and looked devastated for a moment, utterly destroyed. 'It broke my heart.'

He stared down at the carpet, looking something close to devastated too.

'I loved him so much, we'd built this life together and were planning children and he goes and does that. I felt like I was drowning. I couldn't breathe, I couldn't—' She paused as agony clawed itself across her face. 'I couldn't understand why he would betray me like that. I still don't understand.'

'Mr Quarshie?' We were into the session and we hadn't even set ground rules about listening, no abuse, no looking to me to take their side, we were right bang in the session. 'Can you give your wife any insight?'

'I was selfish,' he said. 'I was freaked out about getting married, I didn't . . . I didn't want to get married. Not at that point. But rather than let Hella go, I went along with it. And when it got so close there was no backing out, instead of being brave and telling her the truth, I hurt her. She was my best friend and I hurt her. And I'll never forgive myself for that.'

'You didn't want to get married?' she asked.

He shook his head.

'So why did you propose? That big elaborate proposal with the roses and the lights, the table by the river?'

'All our friends were doing it and I could see how excited you were every time one of your friends got a ring on her finger. Everyone kept saying, "it'll be you two next". I knew I wanted to marry you, so I thought why not? I wanted to be engaged to you but I didn't want to get married right then.'

'And you never told your wife this until just now?' I asked.

'No. Never been brave enough. The last thing I ever wanted to do was hurt her so I kind of took the coward's way out and screwed someone else.'

'Can I ask you both why you went ahead and got married if this was going on between you?'

They both looked at each other then, as if seeing each other for the first time. This little snippet of information had obviously changed everything between them.

'She wouldn't let me back out,' he said. 'I wanted to call it all off, I felt so guilty about what I'd done, but she wouldn't let me.'

'Mrs Quarshie?'

'It was less than a week before the wedding, people had already been arriving from all over. My grandparents had already flown in from the Bahamas. His grandparents had already arrived from Ghana. What was I going to say to them? Sorry, it's all off? Because he couldn't keep it in his pants? I couldn't take the humiliation of everyone knowing I wasn't woman enough to keep him faithful. That he had to go looking elsewhere because I wasn't good enough for him.'

'It was never like that!' he said, taking her hand. 'I didn't realise you thought that. It was never about that. I messed up. I was selfish. But none of it was your fault. None of it was me looking elsewhere. You were woman enough for me. You always have been. I was selfish. I was so selfish. It was all about me trying to get out of something without wanting the pain. I used that woman I slept with, too, you know? She had no idea that I wanted out of a situation of my own making so I used her to do the one thing I thought would end it all. I didn't tell her I was getting married and was terrified. I just . . . I used her. And I hurt you. All because I was a coward.'

He'd obviously been thinking about this for a long while, to have so much insight into himself. There was so much to delve into, so much that I wanted to explore with these two, but I had to pick up on something that had been dismissed along the way to this point. Something they both wouldn't have considered over the years.

'Did you want to get married, Mrs Quarshie?' I asked.

'What?' she replied. Her eyes were swimming with tears, but she didn't reach for a tissue from the box in front of her nor from the box at her elbow.

'Your husband said he didn't want to get married. Did you want to get married?'

I had seen her surprise when he said it. It wasn't hurt and surprise, though. It was surprise that he had felt what she had felt. She had been swept along with this as much as, if not more than, he was. She needed to acknowledge that out loud so they could both move on in a more honest way.

She said nothing for a while, possibly waiting to see if I would move on. I wasn't going to because it was an important point. What her silence did do, though, was make her husband look at her. Alarm took over his face as he watched her, waiting for her answer.

'No,' she eventually admitted. 'I didn't want to marry him. When he proposed I felt trapped. He'd gone to all that effort, and like he said, everyone kept saying it would be us next. And I said yes, thinking it'd be all right. That we'd find a way to make it work. I wanted to have babies with him, but I didn't want to get married. Not to him, not to anyone. But once we were engaged, everyone kept putting pressure on us to set a date. I thought we'd be able to stay engaged indefinitely. But my mum was coming at me with "your grandparents would love to see you get married before they pass" and his family are all "grandchildren should be born in wedlock".

'I started to think that if we did it, everyone would get off our backs, but more importantly, maybe I'd change my mind. Once it was done, it would be done and I wouldn't have to worry about not wanting to get married because I would already be married. And it was only a piece of paper, after all.

'When he told me he'd slept with someone else, I thought I was going to die. I felt so worthless, and I couldn't stand the thought of everyone knowing. They'd talk about it for years, I'd never be able to show my face. One week before my wedding he decides to screw someone else. What did that say about me and our relationship? About me as a woman? It was too much. I couldn't cope with calling it off.'

'Do you regret going through with it?'

She shook her head slowly. 'No. I loved him. At the time I loved him. And I thought that would be enough. And it was enough, for a while. For a long while.'

She didn't want to say what was clearly lurking under the skin of all her words, skimming along the edge of every feeling. She wanted me to say it for her. That was why she was here, she wanted someone else to do her dirty work. But I couldn't. Wouldn't. This was why we should have got the housekeeping out of the way first, people in this room really needed to be shown where the exits were and when to put on their oxygen mask and seatbelts because I couldn't actually do it for them.

'Is there something you would like to say to your husband?' I asked gently. She might as well say it now, she was practically there already. He will have heard the use of the past tense of love, he will have understood what she was driving at. Usually it would take several sessions to get to here, but she had been able to see the path a lot quicker – mainly because he had been so honest. He didn't try to deflect or push blame on her, he took full responsibility. Which meant she was free to think what next, instead of defending herself from his covert attacks.

This time, she reached for a tissue, took it in both hands and dabbed under each eye, mopping up her tears, readying for a few more. 'I don't want to be married to you any more,' she said quietly, then looked him in the face. Watched to see what her statement had done to him.

It blew a hole through him. He looked like he had been shot. I knew what that looked like and this was it: horror and shock and fear and disbelief. Most of all disbelief.

I wanted desperately to look away, but I couldn't. I had to keep my eyes on him, looking for signs of extreme distress and not simply this current upset.

'I still love you, in a way, and I still want to be with you to see if we can work this out. But I don't want to be married to you any more. I don't want to be married to anyone.'

Swallowing, blinking back tears, 'How long have you felt like this?' he asked.

'I don't know,' she shrugged. 'I just . . . it was saying out loud that I didn't want to get married. It made me realise that I didn't have to be if I didn't want to be. And I don't want to be. I want to be with you, I want to work this out, but I don't want to be married any more. Maybe we can date or something? Maybe.'

'How are you feeling right now, Mr Quarshie?'

'Like someone's ripped my heart out and shown it to me,' he replied. That night, the night we met, we had a good-natured argument about *Roadhouse* and whether the Patrick Swayze character had ripped out a man's throat or if it was his heart with his bare hands. Obviously it was his throat, but Handsome Man had argued otherwise. The reminder of that argument bolted across my mind before I could stop it.

'And how do you feel about what your wife said?'

'I'm broken. But what can I do? This is all my fault.'

'No one is assigning blame here, Mr Quarshie.'

'Why not? It's true, isn't it? I messed this all up.'

'No, you didn't,' she cut in. 'We both did. By getting married. We'd have been all right if we'd just lived together and had kids. But neither of us said we didn't want to get married, so we've ended up here.'

Their fifty minutes were up, but I couldn't just ask them to leave. Not when I had – inadvertently – been a part of why this was happening. Connections. The world was full of connections and as time went on I was discovering more and more of them. And this connection, as random and fitting as it was, came with a truckload of responsibility. I had to see this through to its conclusion in this session. I couldn't ethically see them again after this, and I couldn't recuse myself because of the damage it would do to Hella.

And there was no way I was going to be able to charge them, either. Even if this was technically the half-price, getting-to-know-you session, I could not take a penny of these people's money.

'If we'd been honest before it got to the wedding week, we might have stood a chance,' she said.

'Are you saying that you think your relationship is over as well as your marriage?' I asked carefully.

'I don't even know. When I started talking, it was just the marriage that was over. But now I'm thinking what's the point of staying together if we're not married? What if there's someone else out there for me, for you? I mean, what if you're meant to be with that skank from Leeds? And I'm meant to be with the owner of Liverpool FC?'

'You wouldn't dare,' he said suddenly. 'Not Liverpool. And not either of the Manchesters. And not Newcastle. Or Chelsea. Never Chelsea. Promise me now, never Chelsea.'

She did know him, love him. Her saying that had got him away from the bleakness, hurt and pain, while making him laugh. It was a shame they were splitting up, they really were a good match, they really did love each other. But marriage had torn them apart. The fear of marriage had made him cheat, the fear of being judged lacking had made her carry on with marriage. The ever-growing weight of their combined fear of the relationship had crushed their relationship. If that wasn't irony, I didn't know what was.

They could fix it, work hard on repairing the relationship, possibly even get back to who they were. But the truth was, neither of them wanted to. Yes, he was devastated, but that was mainly because he hadn't seen it coming. If he wanted to fight – truly walk through all the fires of hell – for the marriage, he wouldn't have been so easily distracted by the football talk. He knew she was right. Once they weren't married any more, what would be the point?

'I always like to end a session with each person in the couple saying something positive about the other person. It doesn't have to be a huge thing, but it does have to come from the heart and be honest. Things like, "makes good tea" doesn't count, unless it's something like, "they have made me tea every single day that I have known them and they make it just the way I like it and always seem to know when I need it because they have listened to my needs". Which one of you would like to go first?'

They both seemed startled that the session was over, that they'd have to step out of this room and begin this new life almost straight away. That's why these things usually play out over several sessions, it gives people the chance to get used to the changing dynamic of their relationship. I couldn't really give them homework and exercises since I wasn't going to see them again, and whoever took over would have their own way of working.

'I'll go,' he said. 'She made me feel normal when I thought I was broken, weird. When I didn't know who I was, she made me feel like I was whatever normal was. And I'll never be able to thank her enough for that.'

Her face quivered, touched by what he had said.

'He loved me. Even when I did my best to make him go away, when I was horrible and hurting, he stayed and showed me that he loved me. He loved me unconditionally.'

'OK, that seems a good place to end this,' I said, shutting my empty notebook. 'You've got a lot of talking to do. Try to remember what you've both said when you have those discussions. Try to be kind to each other.'

'Thank you, doctor,' they both said at the same time. When they left, him holding the door for her to go through first and then shutting it behind them, I collapsed back in my seat.

*Only me that would happen to. Only me.*

A short sharp knock and the door opened again. Jeb was back in the room. 'I left my phone,' he said, staring meaningfully at me. 'Sorry.' He bent to pick up his phone that he'd put on the table beside the box of tissues, still staring at me. 'I'll leave you alone now. Sorry again.'

I nodded. Not sure if he was sorry for not ringing me, for his wife calling me a skank, for me having to oversee the end of his marriage, or for ever meeting me. All in all, I suspected it was the last one.

## 16 May, Brighton

Only the light from the corridor illuminates the room when I stand in front of the bathroom mirror. I'm not looking directly into the mirror. Not yet. I place my hands on the cool white ceramic sink to brace myself. If I can get this over with now, maybe I'll be able to sleep.

*Breathe*, I tell myself.

*Inhale.*

*Exhale.*

*Breathe.*

I look in the mirror. I force myself to stare.

Nothing.

Nothing there.

Nothing is coming.

I think, nothing is coming.

I might be safe tonight.

Tonight, I might be free to sleep.

*May, 2008*

When I opened the door to my office to say goodbye to my assistant Karizma, I found Jeb sitting on the sofa in the reception area. It'd been nine months since the therapy session that ended his marriage and I hadn't heard from either of them. I'd had Karizma send them a list of other couple therapists who could better oversee the end of their marriage so there was no reason for them to get in touch.

And no reason for him to be sitting out here.

Karizma stood up. She'd already packed up her desk and was clearly ready to go but wasn't going to leave me here alone with this man.

She pushed her browny-blonde ringlets out of her face and said, 'This gentleman has been waiting to see you. He said you might see him even though he *doesn't have an appointment.*' She was flashing her 'I'll turf him out if you give me the nod' eyes at me and I loved her for that. She was loyal and fiercely protective of me. No one got around her if I didn't want them to.

'It's OK, I'll see him, briefly.' I smiled at her, not at him.

'Are you sure?' she asked, noticing my smile was only for her. 'Because I can ask him to leave if you'd like.'

'It's OK. I'll see you tomorrow, Karizma.'

'See you tomorrow, Kez.' She picked up her bag, turned off her computer and then walked out the office, shooting daggers at Jeb as she passed him, just so he'd know she would come for him if he got out of hand. Goodness knows what she would have said to him if she knew what he'd already done.

I stood back against the door and swept my arm to show him that he could come in.

He seemed altogether too big for my office, but also perfect for it. As though he was simultaneously not meant to be there and at the same time shouldn't be anywhere else.

I sat in my chair and picked up my notebook and pen. I indicated to the seat he sat in last time. 'Please take a seat,' I said all business. I was completely ignoring how my stomach had dipped when I saw him sitting outside and how my heart was racing now. My body was a betrayer, it always had been when it came to this particular man. I couldn't trust it to stay aloof and detached. At all. I had to engage my hardened heart and analytical mind for this.

'I'm not sure it's a good idea for you to be here, Mr Quarshie,' I said. 'Ethically, I can't be your therapist.'

'I didn't come for therapy, I came to apologise – properly,' he said.

'Well, that was a wasted journey. You have nothing to apologise for.'

'I kind of do. I didn't call you. Although I'm sure you understand why now. I was going to. But when Hella refused to let me end our relationship, I couldn't. Even though I wanted to. Very much.'

'Sure,' I said.

He reached into his inside jacket pocket and that simple motion made my heart swan-dive off the highest platform. I was a ridiculous person. He had literally moved and my body was all for jumping him. He took out the brown leather rectangle of his wallet, and flipped it open. He then used his thumb and forefinger to fish out a scrap of paper from behind the picture of a big bulldog. I recognised the scrap of paper straight away. The two folds, from where I'd folded the two ends to meet in the middle, were a mottled blue, I presumed, from the amount of time they'd spent in his jeans pockets. It was bashed, the edges worn. 'I've kept this all this time,' he said.

'You do realise, don't you, that you keeping that shows that you – metaphorically – had one foot outside your marriage? You weren't completely in your relationship. And that probably contributed to it falling apart.'

'Don't therapise me, Kez,' he said good-naturedly. 'I kept it because I wanted something to remind me of you. I'm showing you it now because you meant something to me. What happened between us was special and it meant a lot to me.'

I wasn't going to say it meant a lot to me, too, was I? Even though my heart was doing a happy dance and the space between my legs was gently throbbing at the memory of being with him. It wasn't just the sex that I was remembering, it was the chat in the garden, his kissing me goodnight after he'd walked me back to Sylvie's place, the way I felt completely at ease with him.

'Are you trying to say I wasn't just some skank you shagged in Leeds to end your relationship?' I said, bringing this back to reality.

'Hella was mortified when she found out.'

'You told her?'

'Of course,' he said. He frowned. 'Why wouldn't I? I'm fundamentally an honest person, I just didn't behave very well with you. But yes I told her, as soon as we got home. She was mortified, then pissed because you weren't a skank and are actually beautiful as well as intelligent, and then she couldn't stop laughing.'

'And she's not angry with me or going to report me for unethical behaviour?' I asked, terrified that I was going to lose *another* job because I was me.

'Why would she? We went home and had some of the best conversations we'd had in years. We talked for hours. Then we rowed and shouted and then cried and cried. But all of that started here, with you asking the right questions. She's not at all pissed at you. Me, a little still, yes, but not you.'

'Well, that's good to know she's doing OK. She was at breaking point when she walked in this room. It wasn't obvious, she's very good at covering up how she feels, but she was on the verge of a breakdown.'

'That's what she said recently. She hadn't acknowledged how low she felt because she was so good at carrying on no matter what.'

'Well, thank you for the update. I've got to meet someone soon, so

86

if you wouldn't mind showing yourself out?' I said, because I realised where this conversation was going. He had been at pains to reassure me that his ex was fine and that she knew the truth about me because he wanted to start something with me. And that couldn't happen. It was a bad idea.

On any and every level that was a bad idea. I had made some unwise decisions with him that night in Leeds and I'd compromised my ethics in that session with his wife. I was lucky that I hadn't got pregnant, hadn't caught a disease back then and hadn't been hauled up in front of an ethics board in the present. As it was I was carrying around the guilt of not being completely honest with my supervising therapist about the Jeb and Hella session. I described what had happened, how I hadn't followed the procedure that I had set and how they'd skipped over several potential sessions to get to the breaking-up part. I had also said I had been sad for them, without mentioning my one-night stand with the husband a week before their wedding.

I was sure she'd known I was keeping something from her because she repeatedly asked me why it had bothered me so much, and I'd continually fobbed her off with things like, 'I just really related to them'. How was I going to explain it all to her if I got involved with him now?

And anyway, did I want to get involved with him? This big cheat of a man who had kept the number of a woman he'd screwed and lied to nearly ten years ago?

I looked him over – from his skin-fade haircut to his giant feet; his large hands to his easy smile; his soft brown eyes to his thick thighs. Did I really want to get involved with him?

*Fuck yeah.*

He was someone I'd been lusting after for years. Years and years. He was someone I had convinced myself I was in love with.

Of course I wanted to be involved with him.

Whether I *should* get involved with him was another matter altogether.

'If you wouldn't mind showing yourself out?' I repeated and got up so he would, too. The way he sat was too tempting . . . I was physically restraining myself from going over and sliding onto his lap.

He stood and that was just as heinous. I flashed back to standing on tiptoe to kiss him in the bedroom, to him pushing me against the wall, to his fingers stroking me, to him ordering me to take off my knickers. All of that flashed through my mind, trilled through my body, and I had to take a step sideways so I was out of the undertow of being around this man.

'Are you married or something?' he asked.

'No, not that it's any of your business,' I replied harshly because I was telling myself off in my head. I was reminding myself of the seriousness of this situation. How I wouldn't be able to support myself if I lost this job.

'Are you with someone? Dating, engaged or anything like that?'

'What's it to you?' I replied.

'What do you think it is to me?' he said, frustrated. 'This is me calling. Yes, nine years later than expected, but this is me calling. I want to go out with you.'

'How's your wife, Jeb?' I asked nastily.

'Doing a lot better now she's not married to me,' he said. 'I moved out six months ago. Still see our boy every day, so I still see her every day, but she's fine. I'm fine. We're divorced.'

'I don't think she'd be fine if she found out you were dating me,' I said. 'I don't think she'd be fine at all.'

It was almost dark outside now, and I usually put on a couple of sidelights for my evening sessions, but I didn't want to do anything that might make him stay any longer than absolutely necessary. The longer he stayed the harder it got to keep him away.

'She would. I know she would.'

'Of course you do.'

He reached into his pocket and retrieved his phone. He tapped a few buttons and then said, 'She has a voicemail message for you.' A microsecond later, his wife's voice filled the room. 'Hi Skank From Leeds! I'm really pleased you're listening to this recording because I told Jeb he would have my blessing to date you if you were at all worried about how I might feel. If I didn't feature, then he wasn't allowed to play you this message and he wasn't allowed to date you. Well, I couldn't stop him, but I'd always think you were bad vibes and would be cautious about you around my son. But look at you, caring and stuff about me. He's an annoying so-and-so sometimes, but he is a good man. So if you like him at all, then you can give him a chance knowing that I'm all right with it.'

The voicemail recording clicked off and he repocketed his phone as we stood in silence in my rapidly darkening room.

'So there you go, you don't have to worry about Hella, she is thriving now that she's not married to me.'

'You keep saying that. I suspect your confidence has been knocked pretty badly by the break-up of your marriage. I know you were blindsided by it. Are you perhaps trying to make yourself feel better, more powerful, by trying to jump into another relationship straight away? Do—'

'Don't therapise me, Kez,' he interrupted. 'I have stayed away from you all this time because I wanted to make sure that it wasn't a rebound thing. I wanted to call you all those years ago and I'm doing it now.'

He came nearer to me, so close our bodies were almost touching, pulling me straight back into the slipstream of being around him. 'If you ask me to leave, I will go.'

I stayed silent because my treacherous body had already got my meant-to-be-hardened heart on side, if I opened my mouth it would be saying all sorts.

'You don't even have to say it,' he added. 'Just nod or shake your head.' He stepped away a little, so he wasn't crowding me. 'Do you want me to go?'

My breathing had become shallow, my hands and body clammy. A stress response to the two parts of me – my mind and body, my psyche and my physical form – battling over this. Both sides believed what they wanted was best for me.

I paused a little longer, trying to get myself to a place where saying 'Yes, I want you to leave' might win.

'I will go, if you want me to. I will not argue and I will not bother you. Just nod or shake your head – do you want me to go?'

*No.* I shook my head. *No, I do not want you to go.*

I finally faced him then, looked at him without the filter of professionalism and distance and being pissed off that he didn't call. Without that filter, he was that man I met at a house party a squillion years ago when I was naïve and the world was a very different place. When I was on the verge of accepting the job I had before this one and I had no idea what it would turn me into. When I saw him like that, he was divine.

'You want to be with me?'

*Yes.* I nodded. *Yes, I want to be with you.*

He grinned, overtly relieved and happy.

'Take off your knickers,' he ordered. Just as fiercely as last time. And just like last time, lust gushed through me.

I didn't move.

He lowered his voice, 'I said take off your knickers. *Now.*'

Keeping eye contact, I reached under my suit skirt and did as I was told.

His grin widened, looking as though he could devour me again. I moved forward, stood on my toes and kissed him, like last time. He hungrily kissed me back, grabbing me tight and lifting me off my feet as he pushed his tongue in my mouth and kissed me like he'd been waiting a lifetime to do so. Still kissing me, he gently pushed me backwards until I was at the edge of my desk. He pulled away from kissing me to put his hand under my skirt and to stroke the full length of me, pausing to push beside my clitoris. I cried out in pleasure, in the longing and waiting I'd done for this. It was as if all this euphoria had been locked up inside me, waiting for the right key to open it.

'You like that?' he murmured as he slipped his fingers inside me. 'You like that?'

I tried to grit my teeth, to not give away how much I wanted – *needed* – this, but it was pointless. In this moment, I was his. My body was his to play with. He took his fingers away and then stepped back. I sat on the edge of my desk, trying to recalibrate myself, trying to breathe while he stared hungrily at me as he unhooked his belt buckle, unbuttoned then unzipped his trousers. Once he was free, he came back for me, grabbed me, spun me around so I was facing my office chair and window. I put my hands on the desk as he pulled up my skirt, opened my legs with his knee and roughly entered me.

'You like that?' he murmured as my whole body sighed into a loud moan.

I'd forgotten. I thought I'd remembered but I'd actually forgotten it was like this with him.

'You like that?' he asked.

'Yes,' I panted. And he pushed harder into me.

'You like that?'

'Yes.'

Harder.

'Yes.'

And harder.

'Yes.'

He drove himself into me, each stroke powerful and strong, until I was almost sobbing with ecstasy, my body so weak I wasn't sure my legs would keep me upright much longer. Jeb started growling as he came closer to making me orgasm, pushing me to the place he wanted to take me, so I reached out, pressed my thumb near the base of his erection. That little move caused him to howl in surprise, grip my hips tight and climax well before he was ready. The rocking motion took me with it, and moments later I was loudly orgasming too.

'What did you do to me?' he asked as he pulsed with the final part of his orgasm, still clinging onto my hips. 'What did you do to me?'

'You like that?' I replied, breathing hard. He withdrew from me, and I turned to look at him as he tucked himself away. 'You like that?' I repeated, laughing slightly, the hedonism of what we'd just done pumping through my veins.

He rested his forehead and nose on mine. 'I like that,' he whispered and kissed me. 'I like that and I like *you* a lot.'

'Glad to hear it,' I ribbed.

'Are you going to date me, then? At some point become my girlfriend?' he asked.

'Think we might have skipped past that bit, don't you?' I replied.

'No, no, we haven't. Not at all. I want to do this properly, go on dates with you, be your boyfriend, be your partner . . .' He left silence to fill in the space that said, 'be your husband' because we both knew there was no way he should be saying something like that. Not right then and especially not in that room.

'All right,' I said. 'If you want to. Then yes. Yes.' And I meant it, too. About all of it. Even the husband part.

## 16 May, Brighton

I've been OK tonight. I'm free. I'm not deluded enough to think it'll be like this again, but tonight, I'm free. I can lie here in bed and go to sleep. Maybe even dream.

I pull the duvet up over my shoulders, snuggle my head down onto the pillow, appreciate the slight give as I find the perfect spot. *Sleep. I need sleep.*

I'm just drifting off when Arie lets out the loudest cry I think I've ever heard on a baby. In response, my eyes fly wide open.

*Oh yeah,* I tell myself, *that's why I'm not sleeping tonight.*

# Brandee

**BrandeeH**

**@Brandee2ees | Joyn Inn Video | Status: Joyn Only Me |**

*\* April 2021 \**

OK, hey, it's your laydee, Brandee with the two ees, coming at you. Completely forgot to do part two of how my BF became my BF. So, I told you how Moe just appeared in my class at school? Turns out, he had moved to Brighton.

This is some major tea explainage so I hope you've got your tea.

Right, so. Moe's parents are Hella and Jeb. Jebediah. I always call them Mrs Q and Mr Q and she always says she's not Mrs Q any more, she's Mrs B. Anyway, they were married way back when. Maybe last century even.

Just before they say 'I do' Jeb meets My Kez at a party. I think there was definite doing of the do going on that night. Anyway, they don't see each other again. Jeb tells Hella, she forgives him, they get married, reh, reh, reh. They have a child, Moe.

Are you following me so far? There's NO hope for you if you're confused now.

Right, so, time goes on, Jeb and Hella are going through a hard time, they go see a therapist. Got to respect them, their marriage is in trouble and they get help. We should all do that. Well, they show up and who is their therapist? My Kez! Can you believe it?! She talks to them and they decide they're going to split up. Then a year later, My Kez and Mr Q get together and get married and have babies.

I KNOW how it sounds. It seems like the ultimate side-chick story – pause to side-eye the royal patron demon of side-chicks – but it isn't. If you talk to Hella, she's like, 'My Kez is cool. She didn't do anything wrong and wouldn't go near Jeb until I was cool with it.'

My Kez wasn't a side-chick but kind of was. I told you it was messy, but also so not messy. Everyone's loving each other up all the time. They're kinda weird for olds like that. My Kez is always like, 'I didn't know Hella existed when I met him' – hence why I think there was definitely doing of the do going on at that party – 'but I wasn't going near him until she said I could.'

Where was I? Oh yeah, so they get married. And then Hella marries a guy called Richie B. So, it's all cool with everyone married to everyone else and Moe coming down to Brighton for his access visits and stuff.

Then Hella gets a job offer to do a sabbatical in Canada. A whole year, living abroad. And she's like, 'I can't do it. Can't take Moe away from his dad.'

95

And his dad's like, 'OK, I don't want you to miss out so I'll come to Canada for a year.'

And Richie's like, 'My dude, you're cool n' all, but where you going to be living when you're in Canada for a year? Cos you ain't living with us.'

And then Hella's like, 'Nah, I'm being selfish, I can't take Moe out of school for a year so I can go be this big career woman.'

And Richie and Jeb are like, 'This is what you've wanted all your life, course you have to.'

And Hella's like, 'No, mothers have to make these kinds of sacrifices.'

And then My Kez is like, 'Moe will come live with us for the next year. We live near an airport, during the half-terms you can come visit him, during full-terms Jeb will fly him out to you. And you get to do the career woman bit child-free and we get to see a bit more of Moe.'

I wasn't there, but I can just imagine what My Kez's face was like cos she has no time for nonsense. I bet she was sat there going, 'these people are mad'. Except she'd never say that cos she's a therapist, so she knows what mad is.

Anyway, the other three were like, 'Oh, yeah, why didn't we think of that?' and that's what happened. Moe ended up in my school. Hella's job got extended to two years, he stayed for two years. Then she comes back and he's like torn cos he wants to live in both places, so spends more of the week in Brighton, goes to London on the weekends and holidays. But they're all really cool and laid-back about it.

So that's how he became my BF. He moved here when his mum was in Canada and we met again at school after meeting in the park and we became BFs.

Yeah, that story could have been that short. Oh well. It's a good thing you like watching my vids, ain't it?

This vid is set to private to edit out names later.

Peace In.

# Kez

## 17 May, Brighton

'Mum, hear me out,' Jonah says as he enters the kitchen wearing his Black Panther pjs that are too small for him. He's shot up recently but isn't willing to give up his favourite clothes. These pjs that are pretty much pedal pushers that end mid-calf, and above his wrist and just about skim his stomach, are the ones I'm having most trouble separating him from. I can't find replacements in his size, so he isn't letting them go. Jeb doesn't help – he regularly encourages our eleven-year-old to hang onto them for as long as possible. 'Mum, hear me out,' he repeats. 'I heard a baby crying last night. It sounded like it was in the house. Ergo, I think the house is haunted.'

Jonah has thought the house is haunted ever since he and his father watched *The Woman In Black*. Not enough side-eyes for the man I married sometimes. Not nearly enough.

'The house is not haunted. There *was* a baby crying in the house last night.'

My son squeezes up his face, narrows his eyes suspiciously. 'Why is there a baby in the house?' Then he spots the bottle steriliser on the side, the bottles on the table, the change bag sitting near the cooker, the

98

organic formula standing by the kettle. 'Why is there a baby in the house?' he asks again.

'There's a baby in the house?' Zoey questions as she enters the kitchen.

'Yeah,' Jonah says. 'That's what the story is. I think the house is haunted and the 'rents are just fronting up, trying to make us believe it's not.'

'There *is* a baby in the house,' I repeat.

'Well, where is it then?' he asks triumphantly. 'Where is this baby?'

'Your father's taken him out for a walk around the block. They'll be back any minute now.'

'A likely story. A walk you say? Be back any minute, you say? Sure, of course they will.'

'They will.'

Zoey is less suspicious than her brother; she wanders into the kitchen, goes to the green and gold tub of organic formula, picks it up, examines it. I see the thought, 'Interesting' cross her face before putting it down to reach for a glass. She's still examining the baby paraphernalia when she goes to pour herself a glass of water.

'Looking a bit sus now, Mum,' Jonah tells me when Jeb and the baby don't appear. 'Just admit there's a ghost and we can all move on.'

Thankfully, Jeb's key slides loudly into the front door. Arie, the seemingly angelic child, actually had no chill past one a.m. He wanted milk, he wanted a nappy change, another nappy change, a cuddle, a walk around being jiggled, to vomit on my shoulder, to vomit on Jeb's shoulder, some more milk, more jiggling, more nappy change. In desperation, Jeb had taken him out for a walk at six a.m. During all of this, I didn't actually say, 'and you wanted to go back to all of this with baby number three?' but I was sure he could feel it.

'Good morning, everyone,' Jeb says, the sunshine back in his voice and face. His unofficial role in the mornings is to get us all going, to keep us all buoyed while I sort out breakfast and snacks and water bottles and uniform crises and bag packing, before Jeb leaves the house with them to go to school. Jeb is holding Arie, who has his eyes closed and looks very much like he's only just nodded off, in the crook of his arms.

'Wow, there is a baby,' Jonah says, going towards Jeb. 'Is he our brother?'

'I told you,' Zoey says. 'I knew something was going on and I told you she'd got a bit bigger.'

'You cheeky so and so,' I say.

'I told you they were up to something,' Zoey continues. 'You don't think she was really doing a book thing with Aunty Remi yesterday, do you? She was in hospital having another baby.'

'I was not!' I exclaim. 'And come, Zoey, you're meant to be clever, look at the size of that baby, do you really think he was born yesterday?'

Zoey shrugs. 'Could have been.'

'He was not born yesterday,' I say. 'Tell her, Jeb.'

Jeb shrugs like his daughter. 'Could have been.'

I glare at him across the room. We have had no sleep, we have this new challenge to deal with and he's out here making 'jokes'. In response my husband fixes me with his large brown eyes and then slowly moves his mouth up into a wide, teasing grin. My insides instantly turn to jelly. Even now, all these years later, he can do this to me with a look, a smile. 'You like that?' he mouths at me over the heads of the children.

I roll my eyes and look away. Of course I like that. When it comes to this man, I like pretty much everything he does.

# Brandee

**BrandeeH**

**@Brandee2ees | Joyn Inn Video | Status: All Joyn Inn |**

***May 2021 ***

## >>Why do you always

## sign off 'Peace In'??<<

I'm just going to answer this question real quick. I say it because I wish everyone Peace In all things at all times. I have had so much chaos in my life, so often I wanted peace, just simple peace. Not just outside, inside, too. Especially inside. That's it. Does that sound weird? Too bad if it does. Peace In, babies, Peace In.

# Kez

## 17 May, Brighton

Zoey now accepts that Arie isn't a baby that I have given birth to. Mostly. She is still suspicious, while her brother has released his suspicions about there being a phantom baby and is harassing us about how long Arie will be here for.

To my latest *I don't know* reply, he declares: 'I have big brother duties to plan for. Man needs to plan.'

'Just assume he's here for a while,' I respond. 'My friend didn't say when she'd be back. So we're looking after him until then.'

'Where do you think Brandee's gone, then?' Zoey asks.

Alarmed, I glance at Jeb, who is just as startled.

Cautiously, I question, 'Why do you ask that?'

'He looks just like her,' Zoey says, looking us both up and down like we are simple.

'Exactly like her,' Jonah says. 'Didn't you know?'

'Yes, we knew,' I say. Jeb is silent – and busying himself with other things. This is a conversation he is not getting involved in. 'I wasn't sure you did, though.'

'What do we call him?' Zoey asks.

'His name's Arie, so Arie will do.'

'No, I mean, when people ask, what do we say? Shall I say he's our brother? Brandee was kind of like our sister when she lived here. But if he's her son, then he can't really be our brother. Maybe not our brother.'

I glance at Jeb who is still finding busy work in moving things around near the sink. Not actually washing or anything, just moving them around. 'You can say he's your parents' friend's child.'

'I think I'll just say he's my foster brother,' she says. She's obviously been having a whole internal conversation exclusive to the one we are having together. 'Yeah, that'll be best.' She looks at me as though I've magically appeared in front of her out of nowhere. 'I think I'm going to call him my foster brother.'

'If you want.'

'I want.'

After throwing down the rest of their breakfast, the pair of them coo over Arie so much I have to order them to put the baby down and get ready for school.

I'm just coaxing a perfectly warmed bottle between Arie's lips while his glossy brown eyes stare up at me, when Jeb enters the kitchen in search of his keys. Once he has them in his grip, he comes over, starts to make faces at Arie. 'OK, my little boy, you be nice for My Kez, yeah? Yeah?' Arie giggles in return, waving his hands around.

'Are you going to be all right here on your own?' Jeb says to me once he tears his attention away from the child. 'Do you want me to stay home today?'

I shake my head. 'I'll be fine. We'll be fine. I've got a couple of things to do today, so we'll be fine.'

'Call me if you need some help,' he says and drops a kiss on top of my sleep-scarf-covered head. 'I know she'll tell me to do something unpleasant to myself, but say hi to Brandee's mum for me.'

'How . . .?'

'You're playing detective, of course you're going to start with her mum. I'm sure it'll be a wonderful meeting of the minds. Take care and call me if you need back-up.'

'I will. Bye, Zoey, bye Jonah. Love you. Have a nice day,' I call.

'Bye, you too,' is the response from the corridor.

And then they're gone. Swept out of the house on the tidal wave of morning rush.

There's silence, the hush after the storm. Arie uses his tongue to push out the teat of the bottle, not hungry any more.

He stares up at me for a beat, two beats, openly assessing me and my abilities. Three beats and he lets out a loud, desolate, bereft wail.

Clearly I've failed that test.

# Brandee

**BrandeeH**

**@Brandee2ees | Joyn Inn Video | Status: All Joyn Inn |**

*\* July 2021 \**

Really want to talk about this because it bothers me sometimes. Might delete later.

I get really depressed and low. Then I get all hyper-anxious. When I was nine, I was kidnapped. It wasn't anything too bad. I mean, it was bad, yeah, but I don't think I was SA'd or anything like that. But sometimes, if I'm out and people come up to me, I get scared they're going to do something to me like that lady did.

Yeah, it was a lady. Woman. She had been following my mother's blog as it was at the time, and she was in the local park when she saw me. I think I remember her saying the pictures my mum used to post showed her which park we used to go to, so she came to see if I was that thin in real life.

Oh, lightbulb! This is what My Kez meant about predators bringing things into real life. I kind of thought she meant the pervs would start leering on kids in real life, but if you post identifying things, then they'll know where to find these kids. Oh. I feel a bit sick now cos that's what happened to me.

She came to the park – not the one I met my BF in. As usual, Mum was surrounded by her fans, people asking her questions, wanting to be with her, just wanting to be around her. I was playing on my own because none of the other children would ever play with me. Ever! I think they all saw my picture too often and hated me. Don't know if that was true, but that's the impression I got.

I was on my own and this lady came up to me. She was smiling and she acted like she knew me. So many people knew me. They wanted to have their pictures taken with and to chat to me. Guys, the number of people who told me how inspiring they found my mother! She was really nice and said I had pretty hair and a pretty smile. She asked me if I wanted to go for a walk and I thought, why not.

She took me out of the park and to her car. And she asked me if I wanted to go for a ride. At that point I'm a bit, maybe I should wait for Mum, but the lady suddenly looked a bit cross. Her face went all pale and she kind of narrowed her eyes a bit like that, and did her lips like this, like she was about to shout at me.

The most messed up thing is that I kind of thought I owed her. Mum was always making me sit on people's laps, and they were always cuddling me and telling me where to stand, when to smile. We went to people's houses. None of that was new. So I got in the car with her and she took me to her house.

Do you want to know the weird thing? I don't really remember it. I mean, I do. And I don't. I remember she had this gold and white and red wallpaper and this weird mustard-yellow carpet. She dressed me up in these weird like doll-looking clothes. And she fed me stew with these really thick, bitty sausages. And gave me ice cream afterwards. She said she was going to feed me properly cos all Mum ever gave me was waffles and fish fingers. That wasn't all she fed me, not at all, but it was what Mum talked about giving me on her blog and stuff. She was trying to make mothers who didn't have time to cook feel better, and the woman who took me believed it was the truth. I remember all that. I remember not being scared. Not even when she said I was staying the night. I thought she'd asked Mum. I think she'd told me Mum said it was all right. And I just believed her. She put me to bed in this room with lots of frills and cushions and fussy patterns. I think that's why I need my life and house to be as uncluttered as possible. Wow, haven't really made that connection before.

She took me back to the park the next morning, left me there and drove off. I never saw her again. She was a white lady, yes. And she had pale, pale skin when she was a bit angry with me. But I don't really remember anything else. I can't hear her voice or properly picture her face. I remember bits of her house, but what I mean when I say I don't remember anything, I mean, I don't remember what I felt. I don't remember where her house was and that made the police so angry. 'How are we supposed to catch her when your daughter is protecting her?' one of them said.

'Watch your tone,' Dad told him. And I thought there was going to be a fight.

I'm scared sometimes that she did something to me? That maybe someone came and did something to me? I don't think they did, but I'm scared about why I don't remember. I spoke to BF's stepmum about it and she said we remember everything. Studies have shown that. But we can't recall everything. We don't have access to it at will. She said sometimes the mind protects you from stuff by putting it in a little corner, out of the way so you don't go upsetting yourself by it constantly playing in your head.

She said if the woman did do something to me other than brush my hair. Oh I didn't mention that, did I? She said every time she saw a picture of me she wanted to take a brush to my darn hair. She didn't say darn, what she did say would get me banned.

She tried to brush my hair, and she broke her brush, so she left it alone.

I don't know. Maybe she did do something? My BF's stepmum did say if something had happened, I would probably have remembered at least some of it by now because I have a life full of triggers. Something else would have triggered that memory. Ha! That's me, untriggered.

For ages, ages and ages, I thought it was my fault. That if she had unalived me or something like that, it would have been down to me. But my dad told me it was Mum's fault. She should have been looking out for me. My BF's dad said the same. He's cool, you know. Not as deep and theorising with that stuff as his wife, but he's good to talk to. He always makes me feel better. It's so weird how he's like the big version of my BF.

Phew! That was a lot. Just had to share. My head keeps going back to that. It's making me depressed and anxious at the same time. Do you know what it's like to feel scared all the time? That's what it's like for me sometimes.

I'm out. Peace In.

# Kez

**17 May, Brighton**

Brandee's note is preying on my mind like a lion feasts on an antelope's carcass; her number being out of service is worrying me like vultures pick over bones.

None of her social media pages have been updated publicly for nearly six months now. She'd been a prolific poster, daily updates, aspirational videos, behind-the-scenes content, inspirational quotes and sponsored posts. And then they stopped. Just stopped. The final post had been one for a sportswear brand called Traits. High-end workout gear and gym equipment. She made quite a few videos for them and posts, and her stories were full of the events she went to. They sponsored holidays and parties with other influencers and then nothing. Nothing. Quite a few of her fellow influencer friends are still sharing content including the Traits products. But not Brandee.

When her social media sites didn't yield anything obvious, I did searches on the internet and there is chatter – a lot of rumours and conspiracy theories – about how and why she just dropped out of sight. That she'd got married, that she'd been whisked off to live on a desert island with a prince, that she'd had a mental breakdown and was now institutionalised, that she'd been kidnapped and trafficked. That last one made my blood run cold. Because it wouldn't have been the first time something like that happened to her.

Her mother hadn't wanted to listen to anyone when they warned of the dangers of sharing every single detail about her daughter's life. Her date of birth, her school, where they liked to go together. She didn't want to hear how it was opening her daughter up to predators. In response to concerns raised, she had written articles for her blog, *For The Love Of Brandee*, claiming people were jealous, were trying to stop her earning a living, didn't like to see someone like her talk about her experiences of motherhood. For every one negative comment, she got hundreds of positive ones. For every article she wrote, she got more people on her side, more people following her blog, more people showing her they loved her. *Rewarding* her.

Seeing her as a psychological case study, it was obvious that Brandee's mum had become an addict to the attention that blogging about her daughter's life gave her. Every time she hit send on a post, she would not know how it would be received, so she would be waiting, ready, poised, anticipating . . . and then when the comments rolled in, the dopamine hit would be massive, it would flood her brain in feel-good chemicals that would have her buzzing for days.

And if she wanted more, all she had to do was post more stuff. Her blog posts achieved hundreds, sometimes thousands of positive comments. A little hit of dopamine for every single one, a little more drug to keep her addicted, to keep her doing what she needed to light up her pleasure centres with feel-good chemicals. Brandee's mother became addicted to the attention. Then came the endorsements, the requests to try out certain products and feature them on her blog, the toys, the clothes, the parties, the holidays sometimes. More attention, more dopamine, more, more, more.

She kept doing it, writing about her only daughter, detailing her life, making a living, making the chemicals that fed her attention habit. She kept on . . . Right up until someone decided to take Brandee off her hands.

The woman, who had probably watched Brandee grow up online, saw her in the park one day, her mother distracted, surrounded by other mothers who were asking her about her blog, and she decided to take Brandee's hand and lead her out of the park and into her car.

It was nothing new, for Brandee, after all. Strangers came and talked to her all the time, they acted like they knew her all the time, her mother talked to these people, encouraged her to hug them, to let them stroke her hair, to sit on their laps to take photos. Going with a stranger was nothing new for Brandee.

The woman kept Brandee for less than twenty-four hours, she gave her dinner – something nutritious, not the fish fingers and waffles crap she'd seen Brandee's mum feed her in her blogs – and tried to comb her hair, then gave her a nice bed to sleep in. She dressed her up in pretty clothes and then returned her to the park at nine a.m. the next day.

They never found out who the woman was. Brandee said she hadn't hurt her and she couldn't remember where the woman had taken her. And Brandee's mother, after all the police attention, the gearing up to take part in a television appeal, the relief that her daughter was home, *got worse*. The whole thing had brought her a bigger audience, more attention; her daughter's kidnap allowed her to move from blogging to the newly popular social media sites to get the attention she now *craved*. She was invited onto television shows to talk about her trauma, she was offered spots on the radio to give parenting advice, she had a problem page in a magazine. She got more. More attention, more dopamine, bigger and better hits.

All of it built on the shoulders of her little daughter who didn't know any better.

I am scared for Brandee.

She knows what the world can be like out there, she knows what people can do when they think they know you because they've seen your face over and over again on their computer screen, their TV screen, their phone screen.

I am scared for her. I am really, really scared for her.

# Brandee

**BrandeeH**

**@Brandee2ees | Joyn Inn Video | Status: All Joyn Inn |**

***September 2021 ***

## >>Does BF stand for Best Friend

## or Boyfriend?!?

## Can't work it out??<<

A lot of you are asking this. And the answer is . . . I don't know!! Nah, only kidding. Watch to the end to find out.

Hey, hey! It's your laydee, Brandee with the two ees. So is it Best Friend or Boyfriend? It's a bit of both. Me and BF have been friends since we were ten. And we became better friends when he came to my school. And I spent a lot of time with him, studying. Newsflash to everyone: we were always actually studying. Then a lot of s-h-1-t went down and we kind of fell out. A story for another time.

Things were bad at home, really bad. Mum was trying to get me to do more and more stuff, pics of me in my bikini and underwear, she was trying to show she'd raised a young woman who was confident in her body or something. By that point, I'd realised it was because those were the posts that got her the most likes and comments, yes, from men. Oh let's just say it, from predators. And she was on Facebook, and had loads of friends so she wanted to post those pictures on there.

I couldn't stay at home because every time I turned around there was a camera or a camera phone in my face. My BF's folks said I could stay – open house for his friends and all that. He needed to clear his head so went to London for most of the summer.

Those few weeks, I got really close to his stepmum and I didn't even realise it but all this stuff came out, s-h-1-t that I hadn't thought about for years. She really helped me through it. Made me feel better about not standing up to my mum.

When my BF came back, we had a big long chat and sorted lots of s-h-1-t out and got together properly.

So BF now stands for Boyfriend. Before it stood for Best Friend.

Hope that helps.

**BrandeeH**

**@Brandee2ees | Joyn Inn Video | Status: All Joyn Inn |**

***September 2021 ***

## >>Was he your first?<<

Why y'all asking that? So you can slut shame me? Nah, I ain't telling on a public vid. Especially when I know nosey Seraphina is lurking somewhere. He's my heart. That's all you need to know.

Peace In.

**BrandeeH**

**@Brandee2ees | Joyn Inn Video | Status: All Joyn Inn |**

*** October 2021 ***

Hey, hey, it's your laydee, Brandee with the two ees.

## >>You didn't finish telling us

## about how you left your

## mother's house and went

## to live with your BF<<

Y'all staying interested in that? Wow, OK. Where did I get to? Oh yeah, I stayed with BF's folks while he was in London getting his head straight. When he got back we sorted a lot of s-h-1-t out. And we got together.

While he was away, I spent a lot of time talking to his stepmum, I'll call her KL cos I can't be using her government name unguarded like that.

We would sit up late at night talking and she would listen a lot. Not many people listened to me at that point in my life. Can you imagine, someone's making you Horlicks and sitting up at night with you and just listening. I had a lot of talking to do, it turns out. I told her lots of things but when I told her about my mum stabbing me, she kind of went weird.

Not weird, weird, but she looked like she was going to cry. You have to know her to know that she never f-ing cries. And then she asked me when was the last time I cried. And I didn't know! I didn't even know. She asked if I cried when my mother stabbed me and I said no. And then she asked about a whole bunch of other times when most people would cry and I just kept saying no. I was, what, sixteen at that point? Finished GCSEs, started A-Levels. And I'm still practically living at BF's house.

It was weird cos none of us really questioned it. I'd just wake up in their house and then go home for days at a time. Then turn up at BF's house. No biggie. And it was good to get some S P A C E from The Mothership.

So BF gets into uni in London and I get into Brighton so we go back and forth seeing each other. No biggie.

And then it was the end of 2019 and you know what's coming. I hadn't really spent much time with my 'rentals up until that point. I'd always go back for Christmas and my birthday and my mum and dad's birth-days, so I went back for that Christmas, and Mum was so nice. She was cool, didn't pressure me, only took photos of us but didn't post them. She didn't write anything new about me, she reused old content. We went to visit family, chilled.

Oh my days, we had the best time! Then the world is getting weird. I went back to stay with my BF's family but started seeing my 'rentals a bit more. It was great spending time with them. Then the world is getting weirder. And we have to make a decision. *I* have to make a decision. KL said she reckoned we were going to go into lockdown, so I would have to decide where I was staying. She said I should go home if I wanted, but there was a place at theirs if I wanted. I was thinking it'd just be a few weeks, so I could go home.

I went back to stay a few nights and then I catch my mum taking photos of me while I'm sleeping. And I knew, just knew, that all that stuff at Christmas was fake. She was just doing fakey-fakey smiles to get me to come home.

What did your number one laydee do? She kept it together, acted for all I was worth until I got back to BF's house and told them I would like to stay for as long as lockdown happened if it happened. And as long as they'd have me if it didn't. And KL was like, 'Oh thank God, I wasn't going to let you go back there to be trapped with her.'

So we went over to get my stuff, and Mum who'd been lying low, thinking I'd be coming back, lost it. I mean, properly lost it. She started screaming and crying and she went for KL. Claws out, like I said. And said it was 'on sight' next time she saw her.

BF decided to move back to Brighton from uni and I had moved in so they changed their whole house around for me to stay permanent, like. My BF's dad, he was a legend. Gave up his office, so we had enough bedrooms.

And they were so cool. They said BF and I could sleep in the same bed by saying everyone could sleep where they wanted but had to be in their own bed by seven a.m. And be discreet.

Their eight-year-old was like, 'What's discreet? Is that like the pants you see on the TV?'

And that's the story.

Peace In.

**BrandeeH**

**@Brandee2ees | Joyn Inn Video | Status: All Joyn Inn |**

*\* October 2021 \**

Seraphina, stop. You know that story I told about why I left is true. And you know EXACTLY what you did to make me stop speaking to you. You know. Don't make me air out all your dirty laundry in public. I will. And you know all those big buck endorsements will go flying out the window.

Do better, woman who gave birth to me. Or just S.T.F.U. so I can trick my brain into missing you by pretending I was ever anything other than a walking payment app to you.

Peace In, everybody else.

**BrandeeH**

**@Brandee2ees | Joyn Inn Video | Status: All Joyn Inn |**

*\* October 2021 \**

Hey, hey! It's your laydee, Brandee – the one with the two ees. I have just signed on the dotted line for a pretty incredible deal, people. It is more money than I can imagine, and it's going to be so much fun. I'll be doing stuff with my other influencer faves and travelling and going to all the big laydee parties. I'm telling you cos I'm really excited about it. Things are looking really great right now. Me and BF are getting on really well. Life is good.

I'm not bragging so take your fingers off the comment button to come at me with your hater energy. I'm just happy. So often I end up posting my sad s-h-1-t and I just want to be positive for a while.

**BrandeeH**

**@Brandee2ees | Joyn Inn Video | Status: All Joyn Inn |**

*\* March 2022 \**

## >>You're out all the time.

## You're living your best life.<<

I am out all the time. And I am having some truly elite times. But you know what? Not everything is as it looks. Sometimes even the smiles are fake cos you've got to put them on to get through. You shouldn't always believe everything you see.

**BrandeeH**

**@Brandee2ees | Joyn Inn Video | Status: All Joyn Inn |**

*\* March 2022 \**

## >>When did you stop living

## with your BF family?<<

Not a simple question to answer. I kind of had a falling out with KL. It sounds like I just can't get on with anyone when I say it like that. But that's not true! I have lots of friends.

KL and I kind of fell out because not long before I started living with them for real, I told her I was going to start posting on Joyn Inn and other social media channels. I've always been on all of them cos I've got to see what The Mothership does, but I said I was going to start posting. And she was like, 'Why?'

I told her: 'Cos I want to say stuff. To the world.'

And she was like, 'There's already so much of you out there, maybe you should think before adding to it.'

So I tell her: 'I'm trying to take back control. If I start my own channel, I'll be able to decide what goes out there. And I can call bs on the stuff she says. And I like talking to people. I just want to do something about me that's by me.'

And she's like, 'I get that, but don't get sucked in, Brandee. It's really easy to get addicted.'

'I'll be careful,' I said, to calm her down.

What do you think, peeps? Have I been careful, or am I addicted?

We didn't properly fall out over it, but I kind of got the impression she didn't approve. As a result, I didn't tell her what I was doing. After the lockdowns, my BF went to live in London and I stayed in Brighton before I moved up here kind of with him. We basically spend all our time together anyway.

Peace In.

**BrandeeH**

**@Brandee2ees | Joyn Inn Video | Status: All Joyn Inn |**

*\* March 2022 \**

Your laydee, Brandee, is doing the hard yards right now, babes. Feeling blue. Yeah, you see me on this here app smiling but what is it I say? Even the smiles are fake. That's especially true right now. At the moment, it feels like I'm getting paid for every smile I fake. That's not good, is it?

Peace In.

**BrandeeH**

**@Brandee2ees | Joyn Inn Video | Status: Joyn Only Me |**

***April 2022 ***

Things aren't great with BF, not going to lie. He won't see this. He's not the guy I thought he was. He's so juvenile sometimes. I swear, he is one more comment away from getting dropkicked out of my life. Am looking for other places to live just in case.

It's these courses he's been doing. Mind and body wellbeing or B Lox as I like to call them. He's spending all this money to improve his mind but becoming a total bleep in the process.

I love him, he's my heart, but enough dysfunction! He's got these friends now, and the stuff they say. It makes me feel sick. Physically sick. Why can't he be like his dad? Mr Q is like the perfect man. Amazing partner. BF was like that. But not any more. I want to shout at him, 'Why can't you be more like your dad?' I'm sure that'd go down well.

Don't know what to do. Can't talk to KL, can't talk to The Mothership, obviously. Dad would NOT understand. Maybe I should talk to Mr Q. He'll know what to do.

**BrandeeH**

**@Brandee2ees | Joyn Inn Video | Status: Joyn Only Me |**

*\* July 2022 \**

Got some great news. Great news. Happy, happy dance. Wish I could share, but it's for my eyes only right now.

# Kez

## 17 May, Brighton

The last time I saw Seraphina, she told me that she would smash my face in if she set eyes on me again.

'It's on sight, bitch!' she'd screamed as her husband, Brandee's dad, held her back. 'On sight!' I have no doubt she meant it, and I'm sure my response, 'Fair enough, bring it on,' didn't help, so going to see her has its risks, but I have to find out if she has heard from Brandee.

I am hoping that time might have mellowed her, but if it hasn't, hopefully she won't kick off with a baby present. There could be nothing worse for her image than a parenting expert caught screaming on camera in front of a baby.

That time she threatened me, we had been over to collect the rest of Brandee's things before she moved in permanently. She'd been staying with us on and off for years, and she was still dating Moe, Jeb's son, at that point. We hadn't been happy about them sharing a house, but giving Brandee a safe space overrode all worries.

Seraphina saw all her life's work, all her endorsements and social media revenue walking out the door with a couple of know-it-alls and lost her mind. She'd run at me, claws out, but her husband had caught her just in time, and Jeb had stepped in front of me to protect me. 'It's on sight, bitch,' she'd screamed, losing all the composure and decorum she'd been known for. 'On sight!'

I place Arie's car seat slightly to the left of the Hamilton family front door, so if she does swing for me on sight as promised, I won't fall on him.

*For Brandee*, I tell myself, before I press the doorbell and then step back. Not quite out of reach, but far enough to make it difficult.

She swings the door open and I notice how she's aged. We've all aged in the pandemic, we've all worn those years on our faces and in our bodies, in our lifestyles and minds, but I don't ever remember her looking this ordinary, I suppose. On her videos and on television she is polished, her alabaster skin smooth and matt, blushered, bronzed, highlighted. Her eyes are ringed with dark eyelashes, her hair is flowing and glossy. Even when she's doing the 'natural look' she is made up. In this version she is wearing glasses, her face is creased and her jowls sag, she has blemishes that are natural and normal, but not what you normally see. Her hair is twisted up on top of her head, and held in place with a satiny purple scrunchie. Behind her ear is a pencil. This version of her looks fake, the other version real.

She double-takes and then puts her head to one side. Then she folds her arms across her chest, rests her weight on one hip before snarling, 'What the hell do you want?'

# Brandee

**BrandeeH**

**@Brandee2ees | Joyn Inn Video | Status: All Joyn Inn |**

*\* December 2021 \* | Repost |*

No talking, just read the captions I'm pointing to.

My mother stabbed me once.

I wouldn't do what she wanted so she grabbed the kitchen knife and stabbed me in the shoulder. You can see the scar when I wear spaghetti strap things.

We lied to the doctors at the hospital that I was running with the knife and fell. We lied to my dad and said the same thing.

I'm scared of her.

# Kez

## 17 May, Brighton

'I, erm, I wanted to talk to you about Brandee,' I say. 'Was wondering if you'd seen or spoken to her?'

A nasty smirk takes over Seraphina's face and she narrows her eyes at me. 'What's the matter, she run out on you, too? Bet she left with your husband, right? Shagging him right under your nose and now they've run off together. Am I right?'

'Erm, not really. Actually, not at all. Jeb says hi by the way.'

She looks like she wants to spit on me but won't waste the saliva. 'So what are you doing here?'

'I just thought you might have heard from her? Even in passing? I just haven't heard from her in a while and I wondered if—'

'Oh fuck off,' Seraphina says and slams the door in my face.

*Well, that was better than could have been expected*, I think as I pick up the car seat with the sleeping Arie who she didn't even notice. 'At least she didn't try to batter me, eh, baby boy?' I whisper. That wasn't at all helpful except to tell me Brandee wasn't desperate enough to contact her mother.

Once I have strapped Arie into the back of my car, I sit in the driver's seat wondering if I should, in fact, go to the police. I know a couple of them from the times I've been consulted on cases that need a profile to help them work out what the mindset of the criminal is. Sometimes I've been asked to profile a suspect they have in custody from the information they have on them. Those officers who I've assisted might be helpful, could be discreet. Would most likely tell me if there's any news on Brandee, if any bodies matching her description have shown up. I don't want to go there, to think that, but maybe I do need to think about it? Work all the angles? Think of this situation as a giant profile that will help me understand what is really going on here so I can start to look for her properly.

A rap-rap-rap on my window makes me yelp and almost hit the car roof from how high I jump in my seat. I slam my hand over my mouth and wait for Arie to respond to my yelp with a loud cry, but nothing. I risk a look around and he's quietly sleeping. I then turn to the source of the sound and find Brandee's dad, Bert, crouched down beside my car, only his head – the top of it – showing. I hit the window button so I can speak to him. 'Hello?'

'Seraphina can't know I'm talking to you,' he says.

I've always been a bit meh about Bert Hamilton. He has never stepped in at any point to stop his wife, to protect Brandee from what was done to her. Brandee only ever had nice things to say about her dad, she told me often that he would protect her in his own way – he was just gentle, and always scared that Seraphina would accuse him of something. He didn't leave because he didn't want to leave Brandee behind, he didn't take her and go because he was terrified of being locked up for kidnapping. He apparently had an 'adventurous' youth and Brandee often hinted that her mother held that over his head, saying that he feared she would get him locked up quite easily because the police would love to put away an affluent Black man. I still found it hard to respect him, but after Brandee explained, I did downgrade him from actively bad to benignly awful to meh.

'Brandee told me you'd probably reach here,' he says.

'When did you last see her?' I ask.

'Two months ago. She asked me to meet her in the park. Gave me this for you.' He pushes a small white envelope into the car.

'What is it?'

'No idea. She said she was going to drop out of sight for a while and to give it to you if you showed up looking for her.'

'How did she seem?'

'Determined.'

'Determined?' That wasn't what I was expecting to hear. I thought I'd hear 'tired' or 'OK', especially since Arie would have been a month old at the time, but determined?

'She was going to do something. I could tell. She had something planned, she was determined to see it through. I don't know what, but I could see that steel in her eyes.'

Maybe I was wrong about Bert Hamilton. Maybe he did know his daughter, and he did stick around to try to dilute and mitigate the worst of Seraphina. Living with an addict, one with an addiction that is not instantly recognisable, must be hell. There are no twelve-step programmes for attention addicts, online engagement addicts, there is no way to get that type of addict into therapy because they were very unlikely to see a problem. If you ever, *ever* challenged Seraphina, she would come at you through her blog, through her posts, through her followers piling on. How do you stop an addict like that?

'I know you don't think much of me,' he says. 'You think I let Seraphina do whatever she wants and Brandee suffered as a result. But I stayed to keep Brandee safe. I stay now to do the same. If she ever wants to come home, I am here. And if I'm here, Seraphina doesn't get too out of hand. I can stop her going for Brandee in public, I can stop her posting the most private of private things online. I don't challenge her directly no, but I take things away, I minimise things. I do my best. For Brandee.'

'I understand,' I reply with a nod. I am ashamed and I deserve to be. I forgot my first rule of being a therapist – nothing is as it seems.

'Let me know when you find her,' he says. 'And tell her I love her.' He checks the house, looks to see if Seraphina is watching, stands up and walks briskly down the street.

# Brandee

**Brandee | Secret video recording | Memory stick |**

*** Recorded: 1 March 2023 ***

Please, Mrs Q, don't look for me. You'll put Arie in danger.

No one knows about him. I did everything I could to keep him a secret. That's one of the reasons why I shut down my social media for an extended time and why I went away to have him. No one could know about him. Not even Moe knows about him.

I can't tell you who the dad is right now, it's complicated.

I don't want to leave Arie, but I have to do this. Even though I know it's dangerous, I have to do it. I have to. Please try not to worry about me. As long as I know you're looking after my boy for me, I'll be all right, I promise.

You're probably going to hear some stuff about me. Most of it will be lies, some of it will be true, but none of it will be as it seems. You used to say that – nothing is as it seems. Please don't believe everything you see, hear or are sent.

It's fake. All of it is fake. Even the stuff that looks real, feels real, is fake. Don't believe any of it.

And please, look after my baby.

# Part 3

Part 3

# Kez

## 23 May, Brighton

Across the road and a bit further around our road, Chris and Ellie Chandler live.

I met them when I thought that, for a brief moment, I could join the parent–teacher group of Jonah's school. I'd slightly been egged on to join by the bursar of the school deciding that, if I wanted to join, she was going to change the joining rules – I would apparently need four signatures of people already on the committee, while everyone else needed two. I apparently was also going to have to be on probation for a year, during which time they could ask me to leave, while 'probation' wasn't even mentioned for anyone else. 'I wonder what's different about me?' I said to Jeb. He had rolled his eyes, and said, 'Why do people always think they can try it with you?' Obviously, when I challenged the bursar in front of everyone about these extra special Kez rules, she was adamant that I had misunderstood what she was saying and of course I had the same joining rules as everyone else.

Chris and I joined the PTG, and while I discovered very quickly it was *not* for me, Chris loved it, and went on to become its head. They have two children – Jasper, who goes to school with Jonah, and baby

Abigail. When Ellie saw me in the street the other day with Arie, she said to bring him over any time I needed a break.

Today is 'any time'.

It's not so much a break I need, as somewhere for Arie to be for a bit while I go and talk to someone. I've tried really hard to do as Brandee has asked. I've left it another week and I have only looked for her online, but since I got that video on the USB stick from Bert Hamilton, I've noticed an uptick in posts about Brandee. I'm sure it's coincidence, but a lot of people are talking about her. And the things she is allegedly doing. I keep reminding myself that she told me this was going to happen, she said not to believe the things I saw and heard. But it is hard. When it is there in your face, when all sources I check seem to say that these rumours are more than rumours, that these rumours are truth, it's hard not to be more than a little scared. It's hard not to try to find her.

There is a guy I know who might be able to give me an insight into what is going on and I need to not be distracted by a baby when I talk to him.

'Come in, come in,' Ellie says with a smile when I show up at her door, baby Arie in his car seat and his neatly packed change bag on my shoulder. I'd forgotten that it is nigh on impossible to go anywhere without a mountain of stuff – spare nappies, spare bottle, change of clothes, change mat, etc., etc. She stands aside to let me in. She pushes her glasses up her nose and says, 'Chris is working from home today. We have Jessie-May over, too?'

'I don't think I know her,' I say.

'Jessie-May Smart? Her parents are Dan and Cheryl Smart? They both joined the PTG? Dan's sister, Lily Smart, works at the school?'

'Ahh, yes, I do remember now.'

As if by magic, Chris appears with baby Abigail, who isn't so much of a baby any more at two, and Jessie-May. Abigail doesn't have the almost white-blonde hair of her brother yet, but she has the same cute little face and button nose. And the happy smile that the whole family seem to share. Jessie-May, who I think is about one, who I do recognise because she's the image of her parents, is another sweet little girl with blonde hair and blue eyes and a wide smile. Chris and Ellie are what they call 'good people' and I'm so grateful for them right now.

'Good afternoon,' Chris says to me. 'Cup of coffee? Tea?'

'Tea would be great,' I reply. I had been on the verge of just dropping and running but if there's anything this situation with Brandee has taught me it's that I need to make more time for people. Pause. Enjoy the company of good people, soak up the reminders of what life is all about.

'So how is life on the PTG?' I ask Chris.

'Don't,' Ellie replies for him. 'They're gearing up for the big end-of-year party and, of course, Chris has suggested they have a big cook-out barbeque. Just so he can get his big oil drum barbeques out.' She smiles as she gives him a sideways look, the deep affection and love between the two of them palpable.

Abigail and Jessie-May are leaning over Arie, fascinated by him. He is looking up at them, equally fascinated it seems.

'I, for one, cannot wait to see you back in the apron,' I tell Chris. 'Sorry, Ellie.'

She laughs, runs her hand through her blonde-streaked brown, shoulder-length hair. 'It's fine, it's fine,' she says. 'But seeing as you're so keen, you can be the one to help clean out oil drums and wash the smoke smell out of the clothes afterwards, yes?'

'Hey, yeah, nope. Those are both Jeb's jobs. In fact, I'm sure he'll be pleased to help out.'

'Jeb knows what's what. He'll love being up there, smoking the meat, throwing back a few beers.' Chris adjusts his glasses and runs his hand over his brown, grey and blond goatee beard as though in deep thought for a moment. 'Has Jeb actually thought about joining the PTG?'

'I think you'd better go before he warms to this theme,' Ellie cuts in.

'I know it wasn't for you, Kez,' Chris says, 'but we could use a dad like Jeb. He'd fit right in. I don't know why I haven't thought of it before.'

'I'll mention it to him, but I wouldn't hold your breath,' I laugh.

I say goodbye to Arie, who has fallen asleep with Abigail and Jessie-May both sitting on either side of him as though guarding him from any perceived or real danger.

'I'm on my mobile if you need anything. I shouldn't be too long.'

'Take as long as you like,' Ellie tells me at the door. 'We'll be fine.'

'Thank you so much. And don't forget to let the school know I'll bring Jasper home with Jonah.'

'I'll do that,' she says.

I feel a bit odd, not having Arie with me. Like I've left something behind. It's actually scary how quickly I – and the others – have got used to having Arie around. It's almost hard to remember a time when he wasn't here and it's only been a week. Arie is well and truly a part of the family now.

Before I drive off, I text Moe.

*Hi Moe, how are you?*
*Zee and Jay have been wondering*

*when you'll be free to come over?*
*They haven't seen you in months and months.*
*They miss you. So do I. Don't roll your eyes, I do!*
*Let me know if you need anything*
*or just fancy a chat. Love you. K x*

I almost ask about Brandee, but then decide not to. If he knows where she is, he'll most likely tell her I'm still looking for her, which will not go down well. If he doesn't know, he'll be worried. The best thing to do is leave it. I don't know the status of their relationship. They were very on and off when they lived in our house, and then that seemed to carry on when they moved out. From her video, it doesn't sound like Moe is the father of her baby, so there'll be that fallout. She said it's complicated. And I'm trying not to think about what that complicated might be.

My phone bleeps.

**All good. Could use 200 Gs, tho.**

*Two hundred grand?* I think, screwing up my face. *He wants 200,000 pounds?* I'm about to text him back when a message comes up.

**I meant, 2 Hs. Mum's birthday.**

He needs £200, not £200,000. Thank goodness.

*Phew!* 😄 *I'll transfer it later.*

Moe replies:

**Safe.**

Then:

**X**

I drive off knowing at least one of my adult children – and Brandee is my child despite me not giving birth to her – is doing OK.

# Kez

## 23 May, Brighton

Larry 'Larks' Whitland doesn't like me. In many ways, that's totally understandable.

His muddy hazel eyes watch me warily as I enter Whitland Garage, his domain. The garage is neat. Everything is put in its place, the shelves lined up with clearly labelled parts, the tyres piled up four high, three wide. Oils and greases, all facing the same way. The stone ground, smudged here and there with slick black oil, has been cleaned up so there is very little trace of spillages even though there must have been loads of it, slicked layer upon layer, car after car, year after year. In the corner is his desk, neat and orderly too. Black-grey box files all lined up, labelled A–D, E–J, K–O, P–U, V–Z. An old computer sits beside the box files, an ink blotter takes up the whole front of the desk, while a pot of pens sits quite precariously on the edge of the desk – one false move and it'll topple onto the ground.

The garage smells of grease, feels like car engines, sounds like the clanging of an ancient central heating system asked to perform without the proper care and attention.

His neatness and fastidiousness probably comes from prison – from being banged up in a confined space and having to make sure everything stays in its place, otherwise there is nowhere to do anything. Nowhere to sit, to think, to even breathe.

I used to see it all the time – people who never thought of where things need to live, who just shoved stuff and things into drawers, who left piles of paperwork and admin just anywhere and simply moved one obstructive, intrusive pile from one place to another would enter an institution. The institution would present to them confined quarters, minimal belongings, and they would be forced to find a place for everything. They would be forced to return things to their proper home. They would then carry that tidiness, the almost fanatical need to keep order, out into the world when they left the institution – prison, hospital, rehab, whatever. There was comfort and familiarity in the routine of putting belongings away, not accumulating too much stuff, not allowing 'things' to weigh you down.

Larks sits on the edge of his desk, rests a foot on the wheelie chair, his navy-blue overalls baggy on his quite solid form. He takes the cigarette he keeps behind his ear, taps it lightly on the desk as he looks me over. He doesn't like me for many reasons, but the main one is that I am a reminder of prison. I used to go into prisons to talk to the inmates, at least that was the official story. A lot of the time I was there to try to get the guards to see the inmates as humans. Once they could do that, once they could understand what someone going through detox or bereavement or loneliness was experiencing, they would treat them a bit more kindly. Which, in turn, would make their lives easier. A bit of understanding and, dare I say it, empathy was ultimately good for the guards. I met Larks when he was in Hawkhurst Prison, which means I am one of those things that drags him back to that time, spins him away from his respectable present into what he tries to avoid thinking of as his shameful past.

'Wouldn't have thought you'd be allowed to smoke in here,' I say cheerfully. 'What with all the flammable, BOOM-able materials in here.'

He looks at the white stick with the beige tip as though he didn't even realise he was holding it. 'I don't smoke in here. I go outside.'

'Aah, I see.' It is his comfort blanket, his worry toy when confronted with an element from his murky past.

'What do you want?' he demands.

'Information,' I reply.

'And why would I want to help out the rozzers?'

'I'm not with the rozzers.'

*Yeah, right, course not*, his face says.

'I'm not,' I insist.

His broad, solid chest moves in one go as he inhales deeply. 'Look, I know I owe you, but I ain't getting involved.' Tap, tap of his cigarette. He lifts it, then tosses it towards his mouth, catches it with his teeth.

'You don't owe me. You honestly don't.'

'Yeah, I do.'

'All right then, you do. You owe and I am collecting. On behalf of myself. Nothing to do with the rozzers – police – I need help. I wouldn't be here if I wasn't desperate.'

'Charming.'

'It is true. I would not be putting you through this if I thought I had any other choice. The police can't help me with this. I need someone with your . . . experience to help me out.'

'And if I help, we're quits?'

'Absolutely quits. I will never bother you again.'

He snorts like he doesn't believe it. I wouldn't believe it either, but we have to pretend in these situations, don't we?

'What is it you want?'

'I'm looking for someone.'

'What am I? The Missing Persons Bureau?'

'Ha-ha.'

I take out my phone, hold it up so he can see. Then I swipe, swipe, swipe so there are different versions of Brandee in front of him. Different hairstyles, different make-up, different personas. 'I know her,' he says.

'I'm not surprised. At one point she was on everyone's phones and screens. She was a really well-known socials star. "Hey, Hey! It's Brandee with the two ees"? That's her.'

'No, no,' he speaks with the cigarette between his lips, his eyes slightly narrowed. He is searching, furiously searching, through his mind for where he has seen her. 'I've seen her. I've seen her.'

'Any idea where?'

'In one of my videos, I think.' He scratches at the stubble on the right of his chin. He points to the computer, sitting black-screened and innocent on his desk beside him. 'Videos.' He mumbles. 'Web videos. Webcams.'

Ice twinkles down my spine. I came to him because I suspected he would be into porn – the extreme stuff – and webcams, the stuff that the rumours online were alluding to. I was hoping Larks would be able to tell me something about who makes them, how he gets them, and, most importantly, reassure me that he hadn't seen any with Brandee.

I feel sick. Standing here, knowing that the rumours I've been hearing online, the stuff that I've been pretending couldn't possibly be true just might be.

'Are you sure it's her?'

'Yeah, yeah. That curly Afro, and the . . .' He moves his hands in his chest area, then remembers I'm looking for her so probably won't take too kindly to what he's mimicking.

'Videos or webcam?'

'The videos were a while back, maybe six months. Just the straight stuff, nothing too kinky. Boring really. That's why I remember her. Dark, but not doing any of the other stuff those birds usually do. Recently, it's webcams.'

'That's the interactive stuff, right?'

'Yeah. She's good. Really good. Knows how to . . .'

'Oh don't stop on my account. Knows how to what?'

'Why are you looking for her?'

'How long ago was the video stuff?' I reply, deliberately dodging his question.

'A while back, like I said. Few months ago, maybe six months?'

'Are you sure?'

'Yeah. It was her.'

'Was she pregnant?'

'Pregnant?'

'Yes, pregnant.'

He looks at me like I am odd. Like certain men don't have that particular kink. 'Nah, not pregnant.'

'So maybe it wasn't her?'

He frowns. 'Maybe. Let me see the pictures again.' I call them back up, swipe, swipe, swipe while his eyes go back to searching his memory while devouring the photos. 'Maybe it wasn't her. Cos this girl . . . the one I'm thinking of, she was on the other side, if anything. Needed a good feed. Skinny body but big,' again with the cupped hands in the chest area. 'Looked like her, though. Looked so much like her.'

'Looked like her or was her?' I ask a bit more sharply than I intended.

'Sorry, I mean, it's really important to make sure it's the right girl. I don't have time to chase down this girl and find out it's not Brandee.'

He looks at my phone screen again, moves his face right up to it. 'It looks so much like her.' He frowns. 'So much like her.' He rubs his fingers over his mouth, over his brow, his eyes constantly search his memory.

'Can you just get your phone out and show me one of the videos? One of your webcam sessions?'

'No!' he spits, disgust oozing like slime from every part of the word, every part of his being.

'It'll be nothing I haven't seen before and it'll stop all this "is it isn't it?" stuff.'

'I ain't doing it. I ain't showing you that.'

'You don't have to show it to me. You look and see if it is her or not.'

'Not with you here, I won't.'

'What, you're wanting me to come back?'

That stops him. 'Wait here,' he says begrudgingly. He crosses his empty garage space and goes into the toilet. He slams and locks the door loudly, to let me know that I won't able to storm in there and catch him unawares.

Minutes pass. More minutes pass. *Is he aroused in there? Is that why he hasn't returned cos he doesn't want me to see what effect the videos have had on him? Is he cracking one out while I wait?*

Eventually, very eventually, he emerges. He has a 'just finished' glow mixed with embarrassment redness to his face and he won't meet my eye. He clears his throat a few times before he speaks, still avoiding eye contact. 'I can't tell,' he admits. 'I mean, it looks like her, but then it doesn't. I checked through quite a few old videos and saved chats and I can't tell.'

'I'll have to look then.'

He colours up even more, so bright, so red, I think he's about to explode. He clears his throat again, stares at the ground. 'I took some, erm, screenshots.' He holds his phone out for me to take and I recoil like it is a wild animal that's about to bite me, like it's something a man has just used to get himself off. I am not touching it. Not even for Brandee.

'Just get it up . . . I mean, just pull it up, I mean, call up the screenshots, I don't need to touch – I mean, take your phone.' *Smooth, Kez. Really smooth.*

After a moment's fiddling, he holds the phone up. The image isn't brilliant, it's fuzzy and colour-drained, but I can see the face of the performer in the video. It's clear from the image what sort of thing floats Larks's boat and I am erasing it from my mind the second I walk away from here. But I understand what he means. It is hard to tell. This woman could be Brandee. She has her build, her colouring and even one of her favourite hairstyles, but, my eyes search and search, until I realise it's not there. The scar on her left shoulder, just beside the collarbone is not there.

Her mother gave her that scar when she was twelve. She stabbed her with a kitchen knife when Brandee refused to make a video with her about her first period, just like an addict would attack someone who wouldn't give them money for their next fix.

'*She just snatched up the knife from the wooden block on the kitchen side and stabbed me with it,*' Brandee told me in the middle of the night. '*She was so angry with me. She said I didn't get to say no to her. Not after everything she'd done for me. Dad was away for work. She'd promised him no more videos until he got home. She promised him that she would let me say no if I didn't want to do something. She was really sorry afterwards. She cried and cried and said she wouldn't do it again. I had to tell the hospital that I was running with the knife and slipped. I don't think the nurse believed it, but the doctor did because she was one of Seraphina's fans. When the nurse tried to say something, the doctor shut her down. We told Dad the same thing. But at least I didn't have to make the video.'* It was that night I decided that I had to get Brandee away from Seraphina.

The scar is missing from the webcam screenshot, which is a lot more lurid, as well. 'It's not her,' I say relieved. 'It looks so much like her, but it's not her.'

'Good, good,' he says, just as relieved as I am, I think. 'I'm going to ask a couple of the lads. Give me your number and I'll call you when I know more.' He pulls his unlit cigarette from behind his ear, holds it between his forefinger and middle finger of his right hand, then taps the top of his head. 'If I hear anything, I'll let you know.'

'OK, fine. Thank you.'

'Of course.'

I give him my number and prepare to leave.

'I'm, erm, sorry, for . . .'

'Like I've said a hundred times before, it's OK.'

'It was nothing personal.'

'I know. Look, I'm going to leave before you start the full apology thing. I've said it's fine, you've helped me out with this, so we're quits. OK?'

'OK,' he says, hanging his head.

'I'll see you, Larks.'

'Yeah.'

Larks doesn't like me because at Hawkhurst Prison, during a group therapy session, he jumped up and punched me in the face.

# Kez

## 6 June, Brighton

It's been three weeks. Three long, torturous weeks without any word or hint of Brandee.

Larks called to say he'd heard that there were videos circulating of her, but he hadn't seen any and neither had any of his friends. It was the same with the internet and social media rumours – lots of talk, many rumours, no actual facts.

*Where are you, Brandee?* I ask several times a day in my head. *What's happening to you?*

'Are you even listening to me, Kez?' Jeb asks. We're sitting at the kitchen table, having our nightly chat over dandelion tea (me) and beer (Jeb) and my mind keeps wandering, taking off to worry about Brandee and where she might be.

I place my hand on his, curling my fingers around it. 'I'm sorry, no. I can't—' I wave my other hand near my head '—focus. I'm scared for her.'

'I know you are,' Jeb takes his hand away from mine to take a sip of his beer. 'But life has to go on while we try to figure this out. I was asking about the job. They called again today, offering two hundred and fifteen thousand? I was asking you what you're going to say?'

'Exactly what I've been saying all the time they've been asking – no.'

I cross my arms across my chest, trying to contain my fury. 'And it really grinds my gears that they keep calling you and telling you how much money is on offer when that's meant to be confidential.'

'I'm just someone who answers the phone that they talk to. It's not really that big of a deal since we're married.'

'But that's just it, Jeb. They would expect me to keep anything I learn in that job confidential – i.e. not tell you. But this, that's also meant to be confidential? They chat all about it to the person who answers the phone and claims to be my husband. It's part of the manipulative way they operate.'

'Do you really think that?' he says.

'I *know* that. It's what we were taught – if you can't get what you want from the person you want it from, target those close to them, get them to do your dirty work for you. They keep adding numbers and telling you because they think there's going to be a figure that will make you pressurise me into taking the job.'

'Or maybe they think we'll actually discuss it instead of it being a flat "no" from you?'

'Discuss what, exactly? Me travelling up and down to London every day? Me being a glorified recruitment consultant who has to decide which psychopath gets the job heading up various government and other departments over another? No, thank you.'

'Pretty sure there's more to the job than that,' my husband says quietly, reasonably, taking another sip of his beer.

'Pretty sure there isn't,' I reply, loudly, unreasonably.

'All right, enough!' Jeb says, slamming his beer down onto the table. The salt shaker and pepper grinder quake, and I jump. 'Just go, Kez. Just go and see him, get it over with. I know that's what this is all about. I know you want to go back to him.'

'You're making it sound like I'm going back to a lover, or something. I do not want to go back to him. If I never see that man again it'll be too soon. But I am desperate right now. I don't know what is happening to Brandee. What if it was Moe, Jeb?'

'I care about Brandee, too. You don't have to "what if it was Moe" me. That job nearly destroyed you. It took everything from you, turned you into . . . into someone who takes risks and endangers herself all the time to try to make up for what happened. It's why you won't even think about this new job. It's why you were not at all bothered when Seraphina was trying to mash you up. It's why you went to see that man who punched you in the face. You were alone with him and didn't even think twice about it. He could have done anything to you, but you just rocked up there and started asking him questions about his porn habits.

'You don't feel things like you should do sometimes, Kez. It's terrifying to watch. It's terrifying being someone who loves you and watching. And it's all because of *him*, but you want to go back to him.'

'I do not want to go back to him!' I shout, then remember the three children, one of whom can sleep through any noise but seems to wake up at the mere sound of my voice, so I lower my tone. 'I don't want to go back to him. You know what he did and because of that I do not want to see him again. *Ever.* But he might be able to help me find Brandee. I've been struggling with myself over that.'

'I know, and it's making you all kinds of stressed. See? Just the thought of seeing him is making you like this. That's why I do not want you going back there. But I do understand you feel like it's your only option.'

'*Our* only option.'

'Our only option,' he mumbles.

My husband is too protective sometimes. After Larks punched me in the face, Jeb said no more prison work. Even though I explained I met more psychopaths in every day life than I ever met banged up, he was adamant – no more prisons. And he didn't understand how I could be around Larks after what he did when, for me, it really was no issue. Larks had thought I was about to reveal something about him to the group, that I would make him look weak and pathetic. I wasn't going to do that. I would never do that. But he hadn't known that, and had jumped up and punched me to shut me up. It was a misunderstanding. I told the prison brass as much but he was still sanctioned. That's why he feels like he owes me – I spoke up for him after he punched me. And I didn't tell anyone what he thought I was going to reveal. But Jeb was having none of it. No more prisons.

So I know this is why he wants me to do what Brandee has asked and care for Arie, stop looking for her. He won't say it, but I know he's thinking it.

And he is right – it must be terrifying to watch me do some of the things I do. But this is different. This is Brandee's life at stake. I have to do everything I can to find her.

'If you tell me not to go, I won't go,' I say to Jeb. There. Let him decide. Let him see that I don't just go wandering into danger for the thrill of it – I am only ever there because I have to be.

'Talk about bait,' Jeb replies, draining his beer. 'Go. Go see him. I know you won't rest until you've tried everything.'

I cover his hand with mine again; this time, though, I am clinging on. Hoping that he'll hold onto me as always. Jeb is my lifeline. He is the reason why I can do all the things I do. The reason I survive. 'I will be careful,' I reassure him. 'I will be as careful as I possibly can.'

'Sure you will,' he mumbles. He takes his hand away and stands to head for the fridge. 'Sure you will.'

# Part 4

# Kez

## 8 June, Central London

I'm not a fan of going into government buildings. Never have been, even when I used to work in one way back when.

When I was first training, I used to come to a building like this one every day. It looks like an ordinary office block, right next to other red-bricked, yellow-grouted buildings near Covent Garden, London. It blends in like the other office blocks, but the windows are mirrored so you cannot see in and behind them there are net curtains that look grubby and in need of a wash, but are actually bomb blast protection.

I have to use the official entrance, since I am no longer a government employee. The male security person and female receptionist who take my details are extremely pleasant. They ask my name, they take my picture, they ask me who I'm here to see. They do all this from behind a large Perspex screen that I'm not sure was there before 2020 or not. Either way, it doesn't seem to hinder their general demeanour and how they interact with me. I know while we're talking, the third security person, who is sitting right at the other end of this bank of desks and not interacting with us, is typing my name into his computer.

Having typed in my name, he is reading all about me. How I used to work for the person I am here to see. How at one point (I thought) I was a rising star who (I thought) would end up running this department. I glance very briefly at him and see his face change. He's got to *that* point in my government employee story. He's seen what happened – the official version – about my fall from grace, about why I left. It's also the reason why the guy I am here to see – Dennis Chambers – would not answer the phone to me if I called. I've had to make the trip to London, leaving Arie with Jeb for the day. He's taken the day off, and despite his saying that he would support what I did, he is not happy about it. But he'll be less happy if we don't find Brandee in time, that's how I have reasoned it with him and myself.

'I'll just buzz up to Mr Chambers's office,' the receptionist says. Obviously she's been given the all clear by the third man to allow this meeting to take place. I like her dark grey suit and tell her so.

'Thank you,' she says, pretending to be flattered. You don't do her type of job and find yourself easily flattered by compliments. She knows very well that she could end up holding a gun on the person saying they like her hair, so she's astute enough to act the part, but not to allow the words to penetrate her mind and thought process at all. 'Take a seat,' she says, pointing to the brightly coloured, modular sofa area that is opposite their desk.

Very few people come without an appointment and therefore need to wait here, so this area is designed to look good but be uncomfortable because no one stays here long – the sofas are angled so you cannot easily sit back, you cannot relax, you cannot easily hide what you're doing from the people at the desk. It's for show, this area.

I don't have an appointment because I know Dennis would not see me if I made him aware that I wanted to meet with him. In fact, I'm not sure he'll see me now, that he isn't as I sit here, uncomfortable and exposed, slipping out the back door and making his way as far away from here as he can.

## September, 1998

'Look around you, people, this is going to be the place you call home for the next two years of your life.' Dennis Chambers was an impressive man. I'd only met him once in the five interviews I'd had, and even then I hadn't properly met him – he sat silently in the corner observing the proceedings. And I got the feeling that he had been at the other interviews, he simply wasn't sitting in the room as I was. There was something quietly commanding about him. He wasn't especially tall, he didn't have the fit body of a man overly concerned with his appearance, but he was neat, his brown hair styled to sit off his slightly lined face. The most impressive thing about him, though, was his self-confidence. It oozed from every part of him. He was good at what he did and he knew it.

I'd decided to take the job my Masters tutor had told me about. It was a wage that I could only dream about, and it would give me the certification necessary to become a proper, qualified psychotherapist in three years.

'Usually, I have twelve people on my training programme, usually, twelve people sit in this room and learn how to become the type of multi-disciplinary clinical psychologists that we need across the intelligence services. We realised a while ago that it was better for us if we trained people to do the jobs we needed rather than waiting and hoping and wishing the right people would fall into our laps. My programme has been running for five cycles. And this is the first year that I have only got three suitable candidates.

'Three. Pitiful. That means, you three have to be nothing short of brilliant. Usually only three people are taken on after the training is complete. Look around you.'

I did as we were told. I took in the large, open-plan office with a bank of twenty desks, nestled in groups of four. At one end was a glass-walled office where Dennis obviously sat, and at the opposite end there were a couple of rooms that, I seemed to remember from the tour we took, were observation rooms. Those rooms had an area with a table and four chairs and a large mirror on the wall, which was actually an observation window for people on the outside to watch what was going on in the rooms.

The two other candidates – a chestnut-brown-haired woman called Maisie Parsons, and a fair-headed man called Brian Kershaw – and I were going to rattle around in this space. I hoped they weren't dickheads because there would be literally nowhere to hide from them if they were.

'This is where you start the next phase of your lives,' Dennis explained. 'I have trained some of the best psychologists in the country and I am only ten years older than you. I know what I am doing. Everything you do reflects on me and I do not like to look bad. Remember that. There is a kitchen down the corridor that we share with another team who are on a slightly different programme. There is also a break room. Don't eat at your desks. And don't mess this up. The room or this opportunity.'

## 8 June, Central London

Dennis has kept me waiting for an hour now. I have sat here without a magazine to read and without checking my phone. This is psychological warfare. Everything about Dennis is to do with psychological warfare. He wants to test you, *constantly*. He wants to dominate, *every time possible*. He wants to win, *always*.

I have not worked for him, with him, under him, for nearly twenty years, but he is still testing me. Subjecting me to his very unique brand of 'training'.

## November 1998

'I had the best wank over you this morning,' Dennis murmured into my ear.

I was making three cups of instant coffee and was still contemplating milk or no milk in mine, when I'd heard him enter the kitchen. It was big enough for six people to comfortably move around in but rather than go to the sink or the kettle, he'd come to me. He'd pushed his body ever so slightly against mine, he'd leant in, and then whispered those words in my ear. Anyone walking in right now would misconstrue what was going on. They would miss how rigid my body was, how my eyes had closed in disgust, how very close I was to throwing up. They would see a senior member of staff pressed up against a trainee and they would assume she was trying to screw her way to the top. I hadn't been doing field work training that long – two months – but I knew how things looked. How something could fit the expected narrative while being something completely different.

I loved this job.

*Hated* this man.

Knew I couldn't have one without the other.

Theoretically, I could report him. I could put an end to this vileness. Realistically, who would believe me? Who wouldn't tell me that it was just a bit of banter, no harm was meant? Who wouldn't imply I wasn't a team player? Who wouldn't decide my file should be marked to spare other departments and people from me? He was senior, I was not. He was known to them for producing psychologist after psychologist for them, I was not.

Reporting Dennis was not going to help me.

'I don't think I've ever come that hard on my own. You should have been there,' he continued. 'It was that cream blouse with the pink buttons that did it. The way the buttons strain across your chest . . . Wear it again this week, there's a good girl.'

'It's in the wash,' I said quietly. It wasn't in the wash, but it was going in the 'never to be worn again' pile along with my black Lycra skirt, my red vest top and my black A-line skirt. The list of clothes I could wear around Dennis was growing ever shorter.

The thing about him was, when he wasn't being a sleaze, when he wasn't telling me the disgusting things he wanted to do to me, he was actually a good trainer. He was attentive, professional, and inspiring. He would explain things in very clear ways, he would encourage independent thought and areas of research. He would always give credit to my and the other trainees' ideas in meetings – even if we'd just contributed a few lines. He would suggest areas of improvement, give you guidance on what would be of interest to you. He was always saying I could go on to do great things, and would show me the sort of positions he thought I would be suitable for inside and out of the intelligence services once I was qualified.

We overheard the other trainees from the other office on this floor talking sometimes and it was obvious from their conversations that they weren't being given even half the attention and help that I and Dennis's other trainees were.

He was the perfect boss.

Except for his sexual harassment.

It was the type of thing that bent my mind into all sorts of weird shapes. He was so good, so dedicated and professional on the one hand, then a total scumbag on the other. He was like two different people in one body. That was also why I knew no one would believe me. How could they when he was Boss of the Year.

'*People are more than one thing at the same time*,' my mum had told me more than once. Dennis Chambers showed me that every day.

## 8 June, Central London

Two hours. I have now been waiting two hours.

The people behind the desk have been watching me, curious as to why I haven't stormed out or approached the desk to ask if they could call him again. Or maybe they're not looking at me because they're curious, maybe they're staring because I've lasted the longest out of all the people Dennis has done this to. I can put an end to this if I just get up, walk over to the shiny metallic desk with its Perspex screen separating me from them and ask for them to call him again. If I do that, if I give in, cry 'uncle' first, he will appear. He will come straight down and give me a look that says he knows I don't have the mental capacity to go up against him; that despite everything I did in the past, I ultimately proved myself to be weak.

I know he's in one of the rooms up there that has cameras trained on reception, watching me.

He is watching and he is waiting.

He thinks I'm going to cry uncle first, which shows, for all his expertise, he really does not know me at all.

## *December, 1998*

You could set your watch by us. Every day at the same time, the three of us who were being trained by Dennis Chambers took the cups of hot drinks I'd made and went to the quiet break room tucked away on the second floor of this building. We worked on the fourth floor, but we found that the second-floor break room was quieter and Dennis was much less likely to appear. In between being The Best Boss Ever, Dennis was bullying each of us in very different ways. He kept making comments about Maisie's intelligence; he kept implying that Brian was a wimp. And he was still sexually harassing me whenever we were alone.

Maisie's family were all in government so, she'd told me, failure was not an option. When I'd hinted – *really heavily* – that she should maybe tell Dennis where to go or threaten to quit, she had looked at me like I had put the kettle on my head and was speaking in tongues. Leaving was not an option. 'Well, at least report him for bullying,' I'd replied.

'Why? I had worse, *much worse*, at boarding school,' she'd said.

'Just because you've had it worse, doesn't mean you should put up with this.'

'It'll be all right. I just have to prove to him I'm more than my looks and it will all be fine.'

Brian's family were all pretty much in the police or involved with the police, so he was another failure-is-not-an-option-er.

'Not a failure to stand up for yourself,' I said to him again. 'In fact, I reckon that's the very opposite of failure.'

'If I go whining to HR or something, he'll think I'm a—' Brian stopped speaking and eyed me up as though assessing if I would tell him off if he said something homophobic. 'He'll think I'm weak, that I'm not a real man, if I complain.'

'Who cares what he thinks? And from all the real men I know, standing up for yourself is pretty much the definition of being a man. Not shouting or fighting, but showing you're not going to be walked all over. That's real man, real woman, behaviour right there.'

'You wouldn't understand,' he replied. 'All of this is easy for you.'

*Is this guy joking?* I thought. 'How is this easy for me?'

He didn't even have the good grace to look uncomfortable. 'He doesn't pick on you, and we all know that's because of how you got onto this programme,' he said with a shrug.

'By being the best in my class and applying for it after a tip-off, like you were?'

'No, well, I wasn't top of my class, but I was headhunted. But that's different from how you got here.'

'On the train to Charing Cross—'

'No, you know what I mean. They had a quota to fill . . . you . . .'

'I . . .?' I questioned as his voice petered out because he was self-aware and enough of a psychologist to notice Maisie, who was sitting opposite him, widen her eyes in alarm before she ducked her head. I didn't see her do it, I just knew from his sudden reticence to speak that she had hit her internal panic button and that was its resulting look on her face.

'You . . . well . . . they had a quota.'

'Yes, you said that.'

'And well . . .'

'You also said that.'

'Look, I'm not saying you're not good at your job, I just know . . . All my family who work in the force tell me that it's all about quotas nowadays. Even when I was going to uni they said – didn't they Maisie, you said they told you, too – that it'd be so much harder for people like us to get into good universities cos of the quotas.'

Maisie was appalled. Absolutely appalled that he was dragging her into this. She had her own problems with Dennis without Brian creating them by telling me what they'd obviously been talking about behind my back.

'Bdbepf,' she mumbled before lifting her coffee – that I had kindly made for her – to her lips.

'So, you're saying you two got here through hard work and on merit, while I'm . . . what? The quota hire?'

'No. That's not what I am saying at all,' Brian said. He laced his fingers through the large handle of the cup in front of him. Another one that I had so generously made.

They rarely made hot drinks, but always accepted them when offered. Was this why? When all along I had been labouring under the impression that we were all in this together, especially with the Dennis factor, they were thinking I didn't deserve to be here? And were they thinking that my making them drinks was a way of me paying restitution to them for not really deserving to be here?

I had to know how much Brian believed this and how much was his frustration at his situation making him lash out. Both were bad, but how I dealt with them would be different. 'Then what are you saying?' I put my head on one side so I didn't seem threatening (I knew that accusation was coming) and pasted a small smile on my lips so it looked like he could talk to me. 'Cos I don't understand,' I said meekly, making myself soft, approachable, weak-seeming so he would feel empowered, emboldened; so he would speak what was truly in his mind and heart.

'I'm saying your being here isn't as straightforward as any of us like to pretend. We all act like you got here in the same way as we did, but we all know it's not true. You simply haven't had to go through what we did to get here.'

I almost laughed in Brian's stupid, clueless face. Of course I didn't. I didn't have both my uncle and godfather regularly ringing up from their Whitehall offices to check on my progress, like Maisie did. I didn't have offers to come and get some behind-the-scenes extra-curricular policing experience, like Brian did from his police family.

I had gratitude that I didn't have a car so I wasn't constantly pulled over by the police for simply driving around, like my siblings were; I was constantly battling low-level, slow-burning anxiety that around the next corner would be one of those racists who wouldn't be satisfied with verbally abusing me but would be intent on kicking my head in as well.

No, Brian, Maisie and I did not go through the same things to get here; Brian, Maisie and I were not going through the same things to stay here, no matter how similar it looked on the outside. What Brian's face – all earnest and open, without one shred of embarrassment – was broadcasting loud and clear was that he believed what he was saying.

They believed this nonsense, which meant, no matter what I did next, they would always think it. And they would always throw me under the bus first if they needed to save their skin. This meant I could not trust them, and I certainly couldn't open up about what Dennis did to me. The fact that Dennis harassed me in private while he humiliated them in public, probably gave credence to their stupid theories – he didn't bother with me because he was stuck with the quota that I represented no matter what.

This was the last drink I was making for either of these two, I decided.

'I'll admit, I didn't go through what you did, to get here,' I said to the man in front of me. 'Did either of you have five interviews in front of six-person interview panels?'

Brian's gaze swivelled to Maisie, whose eyes had done their startled expression again. 'No.'

'Did they require original paper copies of every one of your qualifications for authentication?'

He shook his head in lieu of speaking.

'So, I'm probably right in guessing they didn't ring every one of your teachers and lecturers from high school onwards to get a rundown of your personality and to check those paper qualifications were real?'

Another head shake.

'They went through a lot of trouble – what with all the time and resources they used to check me out – to have me fill this quota of theirs, don't you think? I mean, couldn't they have just got anyone who looked like me without a shred of ability or experience or even the smallest hint of a qualification to fill this position? Seeing as it doesn't matter who does it as long as they look like me?'

'I didn't say that,' Brian protested.

'He didn't say that,' Maisie added, backing him up now.

That was exactly what he said. But what was the point in arguing with them about it? It would just become a case of me being aggressive and not a team player. I dropped my gaze to the table top. 'No, I guess he didn't,' I replied. I stood up. 'I just need to nip to the loo before we go back for this afternoon's session. Enjoy your drinks.' *Cos they're the last ones I'm ever making you two snakes.*

## 8 June, Central London

*I'm not going away, Dennis*, I tell him silently. *I will wait here as long as I need to until you see me. Until you cry uncle and give in.*

*March, 1999*

BUZZ-BUZZ-BUZZ-BUZZ at my front door via the intercom.

*If I ignore it, it'll go away*, I told myself and pulled the duvet over my head again.

BUZZ-BUZZ-BUZZ-BUZZ. The caller was persistent. It wasn't the postman – I knew him and he'd just leave a card through the door – it was someone else who wanted a piece of me. And they couldn't have it. I wasn't currently available to callers.

BUZZ-BUZZ-BUZZ-BUZZ began again, but for some reason it was in a different note. And annoying as hell. It was at times like this I wished I lived with someone. Then *they'd* have to answer the door.

BUZZ-BUZZ-BUZZ-BUZZ. Bad temperedly, I came out into the corridor, picked up the black intercom phone. Before I could say anything, I heard someone from another flat push their button to open the communal front door downstairs.

Growling in frustration, I slammed the receiver into place. Talk about wasting my time. I had very valuable hiding-under-the-duvet work to do. How dare anyone take me away from it.

I was hiding under said duvet until I had amassed enough courage to resign from the training programme. It was ridiculous, really, that I needed courage to leave but that was how it was. I simply needed to not be harassed by Dennis any more.

He'd been ramping up the harassment, saying more disgusting things, pressing himself even closer against me. But, last week, when he'd come up behind me as usual, and I'd braced myself to hear something disgusting, he had cupped his hands on my breasts, pulled me against his body and rubbed his erection against me. I'd frozen, unable to think or move. Horrified. Seconds later, it was over, he let me go, whispered, 'I'm going to finish myself off in the toilet,' and left. I'd been numb and unable to speak for the rest of the day, and then called in sick the next day. And the following few days. Staying in bed had been dull but also freeing. And those days in bed also confirmed that I did not need to get on a train to central London to put up with Dennis's behaviour. I would do something else.

There were lots of jobs out there I could do, while I finished getting my qualifications as a psychologist. I just needed to start looking. In the meantime, I could temp. People would always need temps. I was just climbing into bed again when the knocking started on my front door.

The person did want me after all. How brilliant. Not. I shrugged on my dressing gown on the way to the front door.

Dennis.

That was someone I was not expecting on the other side of my door. He seemed out of place in the gloomy space of the corridor outside my home. And instead of being neatly put together like usual, his crumpled beige rainmac, small-knotted red tie and poorly ironed blue chinos made him look like the dirty old man he was.

'Get dressed,' he said. 'We're going for a walk.'

'Sorry?' I replied.

'Get dressed. I can't be seen with a trainee in her nightwear in her flat. Put some clothes on and we'll go for a walk and a talk.'

'I'm sick.'

'No, you're not.'

'I'm sick.'

'You're not sick and I'm not a sexual harasser.' He sighed. 'Just get dressed and I'll explain everything to you on a walk.'

'Why should I?' I said, even though I knew I was going to get dressed and go for a walk.

Dennis simply stared at me. He also knew I was going to get dressed and go for a walk.

'Why should I?' I repeated because even though we both knew I was going to go for that walk, there was no way I was making it completely easy for him.

'Because I'm asking you to,' he replied eventually. 'Please.'

It was the please that did it. I knew that was something that had been dragged from the depths of his pride. It wasn't a word he said regularly. It certainly wasn't a word he said to the likes of me.

I shut the door in his face without saying another word.

*

Dennis seemed to know where he was going when he led the way out of my building onto the main road but in the opposite direction to the train station. He was walking with purpose and seemed to forget that I was there for a good five minutes so was striding ahead of me. I didn't bother to try to keep up, he'd remember in his own time I was there and he had come to see me not the other way around.

'When I started my training, things were very different,' he said when he did finally remember I was there and slowed down. 'It wasn't pulled out of bed in the middle of the night with a black bag over your head and driven to the middle of nowhere to have an interrogation light shone in your eyes, but it wasn't far off.'

'Right, OK.'

'Things have become a bit more sophisticated since then. But, we still have to pressure the trainees to see if they'll last the course.'

'You still have to bully and demean people to see if they want to become therapists?' I replied. It was the middle of the day, but the traffic was quite heavy, the sound of it loud and intrusive. 'Seems a bit counterintuitive to me.'

Dennis gave me a long, puzzled look, he stared at me for so long I thought he was going to walk into the lamppost we were approaching. 'You honestly believe that you're training to be a clinical psychologist? Just a psychologist?'

'Yes, course. What else am I training to be?'

'It hasn't occurred to you that all of this is part of agent training?'

'No,' I replied. Even though my siblings, my mother and my father had all suggested, joked and outright declared it was, I had said and thought no. Not really. Because to be trained as an agent probably involved shooting guns and cross-country runs in the mud and cold, and those were things this Black woman's body were never going to do. 'I signed up to become a clinical psychologist,' I said. 'You've told me and shown me that we're being trained to work especially with agents and your department may extend this programme to employ us after training to specifically work with agents, but no, it has not occurred to me that this is agent training. Especially because I did not apply to become an agent.'

'You didn't apply at all.'

'What do you mean?' I asked, even though a few things made sense now. In my working life to that point, a few things hadn't added up. How I heard about the position, how I'd had a response to my enquiry straight away and had been immediately offered an interview. I'd flattered myself that I had done so brilliantly on the psychometric tests (how they graded my cognitive abilities, my personality and my job suitability) and had sparkled so much in every other area that they were desperate to have me. Now Dennis was blowing all of my delusions out of the water, but making lots of things make sense at the same time.

'Your tutor, Svetlana Owen, was an operative. Agent. Whatever we're calling it these days. Trained with me. She gives us the heads-up with the students she thinks are resilient enough to enter into training.'

'Are there others? Other tutors who worked with you and essentially dob in their students?'

'Of course.'

'Of course. Just like that, of course?'

'Did you want me to dress it up or something?'

'Well yeah, at least let me think you haven't been following me and people haven't been watching my every move. At least let me live in that delusion a little while longer.'

'I see. Right, well. Sorry about that.' Dennis did not sound sorry. At all. 'The point of this, is, Kezuma, that you are not simply training to become a clinical psychologist. You're all on track to become agents who work mainly on the psychological side of things. Even if you were simply going to be someone who gave therapy to agents, you would be hearing some terrible things. They go through awful things, they experience . . . some of the most depraved things . . . we need to make sure that you're mentally able to withstand what will be thrown at you.'

'Why does it sound suspiciously like you're about to justify something unjustifiable?'

'It's not unjustifiable.' We arrived at the park and he kept walking, heading towards the big supermarket on the other side of it. If he kept on at this pace, in this direction, we'd reach the train station before the one where I normally got on to go to work in no time. 'The weekly psychometric tests you take, tell us a lot about you.'

'Hang on, we don't take weekly psychometric tests. We have to design and create psychometric tests but we don't . . .' My words disappeared into the vast expanse of realisation that had just opened up in

173

front of me. 'We design and create those tests, which is actually a psychometric test in itself. Wow.'

'Once we have assessed the results of those tests, we know which areas are potential pressure points and could result in a total breakdown in the field. Maisie's pressure point is being taken for a bimbo. She is always worried people don't see her intellect and overcompensates. Brian's pressure point is his constant fight with his masculinity. He thinks he's not a real man and, like Maisie, overcompensates. Those are the areas we concentrate on, apply undue pressure to until we see whether the person can withstand it or if they crack.'

'What was my pressure point?' I noticed he hadn't been as forthcoming with that. But it was pretty obvious, now all these doors and windows of realisation were opening around me.

'You think you are very rarely seen as a desirable woman. Any attention you do receive is usually inappropriate and/or unwanted. Pressure point.'

'I think you're using that – which may or may not be a true pressure point – to get away with what you did to me,' I stated very clearly. It was important I made it clear I wasn't fooled by what he was saying about what he did and why he did it.

Dennis was silent for quite a few steps, contemplative almost. 'I didn't say I didn't enjoy it, nor that I didn't get off on doing what I did, just that it was necessary.'

'That's borderline psychopathic behaviour,' I said. *Actual psychopathic behaviour*, but I wasn't about to say that out loud to the psychopath.

'Not in this context.'

'How far would you have taken it? You said disgusting things to me. You brushed up against me, pushed yourself against me, you basically

174

assaulted me the other day. Where would you have drawn the line? At the groping? Would you have ra—'

'It would never have gone beyond what was necessary,' he cut in before I could say the word. 'And what was necessary was where we reached.'

'Why bother coming here?' I asked, genuinely baffled. 'I clearly failed the test, buckled under pressure. What do you want? Surely you'd much prefer if the flake that I am just disappeared? I mean, Brian and Maisie clearly have the right stuff. I do not. No need for a big long chat about it. What's it that you lot call it? No need for a debrief. I will simply disappear.'

'You passed – stayed as long as necessary, then left. We need people who have the ability to stay the course and then walk away. That ability keeps you safe. Sometimes keeps you alive. Getting involved, hanging around too long, does not keep you safe.'

There was a small, warm wave of satisfaction that I wasn't a failure, I actually had good instincts, but still. 'What if I don't want anything to do with all of this? Finding all of this out has not been the best experience. Working with you has been terrible. Maybe Kez just needs to go back to her life pre-experimental rat days.'

'I don't think you'll be able to do that. You've got a taste for this now. I don't need a psychometric test to tell me that. You've got the taste for it and more than that, you're good at it. You're a bright girl, always have been, but with this, you're exceptional and you know it. And you're not the type to give up on the things you really want.'

'And I don't need psychometric tests to know someone who is good at getting people to do what they want when I talk to one, Dennis. Especially someone with psychopathic tendencies. You know I love mysteries, like to work things out, so you show up after assaulting me, tell me spurious stuff, talk me up like I'm the heroine of this piece, and bingo, no awkward sexual assault chats with bosses necessary.'

'I respect the cynicism, but that's not what I'm doing. I think you could be a fantastic clinical psychologist. When our department expands, you'll be brilliant at dealing with agents and helping us construct the tests to decipher who we do and don't want working across the services. The change in our department status offers so much scope and you will be an excellent part of it. I want you to return and finish the training. Decide then if it's for you or not.'

'I'll think about it,' I said.

'Think fast. When I leave, the job leaves with me.'

'Haven't all the fancy tests told you I don't do well with ultimatums?'

'Yes, they did. And I need you to know I don't care.'

## 8 June, Central London

Three hours. I didn't expect him to keep me waiting this long but here I am.

The people behind the desk will be charging rent soon. I know, from the way they've frowned and blinked at their below-desk screen, that they've contacted him a couple of times now to remind him I'm there. And I'm sure he's told them he'll be right down. And then not appeared. The confused looks on their faces tells me that they've never seen a grown man play out his contempt for a visitor for this long.

*That's the way Dennis rolls*, I'm tempted to say. *That's what he's like*.

I remember at one point I hated him but I thought that hatred would go away. But even when he stopped sexually harassing me, I didn't stop hating him. Liked the job, hated him. It eventually changed to hated him, hated the job.

Because I saw what he was capable of and knew that I could never trust him not to revert to that; and I saw what the job could do to you and I could never forget that.

As it turned out, I didn't have any idea what Dennis was capable of. I misread him. Completely. And because I misread him, because I stuck around that job, someone died.

## June, 1999

Even through the earplugs and the ear defenders and the sound of my terror roaring in my ears, I could hear the sneer in Dennis's voice as he said, 'For pity's sake, Kezuma, it's not going to bite you. Pick it up.'

'I don't believe in guns,' I said to him because this had gone far enough, and I needed to speak up. I was not going to do this. I didn't care if he sacked me, or put a note in my file. This wasn't going to become a part of my reality just because I had chosen to stay in this stupid job. And, much as I loved the work, still hated Dennis, it was a stupid job if they wanted me to participate in this stuff.

'Guns are a fact of reality,' Dennis said patronisingly. 'How can you not believe in something that actually exists and you can see, touch, hear and probably taste if you were so inclined?'

'I don't believe in guns being a part of my working life,' I replied tersely.

'Oh stop being pathetic!' he snapped. It was almost as if he had no patience with me any more since he'd been forced to stop sexually harassing me in the name of Queen and country. 'Look at Brian. A more unmanly man you could not get, and he's picked it up. He is, as expected, holding it like a nine-year-old girl would but he's picked it up. And Maisie, she's picked it up, too. Of course, she's holding it like it's a make-up compact and she's going to check out her reflection a few more times before thinking about aiming it at the target, but she too has at least picked it up.'

Dennis hated everyone, probably even himself, but he was going to give one of the other two a complex with how he treated them because they hadn't reached rock bottom yet. Rock bottom being the moment when they either walked away, broke down or told him where to go. The moment they did that, he would stop the torture. But, because they kept trying to prove him wrong, working and working to show him they were good enough only for him to move the goalposts, this was going to continue for them. I – the quota hire herself – had been in that situation so many times over the years, starting at school, so I knew all about how goals, requirements, parameters were constantly being shifted to suit whoever was testing you.

I – the quota hire herself – could have told them that those goalposts Dennis was throwing up would be continually moving until they gave Dennis what he really wanted: stand up for themselves or show they could stand up for themselves if push came to shove in a field situation. I could have told them, but they thought I had it easy, so I kept my mouth shut and left them to it.

Brian's ears were burning with shame at what Dennis had just said to him, Maisie's cheeks glowed red. 'Think that's a bit harsh,' I said. They were snakes but I did feel for them sometimes, it was not pleasant to watch Dennis continually grind them down. 'I'm pretty sure both of them have handled guns before and know what they're doing. Unlike me.'

Dennis's disgust and contempt swept over me as he looked me up

178

and down from behind his protective goggles. 'Thank you, Miss Defender of The Weak and The Pathetic,' he replied scathingly. He then turned his sneer on the other two. 'Or is it The Pathetic and The Weak? I'm never sure which one of those names they're both acting out on any given day.'

When he was finished making Brian feel so small his bright red ears looked like they might catch fire, and making Maisie feel so pathetic I could see the glow of her humiliation from across the room, Dennis returned to me.

'Pick that up,' he ordered. He was looking at the black handgun lying on the shelf at the head of the shooting lane I was standing in front of. His voice had an edge to it that told me not to argue. He was normally nasty, but this was dangerous. This was *threatening*. I could sense that it wasn't simply my job on the line if I didn't do as I was told. *'PICK IT UP!'*

Both of the other two stopped to stare at us.

My fingers brushed against the hatching of the handle and my stomach flipped. This was not something I'd ever thought I'd have to do. Growing up in London, sheltered from many, many bad things by parents and the schools I went to, guns were not things I ever really thought about as a reality in my life. Let alone being ordered to pick one up. My fingers closed around it properly and the cold from it seemed to ricochet through me. But I lifted it up under Dennis's cold, contemptuous gaze.

'Get used to the weight,' he said, his voice still harsh enough to scrape away any semblance of control I deluded myself I had over my life for the next few minutes. 'Realise that when it's in your hands like this, that is the time when you have most control. That is when you have to master it. The weighting will shift according to how you hold it. Get

179

used to it, learn it, lean into it, hold it lighter, tighter. Always focus on how it shifts, how the weight balances itself in your hand. You do not want to be surprised by the weight of it in a high-stress situation. You do not want it to slip or tip or shift. Master how to control it in different moments, with different movements. That's it. Get to know it.' He stepped closer to me as I continued to manipulate the gun, feeling the weight of it shift and recalibrate according to how high or low or right or left I held it. 'Now remember, everything you've just got used to will change when you're in a situation where you will need to use it. Your adrenaline will be pumping, you'll have blood gushing in your ears, your muscles will be tense and strong, it'll feel lighter than it does now. Your brain will have to compensate for that. When you shoot it now, it will be very different from when you're in a life-threatening situation.

*I don't plan on being in a life-threatening situation*, I thought.

'Now, place your feet a little apart, push down into them so you are on an even keel. Now raise the gun and aim at the target.'

I did as I was told.

'Loosen your arms, don't lock your elbows. The recoil will have less of an impact if your arms are looser. Not too loose, you're not playing scarecrow. That's it, hold yourself together. Now aim again. Have the gun slightly lower than where you're aiming. The recoil will cause the bullet to go up slightly. Now, once you've set your aim, pull the trigger. But don't dramatically pull it like they do in the movies. Squeeze it, slowly, carefully. Squeeze. Just think, squeeze not pull.'

His words were echoing in my head as I followed his instructions to: 'Squeeze. Squeeze. Squeeze.'

The recoil wasn't as strong as I expected and the gun was still in my hand by the time I had squeezed the trigger. A piece of shrapnel or something snapped up and hit against my goggles. My eyes quickly sought out where on the person-shaped target my bullet had struck. I looked and looked but couldn't see any tell-tale signs that I had hit the target at all, let alone the centre.

Oh.

Dennis asked conversationally, 'Did you close your eyes when you fired the gun?' He was furious with me but keeping it under control.

'I . . . erm . . . might have done? Possibly. Yes.'

'I hope I am never in a life-threatening situation with you,' he sneered.

'I hope I'm never in a life-threatening situation,' I replied.

He ground his teeth together for a moment, his fury causing his demeanour to drop. 'Do it again,' he said. 'Do it again and again and again and again. Until you get it right. Until you ALL get it right.'

'But—' Maisie began.

'Until you are all hitting the centre target first time, you're not leaving.'

'But—' Brian cut in.

'UNTIL YOU ARE ALL HITTING THE CENTRE TARGET FIRST TIME, YOU'RE NOT LEAVING,' Dennis shouted.

The other two didn't need to say, 'Thanks a lot, Kez,' for me to hear and feel it loud and clear. And I got the distinct impression that it wouldn't be a good idea to be in a life-threatening situation with either of them any time soon.


## 8 June, Central London

Three and a half hours. Other people have come and gone. Some have even sat near me, and then got up to be seen by the people they are waiting for. Not me. I am still here. Still being tortured by Dennis Chambers.

## July, 1999

When I exited the basement gym at work, Brian was, I noticed, waiting for me. His lean body was resting against the railing at the edge of the pavement and he was holding two cups of coffee. He grinned when he saw me and I had to pause then turn back to check behind me to see if there was someone else he was smiling at like that. But no, it was me with my straightened chin-length hair and my gym bag hooked high up on my shoulder, he was grinning at.

He held out the coffee to me and widened his smile. 'I realised recently that I have never made you or bought you coffee,' he said. 'I want to make up for that.'

'There's really no need,' I replied.

'There is. And there's a need for me to apologise for what I said to you, too. I was very much in a bad place. I allowed my frustration, my fear, to overwhelm me and it resulted in me saying some truly hurtful, hateful things to you. None of it was to do with you personally, although I made it sound and feel personal. I apologise. It was out of order on so many levels.'

I looked behind me again, checking that he was indeed speaking to me. 'What's brought this on?' I asked, truly flummoxed. I could count on no hands the amount of times someone who had been rude, arrogant and downright racist to me had apologised. And not the type of apology you dished out because your mum forced you to on pain of permanent no food and early, *early* bed. A proper apology. One that was substantial enough to hang something on.

'A lot of things. One of them being Maisie's godfather coming to take her to lunch and seeing Dennis practically fawning at his feet. He's not pleasant to her, but unlike you, unlike me, it doesn't matter. She will always land on her feet.'

I half nodded because was this fella really telling me that he and I were the same?

'And so will I,' he ploughed on. 'I realised that. If I really wanted to, my family will find me a way into the force.' He looked down at his coffee cup. 'I'm sorry. I was horrible. I know you're here on merit. And merit alone.'

'I'm not sure what to say. So, I shall get myself off home and start the required reading,' I said. His earnestness was a bit overwhelming, what with me not being used to this type of thing happening – ever.

'Can I walk with you?'

'If you want,' I said with a shrug.

'Can I ask you something?' he began as our footsteps almost automatically fell into sync.

'Something other than "can I ask you something?" you mean?'

'What?' he was confused. 'Oh, I see, yes, other than that.'

'Go on then.'

'Do you want to go for a drink, maybe dinner?'

I stopped walking, screwed my face up at him. 'That sounds like you're asking me out,' I said.

'That's because I am.'

'We work together.'

'Lots of people meet their partners at work.'

'OK. But, well, I have a boyfriend.'

'You do?'

'I do.'

'How come you never talk about him? Or have him meet you from work?'

'Because I come to work to work, he is something separate.'

I did not, in fact, have a boyfriend. I was still – *still* – smarting from the encounter I'd had a year earlier when I'd had sex with a man at a party. Between the sex and the chat in the garden afterwards, I'd managed to fall in love with him. That was the only way I could explain my continuing, enduring obsession with him. Love. Irrational, all-consuming, illogical, passionate love. And, no matter how many times I told myself I was moving on, I hung onto the hope that I might meet him again. I wasn't shunning all other viable suitors while I waited for the impossible to happen, I simply did not want a boyfriend at that moment, especially not one that was Brian-flavoured.

'He could come out with us. Make it a threesome.' Brian cocked his eyebrow, to see if I had understood his pun.

'Again, Brian, we work together. Those are lines I don't blur.'

'Fair enough . . . It would be nice to meet your boyfriend though.'

'I'm sure it would. I'll think about it. But, I like to keep work separate from everything else. Life is just easier that way.'

'You really would make a good agent,' he said, sounding impressed. 'You've got all that compartmentalisation stuff sorted already.'

'I thought we all had.'

'Not quite.'

'Well, good to work on it, I suppose.'

'I haven't offended you, have I? By asking you out?'

'Why would that offend me?'

'I don't know, you might not like being asked out. The whole work, compartmentalisation thing.'

'No offence caused or taken.' At the tube station, I paused to fish my travelcard out of my pocket. 'Brian . . .' I was struggling with whether to tell him or not. Just because he'd been nice and had apologised, didn't mean he couldn't revert to type on the turn of a pin. Didn't want to risk him telling Dennis I'd told him or blurting it out in a fit of anger. But then, I hated seeing him or anyone suffer.

'Kez . . .?'

'Look, I'm going to tell you something that you can either take on board or ignore. Either way, it's cool.'

'Sounds ominous.'

'Stand up for yourself. With Dennis, I mean. Stop letting him get away with the way he speaks to you, the way he treats you. He won't give you respect until you stop letting him treat you like dirt.'

'It's not that simple,' he replied. 'I can't just . . . That's not how things work for people like me.'

'Are you going to tell me I'm a quota hire again? Cos if you are, you can have your coffee back and take it with you to the far side of—'

'No, no, I'm not saying that. I'm saying . . . I'm not very . . . In my family, they're all coppers. They're all real men. No one questions whether they're men. No one raises an eyebrow wondering if they could be, *you know.*'

'And so what if they did question it? Pretty sure being "you know" is not a big issue. It's basically just another facet of who a person is. No drama.'

'It doesn't work like that in my family. They . . . I'm not an alpha male like they all are. That's why no one really minded me doing this. Psychology isn't really . . . I would have embarrassed them if I'd gone down the same route as my older and younger brothers. I work for the government, so it's not so bad, and I don't show them up by doing my "woo-woo" psychology stuff in their faces. They give me a hard enough time as it is. They've always said I need to toughen up. I can't go crying to Dennis about the things he said. I have to take it. And when he sees that I don't care about the things he says and that I'm not going to quit, he'll stop.'

'He won't. The thing about terrible people, Brian, is that they have no bottom. They have no end when it comes to their terrible behaviour. Dennis will not stop until you make him. The fact you don't speak up makes him know it bothers you. Same with Maisie. Until the pair of you speak up, he'll keep going. There is no bad for him, here. It's you two who are suffering.'

'Maybe you're right,' he said. 'I'll think about it.'

'You do that. I am now going to get on this tube and stink out the place before I get on the train to stink that out as well.'

'You don't stink. You smell nice, actually. Like you've just got out of the shower.'

'I have just got out of the post-workout shower, but I'm wearing my work clothes from earlier so I kinda need to change.'

'Sure you don't want me to come and give you a hand?'

'Erm, no thank you.'

'Fair enough.'

## 8 June, Central London

I'm entering my fourth hour sitting here. The receptionist with the nice grey suit asks if I want a drink and I tell her no, thank you and I'm fine. I have to tough this out. Dennis really is trying to punish me but Brandee is too important for me to give in. What he's doing is irritating, annoying as hell, but I have to suck it up. I have to wait for him to be ready to speak to me.

*June, 2000*

Our small Tequila glasses loudly clinked together, and we could hear them above the thumping beat of Obsidiblue, the café bar we were in.

'To us,' Brian said.

'To us and our brilliant, qualified selves,' I added.

'Yay!' Maisie finished.

We all downed our drinks and slammed the glasses down onto the table, before snatching up the slices of lime and jamming them into our mouths.

'That was close, don't you think?' Brian said as we discarded our sucked limes and then reached for our real drinks. 'There were times when I wasn't sure we'd all make it.'

'Thought failure wasn't an option for you two?' I replied.

'It isn't. But that doesn't mean you can't have doubts about your ability to stay the course.'

'OK, Bri-Bri,' I said, ruffling his hair. 'Soooo deep, aren't you?'

He patted my hand away. 'Are you seriously saying you've had no moments of doubts?'

'I've had loads of them,' I replied with a happy shrug. 'But that's nothing new for me. The trick is to feel the doubts and do it anyway.'

'Now who's deep?' Maisie shouted above the sudden music volume increase. 'So, are we like, agents or something now?'

'Well, if we are, half the bar knows about it now,' I laughed.

'I'm serious,' Maisie said, leaning in so we could hear her without her telling everyone in the bar our business. We'd found this place not long after Brian apologised, and we'd started having a laugh together. He'd started to buy and make me coffee, but I was careful to turn down all offers to go for a drink on our own, even as friends. I did not want him to get the wrong idea or think the parameters of our relationship would change. Maisie, not wanting to be left out, had started joining us for coffees. It took her a little while of sitting there with no drink in front of her to realise neither of us were going to make it for her, so she started pulling her weight in those stakes. Once she was on board, we'd occasionally go for a drink in this place, Obsidiblue. A café that served alcohol and had a late licence. The music was too loud, the drinks came in grubby glasses, the service was less than stellar, but it was tucked out of the way and a good twenty minutes from work, so we kept coming back.

And now we were celebrating completing the course, being certified and starting work in the new department Dennis was heading up. We'd been expecting final assessments in a month's time, but obviously nothing was ever that straightforward with our line of work. They'd been assessing us and had decided we'd passed. We still had to *do* the final assessment, obviously. And officially pass. If we didn't, they would rescind the 'you've passed' thing, but all things being equal, we were there. We'd made it. We could now enter proper agent training, I assumed, or continue as clinical psychologists for the intelligence services.

Brian still hadn't stood up to Dennis. He still let him call him names, talk down to him, question his masculinity, imply stuff about his virility and how it linked to his sexuality. It was painful to watch, especially as Brian and I were now good friends. I did speak up as much as I could, but sometimes that whipped up Dennis's ire even more – mocking 'Manly Brian' for needing a woman to stand up for him. No matter what I said, Brian was still determined to 'be a man' and tough it out. Maisie had dealt with her problem with Dennis the old-fashioned way – she got her godfather, uncle *and* father to put pressure on Dennis, who duly backed off.

*'You see,' Dennis told me in the kitchen, 'all of you need to end the pressure in ways that suit your personality and circumstance. That's what will make you a good agent. You were about to duck out, Maisie used her connections.'*

'And Brian?' I asked.

*'You think about Brian and his personality. From all the psychometric tests he's written that you've taken, how do you think he's going to relieve the pressure?'*

Blow. For Brian, as wound up as he was, blowing was most likely the only way to relieve the pressure. I hoped, though, that I was wrong. That being inexperienced was having me see an inevitable end that did not need to be inevitable. 'Why don't you just give him a break?' I'd asked.

Dennis had stared at me with the eyes of the psychopath that he was. 'He needs to be able to use all the resources available to him. He could walk away, like you. He could use his connections, like Maisie. He could stand up and tell me to stop.'

'Or you could stop.' It was as if that option hadn't occurred to Dennis.

'The fact he is letting this go on makes me question whether he'll pass final assessment at all.'

'If I wasn't a lowly trainee,' I'd said in response, 'I would think you were trying to push my buttons to get a reaction from me, possibly to find out if I'm sleeping with Brian.'

*Dennis had grinned. 'And that is why you're my favourite.'*

I'd been overjoyed when Brian had passed the assessment, but with every day, I did wonder when he was going to blow.

'So, how drunk are we getting tonight?' Brian asked.

'Not so drunk you make a pass at Kez,' Maisie smirked.

'I wouldn't do that,' Brian snapped at her, baring his teeth in a way that he wouldn't dream of with Dennis.

'Peace, everyone, peace,' I said. 'This is a party. This is us on the next stretch. We need to chill and celebrate at the same time.'

'To us,' Maisie said, raising her large white Chablis.

'To us,' Brian and I intoned, sipping our drinks.

'And just so you know,' Maisie said, 'when I get my brand-new job running this whole unit, I am going to disavow all and any knowledge of you two. Nothing personal. Just want to forget ever meeting Dennis, and you two are casualties in that.'

'Fair play,' I said. 'Won't be difficult to forget you, Maisie.'

She choked on her wine, then laughed at my grin.

'I won't forget you, though, Bri-Bri,' I said. 'Couldn't forget you if I tried.'

'You either, Kez,' Brian said, blowing me a kiss. 'And I'm sorry that you've finally come round to seeing how amazing I am, but, darling, I have a girlfriend now. She is pretty incredible.'

'I'm glad,' I replied. 'I'm really, really pleased for you.' I picked up my glass of red wine. 'To us,' it was my turn to declare. 'To us and all who will fall at our brilliance.'

## 8 June, Central London

My heart turns over like a flipped pancake when I see him. He has the same beige rainmac he has always worn. It does not look twenty-five years old, though, so I am guessing he has replaced it over the years. His hair has thinned and greyed, his frame is slightly stooped at the shoulders, his face is worn. Around his eyes are what I would think are lines of worry, regret and guilt if he was a normal person.

He has his black bag – probably with his laptop – on his shoulder, and a newspaper wedged under his arm. He approaches the reception desk, speaks to the woman with the nice suit. 'Ms Wedgner, sorry, Charlene,' he says, 'I'm out for the rest of the day.'

She smiles, her rosy cheeks filling out and making her seem younger and cuter than her years. 'Your visitor is still waiting,' she says, nodding over at me.

'I know,' he replies. 'Thank you. I will see you tomorrow.'

'Bye.'

He nods to the male guards/receptionists and strides across the marble floor. He slows for a microsecond as he approaches me, then speeds up, his way of telling me that I should follow him because he will speak to me.

*October, 2000*

'Brian,' Dennis's voice was harsh enough to cause all of us to freeze. 'Kezuma's interrogation, what did you think of it?'

'Well . . . well . . .'

'Today, Kershaw. Today.'

'Well, she—'

'Will you just spit it out! I mean, we all know you're a spitter not a swallower, so get on with it.'

I cringed. Hard. I could not stay silent. I had to say something. Something, anything. I'd been thinking lately that I was going to have to go to the people above Dennis because his behaviour was intolerable.

'What did you say to me?' Brian said quietly.

Maisie's eyes did the jerking wide thing, and I bit my lower lip – my anxiety response.

'Ah, the spitter speaks. What is it? Was I wrong? Are you a swallower?'

Brian, who had been sitting back in his seat, his yellow notepad resting on his knees, stood up, not acknowledging that his notepad and pen had fallen to the ground. 'What. Did. You. Say. To. Me.'

I'd been hoping it wouldn't come to this, that it would not happen. That when I was vaguely profiling him all that while ago, I'd been completely wrong.

'Sit down, Kershaw,' Dennis said. 'Stop embarrassing yourself. Before you know it, the girls will be on their—'

Dennis didn't see it coming. I did, Maisie did, but Dennis didn't. And when Brian's fist connected with Dennis's cheek, nose and upper lip, it knocked him clean off his feet.

'WHAT! DID! YOU! SAY! TO! ME!' Brian roared at Dennis. Maisie rushed to Dennis, tending to him and leaving me with the raging bull that was Brian. He was boiling mad, every muscle, sinew and cell in his body tensed, his face so red I feared it might actually burst into flames. 'SAY IT AGAIN, BIG MAN!' he screamed at Dennis. 'SAY IT AGAIN!'

I had never seen anyone this angry before. I'd seen fights, of course, you didn't go out in London of a Friday night and not see people get into it, but never had I seen anyone in a work setting become like this. Utterly terrified, I approached Brian, and placed a hand on his shoulder. My heart leapt over several beats when Brian shrugged me off. 'Brian, Brian,' I said, despite my fear he was going to punch me next because his rage, rather than lessening, was growing. 'Brian, Brian, look at me, look at me.'

Eventually, my voice seemed to filter through his anger and he swung towards me. 'Brian, calm down now, yeah? You've done it. You've stood up to him. It's time to be calm now. Yeah? Be calm. Be calm.' I had my hands up, showing him I wasn't a threat. His rage was still boiling, so I wondered how much of me he actually saw, and how much was just my calming voice filtering through.

I realised when Maisie and Dennis didn't stand up, that they were staying down so as not to enrage him further. Dennis becoming full size again would be the challenge that might just tip him over to the point of him not being able to stop. None of us wanted that. I wasn't sure what his stressor had been, why this time was different with Dennis and Brian, but it had potential to spiral.

'Come on Brian, let me make you a cup of coffee,' I said, still making my voice as soft and soothing as possible. 'You know I haven't made you a cup of coffee in ages. Let me make you one now, yeah? Yeah?' I took a chance and reached out to touch him again, this time he didn't shrug me off. He was still glaring at me, but he didn't want me away from him. 'Come on, coffee. These hands have not made coffee in an age. I'm not sure if you noticed that? They are willing to go back to work, especially for you. OK? I promised myself a long time ago that I would not be making coffee at work again. But I'm coming out of retirement to make you a coffee. OK? Come on, right this way. Right this way to coffee heaven.'

I noticed a small shift in his demeanour, a slight relaxation.

'What? Too much?' I said with a smile.

A little more loosening, a little letting go.

'You know me, always too much.'

Finally he relaxed, unclenched, became something approximating Brian again.

'Come on, come on, coffee.' He dropped his fists, and dropped his shoulders, and softened even more. *Oh, thank God*, I thought, the fear and sickness subsiding only a little. 'Come on, this way.'

Again, he didn't flinch when I touched him and when I gently nudged him towards the door, he moved. Over his shoulder, I locked eyes with Maisie. We were both horrified. This wasn't meant to be happening. We weren't meant to be in this situation, but Dennis's ego and Brian's issues had dragged us both into this place of fear. And I was scared of what would happen next. Now that this barrier had been breached, what were we going to have to confront next?

*

'What was that about?' I asked Brian after he had sipped half a cup of strong black coffee. Away from our office, he had calmed down even more. After the coffee, he was almost back to normal.

'You've been telling me to stand up for myself for years. This is me standing up for myself.'

'Is it heckers! What's really going on, Brian? If you were someone we were sent to profile, this has "external stressor" written all over it. What's going on?'

His fingers whitened as he gripped his cup so tight I feared for a moment he might crack the ceramic. 'She dumped me. Micah. She cheated on me and then dumped me. What he said got to me.'

'Oh, I'm sorry. I know how taken you were with her.'

He shot me a poisonous look, his contempt plain. 'I wasn't "taken with her". Who speaks like that at your age? I was in love with her. I've put myself into debt to buy her an engagement ring. I went to propose and she tells me she's found someone else. Someone more "masculine". I'm not manly enough for her, apparently.'

'What does that even mean? How can you not be manly enough? What is manly enough?'

'The guy she was shagging. Alpha male, apparently.' He shook his head. 'I loved her, gave her everything she ever asked for. And she finds someone else. We were looking at places to live. Dennis just got to me. Reminded me that she's probably been saying stuff like that behind my back. Laughing at me.' He ground his teeth, his jaw undulating under his skin like rats in a sack.

'I'm so sorry. What are you going to do?'

'Go punch Dennis again, I guess.'

I smirked. 'No, seriously, though, how are you going to navigate this?'

'Shouldn't you be telling me, Miss Psychotherapist?'

'As you well know, psychologists can't tell you what to do, only show you how your behaviours and thoughts influence the situations you find yourself in. And then together we formulate a plan for helping you deal with whatever it is that is causing you distress.'

'You really are taking all of this seriously, aren't you?'

'Yes, why, aren't you and Maisie?'

'Maisie's counting down the days until she can legitimately move on to her next government job. She wasn't kidding when she said when she's running a unit she'll disavow us. And me? I thought I'd be living the *Spooks* and James Bond lifestyle by now. When I found out what we were really going to be a part of, and what we'd really be doing, I thought this was going to be my chance to show my whole family I wasn't a loser who got themselves a cushy job, I was going to do something legit.'

'Why do you care so much what they think?'

'They've told me who I am since I was small, I can't just shake it off. Not care what they think. It doesn't work like that in the real world. It just doesn't. I want them to think well of me, to look at me and see someone important like they do my brothers. I just want to be someone.'

'You are someone.'

'No, I'm not. To the people who count, I'm not.'

I wasn't sure how to convince him he was wrong. Or even if I should. What did I know about it? My parents, my family, for all their faults and foibles, had always made me feel like someone important. I didn't even notice that until I was surrounded by people who did terrible things to try to prove their worth. To make themselves feel important and seen. I couldn't even begin to understand Brian's life. His personality. What growing up to be him must have been like. What having the woman he loved discard him in such a way must do to the raw, open wound of his need to be seen. I could tell him all the right things, but he would never believe them from listening to them. He had to live the words, find a way to have their meanings shape his reality. And that could only happen if he heard the words. If what I was trying to say to him somehow found its way into the centre of his being, his metaphysical heart, his soul. Only then would he believe.

Right then, he wasn't even open to the idea of that process. Right then, Brian was hurting and nothing anyone said would change that.

'I understand,' I said to him, patting his shoulder in a way I hoped wasn't patronising. I didn't understand. Not really. But I wanted to. What I was doing became even more important then. I had to understand people like Brian so I could help them. What was the point of all of this training, all of this learning and all of this work if at the end of it, I couldn't help people who were truly hurting. I knew at that moment that the profiler work would always come second to the therapy work. Profiling would help, of course it would, but being able to help people, being able to take their mental hands and help guide them to the path of freedom through therapy was the most important thing.

It was becoming clearer and clearer that Dennis's T.H.I.U. (The Human Insight Unit) wasn't the place to be. I couldn't help anyone here, not really. I had to find my true calling. Find somewhere I could help ordinary people, not just ones who had these fantastical jobs. I worried, too, what going into their minds, putting myself constantly in their mindset would do to me. How much of my humanity would I lose to start to understand theirs? This place was not for me. I had to do something about that.

## 8 June, Central London

'What part of I never want to see you again, didn't you understand?' Dennis hisses to me. We are alone. Properly alone. I could make a quip about the fact we are down a passage to a mews property in central London and we may as well have signs on ourselves saying 'SPY' and 'FORMER SPY', but I don't. He is too angry to appreciate it.

Up close, Dennis looks tired, exhausted, defeated. His lines are like craters, his skin mottled, his eyes dulled and sunken. I would think it was guilt that had done this if I didn't know him. Guilt doesn't penetrate someone like him.

'*PICK IT UP!*' Dennis's voice and words suddenly echo through my head. Being this close to him has unhooked that memory, that time. I underestimated the impact proximity could have.

'It's good to see you, too, Dennis,' I reply.

'I told you to stay away from me. From all of this.'

'You're sounding quite hurtful there, Dennis. I'm sure you don't mean to. Anyone who didn't know you better would think you didn't want to see me.'

'This wasn't the agreement.'

'I wouldn't have come if it wasn't important,' I say, hating myself for the tremor cracking my voice now I know he won't be mollified. Now I realise he can make me feel twenty-six again. Twenty-six and naïve. And oh so very stupid.

My voice tremor makes him bold enough to get right in my face. 'Nothing is important,' he hisses. 'Nothing.' He steps back a fraction so he can jab his finger at me. 'You were set up for life. You could do whatever you wanted on condition you would stay away.'

'*Pick that up,*' 1999 Dennis shouts in my head. 'What about Brian? Was he set up for life, too?' I reply.

Suddenly Dennis doesn't want to be near me. Suddenly he is stepping away and his anger and indignation fail him.

'It *is* important,' I say with a stronger voice and renewed courage. 'It's vital. And I'm not going away until you agree to help me.'

*November, 2000*

Maisie and I entered T.H.I.U. office to find Brian standing at his desk, cardboard box in front of him, two security guards on either side of him. He was loading the items from his desk into the box, making sure to place everything just so inside it. A place for everything and everything in its place.

'Brian, what's going on?' Maisie asked even though it was pretty obvious what was going on. Dennis sat in his glass-walled office, pretending to type but obviously watching our interaction so he could gather another piece of the puzzles that were Maisie, Kez and Brian. So he could work out how to successfully play us, control us, break us probably. Just like he'd broken Brian.

'I've been sacked,' he said, shifting stuff in the box so his pot plant, a cheese plant I bought him, would fit. 'Sorry, what was it they called it, "giving me the opportunity to pursue other interests".' He gave something that was a cross between a smirk and a snarl, his disgust evident.

'They can't do this, surely?' Maisie said, her horrified gaze shuttling between Brian and me. 'Surely.'

It'd been a month since his outburst. Dennis ended up with a bruise that faded quickly and we'd all not talked about it. Brian had apologised to Dennis behind closed doors and told us he'd be required to talk to someone about his anger and his actions. We'd heard nothing more about it.

'They can do what they want, Maisie,' Brian replied. He placed a black stapler into the box, even though it wasn't his. 'Like me, I suspect you're going to find that out the hard way.' He looked Maisie over, clearly remembering her catalogue of connections, her family tree of protections. 'Well, maybe not you, but definitely you,' he said to me. He wasn't being nasty, he was being honest and realistic.

'But I thought all that from last month was sorted. You apologised. Is this really about what happened?' I asked.

Brian stopped packing for a moment and fixed me with a grim gaze. 'See, it's language like that – passive and refusing responsibility – that has proved my inability to do this job,' he stated, clearly mimicking what he'd been officially told.

'That's such—' I began.

'I've been having psychological testing and therapy since I did what I did. I've been told enough times that it wasn't something that happened – a passive way of speaking and entirely rejecting my role and agency in the situation – but it was something I CHOSE to do.

'The result of the tests and sessions showed that I am unsuitable for any position in this organisation.'

'That is such bull,' I replied.

'Whether it is or it isn't, I have to leave in under ten minutes or they will have me arrested for trespassing in a government building.'

'I can't believe this,' Maisie said. She went to him and threw her arms around him. 'I'm so sorry, Brian. I'll miss you.'

'I'll miss you, too,' I said. Our hug was longer and at the end of it he gave me a quick kiss on the top of my head, acknowledging how close we'd got.

'I'll miss you both.' His packing finished, Brian hefted the brown cardboard box into his hands and this simple action seemed to cause the two security guards to come alive, ready to escort him out of the building. 'Watch out for the beige-mac-wearing snake in there. He'll do anything to save his own skin – he'll use whatever he can on you. I realise that's what you were trying to tell me now, Kez. I had to stand up to him in a way that fitted in with the system. Ah well, means nothing now, I guess. Be careful.'

And that was Brian gone.

Part of me wanted to march into Dennis's office and scream: 'This is such bullshit!' at him. But the rest of me, the pragmatic side, realised I just had to accelerate my plan to get out of there. Because if Dennis wanted shot of us, he could make it happen, even without something as egregious as one of us smacking him. If Dennis wanted rid of one of us, he could make it happen on the flimsiest of excuses. I had to keep my head down, avoid doing or saying anything that he could over-inflate and use to get rid of me before I was ready to go.

I had to leave. That was all there was to it. I had to leave. And soon.

## 8 June, Central London

'What do you want?' Dennis asks through his teeth.

'Someone important to me has gone missing. I don't know what's happened to her. She was really popular on social media, had a huge following and then she dropped out of sight. And now there are all these rumours about what she's caught up in but nothing concrete.' I notice a small reaction, a tiny, involuntary hitch of Dennis's left eyebrow. He's heard about this, about her. Not good. Dire, in fact. If Dennis has heard of this, that means Brandee is definitely in trouble. 'I need you to help me find her.'

'The police do missing persons.'

'The police aren't the right people for this, you know that. They won't tell me even a fraction of what I need to know. I need to find out all I can about what's happened to her. Why she's disappeared.'

'What is she to you?'

'She's my foster child, I suppose. She's lived with me on and off for the past ten years or so. I need to find her before it's too late.'

'I still think the police are the best people for this.'

'They won't do anything because she left a note saying not to find her.'

'If she doesn't want to be found then—'

'She is a child, Dennis. My child. I am responsible for her. I need to find her before something happens to her. I don't care what her note says, I need to find her. She's been exploited and let down by almost everyone in her life, I need to not be one of those people. I need to find her. Which is the only reason why I am here. I would not be here if she wasn't important to me.'

That seems to get through to Dennis. His mask of anger drops. 'What's her name?' he asks quietly.

'Brandee. Brandee Hamilton.'

There it is again, the slight, involuntary hitch of his left eyebrow. I wasn't imagining it before. He knows about her. I have to stay positive, though. I have to believe that if Dennis and his people know about her, that means they are in some way watching over her.

I can't ask him about it. I can't tip my hand. I need to act like I haven't noticed so he will give me more information. If I challenge him, he will return with 'it's all classified so I can't help you'. If I act oblivious now, he will come back with something, firstly to maintain the image he likes to put up about his importance, and then to make me go away. Giving me something, he knows, is more likely to make me go away than nothing. Right now, I need to hold my tongue and be ready to act on any information he does give, question him once I have all he can give me in my possession.

'Anything you can find will help. But I need the information yesterday.'

'Why is this so important to you?'

'I told you. She is my child and I have a terrible feeling that time is running out for her. I just need to find her. I don't need you to understand this. I just need you to help me.'

'I'll see what I can do.'

'Thank you,' I reply.

'And after this, I don't want to see you again. After this, we are quits and you stay well away from me.'

Considering how nice a person I'm convinced I am, it's amazing, really, how regularly people say that to me.

*March, 2002*

Maisie had upgraded herself in the two years since I had last seen her.

Her hair was glossy, her make-up was immaculate and her clothes were expensive enough not to have had price tags on them in the shops she bought them from. She had taken Brian's departure hard – and my suspicions that she'd been sweet on him seemed to be confirmed. She moped around for two weeks, running out in tears a couple of times, then I arrived one morning to find her desk cleared out. Dennis didn't say a word about it, it was the receptionist who told me that Maisie had cashed in her familial chips and had got herself transferred to another department. She was as good as her word and made no attempt to keep in touch with me. A few weeks later, I heard that she had been appointed second-in-command of a government-connected-but-not-run thinktank, where her knowledge of profiling, behaviour and psychology were invaluable. (I got that bit from the website.) Think-tank money meant thinktank upgrading.

I hadn't managed to leave T.H.I.U. All the jobs I found that were perfect for me, that had the recruiter excited and keen for my experience always came to nothing. Sometimes I would get to the interview stage – a couple of times to the second interview stage – and then nothing. The position would disappear, the job description would change, the recruiter would no longer be as keen on my experience. Nowadays I just applied for jobs to see how quickly Dennis could torpedo it.

Because he did not want to let me go. I wasn't sure why. Maybe because I was the only one who consistently stood up to him? Maybe because, as he had told me more than once, I was his favourite? Maybe because not having a say in when Maisie left had made him decide that when I left was down to him and him alone? I didn't know. But I had my plan in place now, which I'd formulated when I realised what he was doing. I had taken a few more courses at night school to get more qualifications and I was saving as hard as I could. Very soon, I would have enough money to quit my job and still pay my mortgage and bills while I set myself up in private practice. I was going to be a therapist whether Dennis approved or not.

Upgraded Maisie was already there when Dennis and I arrived at Obsidiblue, where Brian, Maisie and I used to go drinking.

I'd tried to keep in touch with Brian because we were genuinely friends, and I had felt badly for him. But he hadn't wanted to know. He wanted to move away from T.H.I.U. and Dennis and all of that, so he'd ignored my calls, didn't reply to my messages, blocked my email address. *Fair enough*, I thought. In my final text message I'd said:

**Call me, anytime you want to talk. I'm always here.**

*

Maisie's glossy chestnut hair was wound up into a chignon, she had expensive, bright-white trainers on her feet and a pricey navy-blue skirt suit. Over her suit, she was being fitted with a bulletproof vest.

Dennis and I stood side by side as we both waited to be fitted with bulletproof vests too.

After all this time of radio silence, Brian had finally called.

Brian had called to tell me he wanted to speak to Maisie, Dennis and me. That he was holding seven people hostage in Obsidiblue and would stay there until we came to talk to him.

The worst part of all of this, I thought as the straps were pulled in tight, squashing my large breasts enough to make me gasp, was that I wasn't surprised. Like him eventually hitting Dennis, I knew this was coming. Which was why I had tried to keep in touch; I had thought I could, somehow, mitigate this.

Maisie and I hadn't spoken, acknowledged or even properly looked at each other since Dennis and I arrived but she'd been expecting this, too. Dennis must have known, but he probably assumed he'd sufficiently broken and then binned Brian to not have to deal with the consequences.

*Did Dennis* really *think he would get away with it though?* I wondered as the police officer in charge spoke clearly and sternly to me. *Did he really not see that Brian was always going to make Dennis, Maisie and me watch his self-destruction?* I had seen it, Maisie had seen it. Maybe Dennis wasn't as knowledgeable as he made out. Or, maybe he just didn't care. He'd obviously done that type of breaking many, many times before. Maybe he'd always been able to move on and leave it to become someone else's problem; watch, hear or read from a distance about the inevitable detonation of someone he had broken and tell himself that it had been for the greater good.

I could tell by his grim silence, which had been in place since he got the call from the police not Brian, that this had never happened to him before. Or, if it had, he'd never had to deal with it up close. It had always been someone else's problem by this point.

'Are you listening to me?' the police officer in charge, who was right in my face, demanded. He was not a Kez fan.

'No heroics,' I parroted, having heard every word even though I had seemed in a different place. 'Defer to my boss at all times once inside. Allow him to make the decisions and moves. Don't antagonise the suspect. Don't make promises unless I absolutely have to. Say very little – again, allow my boss who has the training to do the talking. My one job is to get out of there alive. Which brings us back to the no heroics part.'

'Your boss said you would be able to handle this, especially as you all have firearms training,' he said, his voice a mixture of anger and contempt. To be fair, I did not blame him for his unease.

We arrived before SO19 (the armed police) because our office was quite near by and Dennis had effectively bullied this officer into helping us. On the way out of the door, Dennis had grabbed three bulletproof vests and when we arrived had told this poor sergeant that we were going in. The officer had been adamant that we should wait for SO19 before doing anything because they would have a better handle on things. Dennis had impressively gone into controlling psychopath mode: he'd pulled rank, said we were going in whether this guy liked it or not, but it would be better if he helped us – he'd somehow managed to work out this officer was former SO19 – because we needed someone with this guy's experience on our side. When the officer had still refused, Dennis had taken him to one side and spoken to him again. After that, we were being helped into bulletproof vests and I was getting a talking to.

'We tried to talk to him, hoping we could resolve it quickly but he insisted we get you all down here.' The officer looked shamefaced for a moment. 'He shot the owner but won't tell us if he is alive or not. He is not bluffing.'

*Of course he's not*, I thought. *Anyone who has spent time with Brian would know he is not the bluffing kind.*

'Arresting him, stopping him, is our job,' the blue-eyed policeman said, staring straight into my eyes all of a sudden. 'Your job is to get out of there alive.'

For the first time, it seemed like he was seeing me and he actually cared. While he'd been the one to contact Dennis and Maisie – he knew I was the person who Brian had called . . . so he suspected that while all of us were mostly likely going to end up dead, I was pretty much slated as the one who was *definitely* going to meet my end and he didn't want being unpleasant to a dead woman walking on his conscience as well.

If I were to profile him, I would say he was not too dissimilar to Dennis in that he had broken men before, but unlike Dennis he some-times felt bad about it. He usually stopped before it got to this stage. One detonation was enough and he would pull it back before it went nuclear. I wondered, too, if he knew Brian's family. If he knew that none of this would be happening if Brian had followed in their foot-steps, had become a police officer, instead of trying to forge his own way in the world.

I considered, as well, how they would cover this up. But that was a fleeting thought. A fleeting thought of what they would say about the way I was about to die. What the story would be, what they would tell people my job was and about Brian's training. About how he had been trained in firearms by the government.

Dennis started the long short walk towards Obsidiblue's door, then Maisie and I followed. We still hadn't spoken to each other, we neither of us had really acknowledged each other. I wondered if him not calling her direct was because he didn't have her new number? She had changed it at the same time she ditched us to go on to her new life – she hadn't been messing about when she walked away and I could respect that level of scorched-earthing your background in the name of getting ahead. I wished Brian had had that opportunity. From all the things he'd said about his family, though, I knew he'd never get that chance after he left his job in the way he did.

The door gave a little resistance when Dennis pushed on it. He paused in the open doorway, hands up to show it was him and no one else. I couldn't see through Obsidiblue's darkened windows so I assumed when Dennis said, 'It's just the three of us,' he could see Brian and his weapon.

A moment.

A pause.

I braced myself. Readied myself to hear the crack of a bullet being fired, to feel the impact of Dennis's body as he flew backwards when Brian shot him. I had braced myself for one of us to be shot on sight, I realised.

Dennis raised his hands higher, Maisie and I did the same as we stepped into the gloom. I shut the door behind me.

The place had been upgraded since we'd last been in there. The bar, a highly polished dark blue marble, had been moved so it was right at the back of the space, beside what looked like a new corridor and access to the toilets. Its top was a weathered copper, edged with lights; the drinks selection behind the bar was now displayed on backlit shelves. The main space was now furnished with soft-backed bucket chairs around circular wooden tables, and four low sofas in luxurious material, which sat perpendicular to the longest wall, creating a booth feeling. The walls were now decorated with gold-flock wallpaper, twinkly chandeliers hung from the ceiling. A large wicker basket held board games, beside a metal stand with magazines and newspapers right at the back. This was a place to come and relax, enjoy yourself.

Brian stood to the left end of the bar, his black gun pointed at the head of a young woman who was eighteen at most. She looked like she had only just finished school, probably just finished her A-levels and had come out for a drink with her friend. Probably one of her first legal drinks. The person I assumed was her friend sat on the floor in front of the bar, her hands on her head, fear etched into her face. Beside her were four other people, all of them sitting with their hands laced together on their heads, the same fear on their faces. The girl that Brian stood behind with a gun at her temple had an expression that was beyond fear; she seemed to have accepted that things were not going to end well for her and so had divorced herself from this reality.

Her long, shiny black waist-length plaits were loose around her face, her brown skin looked as though she was just coming out the other side of puberty and acne, and her beautiful soft features reminded me of the candid shots of the models who graced the catwalks.

'What are you doing, Brian?' I said, completely forgetting what I'd been told by the police officer outside.

'Turn around all of you so I can see you aren't carrying, then get down on your knees.'

We all turned – amusingly if we weren't in this situation – in synch.

'I'm not getting down on my knees,' I told him as the other two did as they were told. 'One, I won't be able to get back up, and two, if you're going to do me in, I'd rather stand for it.'

I saw it. A glimmer. A glimmer of the old Brian, exasperated and amused by me for a fraction of a moment of a second. He was still there. I could reach him.

'Do you want this girl to die?' he said. The old Brian was brushed aside, this one was back in charge. I saw and felt the other hostages flinch. They'd seen him shoot the owner – who was nowhere in sight – they knew he had it in him.

'No, I do not, but I can't get down on my knees. You remember how bad my back was, how painful my knees always were. It's only got worse.'

'Sit then.'

I reached for a chair.

'On the floor,' he snarled.

I got down on the floor, the other two still kneeling beside me. 'Oh, just sit down,' Brian said to them. 'All of you sit down.'

Dennis and Maisie did as they were told and we all sat there staring at him. I'd already gone beyond the bounds of my experience, there was no way I was going to do any more. In all the hostage negotiating we had done, I'd never been taught how to talk to someone who was a friend.

'What's this all about, Brian?' Dennis asked. 'Why are you doing this?'

'So you do know my name?' Brian replied. 'It's just, I thought you only called me Spitter and the like because you didn't know my name.'

'He didn't mean anything by it,' Maisie said, her voice as cool as ice water, proving her upgrade was total. 'He was just doing his job. Like he used to make me think I was stupid and all I had going for me was my looks and my posh accent, and the way he used to touch up Kez.'

I didn't dare look away from Brian, but I wanted to say, 'you knew about that?' to her.

'It's how he operates. It's sick and it's wrong. But it's not personal,' she said.

'It really isn't,' I added. 'It's him. It's all totally about what's wrong with him.'

'He sexually harassed you?' Brian asked, his frown so wide and deep, it corrugated the top half of his face.

'Yes. For months he would say disgusting things to me. Press himself against me. Once he actually assaulted me by grabbing my breasts while rubbing himself against me. I think he would have gone further if I hadn't decided to quit. When I stood up for myself by doing that, he took the pressure off in that way and stopped.'

'He's a sick bastard.'

'Yes, he is,' I agreed.

'He is,' Maisie agreed.

Without warning, Brian swung the gun away from the girl in front of him, and towards Dennis. From this distance, this angle, Brian wouldn't miss. Especially not after all the training we'd been given. 'So you agree, I should just shoot him and make the world a better place?' he said.

Maisie hesitated, I hesitated. We were both meant to say emphatic noes, we were both meant to defend Dennis. But that was a hard thing to do considering who he was, what he'd done and why we were all in this situation.

Brian started laughing, the sound bitter and desolate. 'You see that, Dennis? Even with a gun on you, they're not rushing to defend you.'

He laughed some more. 'How much of a terrible human being must you be that neither of them wants you to live.'

'What's happened, Brian? Why are we here?' I asked, trying to push down my guilt and shame that I didn't leap to Dennis's defence.

'Yes, why are we here?' Maisie asked.

'Are you asking what's my external stressor?' he mocked. 'What life event has brought me to this situation where suicide by copper is probably the only way out?'

'Yes,' I managed. Brian understood the workings of all of this like we did. Like all of us, he could see his problems but not how to stop those problems controlling him. Maisie had fallen silent although she looked as scared as any of the other hostages.

'They're getting married. My girlfriend who was about to become my fiancée is marrying the "man" she screwed behind my back and then left me for.'

'I'm so sorry, Brian,' I said. 'I'm so sorry. That must make you feel terrible. But there are plenty more people out there who would appreciate your Brian-ness. Maisie had a big old crush on you for ages.'

'What?' he said, turning his attention to Maisie but keeping his gun on Dennis. 'Is that true?'

Maisie kept her gaze lowered and her hands on her head.

'Yes, it's true. She won't tell you now that she's super important, but after you left she was inconsolable. She cried all the time, she was horrible to Dennis, and it wasn't two weeks before she shipped out. Yes, she had a huge crush on you. And that's because you're a good person. Lots of women out there will find you attractive. Just because one stupid woman decided to—'

'It was my brother,' Brian interrupted. 'She was sleeping with my brother and then she left me for him. And now I have to go to their wedding, cos, "no hard feelings". My brother is younger than me but more manly than me. And he was the only one I could get a job with because after that fucker got rid of me, there was nowhere I could go. I couldn't get a job. Fell into a depression. Started drinking. Got into too much debt. Lost my flat, my car. Self-respect. Everything. I had to move back home to my parents. Like a little kid. And who's the only one who can give me a job in their business as the glorified teaboy?'

'I thought you said your brother is a policeman?' I replied. Not the point, at all.

'Yeah, he is. Was. He doesn't do that any more. He set up a business. Got information from me, got me to—the point is, I work for him and he got his wife from me.'

I wasn't sure what to say, how to make him feel better, do what was necessary to get the hostages out. I paused, waited for Dennis to say something. Anything to show me what I should do next. What we should do next. Because Maisie and I had engaged him more than Dennis – the expert, the person we were told to defer to – had.

'Brian,' I eventually said, 'why don't you let those people go? You don't need them. You have us now. Let them go. Let them get the guy you shot some help. Please?'

'No. No one leaves until I say so. This is my rodeo, as Dennis used to say. I get to say what happens and that includes when people leave.'

'Come on, Brian, please? Let them go,' Maisie encouraged. 'They don't need to be here. They don't need to hear all our business. Let them go.' I had underestimated Maisie. I thought now she had gone she would not be interested in helping people. 'We won't leave you until you say. This is your rodeo. It absolutely is. We just want you to give yourself some proper space.'

'I know you don't want everyone in here knowing everything about you. I'm pretty sure you just want to talk to us. That's why you called us. We're the people you want to spend time with – not this lot. Go on, let them go.'

I could tell we were getting through to him, he was wavering. Suddenly, he tipped his chin towards the people in front of the bar. 'You, you, you and you, get up.'

They did as they were told, some getting up quicker than others. I'd done a quick assessment on them when we entered the space and knew that none of them were the hero type. Thankfully. Brian would definitely start shooting and I wasn't sure when he would stop. The young girl who had been sitting beside the adults didn't move as she hadn't been given a potential golden ticket out of there. 'Put your hands on your head and then leave before I change my mind. Any one of you look back and you won't be turned into a pillar of salt, you'll be turned into another four-letter word.' None of them moved, clearly thinking it was a trick. 'You can stay if you want. But they seem to think you want out of here. So go now or stay. Makes no difference to me.'

When they started to move, I opened my mouth: 'Why don't you let the girls go as well, eh, Brian? You don't need them. And they are too young for this. Way too young.'

'Yes, let the girls go,' Maisie said.

'The girls stay,' Brian replied. The edge to his voice, it was nasty. Something was fighting to break through with Brian, I could see that now. Something that I didn't want to acknowledge. If I did then it would make the outcome of this even more bleak.

'Come on, Brian, just. They've seen enough. Just—'

'They stay,' he stated firmly.

In the stillness that followed the departure of the other hostages, I examined Brian. He was tired; exhausted in that way when it seeps into your bones.

'Do you have any idea how hard it is?' Brian said. 'How impossible it is to be a man in this world?'

I shook my head. 'I don't know. But I can imagine. And I can listen if you want to talk about it.'

He snorted derisively. 'Listen. Talk. Listen. And listen again. Isn't that what we were taught? What good does it do? *Really?* What good does any of it do? What is there out there for me? Nothing. I have nothing. Why do I fight it? Why do I spend every day fighting it?'

'Fighting what?' I asked.

Brian needed help, we all needed help at some point, whether or not we liked to admit it. And help could change everything. It could save Brian. More than anything I wanted us to save Brian.

'I can't do it any more you know?' he said. 'I can't do this any more. It would have been fine, I could have kept going, I could have pretended I didn't mind about him and her but now they're going to get married. They're going to do what me and her were meant to do. And I can't take it any more.

'Every time I tried to work out what I did wrong, what I was meant to do to make things better, to get her back, it would bring me back to him. To the man who ruined my life.'

'I'm not sure it's that simple,' I said, hating myself for partially defending Dennis.

'Don't defend him, Kez. Don't defend him. He doesn't deserve it. He doesn't deserve anything but a bullet between the eyes.'

That made my stomach fall away, and I could feel the effect it had on Maisie, too. It sounded certain. Final.

'I'm not going to do that, though,' he continued. 'I'm going to show him. I'm going to turn back time and show him that I am a man. I am a real man. And then, he'll tell me that I am a real man. That I am manly. That I can show a woman a good time. And he'll give me my job back. If I get my job back, if I stop complaining about him, then she'll come back to me. She'll see I am man enough for her. I am more than man enough.'

*Oh no.*

*Oh no, no, no.*

That was why he wanted the girls to stay. That was why he was doing this.

He thought he could rewrite history. He thought he could redeem himself. He thought that was in any way possible.

'Pick one,' Brian said. 'Pick which girl it's going to be who will help me get my life back.'

I lowered my head, scared of telling him no. Because Brian was trapped in the midst of a delusion. He'd obviously had a breakdown. And he had a gun. I could not tell him no without risking all our lives. There had to be a way out of this. A way to stop him.

'It won't work,' Dennis finally spoke. 'What you're trying to do, it won't work. You can't turn back time. You can't do it again. You know that, Brian. You know you can't go back and change things.'

'I can try.'

'You can't try. You did nothing wrong, Brian.' We all turned to look at him then. 'You did nothing wrong. You just weren't up to the job. I had to prove that to you. And your pressure point was your masculinity.'

*What in the holy hell?* I lowered my head again because my eyes were wide with alarm. *What the hell is Dennis doing? Brian does not need to hear this sort of stuff.*

Dennis lowered his hands, rested them on his shins. I spotted the gun strapped to his ankle and whipped my gaze away so as not to draw attention to it. Brian hadn't had a chance to search us properly, being on his own. Was Dennis really going to do it? Was he really going to shoot Brian if he had to?

'I asked you to pick a girl,' Brian said to me. 'If you won't, then I will. This one will do.' He grabbed the arm of the girl standing beside him tight enough to make her flinch. She had reached a sort of zen-like state before, now she was incredibly frightened.

'Don't, Brian,' I said, moving to get up from my seat on the floor.

'Sit down!' he shouted. 'Sit down and don't move!'

'Bri—'

'And shut up! I am sick of hearing your voice! I am sick of you telling me what to do, what I think, how I feel. Just shut up! I'm going to do this thing. It's what men are programmed to do and it's what I'm going to do.'

His grip tightened on the girl in front of him so much that she cried out in pain. He started to back away, dragging her with him to the door to the back room. I looked at Maisie, who was wide-eyed with horror.

I knew Dennis would move then. He would act. He would grab his gun, he would stand up, he would tell Brian to stop.

'Do something,' I hissed at Dennis. Brian would probably have to put down the gun to do what he was planning to do so leaving himself vulnerable to being rushed by us. But we didn't know what the back of the place was like, how quickly we'd be able to find him before he hurt this girl. And no matter how far he got before we stopped him, he was going to further traumatise this young woman, he was going to change her life in a way that would mean she would never be the same again.

'Do something,' I hissed to Dennis again. I turned to him this time and he was immobile. Frozen. *Petrified.*

He had blanked out and wasn't going to snap out of it. Not in time. Neither was Maisie.

Closing my eyes for a moment, saying something like a silent prayer, I reached for Dennis's gun and got to my feet.

'Brian, stop,' I said, the gun in my hand but not properly on show. 'Please, stop.'

'Sit down,' he ordered, holding his weapon to his hostage's head.

I raised the gun. Its weight similar to the one I'd learnt to shoot with. I hadn't fired a gun, nor even touched one since that day Dennis made us all stay until we could hit the centre target first shot. I did not want to do this, but I could not let Brian do what he was about to do, either. 'Please stop, Brian. *Please.*'

He laughed, the scornful sound gurgling out of him like dirty water coming up from a blocked drain. A hideous, bilious sound. 'Are you going to shoot me, Kez? Really? The woman who doesn't believe in guns is going to shoot me?'

'Just let her go.'

'*No*,' he spat. He moved the gun away from her head and instead decisively aimed it at me. She, instinctively, threw herself onto the floor beside her friend, they immediately hugged each other, their eyes closed and heads down, creating a protective cocoon.

'Please, stop this,' I begged.

'No.' He narrowed his eyes, increased his grip on the gun handle.

And I knew . . . I knew what was going to happen next.

He was going to shoot me.

Even though he liked me, even though I was his friend.

He was going to shoot me.

And kill me.

Then he was going to hurt that girl after killing her friend, because neither Dennis nor Maisie would stop him.

Then he was going to kill Dennis.

Then he was going to kill Maisie.

Because he hated Dennis and wanted him dead.

Because he wouldn't be able to let Maisie live knowing what he had done.

Then he would turn the gun on himself. Because he wouldn't be able to live with the shame and guilt of what he had done. He wasn't far enough down the track to not feel anything about the things he had done. That was obvious from him letting me sit on the floor, rather than kneeling. That was obvious from him being shocked that Maisie had a crush on him, that Dennis had harassed me.

That was obvious from him thinking he could somehow go back and rewrite things.

But even though he wasn't too far gone, he was gone enough to be dangerous.

Deadly.

To brutalise someone, to kill four people before he killed himself.

I pulled the trigger.

Pulled the trigger before I was even properly aware that the rationalising I had been doing, the mapping out and profiling I had been doing was me gearing myself up to do it before the cascade of events began.

I pulled the trigger.

The recoil nearly ripped my shoulder from its socket.

And the bullet hit Brian in the chest. Right at the centre. Like I'd practised and practised to do. No arm shot, no leg ricochet. Dead centre.

He stumbled back . . .

. . . looked down at his chest in shock . . .

. . . fell back . . .

. . . stopped moving.

Stopped moving.

His eyes were wide open, staring unseeingly at the ceiling and chandeliers. His body was soft and still.

He was gone.

Brian was gone.

And I did that.

I killed him.

And I could never, ever undo that.

# Part 5

Part 3

# Kez

## 14 June, Brighton

Dennis is waiting for me outside the entrance to Hove Park. I saw the
mound-like shape of his body leaning against the looming terracotta-
red brick gatepost and had paused momentarily as I pushed Arie's
pram.

That Dennis is not only here at this park but knew exactly which
entrance I would be leaving by is disturbing. This isn't the park nearest
to my house. It is the one I used to come to because Moe had football
lessons here. So after I had Zoey and then Jonah, I would bring him for
his football and then walk around with them while they slept/cried/
played in the sandpit/tried to eat mud. It was where Moe met Brandee
and I met Remi. I'd started bringing Arie here because it was a park I
knew and liked. If you were looking for me, you'd go to the park a few
roads over from our address, nearer the seafront. There's no way you'd
come here on a whim.

Dennis wouldn't be here if he hadn't found something important,
but the thought of that battles with my anxieties of him knowing *pre-
cisely* where I would be. Does he have me under surveillance? The
thought hadn't occurred to me before. I thought I had left all of that
behind when I left T.H.I.U. But maybe I was still being naïve in

thinking they'd only keep the vaguest eye on me in case I got up to something unsavoury. Actually, I was being completely dense – they wouldn't have offered me that job they keep increasing the salary for, unsolicited, if they hadn't already decided I was not a security risk. And they could only have found that out by observing me. Spying on me.

It's been a week since I went to see Dennis. Arie has been with us a whole month now and everyone has got used to the lack of sleep, the having to make childcare plans during the day, the nappies and bottles and changing clothes and baths and baby giggles that fill the whole house. He is pretty much one of our family.

'I thought we agreed I'd come back to London for anything you found or you'd phone me if you found nothing,' I state. I don't drop my pace or stop when I pass him, I keep walking and assume he will keep up – just like he used to do with me.

'It couldn't wait,' he says, sounding a little sheepish. That causes my internal antennae to tingle. Historically, Dennis never showed any urgency with anything, no matter how life or death it was, unless it would directly benefit him. So why is he acting like this is bordering on an emergency?

'You found something then,' I say, enjoying having the upper hand on him. He wants attention in a very specific way from me and I am withholding it.

We have a fucked-up relationship, Dennis and I. We haven't even seen each other in nearly twenty years and we are still like this. But it is his doing, his fault that we are still in this dance, that we relate to each other like this. I've never discovered what he gets out of it but the therapist in me has told me there is something specific there for him, just as the behavioural scientist in him would have told there was a reason for it, too.

I *never* think about what it is exactly I get out of it. It must be something because when the music starts playing, I lace on these particular dancing shoes; I still tussle with him.

'I found something and I found nothing,' he replies. 'It's something and nothing.'

'OK,' I respond. I have been around Hove Park twice and I have walked all the way up here from my house pushing this pram because I have been thinking. Reordering. Reframing. Rethinking. There is a thread running through all of this and I have been trying to work out what it is. I have watched all of Brandee's videos several times, trying to work out if there is a secret code, something she was trying to say in the lead up to her disappearance that I have missed. There is something, but I cannot decipher it yet.

That is what is on my mind and I am not going to play Dennis's games. The therapist in me does not care what he is getting out of this messed-up dynamic we have going on. Either he tells me what he's found or he goes back to London and we don't speak again for another two decades. Yes, I need his help, but he doesn't get his jollies from me in return. Dennis owes me. It took me a long while to realise that.

'About nineteen months ago, a company that makes Traits sportswear started to take an interest in Brandee's channel. They started sending sponsorship opportunities her way, advertising on her channels, all pretty legit and open and upfront. It wasn't only her. They started to target pretty, popular young women who had a substantial following.'

I had noticed her 'content' had changed. A lot of travel, a lot of dining out at lavish restaurants. And in the videos she wore nice clothes. Not necessarily designer, just not the fast fashion she'd origin-ally been able to afford. Slowly, slowly she'd started to come up, I noticed. But I didn't pay that much attention, I suppose. I didn't approve of her putting herself online like that, not when she'd been overexposed most of her young life, so I stayed away. I logged on every so often and that every so often had dwindled to texting her. Keeping up with her in real life – even if it was by text and call.

With all the recent watching I was doing, I had noticed her videos started to become top/face-based. I noticed she had started looking a bit puffier after a period of glowing. That was clearly when she'd been pregnant, and if I'd paid more attention, had logged onto her channel, I might have noticed.

I hadn't been on the ball with keeping up real-life contact with her this past year or so. Nor with Moe. Jeb's company was going through redundancies so I was propping him up while trying to plan for how I would be able to bring more income without taking the job I'd been offered. I was starting to put out feelers for maybe going back into therapy work as well as the consultancy work, so was trying to refresh my qualifications. And then Zoey and Jonah were going through things – hassle at school that I had to deal with, crisis of confidence about their drama and sport. The house needed repairs that were going to get more serious the longer I left it. I was getting older and suddenly aware that I might be hitting the menopause soon, and the joys that came with that. There was a lot going on, so as long as Brandee responded to texts, would answer when I called, I'd logged her in the 'OK for now' column of my life. Same with Moe.

I had completely forgotten – wilfully forgotten – that from a dis-tance, almost anything can be faked.

'Brandee seemed to get out before the next stage,' Dennis explains. 'It's complicated. There is the legitimate side of the business. The sportswear, sports gear, the online wellness academy. All legit, upfront. They are the ones who get these young women to endorse their products. The business gives them clothes, sends them on lavish trips, takes them to restaurants, invites them to parties, all the next-level lifestyle stuff young people aspire to and lap up.

'And then, when the young women are used to this lifestyle, the clients start to criticise the engagement they are getting. They start to make demands about wanting bigger numbers responding to their products.

'Which leads to the women having to do more and more extreme things to get the type of attention that will satisfy their sponsors. They start off wearing more and more revealing clothes, doing more and more daring things to get that all important "engagement", to try to get the numbers up. They'll obviously sprinkle these videos with vulnerable ones, the "no filter" content that shows they're still the same old girls, but the videos are always heading in one direction . . .' Dennis stops talking, takes a big intake of breath that puffs up his cheeks and then he pushes all the air out again. 'It's all heading towards private webcams.'

That stops me walking. I grip the pram handle tight. Super tight. When I spoke to Larks in the garage, he had talked about webcams. The girl he thought might have been Brandee was on her following and followed by list. Her name was Krystal. She was Brandee's age and she had a page similar to Brandee's. Her content had got more risqué faster than Brandee's, but I had seen evidence of where it had ended. That could well have been Brandee.

Dennis continues, 'Which is always heading towards in-person contact.'

'But not Brandee.'

'Not Brandee. Possibly because Brandee got pregnant and shut down her accounts rather than . . . Let's say she could have carried on pregnant and would still have had an audience on private webcams.'

'This is hideous, even if Brandee isn't a part of it.'

I start walking again, keen to get home before Arie wakes up and wants to be carried home while I push the pram one-handed. That has happened before and it is not fun.

'It gets a bit complicated though,' Dennis continues. 'The main company behind this have another side to their business – deepfakes.'

I had heard this term used, had seen that some celebrities had had their faces grafted onto other people's bodies. I'd heard people say they need to update legislation to prevent what was happening. But like most things, life got busy. The world was eating itself, society was falling apart, I didn't have the bandwidth to deal with celebrity problems. 'Deepfakes' didn't sound like a problem I had to worry about at all. Even after I saw a TV drama or two where deepfakes were used to frame people for murder and for political gain – it was not my problem. Besides, all of that was made up, it couldn't possibly be going on in the real world. Not right now.

'I don't understand how that would factor in.'

'What these girls—'

'Women. They may be young, but they are women. Do not take away their agency, diminish their standing.'

'What these young women were doing when they were making all this "content", when they were building their followings and fulfilling their commitments with video after video after video, was giving these "clients" blueprints of their faces and bodies, their voices, their mannerisms, movements and facial expressions. The machines – the

Artificial Intelligence – used to build these deepfake images and videos work better the more information they have. These g—young women were unwittingly creating hundreds, if not thousands, of hours of information that could easily be used to recreate their likenesses and basically make them do anything on video.'

'But why would they—?'

Oh.

Oh.

'Yes.' Dennis can tell I understand. 'They can get their images, their likenesses and make them do anything on video. And then put those videos out there if these young women wouldn't do what they wanted behind the scenes. If they said no to anything, they would release these videos, films that are almost impossible to separate from the real things.

'Remember, their followers have already seen them wearing less and less, they have already seen them doing stuff they would never normally do. It wouldn't be that much of a leap to think they are carrying out sexual acts on screen. Especially when their real names are used to label these videos. These girls – young women – even the most sexually confident, would often be terrified of being seen like that. Especially by employers or parents or families or neighbours.

'The choice became: work for us doing this stuff and no one knows, don't work for us and the world will think this is what you do anyway.'

I have to stop again. The thought of it, the horror of it is enough to stop my feet and legs from moving. 'This is a mass sexual assault. This is a hideous type of violence.' I cover my mouth. 'Those poor girls.' I hold my hand up to Dennis. 'I know, I know. They are young women. I'm just shocked. I'm so shocked that anyone would do this. Could do this. What would you do in that situation? There is no way out.'

'I know.'

'What's being done about it?'

'What is there to be done?' he replies.

'Get those girls out of there. What else?'

'As far as anyone is concerned, those young women are there of their own free will.'

'But you know that's not true. They've been coerced. That is coercive control at the least. This is human trafficking. And so-called modern slavery. And that's just with me only knowing the overview of this! Why won't you do something about it?'

'It's not that simple—'

'Yes, it is. It's absolutely that simple. If you cared at all about any of these women you would do something.'

'This isn't my area, Kez.'

'Like hell it isn't. I know everything is connected. This is what your "Insight" unit does – it advises on the psychology behind all of this stuff. You tell them how to deal with the bastards behind it. And I *know* you could make it your area if you wanted to. In fact, you disingenuous slime, those women will be traumatised—'

'Disingenuous slime?' he interrupts. He looks affronted and I know I have gone too far. *Don't bait the bear, Kez*, I remind myself. *But then* . . .

I calm my voice before I speak again. 'Dennis, you know the ones who called their bluff will be traumatised, the others who haven't been able to get away, who are doing this thing, they will have been brutalised and will need to be released from their hell. How is that not your area? Profiling these bastards so you can work out how to take them down is the very definition of what you do.'

My former boss looks pained, he rubs a hand over his forehead.

Guilt. Shame. Or approximations of that because I know he doesn't feel those things. 'All right, there may already be a cross-department operation that we can't bring to its conclusion too quickly because—'

'Because they haven't suffered enough. They were young, independent, making their own money, living life on their terms and when that went wrong, you lot want to make sure they suffer as much as possible before you deign to free them. That will teach them to have sexual, financial and mental agency.'

'Do you want to hear the rest of it, related to Brandee, or do you want to keep playing moral crusader?'

I draw breath, trying to make myself calm enough to hear what he has to say. 'Go on.'

'I got as much information about her as I could,' Dennis begins. I can hear the tremor of something buried in his voice. 'I don't know where she is. It is like she has dropped off the face of this earth. No use of her phone, her credit cards, nothing on CCTV we have access to. It's like she has literally disappeared.'

I don't want to think what this might mean. If she is . . .

'In the lead up to her disappearance, she had some pretty intensive phone activity. Obviously she was spending a lot of money on items for the baby. Expensive stuff, too. Only the best. Organic cotton sheets and Babygros—'

'Hang on, you can see what people have bought, even if they haven't used loyalty cards . . . what am I even asking? Of course you can. Carry on.'

'Her intensive phone activity was to a handful of numbers. Most of them were burner phones so we have no real way to trace their source or ownership—'

'I don't believe that for one second, but carry on.'

'The main one was to a number in the Hove area.'

I stop again, pretty sure what he is about to say but also hoping he won't say it. That he won't ruin my life.

'They're calls to and from your husband's number.'

It's an odd sensation, to have your world crumble around you. To have it happen on a Wednesday afternoon while you're walking back from the park with the baby you found in your car. To have your life be so utterly ludicrous that the end of your marriage is actually the most banal thing about it.

'How long have these phone calls been happening? I assume they're phone calls.' My voice is flat, dead. I am so devastated, everything has shut down so I can't conjure the emotions I am supposed to be feeling to express them.

'Phone calls mainly, yes. Some texts.'

He's never protective of his phone. He has always left it lying around, everyone knows his passcode, the kids use it whenever they can't find their own, and before that when they didn't have their own. Why would he behave like, act like he has nothing to hide but be in contact with the girl we basically fostered?

My husband has always wanted another child. We used to have argument-shaped discussions about it because I would not countenance it. No way. Two pregnancies had ravaged my body, had left me with an autoimmune thyroid condition that meant I had to take medication for life. Had left me creaky and old-feeling and emotionally stressed for many years. I loved my children, but I was never putting myself through pregnancy again.

Jeb thought we could do it, he thought it would be fine. Me, not so much. It always ended the same way with me saying: 'I will happily have a third baby – a fifth child – if you can find a way to carry it.'

Was Brandee, who I counted as one of our children, the way to carry it?

'How long has the communication been going on?'

'Over the past year. Since before she would have got pregnant.'

I feel my stomach dip, that was around the time he and I started to not get on. That was around the time I'd had to do everything I could to save our relationship.

'What else?' I ask. There will definitely be more.

'He has been making payments to her via an account that isn't registered in his name. It took a while to find out the source of the payments. At first we thought it was the business I told you about. But it's him. The payments stopped around the time she disappeared. And, I assume, this one appeared in your life not long after.'

Jeb wouldn't. He just wouldn't. I have lived with him for all this time. I have felt like I have known him for ever. Loved him for a lifetime. He wouldn't do what it looks like he has been doing. He just wouldn't.

'Anything else?'

'No,' Dennis says quietly, almost respectfully. His tone actually causes me to turn to look at him. He must know my life as I know it is over if he is speaking in what is bordering a respectful tone. He must know my life is gone.

'Why are you always present at the worst moments of my life,' I ask him. It's a rhetorical question but I also do want an answer. Why was this man brought into my life? 'You're like the spectre at the feast. Oh, look, Kez is enjoying her life a little too much so here comes Dennis, all spectre-ish to drag her down.'

'You came to me. I would rather you stayed the hell away from me.'

'Yeah, course you would.'

'What do you mean by that?'

'You work it out, Mr Behavioural Expert.'

Dennis's grey eyes try to bore into my head, trying to intimidate me into retracting what I have just said.

I used to think his eyes were a pale blue but they are grey and ice-like. Dennis has no conscience. He is a real psychopath who is trying to get me to take back what I have said because he does not want to admit that he is not as untouchable as he makes out.

Dennis's psychopathy is a trait that I've seen displayed by so many people in the upper echelons of the businesses I consult for. They are there because they have no conscience about doing whatever is necessary to get a company what it wants. They are recruited for this reason. They will do the things other humans – normal humans who know what it is to feel empathy and worry and love – will not do. They have no conscience and will readily twist a narrative to make themselves the victim, to make you the enemy for questioning them. When people used to ask how companies could almost crow about their profits when their customers were freezing to death – sometimes literally – in their homes, I would stop myself from explaining that the company is run by psychopaths who do not see what they are doing is wrong. The company is run by people who do not care who is dying because of them, because the company is about making profit and this is the only way to do it; the company is run by psychopaths by design, so you cannot shame them into caring and trying to help – they expect other people to do that.

I would restrain myself from explaining all of that because people think psychopaths are the ones who plan murders – they do not want to hear that they are probably interacting with psychopaths every day of their lives. Or, at the very least, paying a bill that has been issued by a company that – purposefully – has a psychopath in charge. No one likes to know how surrounded they are.

That Dennis is still head of Insight as it's now called, after everything that has happened, tells me all I need to know about who he really is. He is different in one way, though – he studies people to find their weak spots (pressure points) but also, he can mimic the words, responses and the outward expressions of feelings of normal people. He can pretend to be normal for long stretches of time.

I return Dennis's glacial glare and don't speak, don't try to appease him like he expects. He holds out the file. 'I brought this for you. I thought you might want to read it, see in black and white what I've just told you.'

I don't take it from him, not willing to break the deadlock we have going on with our glares by engaging with him. He concedes, glances away. Probably because he thinks I have sufficient worries and he'll give me this one.

I take the folder from his hand and don't say thank you. A random but significant victory.

Before he slouches away, I ask him, 'Who is in charge of this business empire?'

He stops mid-step, wrestles with whether to tell me or not. Eventually he sighs. 'There is a man called Lucian Powell in charge of it. It looked, at one point, that he was running it with his brother, but there's no real evidence of that now.'

'Are their details in here?'

'Yes, some of them are. What I'm able to tell you is there. Most of it is higher-level stuff.'

'Right.'

'So we're done, yes? You won't be back?' Dennis says.

'Whatever,' I reply. I stash the file in the basket at the bottom of the pram. My mind is already back working out how I'm going to confront my husband about his involvement with our foster child and her baby.

# Kez

## 14 June, Brighton

Jeb is in his office when I finally arrive home.

I'd had to carry Arie back because, as usual, if I was out too long he did not appreciate pram time. I paused to sit with him on the bench on the little patch of green near our house and bounced him on my lap while trying to leaf through the folder Dennis had left me. And it indeed had page after page of Jeb's number calling and texting Brandee's number. It wasn't a number that I had, I realised after checking through my phone's directory. So it was clear he had been contacting her in secret.

I tried that number and that too was out of service.

His reaction to me coming home with Arie, his reticence about me trying to find her was off. It was all off. I thought it was about him being overprotective, but it wasn't that. It was this. These calls and texts and secrets. And then there was Seraphina asking if Brandee had seduced and run off with my husband. She's a crank, as Jeb would say, but what if she knew something? And then there was Brandee saying on her video that the father of the baby was 'complicated'. The strands, these clues had all been hinting at this. And I had been wilfully ignoring them.

Usually, I would have formulated a plan, found a way to go through his phone and computer and anything else to find out the true extent of this. But I do not have time. Brandee does not have time. I am going to have to confront him head-on.

And here I am. Right in front of him.

He has his screen-working glasses on and is completely focused on his computer. Since Arie's arrival, he has been working from home more so he can look after Arie while I look for Brandee. His calls and texts to her had indeed ended the day she disappeared. Did he have something to do with her vanishing, as well? Or was it just about the baby and her?

'Hi,' he says. 'Oh,' he adds, because he was obviously expecting to see me with Arie on my hip. 'Where's my boy?' Those two words, that he's been uttering since Arie arrived, send a chill down my spine now. Was that him hiding in plain sight?

'Arie's with Ellie. She's taking care of him with Abigail and Jessie-May. And Chris will pick up Zoey and Jonah when he picks up Jasper. We need to talk.'

My husband removes his glasses, his face shows that he has clocked how serious this is. He can't know how utterly sick to my stomach I feel right now. If he has been doing what the evidence seems to show he has been doing, then – at the very lowest level – he has been lying to me about Arie and knowing about his existence. At the top level . . . at the top level I have some very terrible times ahead.

'What's going on?' he asks, coming around his desk to stand in the middle of the room. His office is the biggest room in the house. I insisted on it because he kind of deserved it. He'd worked so hard for so many years out of various offices, trying to fit himself in the corners of our old house, that when we moved here, I said he should have this room. I didn't need much space. I liked it, craved it sometimes, but didn't need it. He needed it. It meant he could have everything – his awards, his maps and his printouts, his data – out instead of in drawers and cupboards. Jeb's walls are a beautiful patchwork of him, his thoughts, his insights, his work.

When lockdown arrived, we had to move things around because Brandee was going to be here permanently. This became the children's room, Brandee moved into their room, Moe stayed in his room. We knew that Brandee went into Moe's room during the night, and we told them it was fine by saying everyone had to be in their own beds by the time seven a.m. rolled around. We couldn't stop them having sex, we both knew that, but we did not want them to rub it in our faces.

Did my husband start to desire her, want her, when she was living here?

I have no idea how to begin this, how to continue, how to end it, I realise.

'What's going on?' he asks again.

'Are you Arie's father?' I ask. That's where I'm starting, this is what I need to know. He is fundamentally honest. He will, I think, tell me the truth if I ask him outright. I think. I hope. I pray.

He reacts as though I have slapped him in the face. 'What the *fuck* did you just say to me?' My husband never swears. Not even to talk about sex. He never uses those words, never. Me, I have a mouth like a sewer and have never made any apologies for that. Jeb has never sworn as far as I know, let alone at someone. At me.

'Is that little baby your son?' I repeat, even though I am scared, my heartrate zipping upwards at the rate of knots.

Jeb comes closer to me. 'What the *fuck* did you say to me?' he replies, his voice too angry to convey the shock and disgust on his face.

'I want to know if you fathered that little boy.'

'So because I screwed you once upon a time at a party when you were twenty-two, that makes me a pervert? A predator?' His dark brown gaze drills into me. 'No, I did not father him. I did not lay one finger on that girl. I have never touched her, not even to hug her. You know how careful I always was to never be left alone with her. I never wanted to be having this type of conversation. *Ever.*'

That is true. Jeb is always careful to give women their space, to keep his distance so as not to scare or unsettle them and so he's never accused like this.

'I don't understand why you didn't tell me she was pregnant. Not even when she left me Arie.'

'I didn't know,' he replies.

'But you spoke to her. Almost every day you spoke to her. The phone records show you called her every day. Were on the phone for more than twenty minutes sometimes. How could you not have known? You were giving her money.'

'I wasn't giving her money, not how you mean. And what phone rec—Oh I get it. I see. Your good buddy Dennis gave you phone records and told you I'd been calling her. He didn't show you my phone records, though, did he? Didn't show you I wasn't only calling her.'

'What do you mean?'

'I was calling Moe. But he won't speak to me. So when I called him and he wouldn't answer or would answer for a few seconds, I would call her. Talk to her. Find out how he was. In all those calls she never once mentioned that she was expecting. Not once.'

'Why isn't Moe speaking to you?' I ask, horrified. Jeb and Moe are tight, close. Even his parents' divorce didn't stop him almost hero-worshipping his father. As he'd grown, they'd become friends as well as father and son. I couldn't imagine a situation where they wouldn't be speaking.

Distress. Pain. Agony. Sorrow. All of those things engrave themselves on his face.

*What's happened?*

'When was the last time you spoke to him?' he asks.

'I don't know. I got a text from him the other day. He couldn't come to the phone but . . .' He couldn't come to the phone so he sent me a text saying he'd talk to me soon. That he was fine. Not to worry. Looking back, I hadn't spoken to Moe in months. Whenever I called he was too busy to pick up. Then he would call another time and leave a message to say, 'Yeah, Kez, I'm cool, talk soon, yeah?' That wasn't too surprising. He'd worked so hard to get his dream job in IT, working for a start-up. He'd been super excited when he'd found out, had been excited about saving up to buy a place. And anyway, all of that, his messages and texts, were communication. Seeing as he wasn't the most chatty of boys anyway, I didn't think much of it. Especially when I thought he was talking to and seeing his dad. 'What's going on, Jeb? And why haven't you told me about this?'

Sorrow and agony again.

'What is going on?' I ask, even more frightened.

'It's complicated.'

'Uncomplicate it.'

'I'm not sure I can.'

'Jeb, you're scaring me. Why isn't Moe talking to you?'

'Because,' his shoulders sink and his whole demeanour droops. He moves over to his sofa, drops down into it. He pats his lap for me to sit on it, but I don't want to. This feels too big, too significant to be distracted by canoodling. He may need the comfort of a hug right now, but I need the distance to stop myself screaming at him if he's done anything to hurt our eldest child.

'Why isn't Moe talking to you?' I ask again.

'Because he said as long as I stay married to you, he has nothing to say to me.'

'What? Why?'

'Because,' he closes his eyes, shakes the thoughts free from his mind, 'he hates you. He hates pretty much all women right now, but especially you.'

# Jeb

Jeb didn't know where it came from, how he got here.

He hadn't even noticed, not properly. After the lockdowns, during which Moe had finished his IT degree, Moe had moved out. Jeb had been overjoyed when Moe had chosen to spend lockdown with them – although he knew that was mainly because it was where Brandee was living. He hadn't been sure that Moe was ready to move out, but both Hella and Kez had convinced him that they couldn't hold his son back. If he wanted to live in London while working, they shouldn't stand in his way.

It was then when things began to go wrong: when he and Hella had taken their child shopping for things for his new flat in Croydon in summer of 2021, Moe had said something like, 'It's nice to have my real parents doing this,' and had looked to them for confirmation. 'It's nice to be a proper family.'

Jeb had been about to say something, when Hella had replied, 'If you ever disrespect your S-mother like that again, me and you are going to have a problem.'

Moe had stared at her, wondering if she was serious or if she was just spouting off in front of his dad. But Hella had added, 'That woman

243

has been nothing but loving to you, has treated you like her son from day one and has been nothing but respectful and kind to me. She brought you into her home so I could go and work abroad, and even then she has never overstepped the boundaries of being your parent. And whenever I've not been able to cope, she has stepped in. Don't you dare try to talk her down when she has opened her heart and her home to you.'

Jeb had been taken aback. Shocked but pleased that Hella had come to his wife's defence so passionately. He and Hella had stayed friends since their divorce, they'd had their moments and disagreements, like all people who were once married did, but they always focused on their son and showing him what a strongly bonded family looked like. She had married again but had no other children and she had been more than fine with that as far as he knew. He knew she and Kez spoke and sometimes they slipped into a therapist–patient dynamic that Kez was careful to end as quickly as possible, but he hadn't realised how much Hella thought of his wife.

'Do you understand me?' Hella said to her son as they stood in the homewares aisle of the megastore supermarket near his new place.

Moe had lowered his head and nodded.

Jeb could feel his son's eyes on him as they finished the rest of the shopping in a chastised silence. He was glaring more at Jeb than at his mother. His beef seeming to be with the man married to the woman who got him 'told off' more than the woman who told him off.

Jeb remembers that day vividly. How they'd all tried to pick up afterwards – to be happy and jokey – and how it had fallen short. None of it quite hitting the mark of being a good time together helping Moe set up his first home. And he could feel, constantly, his son sourly, hatefully side-eyeing him. He often wonders if it was then that

Moe's real resentment of Kez started. Maybe the seeds had been planted before then, but that was the day he remembers them visibly sprouting.

The worst part was he was nice to Kez. He would talk to her on the phone, he would come to visit his siblings, he would take the extra £50 she would slip him, but away from her, his resentment – *hatred* – seemed to grow. Moe would call Zoey and Jonah 'your wife's children' and would just about stop short of saying they meant nothing to him because they did. He would ask questions about what jobs Kez was working on and sneer at Jeb's replies. He would regularly ask to see Jeb alone and act as though he hadn't when Jeb arrived. He skipped his last two Christmases with them. The first Christmas he missed with them, he'd seen Hella and Richie and his grandparents on her side, but had skipped anything to do with Jeb. Then he spent the rest of that holiday going away with Brandee – a trip that Jeb and Kez had paid for. Moe knew how much Kez loved Christmas, the effort she went through to make it special for everyone, and she'd been gutted when he said he wasn't going to have time to see them. She hadn't protested, but she had been hurt.

Jeb noticed, too, that Moe had started to make nasty comments about women. 'What's a woman like that doing in politics anyway?' he'd said when a news story broke about an MP who'd received racist and sexist abuse in early 2022. 'With a butt like that, and face like that, she should be online-contenting for the mens, not trying to get into man's business.'

Disgusted, Jeb had countered: 'Don't say things like that. We haven't brought you up to talk or think like that about women.'

'It's true, though?' Moe had casually replied.

'It's not true and you know it isn't,' Jeb had insisted. 'I don't know what's got into you, but you need to get your head straight. Women can be in politics, no matter what they look like. Women can do whatever they want. You know that.'

Moe had pulled a face, shrugged a shoulder. 'If you say so, bruv.'

'I'm not your bruv,' Jeb had snapped. 'Don't forget that. And don't talk down to me. I don't know where all this is coming from, but check yourself, Moses, check yourself.'

To save face, Moe had left the room to get a drink, and Jeb had looked at Brandee. She had been sitting curled up in an armchair in the corner, playing with her phone but obviously listening. She looked up the moment he left the room and locked eyes with Jeb.

'What's going on?' he asked her quietly.

She had shaken her head in obvious despair and then had returned to swiping on her phone before Moe returned.

Jeb had left not long after, worried because this seemed like a path Moe had been on for a while, and terrified that there was no way to turn Moe back. He'd called Hella and she had said the same: Moe was different. There was nothing tangible – a few off-key remarks, the odd sour look, the withdrawal. But nothing she would put her finger on, nothing that would have made her contact him. He was just different. And she wasn't sure if this wasn't his teenage rebellion that never arrived – and they'd all patted themselves on the back about – showing up late to the party.

Maybe being an arsehole was a rite of passage Moe needed to go through. That night, Jeb had mentioned in a vague manner what he and Hella had discussed to Kez. He hadn't gone into detail and had been careful to say Hella had noticed but hadn't called him because it didn't seem like that big of a deal, because he didn't want Kez to go overboard. And she would. If she thought one of her kids was in any kind of danger, she would move heaven and earth to find out why and to fix the situation. And he was still thinking, like Hella was thinking, it was nothing really. So he'd told Kez a curated version of what had happened and his chat with his ex-wife, and Kez confirmed that it was probably them getting kicked in their collective butts by a teenage rebellion that showed up years late.

Months later, he wished that he had spoken to her. Told her everything, even the stuff that seemed trivial, because Kez might have been able to tell him what happened next was coming.

## August, 2022

Moe called him. Asked him to come to his yard. Brandee was living there, too, but the way Moe talked, it was like she was just a visitor. Jeb had begun to suspect, Moe was trying to make it clear to Brandee that he could remove her any time he wanted. That thought chilled and upset him, but by this point he knew to pick his battles and challenges with Moe. Anything could set him off and Jeb wasn't sure what it would be that would cause a fracture so large in their relationship there would be no coming back from it. If he did make Brandee leave, Jeb had decided to find a way to help her find a place and support her financially if necessary. She wasn't their child, but from the time spent with them in lockdown and the years before that when Kez had been trying to help her, she felt like one of theirs. Brandee was one of theirs because she had no one who wanted her beyond what she could do for them. It made him sick and angry whenever he thought of her mother and how she had exploited her childhood to make an income, how her father didn't do anything to stop it. If it turned out Moe was doing similar, he would not be happy. He would have to take action.

Jeb rang the doorbell a couple more times, frustrated because he knew Moe wasn't there. He knew Moe had got him out with urgency and then had gone off to do something else. Not because he had forgotten, but because he liked to mess with him. In a nasty, deliberate way, he liked to mess and antagonise his father.

### WHERE ARE YOU?

Jeb typed angrily into his phone and pressed send before he could delete the message and send a more friendly, placatory one in a normal sentence case. He was done, now. Kez had been due to go out with her friends for an all-day brunch for her birthday, he'd moved work around so he could be at home with the kids. Then Moe had called, begged him to come over to his yard . . . That was it, wasn't it? It dawned on him that Kez had probably told Moe about her birthday plans. And Moe had set about ruining them – using his father's love for him, too. He should have said no. He should have said they could talk on the phone or talk another time. He knew, though, that even if he'd wanted to, Kez wouldn't have let him. She would have insisted he go. Moe knew that and Moe had exploited that. Moe texted back:

### At my local 🍺🍺🍺

Then:

### Why?

Jeb texted in reply:

### You asked me to come to your yard

his anger rising with each passing second. Moe was going to play ignorant, play innocent. He was going to do it so well, Jeb would start to doubt himself or feel bad for questioning him.

It hit him like the broadside of a plank of wood – he was in an abusive relationship with his son. Everything that Kez had ever told him about her friends and the relationships they got into and found hard to get out of sounded like this one. He was even, in a way, being financially abused by Moe. They kept giving him money even though he didn't appreciate it. He didn't technically ask for it, he just made them feel that any shortfall in his income – which he would never reveal the depth of – was putting him at a disadvantage and they owed him so they had to put it right. He never technically asked for anything, beyond responding to what birthday present he wanted – but he always needed stuff that they found out about and felt compelled to pay for. It was complicated, because they didn't begrudge it, they were never asked to do it, but somehow they always *had* to do it. And Moe had stopped pretending to be grateful, he'd stopped saying thank you, he barely acknowledged anything they gave him. And how could you resent giving your kids everything because that's what good parents did, wasn't it? Hella and Kez had mentioned a few times that they should maybe pull back on the allowance and paying for stuff he *wanted* but dressed up as *needing*. They'd said that giving him anything he wanted was teaching him not to stand on his own two feet, it was teaching him that his attention and affection came with a price and that he could, eventually, have his attention and affection bought by someone with deeper pockets.

But Jeb knew his son, he'd told them. His son couldn't be bought. His son had a good moral compass and he wasn't playing them. He wasn't a player. And besides, neither of them felt the guilt he did that his son had grown up with two homes because of him. Because he'd been a coward by not breaking off the relationship before they were almost married, which made him a cheat, which made him a bigger coward by not leaving anyway when he confessed to Hella, his son had grown up with two homes and four parents.

That was why he took Moe's crap. He felt guilty that because of him, he didn't have the stability of a home like he'd had. Hella and Kez had told him more than once, a hundred times probably, that it was better to grow up in two happy homes than one resentment-filled one. But he still felt guilty. Deeply guilty. And that was what Moe had played on.

Yes, he was being played by his son. Their relationship had become toxic in a way that would fool most people into thinking it was normal. And it was hurting his wife. It was hurting him. It was probably hurting Moe on a level he didn't even understand.

Jeb texted again, when it was obvious Moe was going to ignore him:

**_You asked me to come to your yard. Get back here now._**

Moe lived in a six-storey modern block of flats in a quiet cul-de-sac-type road just off the main street in Croydon. There was parking but the streets were quite narrow and, oddly, it felt secluded for where it was. It was a nice enough area, but Jeb didn't like hanging around there. He was never sure which of the neighbours would see him as suspicious and start taking notes, start passing those notes on to the authorities.

**Bruv, I just started a new pint**

was Moe's reply.

Less than a second later, he sent the under-pressure emoji – a laughing face with a sweat drop on its forehead. A second after that, a rolling-on-the-floor-laughing emoji. Then a beer emoji.

**If you're not back here in eight minutes, I'm going. And I'm taking the car payments and the down payment on your holiday with me.**

Jeb jabbed his finger on the send button so hard he was surprised the screen didn't crack. Then he sent a car emoji. A plane emoji. And finally an egg-timer emoji.

Three dots of reply started up . . . disappeared. Started up . . . disappeared. Started up . . . disappeared.

Seven minutes later, Moe appeared around the corner, moving at speed until he saw his dad was still there, at which point he slowed right down. Even from that distance Jeb clocked Moe's relief. Was it the money or the fact his father hadn't abandoned him? Jeb couldn't – probably would never – know.

Moe wasn't alone. He had his crew with him. He'd seen them before, a mess of privilege and unattainable ambition, they dressed in expensively casual clothes, spoke with forced south London accents, moved like they were auditioning for a rap band that would never even look at them because they were all lacking any discernible talent.

'What up, Pa?' the blond white lad to Moe's left said. He tipped his chin in greeting, his sneer of contempt showing up in his hazel-green eyes rather than his lip. He thought himself better than Jeb. Probably better than everyone he ever met.

Jeb checked to see if there was someone behind him. 'You talking to me?' Jeb replied. 'Cos I am not – nor never will be your "pa". Even if you married my son I would still not be your "pa".'

'Burn!' the other lads screamed and fell about laughing. All except the one who'd been humiliated and Moe. Moe glared at his father.

'That was sick, Daddy-o,' the long-faced young man, with skin so white it looked like he was about to keel over, screamed. He raised his hand to high-five Jeb.

'You too, huh?' Jeb said, thoroughly sick of this bunch. 'I'm not your father.' He addressed the hooting, slapping group. 'For the avoidance of doubt, the only one of you who can call me by a parental title is this guy here.' He pointed at Moe.

That sent Moe over the edge. He slapped Jeb's finger away, snarling, 'Look who's come over a comedian. Is that cos you've finally seen you've got clown children with your skank wife, *Dad*?'

Jeb drew back. Horrified. Shocked. And then angry. Very, very angry.

'Don't you dare talk about your family like that,' he said, having to speak over the nasty laughter of Moe's 'friends'. Their vicious merriment was clearly from hearing Moe say this to them before. Probably several times. And now they were impressed because he'd said it to Jeb's face.

'Ain't my family,' Moe replied. 'Ain't no way I'd be related to such a skank. How many members you reckon she had up there, *Dad*?' His spiteful smile spread right across his face. 'Cos you know that skank has *lived*. You know she was doing bits from time before you rocked up.'

The grin of the guy with dark red hair and freckles sprinkled across his pale nose, who stood a head taller than everyone else, widened in pure delight as Moe tore into his stepmother. He was enjoying this.

They all were. None of them were shocked. None of them cared how misogynistic Moe sounded. They all believed it, agreed with it. They all probably encouraged it.

'Don't talk about your stepmother like that,' Jeb said, his calm tone belying the anger he felt. He had realised, almost too late, that Moe wanted him to hit him. He wanted an excuse to go crying to Hella about what Jeb had done. To declare Kez had changed Jeb into someone who would hit his own son. And then he could tell Kez how much she had come between him and his dad.

'Step-Skank, more like,' Moe said. And smiled. Because he knew it was only a matter of time until Jeb went for him. He just had to find the right combination of words, the right button to push and he would separate his father from his wife.

Jeb turned on his heels and began the long walk away from his son. He should have done it sooner. He should have told Hella and Kez sooner. He should have done all of this very differently.

'Don't walk away from me, old man,' Moe said, slapping his hand on Jeb's shoulder, spinning him towards him and following it up with a fist flying towards his face. Jeb, who'd always had lightning reflexes from his days as a trainee boxer, tipped the top half of his body back so the punch missed its mark. When Jeb then stepped back, the momentum forced Moe to tip off balance and land unceremoniously on his face.

His mates, who'd been laughing when the insults had been flying, were now silent as Moe lay on the ground. Jeb didn't bother rushing to help him up, even though that was what his instincts were screaming at him to do. He knew it would do no good, it would cause more harm. And anyway, no one talked about his family like that and got away with it. Not even his precious eldest son.

'She's a skank!' Moe screamed as Jeb continued his harrowing journey to his car parked across the street. 'Your wife is a skank.' He could hear the hate ground like broken glass into Moe's voice.

Jeb had to walk away, had to get away. He slid into the driver's seat, started the car with tears stinging his eyes. He glanced down at his bare forearms and was surprised – genuinely taken aback – that he wasn't bleeding from the way his son's words had lacerated his skin.

# Kez

## 14 June, Brighton

'I called him later, expecting him to have calmed down, to apologise,' Jeb says, talking calmly even though it's obvious he is anything but. My husband is devastated. Absolutely heartbroken. 'But he was worse than before. He was raging, totally off the block furious with me. He started ranting about how I'd ruined his life to be with you. How you had come between me and Hella. Stolen me away. He blamed you for everything, not getting to go to his first university, for not getting the dream job he had wanted, even for Brandee questioning some of the things he said.

'He said you had turned her into a feminist and he hated you even speaking to her because you were constantly putting ideas into her head. He said you kept telling her that men and women are equal, but conveniently forgot that men are always left behind and blamed for everything.'

Jeb closes his eyes because he does not want to keep looking at my face. I'm sure I have put on a neutral face, the therapist's demeanour I wear to make sure my feelings do not taint the therapeutic process, but Jeb knows that every word is a stab to my heart. That my heart is suffering from multiple puncture wounds and I know I'm about to sustain many more of them before he has finished talking. But I need to hear it. I need to hear the unvarnished truth because I need to know everything. All of this is connected to Brandee's disappearance. I don't know how yet, but it is.

'He said in your therapy sessions, you turn women against men, you make them believe that all men are abusers and that you hate men. That was why you broke up our happy home. That was why I was so whipped. He said I'd been emasculated and I needed to get off my knees and stop crawling after a woman who couldn't even keep herself pure and wait for a man to marry her.'

'Where did he get all that stuff?' I interrupted. 'Because that is not normal. That is pure, *pure* hate. That is some of the most radicalised shit I've heard in a long time. Someone has been feeding him that stuff over a long period of time.'

'I don't know exactly where. Maybe his new friends? None of them seemed shocked when he started spouting this stuff. They thought it was funny and encouraged him. None of them acted like they hadn't heard it before.'

'This is the stuff they were talking about on the internet a while back,' I say. The unsettling thing is, I've heard snippets of that stuff before. From the men who begrudged my presence in the companies I consult for. From those who object to me sitting in on meetings to observe team dynamics, from those who resist engaging in any of the exercises (psychometric tests) I sometimes set, from those who completely resent having to talk to me so I can assess whether they are suitable for the job they're in or for the position they'd like. This misogyny, this feeling that men don't get a fair go, always seeps through. It's not me, it's the world they believe we live in, it's the thought that the world is unequal in favour of women, no matter how much quantifiable facts and figures prove otherwise.

I have heard those things before, but never so much of it in one place. Never the full-on rant. Never from someone I know hasn't been brought up to think of women as being inferior to men. In fact, all four of us (Jeb and me, Hella and Richie) had been of the same mind in *actively* talking about equality and respect, about injustice and fairness with the children. Not over the top, just enough to raise awareness, to keep them savvy to what was going on in the world, to stop them being naïve in potentially dangerous situations. How had this happened? Who had dripped all of this poison and toxicity into him?

I say to Jeb: 'I don't know why I thought it wouldn't happen to us. I thought we were immune because we talked to our children. And look where we are now. What happened next?'

'He ended the call saying he was taking away the power we'd been wielding over him by not accepting our money any more and would only talk to me again when I'd left you. Every time I call he asks if I've left you, when I say no, he hangs up and won't pick up again. That's when I call Brandee to find out how he is. See if she was all right, living with him when he was like that. She would tell me what was going on. She admitted to me after the fight that he'd completely run out of cash, that he'd spent it on this course, academy thing and he was flat broke. She said she had some money, but not enough for the debts he'd accumulated. I had someone help me conceal where the money came from I was giving her for him so it seemed like she had a new client who was advertising on her channels so she could "lend" it to him. He hated taking money from a woman, of course, but he was desperate by then. That's why I was giving her money. It was for him. I told her to get out of there if it got too much. To come home to us for a while. Nowadays, he doesn't even pick up the phone – he just texts me to ask if I've left you.'

'Why didn't you tell me any of this?' I know it's not important right now, but I have to know. 'This has been going on for more than a year. Why didn't you tell me?'

'I couldn't. I thought I could sort it, and then I would be able to tell you. Then I'd be able to get you to help with his recovery.'

'What about Hella? Does she know any of this?'

'A little. She helped me set up the money thing because I told her he was too proud to take our cash any more and Brandee had said he had debts. I wanted him to keep in touch with someone. If I told Hella what he'd said, she would have torn him a new one – several new ones – which would mean he'd be completely cut off from the family. I couldn't risk that.

'And I couldn't say all that stuff to you without at least something close to a resolution. Especially not when he continued to engage with you like nothing was wrong. He knew I couldn't say that stuff to you, so he kept being normal with you. And I promise you, Brandee didn't tell me she was pregnant. That she'd had a baby.'

'Moe probably told her not to.'

'I don't think he knew. She told me not long after the incident he was spending more and more time away, disappearing for days at a time. Towards the end of last year, she said she barely saw him. She said he was secretive, said he had a new job that he loved. Then she said, he seemed to have big money to pay off his debts. Which is why I stopped giving her money. Then, out of the blue, she said she was going to get him back. I thought at first she meant get revenge. But she must have meant she was going to get the real him back.'

This situation is so much more horrific than I originally thought. And it is only going to get worse.

'You have to go and see Hella. Tell her everything. All of it. Even that Arie is potentially her grandchild.'

'I'm not sure—'

'You have to go and tell her. You can't say this stuff on the phone. While you're gone I'll go through the phone records and other information Dennis gave me, although I'm guessing he only gave me the bits that were convenient to him and would make a certain narrative play out. I can't do anything about that right now. But I need to go through them and find out about the company Moe started working for. You need to get on the road to London.'

Jeb doesn't move. My fundamentally honest husband doesn't want to perform the honesty in such a difficult situation. He would rather defer this bit, leave it on layaway until who knows when. This is why he ended up engaged, why he fucked me at that party – he doesn't like to have the hard conversations, especially if he is the one who has to start them.

'Jeb,' I say carefully, 'Brandee has disappeared, leaving me – us – her baby. We now know she's probably done that to get Moe back. What do you think that means?'

'To bring—'

He's finally realised: Moe has disappeared too. It's probably linked to his job. To Brandee's close brush with the 'businessmen' who sponsored her. 'You said it yourself, these last few times, he hasn't answered his phone when you called, he has just sent text replies asking if you've left me yet. Before, at least, he was asking you that on the phone. Now he isn't. You haven't actually spoken to him in weeks, you haven't seen him in months. It'd be so easy to fake those text messages. I'm guessing it's the same with Hella. He's been in touch by text, but nothing else.

'You need to tell Hella that her son has disappeared and you need to get her to brace herself for the fact that she may never see him again.'

# Part 6

# Brandee

**Brandee | Secret video recording | Micro recorder |**

*\* Recorded: 5 January 2023 \**

I've taken down my Joyn Inn channel. And the others. There's a lot of shit going on. Urgh, the relief of being able to speak properly now! I don't have to put a 1 in and spell shit out now! Or say unalive instead of kill or S. A. instead of sexual assault.

Freedom.

There's some proper shady shit going on. The Traits sportswear brand people I set up the partnership with began asking for more and more. And I was not up for that, no siree. I remember KL saying that if I felt uncomfortable, to stop. She said when it starts to feel like it did with your mother, even in a good way, stop. Thought she was being over the top, but now look at me. Pretty much in hiding because they want their money back. I delivered everything we agreed in the contract, but they were saying while I stuck to the letter of the agreement, I did not stick to the spirit of it.

They can spirit my left sock.

I mean, I've seen enough dodgy lawyers' letters from Seraphina's friends to know that they were trying it. They thought if they could get me to admit to not upholding my end of the agreement by saying I'll post more for them, that they'll then be able to use that as evidence of me admitting that I've breached our contract. Then they'll have me. Not going to happen to this gal.

They did this to Krystal. She was so panicked at the solicitor's letterhead that she just started posting more and more of their shit. I tried to tell her to get proper legal advice but she was too scared. She thought if she just did as she was told, she'd be fine.

I get so angry when I think about what she's been forced into doing now. Some of those videos are sick.

I just deactivated instead of doing what they said. I have to lie low for now.

Moe has turned into a shit. It's been a long time coming and the way he was behaving with his dad was just out of pocket. I love his dad. And he was finding newer and worse ways to treat him like shit.

The way he started talking to me, too. I called him on it a few times. And he's all, 'I'm sorry, babe, I'm sorry.' I noticed how he stopped saying he wouldn't do it again. Rah.

It's been like this for a while. He's been reading this stuff, watching videos, doing all that academy empowerment bullshit and just getting more and more sucked into that horrible, woman-hating world. Why can't he see all that stuff is racist as hell, too?

This is partly my fault as well. I didn't even think. Back when it was all good with the Traits guys, they asked if I knew anyone who knew computers, so of course I said Moe. He was pretty deep in debt by then. He'd spent all his money on these stupid courses, trying to free his mind and body. Kissing my teeth.

He was also refusing to take money from his parents because he said they were using the finances to control him. Control him? How were they controlling him by giving him whatever he wanted? That's the problem with these online courses that promise you all sorts, a lot of them are illogical and nonsense when you even lightly challenge their basic ideology.

Moe said all this after he tried to hit his dad. Can you believe it? He tried to hit him. He said his dad tried to hit him and he had to put him on the ground. I don't know who he thought he was talking to. His friends might have believed that crap, but I didn't.

I didn't say that, though, cos he was already so wound up. Now he's working for the people who own the Traits company. I did not realise they were the same people who owned the stupid academy courses run by that idiot L King. Since he's been working there he's just got worse. He stays out all the time, doesn't come home for days or weeks at a time. I've moved into the spare bedroom so I won't be disturbed whenever he does eventually get in to crash out.

He hasn't looked at me in weeks. Having said that, even if he had, would he even notice anything was different? Doubt it. His head is just filled with his idiot friends and the stuff he's learning on those courses.

I have to get him back. I just have to. I love him and I need him. Urgh, who knew I would be here when they approached me?

I have to work out how to get Moe back without putting myself in danger. For now, though, I have to keep my head down, get shit done.

Peace In.

# Kez

**15 June, Brighton**

**Name:** Lucian Powell    **Age:** 44

**Address:** Old Town Manor House, Hawksbury, Sussex (owns estate and surrounding land)

**Place of birth:** London    **Grew up:** [Redacted]

**Eye colour:** Blue    **Glasses?** Had corrective laser eye surgery (keeps secret)

**Hair colour:** Brown but dyes blond    **Body type:** Muscular

**Occupation:** Business guru, self-help & lifestyle guru, creator of sports brand Traits, former championship bodybuilder, owns Powell Online Training Academy, owns KlickThroo internet services.

**Relationship status:** Uncertain

**Significant others:** Previously thought to work with brother Ronan Powell but not corroborated.

[REDACTED]

[REDACTED]

[REDACTED]

[REDACTED]

**Significant information:** Lucian Powell is currently known as a life-style guru who runs the Powell Online Training Academy, designed to help young people reach their true potential. Powell focuses primarily on assisting young men achieve their dreams through mental and physical training.

[REDACTED]

Powell has multiple contacts in various industries. His core strength in business seems to be knowing how to form connections. A number of people who have worked with him either move into his home for short periods or [REDACTED].

Powell was previously a championship bodybuilder, travelling the world to take part in competitions. Notable wins: Mr Weightlifting World (2011), Man Alive (2013), Strong Iron (2015).

[REDACTED]

Powell has been arrested multiple times (2011, 2012, 2015, 2017, 2019, 2021, 2022, 2023) on suspicion of domestic abuse. He has yet to be charged or cautioned. All his accusers retract their accusations and [REDACTED]

Powell is currently under investigation for human trafficking. [REDACTED]

[REDACTED]

[REDACTED]

[REDACTED]

[REDACTED]

According to the heavily redacted files that Dennis gave me, there is one person behind all of this: Lucian Powell. He owns the brand that Brandee was working for before she stopped posting. According to the file, Brandee deactivated her account for a while then reactivated it but didn't post, which was how I was able to see all her historic posts.

This Lucian Powell also owns the company, KlickThroo, that gave Moe his dream job in computing.

Lucian Powell is the connecting point in this. And I don't know why. I wonder if Brandee introduced Moe to Lucian and as a result she has felt guilty about what Moe got into? Because the stuff that Jeb said Moe was spouting is the stuff that Lucian pushes. Constantly. But, from the sounds of it, Moe was saying this stuff before he got this job.

Anyhow, if Brandee did introduce Moe to him, I can understand why she felt she had to do whatever she could to get him back.

Lucian Powell is younger than me. From his picture, even this mugshot-type photo, he is handsome. Well groomed, with his (dyed) blond hair neatly cropped to emphasise the structure of his strong face. He has blue-green eyes that penetrate as they stare into the camera, and after studying his face, after locating the type of famil-iarity I see in all faces, I turn over page with the photo – I can't stand to have him staring at me, it's two-dimensional but unbelievably creepy.

His file hints that he is of average intelligence, that his 'genius' is in his ability to surround himself with people who will do what he wants in half the time and to twice the standard that he could do. He is a user. Like a lot of people who are thought of as 'geniuses' he can't actually do anything. But unlike other men – and it is almost always men at this level – who have a fortune and then 'invest' their money in a business only to ruin it by their interference and incompetence, Lucian Powell knows his limitations. He knows that his best bet is to employ other people to do the work for him. To praise them, to value them, to bring them onto his side. Once they are a part of his 'family' as he repeat-edly calls his business associates online, they do not want to leave. They want to stay to be given their regular injection of being needed by him. To get their dopamine hit.

Lucian Powell, whose followers call him L King, is terrifying. Dan-gerous. What isn't in the heavily redacted and deliberately light file that Dennis gave me, is there online for anyone to see.

He is a headworker on a large scale. He knows how to get into peo-ple's heads and to rummage around, and has built a whole business around it.

People like him construct whole worlds based on spurious conspiracy theories.

They know how to speak to people, how to communicate, so they create social media profiles, online communities and real-world personas based on their chosen conspiracy theory. Then they set about turning them into a potentially real theory.

They don't start with pronouncements and certainties, they start in the place where doubt lives by reframing truths. They avoid firm statements about women being less capable than men, they don't declare that Black people are less than. They trick and manipulate. They ask questions, they encourage you to 'open your mind', they speak in reasonable tones, they play to your insecurities, they reassure that your questioning is normal. They nurture you to take a 'Devil's advocate' approach – even with non-contentious issues like 'everyone deserves to eat'. They encourage you to take this approach with everything, absolutely everything in your life and when it comes to certain groups who you're already unsure about, you're supposed to go in harder, question more.

And while you're questioning, playing Devil's advocate, they tell you that there are bad people 'on both sides', that the shades of grey are there because the bad people on the vulnerable group's side are more of a danger to you than the 'bad' no, not bad, 'passionate, patriotic, brave' people on their side. They show you how dangerous the other side are, how honest and upstanding and courageous their side is.

They never tell you what to think. Never.

But at the end of it, where once you believed night followed day, and day followed night, you always question if that is true. You wonder who benefits from you thinking that. You question why it's only someone 'brave and honest and patriotic' and who seems to 'only want the best for you' that is telling you that night and day do not follow each other. You wonder why no one has told you this before. Why no one has trusted you with this truth before. You start to disbelieve the things you've always held true – that night and day are equal. That night isn't better than day, nor day better than night. You wonder who benefits from you believing that, and think that maybe one *is* better than the other. Shouldn't you find the evidence that will prove to you one is better than the other, instead of just being a sheep who goes along with the (wrong) crowd? And who will step into that role of providing evidence? Who will guide you to find that truth?

Yes, Lucian Powell.

With his videos, his podcasts, his social media posts he will tell you what you should believe. Who you should think is better than who. Who is oppressing who. Who is the cause of your problems and how you can 'fight back', take back control, free your mind. For a fee, of course. The questioning part is free, the finding the solution will cost you.

It will cost you your money, your integrity, your friendships, your relationships, your mental stability and, eventually, your soul. They will strip you of every support mechanism that you have.

Lucian Powell hates women. He is racist, ableist, homophobic and transphobic. He hates everyone. He rarely outright says it, but it is there, in coded language, thinly veiled skits, the people he chooses to support and amplify. It is there, part of the DNA of his philosophy.

But it is his hatred of women from which he has built an empire. A business where he manipulates men into paying for access to his theories, he convinces them that he can provide them with the solution to their inferiorities around women. He can help them to elevate themselves, to take command, take control, become that alpha male they know they could be. And once they have been through his programme, freed their minds, improved their bodies, paid to learn how to be a success, Lucian provides them access to some of the most well-known social media faces online. These women are there for them, they smile at them, praise them, carry out their sexual fantasies right there on screen. These men are in control, they can order these women, who wouldn't have looked twice at them before Lucian, to do whatever they want.

And once they have this access, Lucian encourages them to bring others. To bring *paying* others, who he will nurture to join their exclusive, elevated world.

Lucian Powell is brilliant at manipulating people. He is excellent at gathering people to follow him. He is a genius at getting other people to do his dirty work.

The things I have seen online, the words, the theories are almost identical to what Jeb told me Moe was saying. Second wives and step-mothers are skanks who have broken up the family unit. They are the lowest of the low. And if the husband cannot see that, then he must pay the toll. He must financially pay for bringing the skank into their lives, he must suffer emotionally until he sees the error of his ways.

But this does not apply to second wives who are younger and pret-tier than the first wife. It does not apply if the husband left the first wife for the younger and prettier second. It does not apply if the second wife is a trophy, who dotes on her husband and never questions him. It does not apply if the second wife knows her place and shows her husband he is her master in all things.

Lucian Powell's theories have only the thinnest, frailest thread of logic in them, his rules are set in stone until they challenge something else he has said and then they are pliable, and able to be moulded to fit his latest theory. His philosophy is cobbled together from the things he has gleaned from complex theories he has half read and barely understood.

The more I read, the more I accept that Brandee introduced Moe to Lucian Powell. If not him directly, then someone from his world at least, when she was involved with Powell's social-media-buying agency and the sports brand. Before they gave Moe his dream job working in IT, they gave Moe a place in the world where it was OK to want the thing that Moe has wished for every birthday since he was seven – for his parents to get back together. It is nothing to do with me, nothing to do with Richie, he just always wanted Jeb and Hella, Hella and Jeb together so their family unit could be restored.

Moe knows that it is illogical to still want that, especially since his parents have been married to other people longer than they were married to each other, but he still craves it. Those insecurities make him feel 'less of a man'. Those are the doubts Lucian Powell panders to, they are the uncertainties Lucian Powell first of all allows people to think are normal (and they are) that he then he exploits. I bet he bled Moe dry with his 'materials' and 'coursework' and 'grades' in his online academy. Which is why he regularly needed money.

And then, when he found out what Moe could do, how naturally gifted he is with computers, he will have offered Moe a job. Someone with skills like Moe would be useful. Rather than have him as a regular punter, he would have offered Moe a fortune in cash, and a bountiful well of understanding. I'm willing to bet that he will have told Moe a story that is similar to his, he will have shown Moe that he overcame it by seeing the truth, by working hard to restore the order of things, and will have promised to help him get his father back from the harridan who stole him.

It would have been lies, mirroring to make Moe feel safe and heard and understood.

I don't know how long he has been brainwashed by this stuff, but Moe is in deep. And all of that would have triggered something in Brandee. Guilt, mainly. She will have blamed herself for Moe getting sucked in, the things he will have said about me. The pain in Jeb's voice as he tried to reach his son. Brandee would have felt compelled to get Moe back. To bring him home.

From everything I've read about Lucian Powell, he keeps everyone important for his businesses close to him. They all live at his country estate in Sussex. I have seen images of the place and it is massive. It has stables and plenty of room for all his six luxury cars. There's a pool, tennis courts, shooting range. It's likely that Moe is there. If Moe is there, then it's likely Brandee is there trying to get him back.

I have to go there. Speak to Lucian Powell.

I'd rather not, I'd rather sit in my nice house and think of another way to see my children. But it's the only way. The only way to bring them back is to sit down with the ultimate Devil's advocate.

# Brandee

**Brandee | Secret video recording | Micro recorder |**

*\* Recorded: 23 April 2023 \**

Really scared. But I have to do this. I'm going in the next few days. I've taken care of most things. Just one more thing to do and then I'm sorted.

**Brandee | Secret video recording | Micro recorder |**

*\* Recorded: 16 May 2023 \**

I miss him. I miss him so much. But I'm doing this for him, too. I saw her take him. I waited in the shadows until she got back to her car and then I watched her look around, search around, but she didn't see me. I know she'll do the right thing. I'd better not say too much in case someone finds this.

# Kez

## 16 June, Sussex countryside

*'Hi Moe, it's Kez. Just ringing to see how you are? We haven't spoken in about a minute. I know, I know, I'm too old and too square to be using those types of expressions. As evidenced nicely by my use of the word square. Hope you're all right, Moe. All we seem to do nowadays is text or leave each other voicemails. I miss our chats. Call me back when you get the chance. Love you.'*

\*

I'm aware as I drive towards Lucian Powell's previously run-down and now highly modernised estate, that this road I'm on feels a lot like the road to nowhere. It is very isolated here. Deliberately so. And it's unnerving. With every bit of road that is being eaten up by the wheels of my car, the more aware I am of how vulnerable I am making myself by coming here. *'You don't feel things like you should do sometimes, Kez,'* Jeb had said to me. *'It's terrifying to watch. It's terrifying being someone who loves you and watching.'*

But I have to face this person. I have to work out by speaking to him if Brandee is here, if Moe is here, and if there is a way for me to get

277

them back. I am being stupid, coming alone, but Jeb is still in London with Hella and anyway, bringing him would not be a good thing to do. I need to focus, I need to not be worrying about what he is feeling. What he might do. And I mustn't tip my hand that I know how much Moe hates me. That's why I continue to leave voice messages. Moe can't know yet that anything has changed.

Arie is with Ellie and Chris again. I feel bad imposing on them, but they have said they don't mind and this is only going to be for a few hours. I tell myself that as the building, a dark red structure with turrets and grounds that go on for acres, comes into view. I saw it on the map, on the internet, but I hadn't quite appreciated its sheer size.

It is a beautiful place, the type you'd expect to have been turned into a spa retreat, not somewhere a terrible man forces young women to have sex on camera for a paying public; where he creates deepfake pornography to blackmail the women whose likenesses he has stolen, all the while running his male empowerment courses.

When I think about it like that, I get again that feeling of impending danger that seems overblown yet completely rational. It's the feeling I had when I was walking across the car park the night this all started; the sensation that I'm about to die that I had when I walked into Obsidiblue the day that Brian did die.

My stomach falls away, my sensibilities falling with it. I'm about to slam my foot down on the brake, I'm about to execute an emergency stop. Turn around, speed off in the other direction.

*I don't want to do this.*

*I shouldn't do this.*

At interludes like this, my former supervising therapist from when I was a therapist would probably tell me to look at what I am reproducing in my life that is throwing up these feelings of deep terror. She would ask why I am putting myself in this situation when I could be going to the police, asking them to investigate, begging them to get my children back. She would ask me why I am putting myself in danger when there are other options.

And I would say . . .

I would say . . . There aren't other options. Not in real life. On paper, in theory, yes. In real life, no. People like Lucian Powell aren't able to carry on for as long and as successfully as he has without having people who will protect them in all walks of life in their pockets. They are very good at looking after number one by making sure they never take the fall. Are never forced to make the kill shot.

I slow the car, indicate even though there is no one around, and pull over. I open the car door, unclip my seatbelt and get out. I have to rest my hands on my jeans-covered thighs. I have to breathe.

*Breathe.*

*Inhale.*

*Exhale.*

*Breathe.*

Did I have to do it? Did I have to take the kill shot?

Did I have to kill Brian?

I don't know, *I don't know.*

I pulled the trigger and he died. I hadn't been aiming for his heart. I didn't aim for his head. But where had I been aiming? Would wounding him have stopped him?

*I don't know.*

He was determined, resolute in killing me, killing Dennis, killing Maisie, brutalising that young woman and then probably killing her too because his guilt would have been overwhelming. But did I have to kill him?

I don't know. I just don't know.

Few people know how the terror of maybe having made the wrong decision walks with me every day of my life. That inside, I am a scared little girl who wants someone to scoop her up and tell her that she made the right choice. That there was nothing else she could have done.

My supervising therapist never knew I felt this. She knew I'd been at the scene where someone was shot and killed. But, outside of Dennis and Maisie – and technically those two young women whose names I was never allowed to know – the only other person who knows that I was the one who pulled the trigger is Jeb. I have never revealed to him, though, about desperately wanting someone to tell me I did the right thing. And I have never told him – or anyone – that I see Brian's face all the time. Not just in a crowd, or as a fleeting play of light, I see his face on every new person I meet. I see it on the people I've known for years. I haven't confessed that when I can't sleep at night it's because I know Brian is lurking somewhere in a reflective surface, waiting to frown his pain at me. Brian haunts me, every day, *everywhere*.

With effort, I stand upright. Push Brian's face away. I can't allow myself to get sucked into my own head like this. Scared or not, terrified or not, I have to talk to this man. I have to find a way to persuade him to give me back my children. Adults they may be, but they'll always be my children and they'll always be the reason I do whatever is necessary to protect them. And if that means confronting this man as I pretend to be the woman who isn't haunted daily, hourly by the face of the man she killed, that's what I'll do.

# Brandee

**Brandee | Secret video recording | Micro recorder |**

**\* Recorded: 18 May 2023 \***

I'm in. They made a BIG deal of bringing me in to their base of operations. Going on about how they always find people. 'No one escapes us. We are elite, we are everything. L King knows everything, L King is everything.' He actually said that shit with a straight face as well.

I have to keep my voice down, whisper. They honestly think they're all military and shit, but that was literally the most pathetic search I've ever had. I've had searches to get into clubs that have been more intimate than my smear tests, but OK L King and your military guys! My heart was pounding, I thought I was going to get caught. But nah, L King's men didn't find this micro recorder. All the better for me, I suppose, cos I need to get as much evidence as I can.

When I get it, I am going to march down to that police station and throw it in their faces. When I have this stuff on camera, they can't fob me off like last time. They don't know how much it took to go in there and report stuff last time. They were all, 'She's an adult, we can't investigate if there's no sign that she's being coerced.' Then there was the one in the corner, smirking and saying, 'It looks like she's enjoying herself!'

'She doesn't look like she was enjoying herself,' I wanted to scream at him. She looked terrified. She looked like she was in a great deal of pain. If they'd ever been scared, or if they'd ever cared about anyone, they would be able to see that. Krystal wouldn't do that stuff. Not on camera. Not when anyone she knows could see. *Bastards*.

That stuff was bad. I'm not trying to kink shame, but I know Krystal wouldn't do those things unless someone was forcing her. And I know she's here. And I'm going to help her. The only way I can do that is if I can get evidence about what L King is up to.

The game plan is to act like I'm going to go along with it. Like I'm going to join them and film stuff. I might have to do it. I don't want to, but it's no different to what my mum used to make me do. I just have to put myself into that space. Step out of my head and think what I'm ultimately doing it for.

Peace In.

# Kez

**16 June, Sussex countryside**

Up close, you can see that this property is not like the others in this area that have this much land. This place is ringed with a high, red-brick wall, built with weathered materials to make it look as if it was always like this and not that the previous boundaries were woodlands or a stream. Barbed wire, studded at regular intervals by security cameras, sits on top of the walls like an open threat. 'Foreboding' and 'intimidating' were the aims of the modernising process. They want people to think twice before entering, they want visitors to worry that they may never be allowed to leave.

Monogrammed front gates, which appear to be the only entrance and exit, held together with a three-foot-high iron L and P, greet me when I arrive. I expect to have to speak into an intercom or something, but the gates open for me and I drive into the white-gravel circular driveway and park my car by the front door. There is more than enough room for anyone to pass, so I gather my courage, which is seriously wavering by this point, and switch off the engine.

I'm met by a tall, thick-necked blond man who has spent many an hour in the gym, and now has the attitude and mannerisms of an unsmiling nightclub bouncer. He glares down at me as I say, 'I'm here to see Mr Powell, my name is Kez Lanyon.' Those seem to be magic words because he steps aside to let me into a hallway that is every bit the stately home it used to be – twenty-foot-high ceilings, expensively laid and polished stone floor, sweeping staircase.

The silent man moves away to the small table that stands next to the staircase, picks up the receiver of the gold telephone and speaks quietly into it. He speaks so quietly, I can only make out my name before he listens, then hangs up.

The man, who still hasn't spoken to me, indicates to the left, and starts to lead me through the house. We pass a large open reception area with plush white sofas and a low wide marble table facing a large screen on the wall. We walk down a corridor that is dark with wood panelling and framed paintings of people who could be Powell's ancestors or could have come with the house. For someone so well-known and constantly 'out there' Powell is impressively oblique. No mentions of his family, his history, or background – not even in Dennis's files. I have no doubt that Dennis knows more than is in those files, but for me it's almost impossible to find out anything about Powell from before 2004. From the lack of information out there, it's quite possible that he was spawned, full grown. Which is even more disturbing when you consider that his fortune has been essentially made from exploiting, sorry, *enlightening* people online: he has entered their homes, their lives, their minds and they know next to nothing about him. Hundreds of thousands of people who have signed up for his courses, who listen to his talks, who pay him to advise them, who eventually pay to have their sexual fantasies realised only know about him what he has decided they need to know.

We turn a corner and I realise that this guy could be taking me anywhere. He could do anything to me. And no one, except Ellie and

Chris, would be able to tell people where I went. And all they know is that I had a meeting in the Sussex countryside.

*Maybe I should get my phone out, turn on tracking*, I think as we arrive in front of a large, thick dark wooden door that wouldn't look out of place in a dungeon. The man knocks briefly and opens the door without waiting for a response.

Lucian Powell's office is such an exercise in overcompensation that I'm embarrassed for him and embarrassed for me who has to act like I can't see his inferiority complex in every single thing in this place. From the giant flat-screen TV, around which is arranged a white leather sofa suite, to the double-life-sized portrait of Lucian Powell standing, legs apart, chin raised, arms folded, beside his gold sports car to the oversized dark wood desk, his feelings of inadequacy ooze from every millimetre of this room.

Behind his desk there is a wall of screens that show other parts of his house and grounds: the front gates, the pool, what looks like a common room, with a few people milling around in there, what looks like a computer room with several people at different stations, bedrooms that are empty, bedrooms occup— the screens, which I've obviously been staring at, suddenly go black and blank.

'Mrs Adu-Quarshie,' Lucian Powell says and stands. 'It's a pleasure to finally meet you.'

He does not offer me his hand to shake because, from what my reading and research of the last twenty-four hours have told me, he only shakes the hands of equals, and since only men – certain men at that – can be his equal, he will not be proffering said appendage to me, a woman.

'Please, take a seat,' he says when I don't respond to his greeting.

He has used my full married name when I gave the silent man at the front door – the one who now stands just on the periphery of my left eyeline – the name I use ninety-nine per cent of the time. He knows who I am and why I'm here, which is not good news for Brandee, Moe and me.

I sit on the edge of a heavily padded bucket chair, and take him in. He has grown a fuller beard since the picture I saw of him, and cut his hair shorter. He wears tinted shades and has an extinguished cigar resting on the ashtray by his closed laptop.

'As I told the man who brought me through, I'm Kez Lanyon.'

'I know who you are, Mrs Adu-Quarshie. You don't mind if I call you, Mrs Adu-Quarshie, do you. I find it odd when women don't use their legitimate names.'

'Legitimate names?' I reply.

'The name through which you are conferred legitimacy with when you marry. I find it odd and disrespectful that women shun that legitimacy by not using their husbands' kindly given names.'

'Legitimacy with?' I ask because, well, what the hell is he talking about?

'Did you know that married women were the first to be given the vote? It suggests that even back then the general wisdom was that marriage conveyed something important – legitimate – to a woman when it brought her under a man's physical and intellectual protection. Don't you think that suggests a woman should honour her husband and the sacred institution of marriage by donning the mantle of protection and legitimacy that comes with a man gifting her his name?'

The worst thing about Lucian Powell is the fact that he thinks he's clever. He throws in 'facts' from history, he uses 'don', 'convey' and 'mantle' then tops off his act by squeezing his face into what he thinks is an intellectual shape while templing his hands. He is not clever. At all. The first women allowed the vote in national elections in the UK had to be over thirty and either have already voted in local elections or be married to a man who had voted in local elections. Those were details he most likely didn't know or wasn't able to twist to fit his nonsense so he deleted them.

I sit back in my seat, and briefly examine my nails. 'To be honest, I've had this discussion on a much more intellectual level, with people who have brought up the philosophical as well as physiological aspects of name changes and even they didn't convince me not to use my birth name, so I have to demur on this conversation. As I say to everyone, including my family, you are free to call me what you wish, and in that moment I'll decide if I'll answer.' I smile at him. How long will it take him to realise I have called him stupid and told him I am not going to be cowed by him?

Not long. Behind his shaded glasses, I can feel his eyes flash as his facial colour rises. A rich seam of anger has been mined by that humiliation. He carefully removes his glasses, all the better to glare at me with, folds them and places them beside the ashtray and laptop.

'Why have you come here, Mrs Adu-Quarshie?'

'I've come to see my children.'

'And you think they're here?'

'I *know* they're here.'

'You know that, do you?'

'Yes.'

'And do you know why they're here?'

'To be honest, I don't. I have my suspicions, but I don't know for certain.'

'I have to admire a woman who knows when to admit she hasn't the intellectual prowess to fully grasp the underlying nuances of a situation.'

More pseudo-intellectual speak. 'I'd like to see my children, please,' I state.

'As I understand it, Brandee is not your actual corporeal child and Moe . . . Moe isn't communicating with you right now.'

*Corporeal.* Wow. 'Brandee is my child; and Moe isn't talking to my husband, he has been communicating with me. I just haven't seen either of them in a while so I thought I'd drop by.'

'Rude. Just dropping by.'

'You could take it like that. May I see them?'

'You want to see them, yes?' he asks.

'Yes.'

He reaches out, still keeping eye contact, and picks up a small silver remote. Without looking he clicks on the screens behind him, for one moment, for one second, then clicks them off again. 'They were up there. Did you see them?'

I stare at him, a small modicum of admiration blossoming. *Well played*, I want to say. *That got me.* 'Not properly, no. I just want to see them,' I tell him.

'It seems to me that they don't want to see you. Is there any reason for that?'

'How did you know my full name?' I ask.

'Excuse me?' he replies.

'My full married name, how did you know it? We never use the Adu part of my husband's name, ever, so how come you knew it, especially when I only gave my name? Brandee doesn't know it at all, and Moe has never used it – it's not on any of his official records. So how come you know it?'

Lucian Powell sits back in his seat, openly enjoying this new-found power he has over me. He steeples his hands and presses his lips to the top of them. 'You really have no idea who I am, do you?' he says.

'I really don't,' I admit. I have a feeling, one that is prickling sweat down between my shoulder blades that I should know him. I should have searched harder for background info on him.

'Interesting,' he says, thoughtfully, before pressing his steepled fingers against his lips again. 'We should have met a long time ago,' he says.

'Why? And when?' I ask because there is no point pretending I have a clue what he is talking about.

'We should have met in 2002, when you and two other people killed my brother, Brian.'

# Brandee

## Brandee | Secret video recording | Micro recorder |

### * Recorded: 20 May 2023 *

L King doesn't want me to do webcam work. He doesn't want me to do the love fraud stuff on the phones, either, but he does want me to hang out with him. He said it's because I evaded him for so long; dared to defy him. He finds that fascinating, apparently. He finds me fascinating. So he wants to get to know me. I'm not stupid. I totally think it's because he wants to get at Moe by getting close to me. But I'll take the W, I guess.

## Brandee | Secret video recording | Micro recorder |

### * Recorded: 24 May 2023 *

I saw Krystal. We passed each other in the corridor and she didn't even recognise me. Or if she did, she thought it wasn't real. She looked straight through me as the man who was with her pretty much dragged her along cos she could barely walk. I'm trying to convince myself I didn't see track marks on her arms. You can't see them in the cam vids I saw before I got here, so maybe they're new. She did not look OK. But I have to keep focused. I have to remember why I'm here.

I hate it here.

The room they've given me is nice. Beautiful even. It's got an amazing en suite, the bed is huge, the windows are incredible, even if they do have metal bars on the inside and outside. There's a TV screen, where I can only get certain channels. No streaming. No books, either. Only the magazines that feature L King and his businesses. If I'd booked this place for a holiday, I'd be well happy. But it's hideous, this place. Hideous because I know what else goes on here.

I haven't seen Moe.

I hate it here.

## Brandee | Secret video recording | Micro recorder |
### * Recorded: 27 May 2023 *

L King took me on a date – to his private dining room. Made a big deal of it. Left me a dress to wear on my bed. This stupid satiny pink thing. 'It's the height of femininity, don't you think?' he said when I sat down to dinner wearing it.

I said, 'It's all right.'

And his eyebrows twitched, and his mouth twitched. He doesn't like women disagreeing with him. But I am not going to last long if I give in and make it easy for him, am I? If he thinks I'm no challenge, he'll have me in front of the cams and scamming men on the phones in no time.

He told me all about his businesses, the legitimate side of it. He talked and talked and I looked bored. I could tell he was pissed off by the end of dinner when he 'walked me home' because I hadn't asked a single question. Maybe because I had no interest in it?

At my bedroom door he leant in for a kiss. Actually leant in. With his stupid shades on and that bull he spouted at dinner, you think I'm going to kiss you? Not in this lifetime, buddy. I hope when you see this you're in court, idiot face. Cos not in this lifetime or the next, mate. Have you *seen* you? Have you listened to you? Have you been around you? Why would I want you anywhere near me?

Like I ever would. Ever.

I put my head down, and said goodnight. I could feel his anger. But he wanted a challenge, and here I am.

# Kez

## 16 June, Sussex countryside

Brian had two brothers. I remember, he would talk about them every so often. They weren't close and, from what he said, they were in the police, like their father and his father before him. If that is the case, then what happened? Because this is not a man who is in the police. I mean, yes, he'll have 'contacts' in the police, but not even he could get away with this in-yer-face lifestyle while walking the beat.

'*I thought you said your brother is a policeman?*' I said to Brian on the day he died.

'*Yeah, he is. Was. He doesn't do that any more. He set up a business. Got information from me, got me to— the point is, I work for him and he got his wife from me.*'

The business based on psychological techniques, ways of communicating, speaking to insecurities, strumming on prejudices. All things he got from Brian. Dennis will have known this. And he's let me walk in here, knowing exactly who this man is.

I'm woozy. Like when I was pregnant and had been out in the sun too long.

I'm woozy, like the world has shifted on its axis and I've stayed in the same place so I am out of place and about to leave this consciousness.

I'm woozy, watching as Brian's face imprints itself perfectly over this man's features.

'You really had no knowledge of my existence, did you?' He leans forward onto the desk, clasps his hands and glares at me with his dead brother's eyes. 'I'm perplexed. Everything I've ever heard or read about you has you down as this empathetic being who cared for everyone who even looked in her direction. None of that for Brian, eh? Not a second thought for the family that was left behind? Hated him that much, did you?'

I'm still feeling woozy, lightheaded, floaty and ready to pass out, but I can't let him get away with that. 'I never hated Brian. I liked him. A lot. He was my friend. We were quite close, I tried to keep in touch with him after he left—'

'After he was forced out.'

'Yes, after he was forced out. I tried to keep in touch. I called him, texted him. I had a soft spot for Brian. I liked him.'

'Not enough to come to his funeral, though? How do explain that, Brian's friend?'

'I couldn't.' I inhale deeply. 'I just couldn't. He was the first person I knew that had died. I just couldn't—'

'The other two came along. They made nice. They hugged my mother, shook hands with my father. They came and paid their respects. And then there was you. Nowhere to be seen. No card, no flowers, no call. Just absence. At least the other two didn't claim to be his friend.'

Dennis.

Maisie.

They forced me to agree not to go to the funeral because they couldn't trust me not to tell the truth about what happened. We agreed we would all stay away. One of the bigwigs would go, show how important Brian was, smooth things over. But those two went. And neither of them let me know, either. The bastards. The utter, utter bastards.

'I'm not claiming anything. He was my friend.'

'And you couldn't suck it up to say goodbye to him? I don't buy it. I don't buy it at all. Unless you had something to feel guilty about? Unless the official story about him being shot in the tear gas confusion wasn't the truth and you have something else that needs to be confessed?'

I am silent. What happened after the shooting, what it was twisted into and then what became the official story silenced me. I have been trapped in a lie for twenty years. This is not the time to start telling the truth. I relax my face, my body, my hands, my mouth, my mind. I relax so I can allow his words to wash over me. So nothing he says will trigger a guilty look on my face.

'You didn't show up at the funeral,' he accuses, his eyes boring into me. 'And then you were a no-show at the inquest, which of course was private because it could damage national security or some such nonsense. I felt sure I would see you there. As a witness. But no. The official version is trotted out and none of you have to give evidence. If I didn't already know it, that just showed me – we are controlled. A wokespiracy has us. It is controlling those who can't see it. I can see it, though. I can see it all. And I know there was more to what happened to my brother than what we were told.

'Not even my father could find out what *really* happened. That girl who was in there, disappeared. No show at the inquest, no show in her life. She just upped and disappeared. They don't use tear gas in such small spaces. No. Something went on. Something they wouldn't even tell his own father. One of theirs. That was when I knew. That was when I was set on the path to exposing what wokeness is doing to our society. Originally, I just wanted to help men to see that they could have any woman they wanted. But after what you three did to my brother, how The Establishment covered it up, my new mission was born.'

He is the brother who cheated with Brian's girlfriend. He is the one about whom Brian had said they were going to work on things together. I understand now. Brian gave this man the tools to start his little business, which I bet was just a range of techniques to harass, coerce, and manipulate women into bed. Brian knew all about pressure points, he knew all about how to read people, how to shift people towards doing what you want. He knew and he showed his brother. His brother probably tried it out on Brian's fiancée-to-be among other women. I am guessing that he didn't marry her in the end, but by then, he'd done sufficient damage to Brian to break him.

When we agreed not to go to the funeral, I shut myself off from thinking about Brian's family. I couldn't stand it. I couldn't stand to look at their faces, knowing what I had done and never being able to tell them. To explain. I had erased Brian's entire family and world from my mind and focused on helping others. With therapy. With having an open house so children who weren't happy at home could have somewhere to crash for a few days. With taking care of Brandee. I thought I could shut them out and pay my penance by doing good elsewhere. The universe doesn't work like that. The universe wants me to remember. To pay.

'My father was never the same after Brian died. He was his favourite.'

That is a lie. But what can I say?

'I'm sorry to hear your father is still suffering.'

'Are you?'

'Yes, yes I am.'

'Then tell me the truth. Tell me what happened to my brother. Tell me who pulled the trigger, who took him away from me. Tell me and help me relieve my father's suffering.'

'It sounds like you know everything there is to know,' I reply.

'Who pulled the trigger?'

'I can't tell you anything more than was in the original report,' I say.

'And that is why your "children" need to stay here to work off some of the debts they have accumulated.'

'This is nothing to do with them.'

'This has *everything* to do with them,' he snarls. 'And the fact that you can't see that, reveals everything to me about how clever you really are. You tell me what really happened to Brian, and I let your "children" come home unharmed. If they want to. I am not holding them hostage. They have been free to leave at any time.' He is speaking for the microphone he thinks I am carrying. I am not carrying one, nor am I recording him. How could I when I don't know how much trouble Moe and Brandee are in? How could I record anything that could be used against them at some point?

'If they are free to leave, then they could come with me now.'

'They could. If they wanted to. I suspect they would be more likely to come with you if I told them you had given me a vital piece of information I have been chasing for years – who pulled the trigger that fired the bullet that killed my brother?'

'And what would you do with that information?' I ask. 'If it was theoretically available?'

'Ask them why, of course. Ask them if there was no other way,' his mouth says. His face, his eyes, his whole body tells me that he will kill them. He will do anything he needs to kill them.

Kill me.

'I'll see what I can find out,' I say to him and stand up. This is over. There is nothing more I can get here.

'Mrs Adu-Quarshie, it's been a pleasure. I look forward to conducting more conversations with you in the future when you have the information I require.'

I say nothing.

Here I am having to choose again. Having to decide who lives and who dies. Except to save my children, it looks like I am going to have to take Brian's place.

# Brandee

**Brandee | Secret video recording | Micro recorder |**

***Recorded: 16 June 2023 ***

He was pissed today. I couldn't work out what had happened first of all. He was walking back and forth in my room, ranting about women disrespecting him, people lying to him. People thinking he was stupid. And then he said, 'Do you want to stay here?'

I said, 'Of course.' What else am I going to say when I'm in a place with literal bars on the windows and barbed wire on the top of the walls?

He looked so relieved. Relieved! He actually thinks I like him and like it here. I'm a better actress than I thought. If he knew the stuff I'd got on him now. Just a little while longer and then I'll have so much evidence the police can't ignore it.

And he is stupid. Just need to say that. He *is* stupid.

# Kez

**16 June, Brighton**

'This is all because of that shooting twenty years ago?' Jeb asks.

I am staring out of the kitchen doors, watching the sun cast its light across the grass and garden toys that we really should have rehomed these past few years. We'd been grateful for them during lockdowns, but they are defunct and unneeded now.

'Yes, this is because of that shooting twenty years ago.' Jeb is the only person I have told that I killed a man. That I killed my friend. Brian. 'He says he'll let them go if I tell him who pulled the trigger. He says he only wants to talk to the person who did it. Wants to find out if there was no other way.'

'Do you believe him?'

'No. Not about any of it. I don't think he'll let them go, no matter what I tell him. He'll probably try to . . . Well, let's put it this way, you don't go to all this trouble to find someone to talk to them.'

'And that bastard Dennis didn't tell you?'

I hold my hand up. If I think about Dennis, I become incandescent with rage. He set me up. He wanted me to be hurt. Possibly killed. I hadn't gauged accurately how much he hated me. Not even by a long shot. 'Don't mention that man's name in this house. I will deal with him when the time comes.'

'What are we going to do?' Jeb asks.

'There's only one thing I can do, I have to tell him the truth. Say it was me.'

'You can't,' Jeb declares. 'You just said he's going to kill you.'

'How are we going to get them back then, Jeb? How are we going to get Moe and Brandee back? Do you want to be the one to tell Hella that her son is living in a compound with barbed wire and a shooting range? That he's being brainwashed by that man and pretty soon we won't know who he is? Do you want to tell little Arie there that his mother's not coming home?'

'You can't tell him it was you.'

'It looks like I'm going to have to.'

'All right, it's enough now. I'm going to get Richie and a few other men together, go down there and get them back myself. I'm not going to sit back and let this go on any longer.'

'A group of Black men storm the house of a rich, successful – famous – white man who has family in the police. A place that definitely has guns. How do you honestly think that is going to work out?'

'Is there really nothing else? What about the other person that was there? Maisie? Maisie. You said she was a bigwig now. Can't she do something to help?'

'Yeah, yeah. She was my next port of call. But I have to be prepared to tell him. If she can't help, and Dennis clearly won't help. I'll have to tell him that it was me who pulled the trigger.'

'Don't say that. Let's not think about that until we have to.'

Jeb, love of my life, always with the avoiding of the hard conversations. And in this instance, I don't blame him.

# Moe

## 17 June, Sussex countryside

For Moe, it was that one photo that proved his whole life could have been so different.

He could have had his ma and his pa in the one house, together. They were two of the coolest people you could ever meet and he only has fragmented memories now of the pair of them together: a birthday where his mother tried to hide the fact she was blowing out the candles for him when he couldn't manage it; a Christmas where his dad took him around and around the block on his new bike.

But these were fleeting things, GIFs in his mind that he could only have a few seconds of. He wanted more. He would rather remember than hear about the time the chip pan caught fire while his mother was making saltfish fritters, he wanted to recall not imagine his dad trying to be a drum'n'bass DJ then getting booed off by the partygoers he tried his skills out on – in his own house. There were so many memories his parents would laugh about that he simply couldn't remember. The later memories, the ones that had stuck in his head, all have *her* in them.

And it all comes back to this one photo. This photo that showed everything for the lie that L King had told him it was. You could trust no one. Especially not women.

Moe stares at the four computer screens in front of him. He has the biggest bank of computers in this room where the other programmers and coders sit. He's the only one of the five others who lives here, too.

He's lucky, L King likes him. He pays him more than anyone else in this room, because he's good at what he does. He's good at coding, programming, creating systems that work. Moe thinks in code sometimes, he thinks he probably always has. He finds all of that stuff easy and L King appreciates that.

In front of him are four videos that he's been working on. A couple of the others – the newer recruits who haven't been asked to live here – have put them together. They're OK, not brilliant. Not bad for people new to this work. It's easy for him to see where he can fix things, frames missed, codes not properly rendered. It won't take him long to sort it.

When he first started working for L King, he was working on the academy website, making it more robust, more user friendly, a better experience. He also made it easier for people to sign up, then he set it up so once you'd signed up, the site came back to check on you, see if you were ready to progress to the next level, encourage you to stick at it so you could see the truth. All of these were things Moe had wanted when he'd first come across L King's videos.

Originally, one of his friends had forwarded a few vids to him, saying, 'The truth, right?' and Moe had begun to see. For the first time in his life, he'd seen something that seemed to understand the thoughts he had, the struggles he had, the doubts that plagued him. His dad never seemed to suffer from these worries, neither did Richie. His mum wouldn't understand and Kez . . . Kez was something else.

L King had been impressed at what Moe had done in such a short amount of time on his website. And he especially loved that Moe had already completed the academy. It seemed like fate, he said. Fate had brought him Moe, the perfect person to take his business to the next level.

And that next level was the videos. The photos.

Moe watches the way the woman on the screen moves, how the shape of her face doesn't quite fit the visage placed on top of it. He'll have to fix that.

When L King had first shown him what he was doing, Moe had been dubious. It didn't seem right, putting one woman's face on another woman's body. Especially as some of those videos were porn. Extreme porn at that. He hadn't felt right about doing it. But L King had explained that these women put themselves online, knowing that those images could be scraped by Artificial Intelligence programs from those sites to be used elsewhere. He explained that this was actually a good thing. It would help the men who weren't as lucky as him, who didn't have a beauty like Brandee on their arms, in their lives. These videos and photos, L King explained, would reduce violence against women – if men were able to live out their fantasises online and in private, then they wouldn't have to go out there to hurt women in real life. But these fantasies had to be believable. They had to have the faces of the women these men knew so they wouldn't think they were fake.

Besides, L King said, 'We wouldn't ever do anything without talking to the women first. Getting them to sign a disclaimer. Getting them to agree to it.'

That made Moe feel better. If the women were agreeing to it, then that made it all right. Consensual. Obviously they had to keep it secret. L King wanted to create his own line of deepfakes – Made-For-You Moments, as he called them – that would help men and eventually help women. Also, other, less superior deepfakes were getting bad press out there, so best to keep it on the down low. When L King had said that, Moe had almost asked him if he knew what 'down low' meant. But he didn't. L King would have got angry, would have thought Moe was disrespecting him when he wasn't. He would have simply been point-ing out that 'down low' referenced a particular type of sexual activity that was so different from this, but he understood what L King meant so had said nothing.

In the following months, their output of Made-For-You Moments had increased and Moe had been working flat out, round the clock to get them done to the right standard. Moe was careful to check the release contracts he was given for the women's faces before work would begin. And then he noticed that some of the women who he had releases for, who he made videos of, would show up at L King's pad. They would arrive in the house, they'd be given their own rooms, they would be given a choice of where to film their online interactive camera work.

L King had been right. All of this was fine. It was going to do so much good out there.

L King been right, too, about stepmothers. When L King talked to him about family when they first met, Moe had confessed to having a stepmother. He knew how L King felt about stepmothers. Knew that they were different from stepfathers, who were heroes taking on single mothers. Stepmothers, L King said, were suspicious, you always had to be cautious about those second wives and what they'd done to get there. L King's own stepmother had been dodgy, he explained, maybe Moe's was, too? Moe had been non-committal in his reply.

He knew the truth about stepmothers, but Kez was all right. She had always been nice to him, cared for him. And he liked her, probably even loved her, but her place in his life did bug him sometimes. Because no matter what she did, how wonderful she was, it didn't change the fact she was one of the reasons his pa hadn't got back with his ma. And he couldn't help hating Kez a little for that. Seeing what L King had revealed about stepmothers had helped him find a space and a reason and understanding for his conflicting feelings about Kez.

When Moe had started working long hours for L King, he had said again that he had contacts who could look into Moe's stepmother's background for him if he wanted. This time, he'd said yes. Because the things that annoyed him about women, about Kez in particular, had become like an open wound into which salt was constantly rubbed. His dad was whipped, he was weak and he was cowed by his wife and her children.

Weeks later, L King had come back. 'I'm sorry, man,' he said, slapping Moe on the back. 'I'm truly sorry.' He'd handed Moe the photo.

Moe gets it out of his pocket now. It's crumpled, because he keeps it with him always, but it's still clear. Kez, young, with straightened, shoulder-length hair, slimmer than she is now, sitting outside a café, laughing. Across the table from her, laughing too, Jeb. He has longer hair than he has now, a neat afro that gives him a 1970s vibe. Jeb has his hand, tenderly on Kez's cheek, the pair of them are clearly into each other. The image itself is slightly fuzzy, but the date in the corner of the photo is clear: 2002 : 07 : 03

Two years after Moe was born.

Five years before the counselling session when Kez and Jeb supposedly saw each other again after meeting at a party.

Despite everything that they'd claimed over the years, despite promising they didn't get together until after Hella and Jeb were fully divorced, this photo clearly showed they'd been sneaking around with each other for years. *Years.* Which meant, when they walked into that room to get marriage counselling, Kez had set out to split them up.

Kez had purposefully broken up his family. And Moe could never, ever forgive her for that.

# Part 7

Part 7

# Kez

## 19 June, Brighton

'So you went to Brian's funeral,' I say to Maisie.

Maisie lives over on the other side of town, near Roedean, the world-famous girls' boarding school, where the houses are vast and yet you feel secluded, that you're not really a part of what goes on in Brighton or Hove. She still works in London, though, has a big government job, which is why she calls herself MJ Hudson (her husband's name) now, instead of Maisie Parsons.

She was about to come jogging up her driveway, dressed in black, neon-pink-edged über-expensive running gear, her chestnut ponytail swishing, when she saw my car parked there. It's a nice car, but around these parts, it is distinctly down at heel. I'm leaning against my car, staring at her. I haven't been this close to her since we passed each other in the Lanes five years ago. It was one of those hot summer days, the Lanes, essentially an alleyway of quirky shops and cafés, was rammed with people moving in two directions. We'd passed each other outside a metal-grilled jewellery shop, and we'd both done a double-take, realised who the other was, stared in horror for a second, two seconds, then torn our gazes away again.

'You went to Brian's funeral,' I repeat. 'You want to tell me about that?'

'Keep your voice down,' she hisses, now pale where she had been flushed from her run. Her sharp hazel-green eyes dart around, checking for neighbours, spy cameras, anything else that might be able to tie her to the events of twenty years ago.

'Why should I?' I reply raising my volume. 'Why should I keep my voice down when you all forced me to agree not to go to Brian's funeral, then went off to it likc nothing.'

'Of course it wasn't nothing.' She marches up to me, ready to punch me one. 'I had to go,' she forces this out through her teeth. 'My father told me I had to go. He said politically, I had to show up to the funeral of the son of a highly decorated police officer. When he was a colleague of mine, I had to show up. I didn't want to be there. I didn't want to hug his mum and shake hands with his dad. Chat to his brothers. But I had to. It was my duty. My father said it was my duty to do that.'

'Was it your duty to lie about what happened, too?' I ask, my voice even louder. Because she doesn't get to Maisie her way out of this. Whether she is Maisie or MJ, she doesn't get to make it anything other than trying to hide her part in the cover-up of Brian's death.

## March, 2002

The gun became an anvil in my hand. After Brian fell, it slipped from my grip. I could taste blood at the back of my throat, my head was full of pain and noise and my legs felt like they would not keep me upright. I wanted to curl in on myself, disappear.

The girl Brian had been holding hostage was on the floor, still cocooned in a ball with her friend and they'd jumped and clung tighter to each other when the gun went off. I didn't know what she had seen. When I pulled the trigger he wasn't holding her, she was clinging to her friend.

I turned towards Dennis and Maisie and they were both staring at me. We could all hear the groundswell of police storming the building. My legs gave way at that point. I fell onto my jelly-like knees and stayed there. I couldn't look at Brian, I couldn't face what I had done, but I also didn't want to look away. Without thinking, I raised my hands, like Dennis and Maisie, knitted my fingers together behind my head.

I was cold suddenly, a chill had descended on me and I was frozen into place. The door exploded, police poured in. Shouting. Orders. 'GET ON THE GROUND! STAY DOWN! DON'T MOVE!'

They ran to Brian, found he was dead. Looked up to see which one of us did it.

My ears were ringing, the sound of the gun had been louder than I realised and now there was an immense noise, numerous people. Swarms of police.

'What happened?' someone in a helmet with a visor shouted in my face. 'Is there anyone else with a gun?' I couldn't move. Couldn't answer their questions. I didn't even really know what was going on.

'He had to do it,' I heard Maisie say, still kneeling. 'Dennis had to shoot him. Kill him. He was going to assault that young girl. He was going to kill us. He was about to kill us all and Dennis had no choice. He shot him.' She was speaking loudly, in a rush. Lying. She was blaming Dennis. The gun was on the ground in front of him, and he was staring down at it. He didn't seem bothered by what she was saying. How she was lying.

'No, Maisie,' I said. 'That's not—'

'He had to do it,' she said loudly, drowning me out.

Dennis nodded. Stared at the gun, nodding. He looked up at the officer in charge. They connected, their eyes came together in understanding. Unspoken camaraderie, mutual acceptance passed between them. 'I had to do it,' Dennis said. 'We tried to talk him down. We thought we could get through to him.'

'We all tried,' Maisie said. 'He seemed to be listening for a while, then he just switched.'

'I had to shoot him. He raised the gun, he was going to kill us so he could go and rape that young girl. I had no choice.'

'That's not what happened,' I said. But it was like I didn't speak. Like the words hadn't left my mouth. They had, I knew they had. I said them again. But they were only listening to Dennis. Not even to Maisie who had started the lie. Dennis was the only one whose judgement they trusted, and the only one they trusted to tell the truth. The officer in charge nodded at Dennis, lapping up his lies and ignoring me who was trying to tell the truth.

The official story was: Dennis was a hero who had saved us all.

The public story was: the police had tear-gassed the room to end the hostage situation, Brian had been shot in the confusion.

My story was: silence. I could never talk about what I'd done. Could never seek true comfort or answers to the questions I tortured myself with because no one could know it was me.

## 19 June, Brighton

Maisie has a pool. Of course she does. These properties are proper displays of wealth, the type that it had always been obvious that Maisie comes from. She is something big in government. Not an MP, that wouldn't pay enough for her to live here. Not your average civil servant – that wouldn't pay enough either. She is something in a nebulous department, much like Dennis, where there is very little transparency or accountability. She is important, though. That's the bottom line and what matters, I suppose, since she has a driver who takes her to work. She also has a husband who is a 'captain of industry', which means from what I could see, that he sits on many different boards and is paid astronomical amounts to consult for these companies. His Companies House returns show that he owns companies that make virtually no money but somehow manage to allow him to live in a house with a pool and eight bedrooms and have a wife who is important in her own right.

Maisie has forced me to come into her house to try, I guess, to keep my voice down. Her neighbours may be far away, but you honestly do not know who is listening. I don't get a proper tour or even a look at her house, she takes me down a side corridor and out into the garden, from there, she marches towards the pool house – set right at the back of the vast garden – and unlocks it to allow us to enter. She doesn't seem bothered that we're wearing outdoor shoes as we walk through the white-tiled changing area, with its hanging hooks, lockers – *lockers!* – and stacks of soft white towels and dressing gowns, into the pool area.

The water is blue because the bottom of the pool is tiled blue and the surrounding tiles are a bright white. There are lounge chairs, with pool toys stacked at one end. The heat in here is almost tropical. You would not need to go anywhere on holiday if you lived here. I wonder how different their lockdown experience was to ours? They had considerable space, unlike us who also had an extra person living with us, they could pretend to be on holiday with a pool and everything, but how did their pool get cleaned? Maintained? And who did their general cleaning? Who replenished the towels and changed the bedsheets? Needs must, I suppose, but Maisie never gave the impression of being a person who would – or could – do those things.

The acoustics in here are echoey and constantly shifting. It's hard to hear anything over the gush of the water pump and the smallest sound bouncing off the tiles. Anyone attempting to listen would have a hard time, which is the point of her bringing me in here. I remember when she thought nothing of shouting our private business out in crowded bars, and now this. Her paranoia has clearly grown since she's seen the things that people can do.

'I didn't go to his funeral lightly,' she says, standing near the deeper end of the pool. 'I told you, my father said I had to go. I had to press the flesh, he said.'

'We weren't talking about that, Maisie,' I remind her.

'MJ,' she counters.

'We weren't talking about that, MJ,' I correct. 'We were talking about why you lied to the police. Which made Dennis lie. And silenced me because no one would believe what I was saying. Why?'

'I had to,' she says quietly. 'I just . . .'

'You just what?'

'I couldn't let you take the blame. They would have destroyed you. I couldn't let that happen.'

'Oh is that what you told yourself? That it's my fault that you lied? Is that why you were able to go to his funeral because at the end of the day, it was all my fault and you could blame me for everything in your head but give Dennis the glory of being the big hero?'

'No!' she almost screams. 'You were right, OK? That thing you said all those years ago, when Brian was calling you a diversity hire, and you told us to fuck off without actually saying it. I didn't want you to be right, and I agreed with him. I mean, we all know that ethnic minorities get a leg up and have it easier when it comes to the plum jobs, we all know that it's people like me and Brian who lose out to people like you. Except . . . except . . . I kept looking around, looking for evidence of what we all knew was true.' She stops talking, pushes her thumbnail into her mouth, runs her teeth across it a few times. 'Except everywhere I looked, I couldn't find evidence of that at all. There were no people who looked like you. The very few that I did see were the ones who went to the same schools as I did because they came from wealthy families. There was virtually no one like you. Not even on the diversity schemes.

'And it bothered me. It bothered Brian a lot sooner, and I know he apologised to you because he told me he was going to. Even when he said he was going to apologise, I was convinced that the odds were stacked against me and not you. He also told me that he was going to ask you out and that pissed me off, too, cos I really liked him, as you guessed.

'I never apologised to you, but I did accept what I'd always believed wasn't true. And once you've seen something, it's really hard to unsee it. And every job I've had, every position I've been in, I've just seen what it's really like. So when the thing happened with Brian . . .' She breaks off, tears flood her eyes. 'When you had to do what you did, I was so grateful. Because I knew, like Dennis knew, he was going to kill us. But neither of us did anything. I kept waiting for Dennis to step in, take charge, end the situation. And he just sat there and did nothing. But I knew they would tear you apart if they found out that you'd killed Brian. There was no way a Black woman would get away with killing a white man. A policeman's son. I knew they would destroy you. Probably put you in prison.'

'I didn't need you to save me, MJ,' I say.

'I wasn't being a white saviour,' she snaps back. 'Yes, I know that term. And that wasn't what I was doing. Not only what I was doing. I was . . . If it came out that you had killed him, trying to save a Black girl's life, that would have become the story. They wouldn't care that Brian had a gun, that Brian had held all those people hostage. That he was going to rape an eighteen-year-old girl to prove a point. That he'd already shot and nearly killed the bar owner. All of that would have been forgotten as they tried to destroy you. The scandal would have stuck to all of us for years. As it is, it still follows me around. People still raise eyebrows, think twice about asking me to do things because of the scandal attached to my name.'

And there it is. The main motivating factor. I don't doubt that she was trying to help me, but the main reason for her lying was to help herself. Save herself. From the word go Maisie profiled as someone who would always put her own interests first. Always. That was why I preferred Brian to her. He was a decent person, a good guy. Until he wasn't.

And that is my fear for Moe. He is a good boy, how long before he isn't? Lucian had turned Brian into a potential rapist and killer without even trying, what is he doing to Moe now he *is* trying? How is he treating Brandee to get at me?

'Did you know Brian's brother is that prolific internet guy who posts those misogynistic, racist, homophobic videos? Has a whole teaching system based on the stuff Brian was saying before he died?'

Maisie – MJ – wipes her tears, moves away, hides her face. 'I might have heard something,' she says.

'And you didn't think to warn me?'

'I would have thought I would be the last person you would want to hear from,' she says.

'Did it cross your mind that Brian might have helped him? Used the stuff we learnt to help him create this system?'

'I don't know, maybe. Possibly.'

'Again, you didn't think to warn me?'

'Again, I would have thought I'd be the last person you would want to hear from. And what is there to warn you about? Brian's brother changed his name and makes cash fleecing people with stupid theories. Why would you even care?'

'He's taken my children, that's why I would care,' I tell her. 'Brian's brother changed his name as you said, and he has taken two of my children.'

That gets her to care for a moment: 'He's kidnapped them? Have you called the police?'

'No, he has not kidnapped them. Not officially. He has pretty much brainwashed my oldest son to hate me because I'm not his biological mother and the girl we kind of fostered has gone to live with him, possibly working for him doing online sex cam work. I spoke to him. He said he'll let them go if I tell him who killed Brian.'

'That's terrible. Really awful. I'm so sorry.' I know she is sorry, I know she means that, but she also pauses, like the self-centred, self-interested person she is. 'You can't tell him that, you know that, don't you? It was agreed that no one outside of the unit would know. That was why we had to be tear-gassed and everything. Everyone outside of us has to believe that Brian was shot in the confusion. Everyone inside of us needs to believe it was Dennis. You can't tell his brother anything other than Brian was shot in the confusion.'

I stare at MJ, the new harder, harsher version of Maisie, for a moment. What I'm about to say is going to scare her in ways she didn't realise she could feel fear. 'When was the last time you spoke to your daughter, MJ?'

'Why are you asking me that?'

'I know she's away at boarding school. So when was the last time you spoke to her?'

'What has that got to do with you?' She's unsettled by the fact I know she has a daughter, that I'm aware her daughter is away at boarding school. It's ironic that she lives right next to one of the most famous boarding schools in the world and didn't choose to send her daughter there. But tradition trumps convenience. Always.

'Nothing. But Brian's brother is coming after all of us. I thought it was just me, at first. I thought he had worked out it was me who had killed his brother because I didn't go to the funeral so was coming after me and going through my children. But no, he's coming after all of us.'

'What are you talking about?' she asks, even though she has stopped moving and looks full of dread.

'Brian had two brothers. One who is quite well known. The other also changed his name so as not to be associated with his crazy brother who almost killed a man and held people hostage. He stayed a policeman, he's risen quite high in the ranks. But you probably know all that already.'

'What has that got to do with anything?'

'Brian's other brother, the policeman, has three children. One of them has just transferred to boarding school. How he can afford it on his wages is anyone's guess. But he does have a very rich brother who might have helped him out.'

MJ doesn't appear to be breathing.

'I guess you only see your daughter in half-term and full-term holidays. Other parents go down and see their children every weekend, I'd imagine? Take them out. Take their friends out. When was the last time you spoke to your daughter, MJ, about her new friends and the new ideas she's being exposed to?'

I stare right at her as I continue: 'Your son, he's at boarding school, too. When was the last time you asked him about what he's watching online? Who he is befriending online? When was the last time you really talked to him about anything?'

The tumblers fall into place in MJ's mind. Things that were random and unconnected slot together; she has a fuller picture of what she did not want to see.

'He's coming after all of us, MJ. Dennis has a wife, I know that, but I'm not convinced he cares enough about her to be as easy a target as you and me.'

'What do you want me to do?'

'I need you to find out everything you can about him. Dennis gave me a heavily redacted, already light-on-details file on him. I need you to find out more. If there's a proper investigation into his activities, about the human trafficking he's involved with. Find out as much as you can that we can use against him. So I can get my kids back, and you can protect yours.'

'It's not going to be easy. I don't have the type of access that would make getting this information easy and without rousing suspicion.'

'MJ, this is your daughter and potentially your son we're talking about. I'm going to get my kids back no matter what, so if I can get helpful information from you, then I will take it gratefully. But I have to do whatever it takes to get them back. You need to think if you can do the same before it gets to that stage with you.'

'I will do whatever I can.' I think she means that, too.

I leave without telling her the rest of it. The stuff I haven't yet told Jeb. This will not end with Lucian finding out which one of us pulled the trigger and killing them.

Lucian Powell wants all three of us dead. He'll simply kill the person who pulled the trigger last.

# Brandee

**Brandee | Secret video recording | Micro recorder |**

*\* Recorded: 24 June 2023 \**

This is worse than I thought. Sadie, Bianca and Mila are all here. I saw them. On his screen in his office. We all went on that trip to the Maldives that Traits sportswear paid for. We all had the best time and came home saying we had to stay in touch. And now he's got them living in his house, working on cams and talking to and texting men to get them to buy them gifts and send them money.

That could have been me. The thought of that still makes me feel ill. 'I'm always fascinated by the way women appreciate the form of other females,' he said when he saw me looking. 'You, yourself, look disgusted. I'm not surprised, you're probably wondering how you're going to compete against them for my attention. The attention of the alpha male is always what females will do anything to get. Tell me, Brandee, what would you do to get my attention?'

Kick you so hard in the balls your ears squeak, I thought.

'Sometimes I feel like an alpha female,' I said, 'so I don't know if I would compete with other females for attention. Alphas don't do that, do they?'

That pissed him off! I've got to be careful, though. I might tip him over the other way.

## Brandee | Secret video recording | Micro recorder |
### * Recorded: 27 June 2023 *

Stupid picnic. We sat in his courtyard and he brought out the champagne and smoked salmon, and blinis and caviar. 'This champagne is older than both of us,' he said. It wasn't, but you can't tell that to someone so stupid. He cracked a few jokes and I laughed, have to keep him on side.

I went back to my room hungry. Stupid picnic.

# Kez

## 11 July, Brighton

*'Hi Moe. Kez again. I just want to tell you I love you. No matter what you hear or are told, I love you. If you see Brandee, tell her I love her too. I love you both and I can't wait until we're together again. Zoey and Jonah send their love, too.'*

\*

The past three weeks, Jeb and I have been living around each other, like two people taking part in a do-si-do square dance – occupying the same vicinity, but not interacting.

We rarely speak unless it's about the children, barely look at each other unless it's to avoid bumping into each other, never touch.

Two days ago I took Zoey and Jonah to stay with my parents as it's the start of the holidays and something we always do. Ten days with my parents, ten days with Jeb's while we both finish up work, then we get four weeks together as a family. Without the children, we can do-si-do even further apart while I try to work out what to do.

Hella calls me several times a day, every day, asking if I have heard anything. Asking when my government contacts are going to come through with the info we need to get her son back. She wants to see Arie, of course, even if he isn't her grandson, but she is too distraught over Moe to do anything but wait for news. She doesn't call Jeb because her fury at him has not subsided. When he revealed everything, she hit the roof. Called him every bastard under the sun before breaking down and crying uncontrollably. She blamed him for not telling her sooner what was happening. She blamed herself for not noticing that he was slipping further and further from her. She blamed me for being this big-time therapist and profiler and not realising what was going on right under my nose. Even Richie got a share of the blame for failing their child, even though, technically, he hadn't done anything.

None of us have blamed or are going to blame Moe. Not until he is home. Probably not even then because we'll be too scared he'll take off again. And not until Brandee is home. This started off as a search for her, and I am not letting any of us forget that we need them both home. Both safe. Both back where they belong.

I have been going over and over the files, checking and rechecking, trying to work out what I have missed. I have missed something. I have. I just do not know what.

MJ has called a couple of times, nothing really to report, but she is relieved it is the summer holidays. Her children are home, they are not seeing any friends – old or new – and she is keeping a watchful eye over them.

I have missed something.

I have to do something.

This is the thought that has overtaken all other thoughts: I have to do something.

Jeb and I lie next to each other tonight, spinning in our own worlds.

I'm barely aware he's here and I'm not even considering what he might be thinking. I am consumed with thoughts of what I have to do.

I know what I have to do, of course. It is simple: I have to go back to that manor, the compound, as I call it in my head, and confront Lucian Powell.

I have to explain what happened with Brian. I have to find a way to make him understand that the stories he has about Brian, the tales he has constructed are not reality. These stories, the fantasies of what his relationship with Brian was like have fuelled him to employ Moe, ensnare Brandee; get revenge on the people who killed his brother. Even though, ultimately, it was Lucian betraying his brother, screwing his girlfriend, deciding to marry Brian's girlfriend that put the gun in Brian's hand.

Lucian Powell is not a man who would tolerate that, though. You do not need to be a professional profiler and psychologist to know that he does not hear anything that might come within shouting distance of damaging his self-image, showing him in a critical light.

None of us likes to be wrong. However, people like him, men like him, will change the world to stop themselves being wrong. They will bend reality, they will provoke vendettas, will get terrible people to do awful things so they are never proven wrong. I have to find a way to get through to him. To reach him so that he will let Moe and Brandee go. And therein lies the rub, as they say: he will not let them go.

He will accept anything I offer – everything any of us offer – to let them go, and then he will maintain his hold over them by keeping them entwined in his life. I need a way to cut the ties, end the brain-washing, remove the blackmail threats.

I feel Jeb move beside me, assume he is rolling over onto his side to get comfortable for sleep, but he keeps moving until he is climbing on top of me, holding himself above me. Once in place, once his body covers mine, he stares into my eyes.

I stare back.

We haven't looked at each other in a while, I haven't appreciated the curve of his broad nose, the lines of his lips, the shape of his eyes in his face. My pulse picks up pace, my skin tingles. Maybe that's why I haven't gazed at him recently – my body does this and I only remember the good stuff. And the bad stuff is what I need to focus on right now.

'Tell me what you're thinking,' he whispers. We've all got used to speaking in low tones because of not wanting to wake or disturb Arie. Even though he is in the room next door, now his nursery, we're still talking quietly. 'Tell me what you're planning. You're planning something, I can tell. What is it?'

'I'm not planning anything,' I reply just as quietly.

*I am not planning anything. I wish I was. I wish I was at the stage when I was merely planning something.*

He doesn't believe me, but he doesn't say that, doesn't start that hard conversation. Instead, Jeb unbuttons my nightshirt, exposing my bare breasts and my naked body, then lowers his hand to slip two fingers inside me.

I try not to react, not to buck as the glorious familiarity of his foreplay finger-fuck blossoms. It's delicious, luscious, insanely pleasurable, but I mustn't get sidetracked.

Jeb pauses, waits for me to push his hand away, which I always do if I'm not up for it. He stares into my eyes, waiting a little longer to see if I will stop him. When I don't do anything but stare back at him, he pushes his fingers deeper inside, then moves them in deliberate, tantalising circles.

*You like that*? he silently asks.

*I'm not going to make a sound*, I decide. *I'm not going to whimper and moan and cry out, like he wants. Needs.*

My emotions are paused at pissed off, stalled at anger. He should have told me. I know why he didn't tell me, but I remain vexed. None of this would be playing out like this if he had told me.

Firmly, carefully, Jeb circles his fingers as he slowly withdraws them, and I have to control myself, stop myself from giving him the reaction he craves.

Jeb needs my vocal, physical, emotional reaction to get off. My pleasure is his aphrodisiac. It always has been. Since we met, he's only been able to totally enjoy himself if he knows I am satisfied. My overt pleasure means I love him, that no matter what else is going on, I love him. Everything else is falling apart, which means he needs this. His body needs this closeness, his emotions need this connection.

He plunges his fingers into me again and my body involuntarily quivers with pleasure, giving me away.

'You like that?' he finally whispers out loud.

I stay silent.

'You like that?' he asks again and silence is my reply again.

He takes away his fingers, immediately pushes his erection into me.

I can't help but close my eyes and sigh.

It's all very well being pissed off and withholding what he wants, but I need this, too. I need this physical relief, this coming together, this touching of my body. I have been tense and stressed, almost locked into one position for weeks, and in these moments my being is experiencing something else; I'm being unlocked.

Jeb has always touched me in ways no one else can. I've never been sure why, and I've never wanted to interrogate it. Jeb 'gets' me on so many levels, he understands me in so many logical and illogical ways. I try to disavow how I took complete leave of my senses when I met him. Unprotected sex when I'd known him less than an hour, practically begging him to call me, being *devastated* when he didn't call, staying away from anyone for years afterwards because I knew they would never match up to him. It was ludicrous and not me. I couldn't even blame it on being young and naïve because years later, when he showed up wanting another chance, I allowed him to seduce and fuck me (again unprotected) in my office, my place of work, where I had been nothing but professional for years. Anyone could have walked in because we didn't even lock the door. Jeb was a weakness. He *is* a weakness. A constant, abiding weakness.

My husband uses his other hand to wrap around the mini twists in my hair, pulling them, tugging my head back, as he stares into my eyes and thrusts inside me.

'You like that?' he asks, a bit more urgently this time.

I say nothing, refusing to give him what he wants. He lowers his head and takes a nipple in his mouth, running his tongue over it before gently biting it. Again, my body gives me away, convulses with the desire that shoots through me. He moves to the other nipple, takes that in his mouth, bites a little harder and the same intense bolt of pleasure strikes. His mouth is back on the original nipple, sucking then biting, just the right amount of pressure, the perfect amount of pain, timing it with a hard thrust and tug of my hair. *You like that?* I can hear him silently ask. *You like that?*

The other nipple, another bite, a thrust, a tug.

*You like that?*

The other nipple, another firmer bite, a harder thrust, a tougher tug.

*You like that?*

'Yes,' I finally whimper. 'Yes . . . Yes. . . Yes.'

I can feel his relief that he can still do this to me, that my body will still respond to him no matter how pissed off I am. That his 'You like that' which means – and has always meant, 'Do you love me?' – has got the answer he wants. *Needs*.

Yes, I still love him.

Of course I still love him.

From the moment we first kissed, probably from the moment we first met, I have loved him.

A weakness. Jeb is a weakness. A weakness that is sprinting inside me, teasing and exciting my senses; biting and sucking and fucking my body until we're both shuddering as we orgasm in a messy bundle of pleasure and bliss and release.

'I want you to move out,' I say before he's even properly withdrawn from me.

'What?' he asks as he lifts himself up and stares down at me.

'I want you to move out. To leave. I need you to leave.'

'No,' he responds and lies down next to me. 'I'm going nowhere.'

'I don't trust you any more, Jeb. I was always dubious about you after how we met, how you lied right to my face.'

'I didn't lie to you. I didn't have a girlfriend, and I *was* going to call.'

'You had a fiancée and you were going to call after you cancelled your wedding. Technically, no, you didn't lie, but this isn't court. You don't get let off on a technicality. I need you to leave.'

I need to remove the weakness that is Jeb so I can focus, so I can get Brandee and Moe home. I can't be letting him screw me to make himself feel better, to make me feel better. Why should either of us feel better right now?

'What about the kids?' he asks.

'They'll stay with my parents for now, so they won't know any-thing's different. When they come back from your parents, we'll sit them down and explain it then.'

'And Arie?'

'Brandee left him with me. I'll take care of him.'

'And what about Moe and Brandee?'

'I'll keep you updated as I'm sure you'll keep me updated if you hear anything.'

'You've got it all worked out, haven't you?'

'If you knew how far that was from the truth.'

'Where am I even supposed to go?'

'To a hotel, I don't know. I haven't thought about it.'

'We can't afford for me to stay in a hotel for an unspecified amount of time.'

'Yes, you can. You have that money you're not giving to Brandee for Moe any more. You've got loads of money.'

That was horrible, unnecessary. And why he needs to go. If he doesn't go, it'll only get worse, I'll only say more terrible, hurtful things to him probably after I've had sex with him. If he goes now, we might be able to salvage the ability to have a decent, civil conversation for the children.

'Is this a separation or the end?' he asks.

'The end. It has to be. If there's no trust, what's the point?' I reply. 'Marriage is all about trust and truth and knowing the other person will be honest with you. That they will tell you everything, even if it's not what you want to hear. Without one of the fundamentals between two people, what is the point of a marriage?'

'Don't therapise this, Kez,' he says sternly. 'Is our marriage over? Is this you asking for a divorce?'

I inhale the scent of my husband, our marriage, our home. It has to be over. It has to be. 'Yes,' I reply. 'I was going to pretty it up, find lots of ways to soften the blow, but what's the point? I'm pissed off with you, you're probably pissed off with me that my past has caused this, so yes, it's over. If I don't trust you any more, then it has to be over and yes, I'm asking you for a divorce.'

'After one conversation, if that, our fourteen-year marriage is over?'

'Yes.'

He exhales loudly; I brace myself for him to shout, to protest, to cry, to climb out of bed and start to pace as he argues back. Instead he closes his eyes, doesn't move.

'I knew you'd leave me one day. I suppose I'm lucky to get the time I've had,' he says.

After his shower, he starts packing. After the packing, he goes to Arie's room, kisses him goodbye, then leaves without saying another word to me.

# Brandee

**Brandee | Secret video recording | Micro recorder |**

*\* Recorded: 11 July 2023 \**

Almost got caught recording three days ago. I was in the bathroom, whispering while filming this as usual, but I thought I heard a noise outside and something told me to hide this recorder.

I took my time, went to the loo, flushed, washed my hands. Brushed my teeth. All the while talking to myself so it sounded like that's what I always did.

I get out into my bedroom and he's on the bed, isn't he? I had locked the door, so clearly that meant nothing and I have to sleep with the chair jammed under the handle now.

So he's on the bed, tight shirt with the buttons open to his waist, stupid tight chinos. He looked ridiculous. I wanted to shout at him, 'Don't you have mirrors?'

Being here is not good for me. I'm scared all the time and then angry all the time, too. I just want to get this evidence, I want to find Moe and then I want to get out of here.

I haven't seen him and I miss him. I obviously can't call him. I wonder if he knows I'm here? If he misses me.

'Just come for a bedtime nightcap,' L King said. He was trying to sound seductive but he sounded like he had phlegm stuck in his throat. I think he thought we were going to do the do but that is not in our cards. Ever.

'Oh, right, well, goodnight.'

He patted to the bed, for me to join him.

'Set your intention,' I said to him. 'A woman has to set her intention when it comes to men. If you move too fast, if you are easily led, he will not respect you. He will not value you. Keep yourself as pure as you can.' I pulled a regretful smile across my face. 'That's what you said in one of your videos, isn't it?'

Whew, he was mad! But how could he argue with himself?

Thankfully he left, but I don't know how much longer I'm going to be able to keep him away.

Have to be extra careful from now on.

# Kez

## 25 July, Brighton

It's been two weeks since Jeb left, and Arie and I have got ourselves into a nice little routine. I take him out for walks, bring him home, play with him, feed him, bathe him.

Then he screams the house down for a good hour.

My neighbours are angels, but even the most patient of patient people would be forgiven for losing it over the noise this little boy makes.

But who can blame him? His mother is not here, Jeb, who he had formed a strong bond with, is not here. I often want to cry with him. I want to wriggle and protest with a screwed-up face, bunched-up fists and big fat tears in the hopes it'll bring everyone back to me.

**Are You Ready To Talk.**

The text comes from an anonymous number. I can only assume that Moe or Brandee have given Lucian Powell my number. I've had three of these messages, and I haven't replied. Of course I'm not ready to talk. Confess. Let him know I am the one who pulled the trigger, I am the one who deserves to die last.

I don't answer the texts because I am waiting for the call.

Obviously, Moe now is aware that Jeb and I have split up, since Hella has stopped calling me, which I suspect is a sign that she has been reunited with her son, at least via the phone. And Lucian knows I'm on my own now, too. Hence the text messages.

Lucian sees me as vulnerable. He assumes I will throw one of the other two under the bus to save myself. He has theorised that if he puts enough pressure on me, now I am isolated and alone, I will be desperate to end this in a way that will get me my old life back.

Lucian Powell considers himself a profiler above the profiling we all naturally do. He believes he can read people, get into their minds and accurately predict their thoughts, habits and future behaviour. However, he never steps away from the profile. He always searches for the clues that prove everyone is like him even in the smallest way: a malignant narcissist will do anything and hurt anyone to get what he wants while maintaining his image as a 'good guy'. He would definitely sell out the other two if he were me, so he assumes I will do the same. It doesn't occur to him that I wouldn't. Or that selling out the other two would only ever be the very last resort, to save someone's life. Not the first port of call like it would be for him.

That is the problem with having only a little bit of the knowledge Brian, Maisie, Dennis and I have. We (except Brian) went on to learn more, to expand our skills, to build on them with other courses, knowledge and experience. His skillset, which Brian had passed on, probably stopped then. It got him what he wanted, he was able to get people to do what he wanted and he has honed that set of skills to build his wealth and reputation and empire. It has worked. But at times like this, having that bit more information about how humans work and don't work would be an advantage.

*

'I need to see you,' Moe says on the phone when I answer the call from an anonymous number. I'm surprised – I'd almost forgotten that this is what I've been waiting for.

'Have you spoken to your father?' I ask.

'Yes. Lots. He said you've split up.'

'Yes, we have. I haven't seen him in two weeks. Is Brandee there?'

He pauses. 'Yes.'

'Can I speak to her? Just for a moment?'

'She . . . she doesn't want to speak to you,' he lies. At least he is still a terrible liar.

'Yes, she does. I know she does. It's really important that I speak to her if you want me to come and see you.'

He pauses for a bit longer then, 'Hello?' She is subdued, muffled. Tired, scared. I dread to think what she is going through. What they've both been through.

'Brandee, I went to see your family when I was looking for you. Your mother hasn't changed, still hates me. I saw the son I'd never met? The one she doesn't really tell people about? You know who I mean?' She has to know what I'm talking about. What I'm trying to say.

'Yes,' she says carefully.

'He's fine. It was great to meet him. And he's fine.'

I can hear her smile and I know she's understood. She knows that Arie is fine. 'OK,' she says.

'Are they treating you OK?'

The phone is snatched away before she can speak. 'Are you going to meet me?' back to Moe. Exhausted, too. Tortured. I can't imagine what they've put him through. How they have spent these last few months messing with his head.

'I love you, Moe. I would do anything for you. Where do you want to meet? Or do you want to come here? You can stay the night. You can bring Brandee. Be like old times. Except, of course, you're now adults so you can sleep in the same room. All night and I won't say—' My babbling is to remind Moe he doesn't hate me. He may not like me all the time, he may wish his parents would get back together, but he doesn't hate me enough to do what Lucian wants him to do. Which is to be the one to pull the trigger. He wants Moe on the other end of the gun; to make me choose between his life and mine. Maybe I can avert that, can stop that trajectory by reminding Moe what home and family feel like.

'London. You know where. Three o'clock tomorrow. No police.'

'Why would I bring police?' I ask.

'No police,' he repeats, robotically.

'No police.'

'And bring the others.'

'No can do. I don't see them, I don't speak to them. If you want them, you'll have to contact them yourself.' Lucian knows I am speaking to him.

'Tomorrow. Three o'clock. No police.' The line goes dead.

# Brandee

**Brandee | Secret video recording | Micro recorder |**

*\* Recorded: 25 July 2023 \**

Haven't been able to record much at all because he won't leave me alone. He's always coming to my room for a chat. He talks about himself, asks me to go for dinner, gives me something to wear and then talks about himself for the rest of the evening. He's exhausting. But something big is about to happen. I can feel it. Something is being worked on.

# Kez

## 26 July, Brighton

'Is this how we're going to see each other from now on? Passing children over in a car park?'

'Depends where you're going to be living, I suppose,' I reply.

My husband and I are at the Cobham services because I'm on my way to London. To meet 'Moe', which I know for certain is meant to be my final showdown with Brian's brother.

I'm giving Arie to Jeb because he is probably his grandfather, despite what Brandee said, and Arie has been pining for him. If what I think is about to happen to me happens to me, then Arie is going to need more care than Ellie and Chris can provide.

These services are relatively new. I remember when we used to drive up north and it took us ages to find services before these ones were constructed. It's early, but post rush hour so the car park is only half full. Most of the cars are parked like a group of cows hunching together in the middle, with a few parked right at the edge near the exit road and others near the building where the restaurants, loos and shops are.

'Where are you staying?' We stand by my car, Arie between us as I hold onto the handle of his car seat, his change bag over one shoulder, another bag crammed with as much of the rest of the stuff he has over the other shoulder.

'Thought you didn't care?' Jeb says. He takes the car seat from me. The sudden loss of weight almost causes me to fall forward. He's grown in the very short amount of time he's been with us, in a couple more weeks he'll need to be weaned. Baby food. I remember the joy and the hell of it. The excitement when they would eat something, their faces reflecting what the new flavours were doing to their tastebuds; the frustration of everything being rejected for no particular reason. Arie's face relaxes into a big gummy grin when he sees Jeb.

*Thanks, kid,* I think. *Way to make me feel valued.*

'I didn't say that.'

'Not directly, no. But you haven't asked. I'm staying with my parents. They're really pleased that their fifty-one-year-old son is not only back in their house, but also about to be twice divorced.'

'I'm sure my parents will be just as happy with my one divorce. Maybe they can start a support group for Ghanaian parents of divorced adult children.'

Jeb laughs then chokes it away, dampens it down. He wants to stay aloof; guarded, cold.

'I left something in my car for you, if you've got a minute or two?'

*Is it a gun*? I go to ask, then remember myself. 'Sure,' I say instead.

We weave our way through the parked cars, heading for his one which is parked on the other side of the bunch. 'This reminds me of when I told you I was pregnant,' I reminisce. 'I don't know why I waited until we were in Holmbush car park, hands full of shopping bags to blurt it out, but I suspect that's all part of the "being Kez" experience.'

'I was so relieved you finally told me.'

'Finally? You knew?'

'Yes.'

'How?'

'I don't know. You seemed different, looked a little different, felt a little different. I just guessed you were pregnant.'

'Why didn't you say anything?'

'Because . . . Because I wasn't sure if you wanted to go through with it. I know we were married, but you might not have wanted it. I was still convinced you would leave me at some point. I didn't want to put pressure on you by being excited or anything before you were ready to talk about it.'

Arie has been burbling quietly and happily as Jeb swings him while we walk. 'Was that the same second time around?'

'Yes.'

'Why?'

'You might not have wanted another one.'

'You're . . .' I have to stop speaking.

'I'm what? Terrible?'

'No. Not terrible. So far from terrible.'

'But you can't trust me therefore you can't be with me?'

'If you can't share something fundamental and essential with your partner, what's the point? And that's not me therapising this. It is me stating a fact.'

'I suppose so,' he says quietly and it's obvious I've hurt him, clawed his heart out all over again. I hate doing that, hate it.

At his midnight-black Volvo, we stop. He's gazing at me, like he did when we sat on that swing, like he did when he came to my office to declare his feelings. I wish he would stop looking like that, it brings on my weakness.

'What was it that you wanted to give me?' I am brusque, serious, focused. No weakness.

Hiding away his hurt, he reaches for the back door handle of the car and pulls it open.

'MAMA!' the children scream and come barrelling out, catching me around the middle, squeezing me to a standstill. I gasp in surprise, in wonder; at the feeling that I am alive again.

My gaze flies to my husband, who is smiling at me like he knew. He knew that I needed this. I needed to have my beating heart, which has been ripped out of my body by their absence, placed back at the centre of my being.

\*

The past two hours have been like another world, a different reality. Since I opened my car and saw a baby Arie in the back seat, I have been scared, tense and on edge.

This was what I felt like after Brian died. After I killed Brian. Tense, on edge, terrified *all the time*. Things got better when Jeb and I got together. I was able to relax, laugh, enjoy life again. Today, I've gone back to feeling normal. Feeling like a human being, not an evil witch.

Zoey has told me all about the drawing she has been doing since their stay at my parents' was slightly extended. Apparently Grandma has asked her to paint a huge mural of Jesus on the wall of the spare bedroom. 'Really?' I asked her.

'Honest, Mum. She's so cool. She lets us do whatever we want.'

'Fabulous,' I replied, a little enviously. My parents are the most permissive, coolest grandparents.

344

'She can't wait for me to finish the mural. She wants to make it where her prayer group meet.'

And Jonah explained how he had pretty much become a chess grandmaster online: 'No one can beat me online but Grandpa still beats me in real life. I'm not sure how that works?'

'None of us could beat Grandpa when I was growing up. You can learn a lot from him.'

'I know. But he does say it's hard to beat me. I am proud of that.'

'I'm proud of you for that, too. Cos Grandpa was the original G.O.A.T of chess among everyone I know.'

'Don't do that, Mum. Don't say things like G.O.A.T. It's cringey.'

'Ooops, sorry.'

We ate terrible food, and played with Arie and acted like we did when we were on a long car journey and stopped at a service station, which culminated in me buying books and magazines and too many sweets from the shop. And a travel pillow – I bought them each a travel pillow even though we have five at home. By the time we walked back to Jeb's car, I was almost giddy with happiness, with the memory of what it was like to be a normal-ish mother with a husband. Pretty soon, I had to go back to being who I was before this interlude.

I grabbed my son, grabbed my daughter, but not right then, not right then.

\*

'When I met you,' Jeb says once all three children are shut away in his car, 'I had this really surreal feeling that I'd met you before. I'd loved you before. That wasn't me, that night. I don't do things like I did that night. The way I pursued you, the bedroom stuff, smoking. That's why I repeatedly asked what you were doing to me.'

'Kez Lanyon, corruptor of men, that's me!'

'I didn't realise it was possible to be in love with two people at once until I met you,' he continues, ignoring my quip. 'I fell for you hard that night we met. That was well before we went up into that bedroom. The whole night, I wanted to see your face, I wanted to be near you. Couldn't believe it when I got the chance to . . .' he lowers his voice, 'to make love to you.'

'That wasn't love-making,' I remind him just as quietly. Love-making is considered, sensuous, tender. Nothing at all like that night.

'Yes it was. That's what I'm trying to tell you. Although it was how it was, it was still love-making. I only did it because I'd fallen for you so hard. I went into my marriage with Hella with an open heart and a deep love for her. I loved her. I would have stayed with her for ever. But when that ended, I knew I couldn't be with anyone else but you. I would have stayed single if I couldn't be with you.'

'Why are you telling me this?'

'I don't want you to do whatever it is you're about to do. I want you to keep yourself safe. But I know you're going to do it anyway. So if you must do this thing, please, do whatever it is you need to – no matter what it is – to come home to your children. I don't want to have *that* conversation with the children. I don't want to lose you, even if I'm not married to you.'

My eyes, which have been trained on Jeb while he speaks, now dart away. He doesn't know what he is saying, how this is going to play out. How doing whatever is needed may well involve choosing between coming home to our children, or harming Moe, his eldest son.

I blow kisses to the children, who wave at me in return, then I turn

346

to my husband. These hours he has given me have been so precious. I will cherish them for as long as I live.

'Thank you for today,' I say to him.

'Kez—'

'Thank you,' I repeat to interrupt him. I need to walk away, escape, otherwise the weakness of being around him will make me confess everything.

# Part 8

Part 8

# Kez

## 26 July, London

At three minutes to three, I turn the corner to Obsidiblue and find MJ, wearing a black trouser suit, hair up in a chignon, stepping out of the back of her sleek black car, the driver taking off straight away. Dennis is already there, standing on the opposite side of the road, wearing his crumpled navy chinos, his ironed white shirt, his immaculately knotted red tie.

*I am not ready for this.*

I've had to park my car a while away and walk here because the exclusion zone in London has grown bigger and bigger since I was last in this part of the city. The streets to get here are very different – new buildings, roads, turns, shops, houses. I would think I knew where I was but would quickly realise that the shortcut I thought I knew is no longer there.

I eventually found the place, and despite all the time I've had to think, prepare, I am not ready for this. I am not ready to walk into the place where Brian died. Where the Kez I was before died, too. Killing someone killed the person I was.

We stand across the road, looking at Obsidiblue, where all our lives changed. Dennis had to let me go in the aftermath. Maisie stopped being Maisie and became MJ, started her new life, promoted away from all of this. Dennis's unit was officially shut down, only to be rebranded and reopened months later. More people, not less. More trainees, more young minds for him to break. Failing upwards as his type always do. I went into the abyss, tumbling down into the horror of what I had done. Then regrouping, rebuilding. Private practice. Working for myself. Treating people one at a time.

'Every offence meant when I say this, I hoped I would never have to be around you two ever again,' MJ says.

'Snap,' I reply.

Dennis doesn't speak. We're beneath him. Truly. I'm surprised he has bothered to show up. He has nothing in his life he cares about except his job. He's married, doesn't have kids as far as I know. I can only imagine he is here to protect his reputation, make sure the story that has been told of him saving young women from a crazed gunman remains intact.

'Dennis,' I say, still staring at the front of Obsidiblue, which is now shuttered with silver slats.

'Kezuma,' he states.

'If we survive this, you and I are going to have a full and frank conversation about how you didn't tell me who Lucian was, but you did do your best to break up my marriage by lying about my husband.'

'I did not lie. I simply presented you with the facts,' he replies.

I turn to look at him and he stares back, that psychopath's stare I know so well.

'And left out the salient parts. Like I said, when this is over, that conversation begins.'

'Whatever you say.'

We both return to staring at the bar.

No bulletproof vests this time. No police on standby. No pep-talk. What was the last one? Along the lines of: *No heroics. Defer to your boss at all times once inside. Allow him to make the decisions and moves. Don't antagonise the suspect. Don't make promises unless you absolutely have to. Say very little. Again, allow your boss – who has the training – to do the talking. Your one job is to get out of there alive. Which brings us back to the no heroics part.'*

No heroics.

Dennis moves first, MJ follows, I bring up the rear. We haven't talked about what we're going to do. We haven't decided or discussed how soon they're going to throw me under the bus of saving their own skins or if I'm going to throw myself under it first.

Lucian Powell owns Obsidiblue, I found that out when I checked Companies House under his original name – Ron Kershaw. He bought it five years ago, but never reopened it for use as a bar. Anyone observing this play out would think Lucian Powell loved his brother. They wouldn't know that he didn't like Brian. Brian was beneath him. Brian was dirt, lower than dirt. He treated his older sibling with contempt and disdain over and over, drained him of all the useful knowledge he had, thought nothing of seducing the woman Brian loved, rubbing it in his face about marrying her. Lucian Powell had nothing approximating love for his brother. He is doing this because it is about him. Everything is about him. His narcissism requires recompense from the people who took away his favourite punchbag.

'It's just us,' Dennis's hands are raised, as are mine and MJ's.

I'm transported back the moment I step inside. The atmosphere, the light, the smell. The heat. The oppressive, pervasive sense of fear that coats everything. Brian's shock as he registered that he'd been hit flashes before my eyes.

I can never forget that face. That moment. The last moment he was alive.

We cross the threshold, step back in time and immediately someone is behind us, shutting and then locking the door.

'Welcome to the last day of your life,' Lucian Powell states with the widest, most predatory grin I have ever seen.

# Kez

## 26 July, London

Brian's brother has recreated the hallway sitting area of his house in here. Plush white sofas are placed in a semi-circle formation pointed at the wall where a huge TV screen has been mounted. The bar is still the same as it was twenty years ago but now it is exclusively stocked with expensive beer, wine and spirits. I have no doubt there will be pricey champagne in the fridges below the bar.

Lucian is standing by the bar, holding Brandee in front of him like a shield. He grips her tight, holding her in place to cover his heart, protect his life. My heart skips when I see her. She is incredibly thin. The pink satin dress she is wearing, something I know she would never pick out for herself, clings to all the bones in her chest, her hips, while her spindle-like arms stick out from the spaghetti straps. She had a baby not long ago, she should still have 'baby fat', she should not be this thin. Her face is a mask of fear, her body a petrified mass because Lucian has a gun jammed into her side.

Behind Lucian, up against the wall, is the big man who showed me into Lucian's house. He has a gun in his hand, but holds it by his side, casually, like he always stands like that with a loaded weapon.

Moe is standing beside the sofa formation, a high table in front of him. All his expensive clothes are a contrasting match to Lucian's – Moe's tight shirt is white, Lucian's black, Moe's fitted suit trousers are black, Lucian's white. They both wear a thick gold chain, shown off by the three buttons open on their shirts, they both have tramlines shaved into the left side of their neat, matching haircuts. They both have expensive shoes. Moe, despite the polish, despite the working out that has bulked him up, looks like he hasn't slept in weeks, possibly months. Dark circles have scored themselves deeply under his eyes. His lips are dry, his fingernails are manicured right back, I'm sure, to hide how much he has been picking at them. The eczema Hella and I used to battle has flared up behind his ears down his neck. These are all signs that Lucian hasn't completely got him. That Moe is still there. If he were showing no signs of stress, was dressed like Lucian and acting like Lucian, he would be lost. It would be nigh on impossible to get him back. It will be difficult as it is now, and he hasn't completely passed into that world.

Moe has a gun. He holds it like the big man, down by his side as if he holds one regularly. On the table in front of him is another gun.

'Hands on your heads, while my lieutenant searches you,' Lucian Powell says. He really is an idiot, this man. I resent that more than anything. He is stupid and he has managed to achieve this, control us like this. The man by the door, Lucian's lieutenant, another thick-set white man with giant hands, lingers over searching MJ, lingers over searching me, barely touches Dennis.

'They're clear,' he says.

I'm tempted to tell Lucian that if they're lieutenants, that would make him a general, not the king, L King as he calls himself. But why enrage him by pointing out his stupidity.

'Hands on your heads,' Lucian orders. We do as we're told.

'Thank you all for joining me here. You were the last people to see my brother, Brian, alive. I want you to tell me what happened to him. Who really shot him? We all of us know it wasn't a stray bullet in the tear gas confusion. One of you three shot him, the others covered it up. Who did it?'

I wait for one of the other two, those snakes who went to the funeral without me, to give it up. Give me up. Sign me up to a bullet-riddled end.

Silence.

We can hear each other breathing, a clock ticking, but no one speaks.

'Tell me!' Lucian orders. 'Tell me now!'

Silence.

Silence.

*Silence.*

The other two really aren't going to give me up. I'm rarely shocked by people, especially not two who have shown themselves to always put their self-interest first.

Silence.

'I will kill this bitch if someone doesn't start talking.'

I lower my hands. 'We're not going to talk until you tell us what you'll do with that information.'

'Put your hands back on your head,' he snarls.

'What are you going to do when you find out what happened to your brother?'

'I'm going to ask the person if there was no other way? If they couldn't have let him live?'

'I think you're going to kill that person. I think you're going to shoot the two who didn't kill your brother and then kill the person that did last. Am I wrong?'

357

He doesn't like that. He doesn't like someone knowing him.

'No,' he bites back. 'I mean, yes. You're wrong.'

'If I'm wrong, why does Moe have a gun? Why do you have a gun? Why do your "lieutenants" have guns? You don't need guns to talk. You don't need to hold a gun on a person to get people to talk.'

Dennis lowers his hands, as does MJ.

'There was no other way,' MJ states. Her voice hooks icicles onto every word that comes out of her mouth. I guess you don't mess with her children and get a pleasant tone.

'He wouldn't have died if there was any other choice,' Dennis states. He is less hostile, but equally definite.

'There really was no other way,' I intone.

'You're lying. You're all of you lying. Which one of you killed him?'

'What are you going to do to the person who pulled the trigger?' MJ asks.

'Yes, what are you going to do to them? You have the answer to the question. Why do you need to know anything else?' Dennis adds.

'If you just want to ask them those questions, then you've got the answer. There was no other way.'

Lucian's confusion fills the room. He doesn't understand. People usually give him what he wants, reply to his questions, wait for him to mete out punishment or reward. No one answers his questions, responds to his demands without giving him what he wants. His self-focus, main-character syndrome doesn't allow for anyone else to resist him. Especially not by giving him what he has asked for. He is confused. The lieutenants are frowning, wondering what is going on. How is their genius leader, L King, confused, stumped by three people who haven't seen the light by working his programme. Two of them women, as well. One of them a Black woman, too.

'Moses,' Lucian says, recovering from his bout of doubt, 'pick some-one to kill. If they won't tell me who did it, pick one and kill them.'

I step forward. 'I did it,' I state. 'I killed Brian.'

MJ steps forward. 'No, I did.'

'It was me,' Dennis says and steps forward.

They're not protecting me, they're simply delaying the moment they are shot. OK, maybe they are protecting me a little.

Lucian has reached his limit of being given the run-around by people he believes beneath him, so jams the gun into Brandee's side, hard enough to make her flinch, cry out. Brian's face when he did that to that young woman all those years ago comes to mind.

This has to turn out differently. It has to.

'OK, all right,' I say. 'It was me. I shot him. I had no choice. I tried to talk him down. We all did. But he wouldn't listen. There was noth-ing else I could do.'

'I knew it was you,' Lucian sneers. 'It was obvious. That's why I've got your "son" here. I've told him all about you. What you do, *mur-derer*. That's why he hates you. That's why he's going to kill you.'

'Moe's not going to kill me, are you, Moe?'

'He'll do whatever I tell him to.'

Lucian has overestimated his influence on Moe. Maybe if he'd waited a little longer, maybe if Jeb and I hadn't split up when we did and Moe hadn't started communicating with his father and mother again. Maybe if Brandee hadn't gone to rescue him. Maybe he would do whatever Lucian told him to.

'Moses, rid me of this traitorous bitch,' Lucian says.

Moe raises the gun and points it at me.

Or maybe, this is another time when I've got the profile wrong, the mind of the person wrong. Like I did twenty years ago with Dennis. I thought Dennis would do something, have a way to stop Brian. But he didn't. He froze. He left it to me.

I brace myself, prepare to die.

'Oh, wait, wait,' Lucian intervenes. 'How about we even up the odds? Make it a bit more like when my brother died. Pick up that gun.'

'No.' Straight up no.

'Pick it up and I'll spare this one.' He shakes Brandee.

'I am never picking up a gun again. I swore on that day it would be the last time I touched a gun.'

'Pick up the gun, and see if this time, when a gun is pointed at you, you have no choice. See if, when it's someone you care about, there really is no choice.'

I stare at the gun on the table. I had no choice. I've told myself that over and over. Whenever Brian appears in my head, in the face of someone I'm looking at, in my most innocuous dreams, I remind myself that I had no choice. He wouldn't listen. He wouldn't stop. I had no choice. There was no other option.

My feet make no sound on the highly polished, wooden floor – a Lucian addition if I ever saw one – as I cross the room to the table. I stare at the gun. It is a black one like the one I learnt to shoot with. It will be heavy in my hand, it will be cold to the touch. It will take me straight back to deciding to shoot Brian instead of letting him kill everyone in the room.

There is another way out of this. 'What if I can prove that there was no other way to resolve what happened with your brother? Will you believe me then?'

'How are you going to prove that?'

'If I can persuade Moe to give me the gun and walk out of here with me, will you believe me that I wouldn't have shot Brian if I hadn't had

360

to? That I would have done anything I could to keep him alive if there was the slightest possibility that he would have listened to me?'

The genius in expensive loafers is stumped. He can't justify any of this if he doesn't at least give me a chance to show that I didn't simply kill Brian. He has to show his lieutenants, who will talk to others, that he has been fair. Even if his plan is to end us all, he can't be seen to be a dictator without mercy.

'You have five minutes. Five minutes. And if you can't do it, then you pick up that gun and you choose someone to die. MJ, Dennis, Moses or you.' He shakes Brandee like a doll again. 'Me and Brandee have things to do, so she isn't on the list.'

'And if I can persuade Moe to put down the gun, you'll let everyone go? Including Brandee?'

'Yes.'

'I have your word?'

'My solemn word.'

'Deal.'

# Moe

## 26 July, Sussex countryside

'This is your chance, Moe, to ask her to tell you the truth. We both know she has been lying to you for years. That she didn't just happen to arrive in your parents' lives when she says she did. She made it happen. Just like she and her friends made my brother die.'

L King's words filtered into Moe's mind as they had been doing all these months. L King had been his lifeline. He had shown Moe so many truths. Had understood him when no one else seemed to. Not about this stuff.

It was clear what he needed to do. He had to talk to Kez. Get her to admit what she did. Once she admitted it to him, she'd admit it to Jeb. And that might make Hella reassess, rethink being with Richie. And if she wasn't with Richie, and Jeb wasn't with Kez, they may just get back together. It was a long shot, but one worth taking.

He, after all, had nothing to lose.

'And if she won't tell you the truth, if she won't admit it, well, this is your back-up.'

L King handed him the gun. It was black and heavy, the gun he'd spent hours and hours learning to fire.

'With this, Moe, she will have to tell you the truth. She'll have to.'

Moe nodded. He knew L King was right. With this gun, Kez would have to tell him the truth.

# Kez

## 26 July, London

'Why do you hate me, Moe?' I ask. I do not have time to make this pretty. 'I love you, I have loved you from the moment your parents let me meet you. Why do you hate me so much?'

'You broke up my family. I know you were with my dad before that counselling session. I know you were with him. They were happy until he met you. And then you got in their heads, by pretending to help them, and you messed with their minds and talked them into breaking up so you could have my dad.'

'That's not true. I don't know who told you that, but it's not true.'

'It is true, I know it is.'

'It's not true. I promise you none of that is true.'

'So how do you explain the pictures then?'

'What pictures?'

'The pictures of you and him. I saw the pictures of you and him together. You were young. He was young. You had long straightened hair, you were thinner. He had an afro.'

'It's not true, Moe.'

'It is!' he insists. 'It is. There are photos and videos. All of them timestamped.'

*Did someone have a camera at that party?* I wonder. *Did someone snap Jeb at that moment he first kissed me?* No one saw us fucking upstairs, but they will have seen us kissing. How would Lucian have got that image? He wouldn't. That's the long and the short of it. He hasn't got that image. It has to be fake. Lucian has gone to great lengths to poison Moe's mind against me.

'The timestamp showed you and Dad were together when he was with my mum – two years after I was born. He was with you. You were together. Cheating on my mum.'

I shake my head. 'It's not true,' I tell him. 'We didn't do that. I told you, your dad told you, we met at a party. And it was before they were married. But it was that one time. He married your mum and I didn't see them again until they were on the verge of breaking up. And your dad and I didn't get together until after your parents were divorced. You know that, your dad has told you that. Your mum has told you. I've told you. It's the truth. You know it is.'

'But I saw the picture. Videos.'

'When I first met your father, in 1998, there were barely any videos made that weren't filmed on a camcorder. Phones didn't have a big enough memory to store photos properly, let alone videos. You had to constantly delete photos and text messages from your phones cos they had virtually no memory. When I met your dad again, I had stopped straightening my hair, he didn't have any type of afro. Anything you've seen is fake. It's completely fake.'

'I know the fake stuff. I've made the fake stuff. It didn't look fake. It looked real. It all looked real.'

'I know it did. And that's the point, isn't it? That's what Lucian does and gets people to do. He messes with things, just enough to make fake things look and feel real. He makes it so you can't trust your eyes and you can't trust the people you know. I have been honest with you all your life. You know that. So have your dad and your mum. None of us have ever hidden how our relationships came about from you. We have never lied to you about anything. You know that I was always telling you the truth about things from a young age. Even when your parents didn't want you to necessarily know something, I said to them and I said to you, if you asked me directly, I would tell you the answer in an age-appropriate way. I am not going to start lying to you now.'

'Kez, I just need you to tell me the truth.'

'I have. I promise you that I have.'

'You sound like you're telling the truth but the pictures . . .'

'I am telling you the truth and the pictures are fake.'

'I'm so confused.' Moe shakes his head. 'My head hurts. All the time.'

'I know it does, Moe. I know. But those pictures are fake. Those videos are *definitely* fake. Come home with me, and we'll work it out.'

'Dad said you're not together any more.'

'We're not,' I reply.

'That's for real?' Moe asks, his line of vision settling on me for the first time.

'It's for real. We have split up. Your father is a fundamentally honest person and he told you the truth.' I hold out my hand for the gun. 'Give me the gun, Moe. Come home and we will get you the help you need.'

'What's the point?' he says. 'Everyone hates me. I hate myself. I hurt my dad. I hurt my mum. I hurt you. Brandee hates me.'

'Do you hate him, Brandee?' I ask her.

Although Lucian has a firm grip on her, she shakes her head. Doesn't dare speak, not with the barrel of Lucian's gun pressed into her side.

Lucian is allowing this conversation to take place because he thinks he has so successfully broken Moe that he will do whatever it is he wants. He thinks that he will be able to get Moe to kill me or me to shoot Moe. Win for him, either way.

'Brandee doesn't hate you. She did all of this for you.'

Moe frowns at me. He is hearing me and that is important, vital. 'Did all of what?'

'When she didn't want to work for Lucian's company any more and you took off on her, she went into hiding. But then she came out of hiding and allowed Lucian to find her, to seemingly coerce her into coming to his compound, so she could make sure you were OK.'

Lucian's shock is felt around the room, even though it is brief. This revelation has unsettled him. 'Nice try,' he says, rallying. 'Brandee isn't clever enough to think of something like that.'

'Ever wondered where the notification that told you where she was came from?'

'One of my foot soldiers,' he replies. He really is pathetic: 'foot soldiers', 'lieutenants' to describe people outside of the actual military but inside your deluded little world. Pathetic.

'Right. And since you didn't manage to get her into your little scheme and she deactivated her account, disappeared from your surveillance for months, you didn't think it at all odd that she popped up again as if by magic? That this foot soldier just "bing" found her that easily? Really? And you're meant to be smart? A genius no less.'

I do not mention that some of those women that Lucian coerced and blackmailed and trafficked will have been her friends. She's not the sort of person who could stand by while the people she loves are hurt. Not Moe, not her friends. After what Seraphina put her through, she will have wanted to save the people she loves. Knowing Brandee, she will have gone there to get information that would be irrefutable in a case put before the police. I do not mention that to Lucian.

'It doesn't matter,' Moe says. 'She's with him now.'

'No, she's not,' I reply. Moe is in agony. I can feel his pain, his mental and emotional torment from where I am standing. Lucian has damaged him, tortured him. He is breaking under the pressure of having his mind, his reality, his certainty about anything and every-thing constantly questioned. I know that is why Lucian made him work on creating those deepfake videos and photos. It has made Moe fragile, he doesn't know what to trust any more. Doesn't believe his eyes, doesn't believe his ears, doesn't trust anything anyone says.

'She is. I saw them. I watched them talking, walking, laughing, eating together. Drinking together. And then they were in bed together.'

'You actually saw them. Physically saw them in bed together with your own eyes, not through video?'

'I watched them from my window. They talked and walked. He made her a picnic in the garden, she was laughing with him and they ate together. I found the video of them in bed later.'

'So you didn't see her kiss him or anything? Just talking and laugh-ing and eating?'

'That was enough.'

'She wouldn't, Moe. She wouldn't do that. She wouldn't go to bed with him.'

'But I saw them. She was wearing the same thing. She was—'

'Moe, you know her. You know she wouldn't,' I say. 'And his ego wouldn't allow him to force himself on her. Other women, maybe, but with Brandee, because you love her, he wants her to give herself to him willingly. He thinks he can have any woman he wants, so it must kill him he can't have Brandee. He thought he could wear her down. Make her his. But he had to make you think she was with him, so you would give up hope. So he could break you.

'He did it to his brother. He thought he could do it to you. He's the reason his brother had a breakdown. Lost his job, lost his life. And he thought he could do the same to you.'

'You speak of my brother again and I will kill this bitch before I kill that runt,' Lucian snarls. 'And anyway, time's up, Mrs Psychologist. You said you would be able to persuade Moses to give you the gun, to walk out of here with you. He is still holding the gun. Which, therefore, means you have failed. And therefore, you have to pick up that gun. And you have to decide. Moses. Dennis. MJ. You. Which one of you gets the bullet from your gun?'

My mouth is dry while I train my sights on the gun again.

'And if you don't choose, I kill this bitch and then kill everyone else anyway.'

*Your brother didn't have to die, Lucian,* I want to say to him. *If you had shown him even the smallest morsel of compassion, he would not have died. You broke him. You and your brother and your father, you started this by constantly making him feel like he was not a man. You made him feel less than because he wasn't leering at girls and women all the time. He wasn't power hungry enough to join the police. He was decent enough to say sorry when he was wrong. He felt things and he felt them deeply. And you hurt him because of that. You used him, and then you discarded him, but not before you went after the one person he cared about more than anyone, the woman he loved. And again, you used his masculinity against him, 'proving' he wasn't man enough to keep her. Deciding you wanted to marry her. Wanting Brian to be happy for you. You broke Brian. You put that gun in his hand, that hopelessness in his head.*

*And now you're doing it with my son. With Moe. You have filled his head with hatred, with fear, with uncertainty and anxiety. You have made him feel less than, you have made him question his masculinity. And you have given him only one way to prove it – get him to kill the woman you convinced him is the source of his pain.*

Get him to kill me.

'When did you decide to use Moe to get revenge on me?' I ask Lucian. 'Before or after you found out what he can do with computers?'

He doesn't reply.

'I'm just curious.'

'Your husband's son could hear my message, he understood. He was able to see that women are prey that have started to think they are predators. You are prey who have forgotten your place.'

'So before you found out what he could do with computers.'

'There is another way out,' Lucian says. 'Let him kill you. And he'll walk free. I'll let him go. I still have contacts high up in the police, I will be able to spin it. You know your friends have no problem lying to cover things up. My lieutenants will say whatever I tell them to say. Brandee here will do whatever it takes to save him.'

I think about what Jeb told me, what he said about doing whatever is necessary to come home to Zoey and Jonah. And what that means. He wouldn't want me to choose myself over his son. The children wouldn't want me to choose myself over their brother. And what about me? Would I choose me over Moe?

Of course I wouldn't.

I step closer to Moe, into his direct line of sight. If he pulls the trigger of the gun in his hand, he will not miss me. He will hit me straight in the heart.

My mouth is dry, parched and I am shaking inside. I do not want to do this. But I have no choice. I cannot let Moe continue to suffer. I cannot let Brandee stay with these people.

'I want your word that if I do what you want, Moe will go free. No prison time no matter what he has done. And you'll get him the help he needs. Proper mental and emotional health help to make him well again.'

Lucian's sinister smile of triumph looms over me from across the room. I can't stand to turn my head to look it, but I feel it all the same.

'I want your word, your solemn word,' I say. 'I need you to say it out loud.'

The chilling embrace of Lucian's grin throws itself around me. He says, 'You have my word.'

'I wasn't talking to you,' I state.

A pause.

One beat . . .

Two beats.

The grin fades, confusion blossoms. He thought he was in control of this. That he was in charge. That all of this was going to play out exactly as he planned.

'You have my word,' Dennis says loudly. 'You have my solemn word.'

In response, I snatch up the gun, turn and fire.

# Kez

## 26 July, London

Jeb is waiting for me when I am finally finished giving my statement and I am let out into the police station reception area.

He is sitting on a moulded blue seat opposite the glass-protected desk, beside two people who look like they have been there for hours. His hands are clasped in front of him, his body is leaning over his knees. I halt when I see him. *What's he doing here?* I wonder. *I thought he'd be with Moe and Hella, and I would have to find him tomorrow to speak to him, to explain everything.*

He gets to his feet when he sees me. And I can't control myself. I dash across the distance and leap at him, launch myself into his arms. He wraps himself around me, holds me tight.

'Hella said you'd want to see me. I wasn't so sure—'

'I'm sorry,' I cut in. 'I'm so sorry for all of it. For all of it.' I cling tighter. 'I love you, I never want to be apart from you. I love you, I love you, I love you.' I need him to understand, it was fake, it was all fake and now all of this has to be real.

\*

*Earlier, 26 July*

Lucian Powell fell like his brother. Backwards.

After the shock of impact, his body dropped backwards like a stone. I didn't shoot him in the chest – Brandee was his shield, his protection from any bullet aimed at his heart. He was taller than her, a lot wider from his bodybuilding, so I went for the space where his shoulder meets his neck, an area that was thick and prominent. It wouldn't kill him, simply wound him, disarm him.

Brandee managed to stay on her feet when he fell and she immediately turned on her heels, pulled back her leg and kicked Lucian in the side. Then she raised that leg again and stamped down on his family jewels. She didn't hesitate, didn't think twice. She was pissed and she was letting it out. She then went to Lucian's gun that he dropped and kicked it away.

I turned the gun in my hand on the lieutenant standing nearest to the door and he dropped his weapon, raised his hands in surrender. I heard the clunk of the gun falling and landing from the other 'trusted lieutenant' too. As I expected, these hard men who had been hand-picked to protect the 'L King at all costs' valued their lives more than they valued him. He talked in his videos about being surrounded by a steel ring of trained mercenaries, but they were, in fact, fantasists like him, playing at being dangerous, radical and hard.

Lucian hadn't ever really experienced this sort of thing, he hadn't been in a battle situation, despite the stuff he publicly spouted. His trusted army hadn't either. They were all imitations of the real thing. They thought, because they had coerced and trafficked and brutalised and mistreated women, because they had mentally groomed and broken young men, because they spent hours firing bullets into paper targets, that it was the same as holding a gun to someone and shooting. They thought the leap to do that was simple.

Until the moment they had to. And then they realised there were a lot of steps between picking up a gun and shooting a gun, there were even more between picking up a gun and firing it at someone who has just shot the reason you are in the situation in the first place.

The screeching wail of sirens speeding towards us suddenly filled the air, their arrival too quick to be normal. I guessed MJ, who was important, had people on standby, waiting to descend.

'No lies, this time,' I said to MJ. 'No lies, no cover-up, no faking.'

She made eye contact with me and her face reflected her unhappiness at what I said. But she nodded.

'I need you to say it out loud,' I told her.

'No lies, no cover-up, no faking.'

'It's better with the truth. It's painful but it's better,' I said.

Lucian Powell, L King, was still groaning loudly in pain on the ground. He dismissed women, denigrated them as inferior creatures and he yet there he was, wailing, howling over what was essentially a flesh wound. A painful one, yes, but in his world and reality and framing of what 'real men' are, he should be sucking it up. He should be toughing it out. He should not be causing so much of a fuss.

Brandee had flown to Moe's side, and was cradling him, rocking him, and he was clinging to her, constantly saying he was sorry. Sobbing and sobbing, repeating and repeating, 'I'm sorry, I'm sorry, I'm sorry, I'm sorry.'

*So am I*, I thought. *I'm sorry, I'm sorry, I'm sorry.*

## 26 July, London

We have checked into a hotel that is within walking distance of the hospital Moe is in. He had to be sedated and will be assessed in the morning because he was in such a state. Hella is with him and so is Brandee. He was going to be questioned, but he hadn't technically done anything, and they didn't know about the 'work' he was doing for Lucian Powell, so at the moment there is nothing to hold him on.

Lucian Powell was taken to a different hospital, one where he could be securely held until being transferred into police custody. There was genuine malice in MJ's voice and face when she told the first officers on the scene who he was and what his operations were. She was going after him for daring to go near her daughter, and I suspected she knew a lot more about him than she had bothered to share with me. Fair enough, I'd thought, as long as they take him down, I'm cool.

I am first in the shower, allowing the water to wash away every bit of not only what had happened in that place, but also in the last three months. Wrapped in a white hotel dressing gown, I slip under the covers and wait for Jeb to finish. We have so much talking to do, I have a lifetime's worth of explaining to do. My head sinks into the pillow and my eyes slip shut. I can't remember the last time I got a proper night's sleep. It was well before this started. In fact, it might have been around the time Brian died.

The shower shuts off, the shower door squeaks open, squeaks shut. I listen to Jeb drying himself off, I wait for him to appear so I can explain. I can explain it all.

*

'It's three a.m.,' Jeb states when I open my eyes. 'On the dot.'

'Jeez, how long did it take you to dry yourself off? I was waiting for you to come back to talk.' I rub at my eyes, stretch my face. 'There's so much to explain.'

'Can that happen after I've made love to you?'

'We've got a lot to talk about, don't you want to—'

'Nope. Not even a little. No. I just want to make love to you.'

'Go on then,' I grin, 'if you absolutely have to.'

\*

'This all goes back to what you said to me that time in my office,' I begin. 'Just before we did stuff on my desk, you told me you were a fundamentally honest person.

'As a fundamentally honest person, I knew you could never pretend to Moe that we'd split up. He would see right through you. And he was in such a bad place, Lucian Powell did such a number on him, I knew that he couldn't take any more lies. He had to know that you had done what he wanted – you had split up with me. I had to make sure you believed it, too. So you would be telling the truth when he asked you if we were still together.

'When I said that stuff to you, that "if you can't trust someone to tell you the truth" stuff, I was talking about me. How I couldn't trust you with the truth of the situation because I had to make you believe that we were separated and on the road to divorce.

'Once we'd split up, Lucian thought I was isolated and vulnerable, which is when he would make his move. The longer he had Moe, the worse it would be, I knew.

'He had Moe brainwashed. It's going to take a lot to get him back.

And it's going to take a long time, but at least he's away from them now. At least he can start to see what is real and what isn't. I'm not sure how he's going to react to being a father, but at least he's free.'

I shift on the bed, trying to stretch my poor beleaguered body. This amount of stress is not good for anyone, but for someone with an auto-immune condition like mine, it's like setting fire to your nerve endings. Jeb shifts with me, slipping his arms around me and pulling me closer, almost as though trying to absorb some of my discomfort and pain.

'Lucian is a cliché, I knew he would try to recreate how his brother died, especially when I found out that he'd bought the place.'

'Brandee said you shot him. She said you made a deal to keep Moe out of prison and then you shot Lucian.'

'Something like that.'

'I'm not going to like it, but tell me what is this deal?'

'I have to go back to him. To the job I had before.'

'To being an agent?'

'No, I don't know. I doubt it. Too old, too cynical, too visible. But I do have to go back and work with Dennis at Insight. He wants me back.'

'But how did you know you could make a deal with Dennis?'

'Lucian had nothing on Dennis and yet he showed up. He doesn't care about anything enough to show up unless he had an ulterior motive. Unless he had worked out a way for this to benefit him. I realised, just before we went in that he had showed up in case he could use the situation to his advantage. That's why he tried to split us up, it was a chance for him to use this to his advantage. To get him what he wants.'

'Raa. Really?'

'Really.'

'And what does he want?'

'Me.'

'What, he's into you?' Jealousy rises quickly in Jeb. It's completely unnecessary, though.

'No. No way. Dennis is not into me in that way. All that sexual harassment, he got off on it, but it was merely a means to an end. He never wanted me to leave my job, leave his unit, but they wouldn't let me stay because I was one of the people who had been there when Brian died. Everyone believed Dennis had taken the shot, but I still had to go. He *hated* that. When I walked back into his life asking for help, he decided to use that situation for his own ends.' I stroke my husband's cheek. 'I realised that as we walked across the street.'

'You don't have to, you know? You don't have to go back to him. You could take that other job and say you can't work for him. Say he can't afford you with the amount of cash they're offering.'

'I do. If Moe is going to get the care he needs and stay out of prison, because I dread to think what Lucian had him doing, then I need to keep up my end of the bargain.'

'I hope you know I appreciate you putting yourself on the line like this for him.'

'He's my child, so of course.'

'And when he's better, he'll see it too. He'll appreciate it, too.'

I smile at Jeb. He doesn't realise there is a long road ahead. Deprogramming Moe could take years. And even if he does stop hating me – which he may never do – he will probably always be wary of me. That's something I will have to live with. I'm hoping, though, that going back to working with Dennis on Insight, his renamed unit, will give me access to the latest psychological treatments, so I will be able to help Moe. I'm going to do everything I can to mend this family. I didn't break it, but I have to mend it any way I can.

'Can you believe we're grandparents?' Jeb says, pulling me out of my hole. I have a reckoning with the past and the present and how they have collided, how they have created this mushroom cloud of horror. But I can ignore all of that now. I can use the best technique I have learnt in all my years of working with the human mind, I can stay in the moment. I can forget everything and focus on being here. On feeling here. On existing here.

'So Moe is Arie's father?'

'Yes. Brandee explained that she'd wanted to tell Moe but he was too far gone into the world of L King and she wasn't sure how he would take the news. She couldn't tell us because she knew we'd tell Moe. So she went through the whole pregnancy alone, knowing she was going to do whatever she could to get Moe back.'

'She's so brave. I wish she'd told me though. I hate that she went through all of that alone. We are going to have to do everything we can to help her now.'

'I told her that. So did Hella. Anything and everything she wants and needs.'

I grin when I think of that little boy, how quickly he slotted into our lives. 'I'm going to miss having him around,' I say to Jeb. 'And, no, I cannot believe that you're a grandpa. I, on the other hand, am going to be known as the cool grams that I am. I will be taking no more questions about the terminology right now.'

'Are we back together?' he asks.

'If you want to be, we are. I wouldn't blame you if you didn't want to. I was pretty nasty to you.'

'That wasn't nasty. Far from it. I was more angry that we didn't have a proper break-up conversation. It was literally you need to leave and then boom, over.'

379

'That was all you. I thought you'd at least argue, maybe shout at me. You know, fight back a bit. No, I tell you it's over, you leave. Who does that?'

'Normal, innit? A woman tells you to book, you book. What's the point in arguing?'

'The point is to fight for your relationship.'

'Why? If a woman is out, what good is me shouting going to do? Change her mind? Change *your* mind? No chance.'

'It would have made me feel a bit more guilty, knowing that I'd hurt you. I mean, you said it felt like Hella had ripped out your heart and shown it to you. Me, it's all "I knew you were going to leave me one day" and off you bounce. Who does that?'

'Me, babe, me. I needed to protect myself.'

'From me?'

'Yes, from you. I've never, and I mean *never*, had anyone hold so much sway over me as you do.' He climbs on top of me, stares directly into my eyes. 'I always ask what have you done to me because I never know where this feeling for you comes from. And I hate it sometimes. I hate being so powerless about you. Because I am always waiting for you to dump me. To decide I'm not good enough for you.'

'Well, what do you know? Same here.'

'*You* think I'm going to decide you're not good enough for me?'

'Always. It began with you not calling. Actually, no, it began with me having sex with you when I didn't even know your name.' I wriggle underneath him. 'Jebediah, you're my weakness. My sweetness and my weakness . . . And yes, I know those are song lyrics before you say anything and I also know that I could not be any more cliché if I tried.'

'You're my cliché,' he says. 'I think that's all that matters right now.'

And when he kisses me, it's like nothing has happened. Nothing has gone wrong. And we can just carry on like the couple we are.

*

I have to be quiet as I stumble into the bathroom. Jeb is finally asleep and I do not want to wake him.

I've been awake next to him, pretending that it is all cool, that now we're together again and the children can come home, everything is cool. I stand in front of the sink, only a little light spilling from the bedroom floor lights into the dark bathroom. My hands are trembling, shaking and quaking as they try to deal with the adrenaline racing through my body. I was fine before. I *thought* I was fine before. I am not fine.

*Breathe*, I tell myself.

*Inhale.*

*Exhale.*

*Breathe.*

I chance a look in the mirror and my heart flies to my throat, choking the scream.

Brian.

Brian is staring at me from the mirror.

His eyes are hollow, his skin is alabaster white, his mouth is a line of disapproval.

I slam my eyes shut.

*Breathe.*

*Inhale.*

*Exhale.*

*Breathe.*

I open my eyes and he's still there. He's still staring at me.

Closing my eyes isn't going to work this time. Willing him away will not work. I know this. I know this.

He's back. Brian, the face I see whenever I can't sleep, who disappeared these past few weeks when Arie was living with us, is back.

I sink to the ground. Pull my knees up to my chest.

Brian is going to be here for a while.

He is here for a long, long while.

# Brandee

'Moe, Moe,' I whisper. He's been sedated and he's been sleeping these past few hours. I need him to wake up now. I need him to see.

I have not let Arie go since Mr Q handed him back to me. I have hugged and kissed and held my son so tight. I have marvelled at how big he is, how familiar he is and how happy he looked to see me. I'd been scared that he would not recognise me, but he did.

I find it hard to believe I'm mother. Me. I'd been overjoyed when the second line appeared on the test, when it confirmed that I was pregnant. But I'd also been terrified. I was and am scared, every day, that I'll turn into *my* mother. That's why I needed Moe back. Obviously, I didn't realise he'd be this damaged, that he would need a lot of help and love and patience to bring him back to us properly. But we can do that.

Right now, though, I need him to wake up so he can see.

'Moe, Moe, wake up,' I say to him.

His eyes crack open a little, but he still seems out of it. The nurse had been kind enough to let me stay even though visiting hours are well over.

'Moe, this is your son, Arie,' I tell him gently.

His face, so tired and exhausted, changes, he's confused.

'Yes, your son. We have a baby together. I had to get you back because I love you. And because your son needs you. He needs both of us.'

Tears prick in his eyes. He understands.

And he's going to be OK. I know we're all going to be OK.

# Part 9

# Brandee

**BrandeeH**

**@Brandee2ees | Joyn Inn Video | Status: Joyn Only Me |**

*\* 7 August 2023 \**

Hey, hey! It's your laydee, Brandee, coming at you after a long time away.

And this is going to be my last update for a while, if not for ever. I'm getting off this video merry-go-round and focusing on things in real life.

In case you were wondering, Moe is stronger. Much stronger. He was in hospital for a while, but now he's staying with his mum. He's getting the help he needs. He has someone to talk to and he's getting plenty of rest. I'm staying there as well so he can see Arie.

He loves that little boy and I love watching them together. He's going to get well again, I know he is. We'll get Moe back. Different, but Moe.

Lucian Powell AKA L King AKA Ron Kershaw, is still on remand. They are unpicking all the things he has been doing and it is going to take some time. It has far-reaching consequences because he had some pretty high-level contacts that were either helping him or looking the other way.

The most important thing is the women he was holding, some of them my friends, are getting proper help and care. Can't imagine what they went through. Scrubbing those deepfakes from the internet is going to take a while, and they may not manage it.

The internet is melting down over L King's arrest. The people who signed up for his stupid academy and paid for courses are all freaking out cos who is going to fulfil their stuff now? Lots of people have come up quickly to fill the void he's left, which is kinda depressing. But, their stuff is not as long-term and established as L King's so hopefully they'll be able stop them before they get too far.

Never mind the book, I hope they throw the whole library of crimes at him. He deserves it.

I saw my dad so he could meet Arie. He was so happy and he told me not to tell Seraphina yet. She would sneak a camera or she would tell the world, and he thinks I should spare myself and Arie that. I totally agree.

And I am doing so well. I have my boy. My beautiful, gorgeous boy. And every day, every day, he makes me smile, truly smile. With him, I am the luckiest woman alive.

Peace In, everyone. Peace In.

# Kez

**18 August, Brighton**

'Are you sure you can't just duck out on this whole thing?' Jeb asks.

We are holding hands outside a big glass building in what is basically the financial district of downtown Brighton because every other building around here houses a financial institution. This building, though, is essentially a government building done up to look like all the other companies around here and it is also where Dennis's Insight unit is now located.

My husband is still not on board with me working with Dennis again, and he's less than thrilled about me coming here on such a glorious day when my new job hasn't even started.

The sun is out and everyone we love is down on the beach. Hella and Richie have come down for the day, bringing Moe, Brandee and Arie, and I've invited Karizma, my old assistant from my private practice days, who was so happy to hear from me and said she was going to try to make it. Sylvie is coming down from Leeds with her husband and children for a few days. Jeb only stopped complaining about me coming here when I agreed to let him walk me to the building. 'He can't actually force you to come into work when you haven't even started yet,' Jeb had said on our stroll into Brighton.

'Technically, no. But he said today was the last day I get to choose an office. If I don't come in today, I don't get to complain about where I work. I'm sure each office is as good as the next, but I want to take some kind of control of this. I feel like I've been railroaded into it, so I need to make my mark in some way. Besides, I would really like to choose an office as far away from him as possible.'

'If you're not at the beach in twenty minutes, I'm coming back for you,' my husband says. 'Security clearance or not.'

'In which reality am I making it to the seafront in twenty minutes even if I set off now?'

He laughs, that big laugh of his that soothes me as much as it stirs me. 'Forty minutes.'

'Forty minutes,' I agree.

*

Dennis, of course, has the biggest of the glass-walled rooms with a solid oak door, on a mezzanine level just slightly above the rest of the bank of desks in this space. I have run the gauntlet of security, secondary security and security badge adventures and have finally made it to this floor. To my new work home for the foreseeable.

There are boxes, everywhere. The room is buzzing with the excitement of the new, the hum of fresh beginnings. There are only three private offices on the mezzanine level – including Dennis's – so I don't know why he made such a fuss about me coming in today. It would literally be a case of deciding if I'm on his right side or left side.

Actually, yes, I do know why he made such a fuss about me coming in today. He did it because he can.

I don't bother knocking before entering his office. He is looking around, searching for a way to display his certificates and other achievements now that he is surrounded by non-nail-friendly glass. 'This place is ludicrous,' he says, clattering his framed doctoral professorship certificate onto the desk. Technically, I should call him professor, but I never have. He's never asked anyone to use that title, either.

'It is what it is,' I say and sit in the chair on the other side of his desk. Orange, suedette, the wrong side of uncomfortable. Obviously designed to make sure people don't outstay their welcome.

'How perfectly sanguine of you,' he replies. 'I notice you are sitting. Is there something I can help you with?'

'I'm curious, Dennis, what was the second stressor?'

'Excuse me?' he replies.

'What was the second stressor that triggered you into doing all of this?'

'I'm not sure I understand,' he states.

'You understand perfectly,' I tell him, an edge to my voice. I wish he would drop the act. 'Don't worry, I'm not going to tell anyone. I haven't even told my husband. If I did, there's no way he would let me work with you.

'I just can't work out what the second stressor was that made you do all of this. Because you and I know that Lucian Powell is way too stupid to pull this off. He doesn't think long-term. If he did, he wouldn't have had the human trafficking and extortion businesses alongside his legitimate companies. I mean, neither human trafficking nor extortion are long-term occupations anyway, but to keep those women hostage at his place where he was running the deepfake porn business alongside the webcams and his sportswear and internet businesses? That is just thick.

'And certainly not clever enough to ensnare my child, end my marriage, put someone in MJ's kid's school. No, that's clever, sneaky, callous, vicious, long-term. And that's you all over, isn't it?' I shrug. 'I'll hold my hands up, you had me completely fooled with all the "I never want to set eyes on you again" and the "that's it you and me done" stuff. But all of this was your doing, wasn't it?'

While I've been talking, Dennis has taken a seat and is staring at me, his face impassive instead of the wary most people's would be.

'What is it that you would like me to say, Kezuma? Would you like some kind of confession?'

'No, I don't need that. I just want to know what your second stressor was? What was it that flipped you into serial killer mode and set you off on a killing spree with other people doing your dirty work? My guess is the first stressor was your wife deciding she was done with you. You don't like people deciding to leave you, do you? That has to be your decision . . . Oh, I get it. Couples' therapy. She suggested couples' therapy and you were insulted.'

He folds his arms across his chest, leans back. 'Brighton wasn't my first choice for an office move, I would have preferred if we stayed in London. But that wasn't an option, apparently. I had to do as I was told.'

'That's not enough to be a second stressor.'

'It was time for you to come home, Kezuma. You'd had plenty of time to get over the Brian incident, it was time for us to be together again. You were always meant to run this place, that's what I was training you for. When I retired, you were meant to take over. And then Brian had his episode and you left.'

I shake my head. 'I forget, I keep forgetting that you're a proper psychopath. You will literally do anything to get what you want. Literally. You could have got my children killed.'

'They're not your children. One is your husband's son, one is a stray you took in.'

'They *are* my children and you knew I would do anything to get them back. It was only meant to be Moe, though, wasn't it? Brandee spoilt your plans, didn't she? She triggered everything a bit too early. She was meant to introduce Moe to Powell and then disappear when Moe was treating her badly. In your original plan, I suspect, I was only meant to find out what was going on when Moe was completely brainwashed, which would make Jeb blame me and leave me, and then I would what, be forced to confront my demons with Brian by killing his brother? And you would be the only person to help me out, to save me from prison? Or was it more simple than that? You wanted me to try to save Moe and then when I failed, I'd turn to you for more help? Promise you anything, as long as you helped me? In that scenario, taking out Brian's brother would just be a bonus, wouldn't it?'

'Lucian Powell is a terrible human being. After all the things he's done, prison is almost too good for him.'

'And what about you? Is prison too good for you? You're no better than him.'

'Of course I'm better than him. He's a common little pimp who got lucky by surrounding himself with people who know computers and coding. Apart from his ridiculous videos, everything that idiot has comes from other people. That's why those "lieutenants" folded when you turned the gun on one of them. He doesn't inspire loyalty.'

'And you do?'

'Of course I don't. But I know what I'm doing.'

'Did you really tell him I killed Brian?'

'How are the nightmares, by the way?' I am able to look at him then, to see the malice behind his eyes. 'Brian still paying nightly visits to your dreams?'

'If I didn't know better, I'd think you were trying to deflect from this conversation with a distress distraction technique.'

'Very good. And that is why you were always my favourite. From all of my recruits over all of the years, you are my favourite.'

'Did you tell him?'

'Of course I didn't. He would never have gone for that. Not Mr Conspiracy Theorist himself. I had to make him work for that information, believe it was all his own idea. I had someone teach me how to create fake identities. I became a "foot soldier" who fed him information about police raids and new gangland threats until he trusted me. Once he trusted me, I fed him information about conspiracy theories surrounding his brother's death.

'I also created a female persona, complete with fake looks that were reminiscent of Brian's girlfriend he stole. That girlfriend left him after Brian died – she felt too guilty about what happened to him. That persona became Powell's confidante. After some gentle prompting, he couldn't wait to open up to her. I knew exactly what he was thinking and feeling and when to give him a prod in the right direction.

'I had a third persona as an investigative journalist who was looking into potential police and state cover-ups, also vaguely linking back to his brother's death. Between the three personas, I gave him ideas on what to do such as putting his niece into a boarding school with MJ's child with the sole purpose of befriending her, such as employing your husband's son after he had been hooked into giving all his money to Powell's "academy". It was all to create enough of a mystery to get you engaged. To remind you how much you enjoy this type of work, how good you are at it.'

'The irony of you using fake personas to take down the L King of fake personas may actually eat itself into becoming a black hole,' I comment. 'But you didn't need to do all that, you know? You could have just asked me to come back to work with you.'

'Would you?'

'No.'

'Needs must then.'

'You still haven't told me what the second stressor was. And don't give me that bollocks about moving to Brighton. It was more than that.'

'My niece, she had a baby boy. Called him Brian. And then I realised he'd been born on Brian's birthday. It hit me, probably for the first time, what had happened to Brian. My role in it. I wanted to make things right and that started by getting you back into the fold. Making things up to you as well as to Brian's memory.'

Dennis and I are still looking at each other. For the first time I see Dennis the real man. He does have feelings, he can understand emotion. He does reflect on the things he's done wrong.

'And if you believe that load of over-emotional drivel, then I'm going to have to send you on a few more training courses.'

I can't believe I fell for that.

Dennis is the most dangerous type of psychopath: he does not feel things like the rest of us do but he *does* know how to fake it so you think he is capable of feeling things. He is like quicksand – you don't realise how much danger you're in until you're too far into it and you're being sucked under. I would bet that story was at least partially true, so he's adapted it to get him what he wants. To show me exactly who he is. Again.

'Don't look so unhappy, Kezuma. We're going to do so much good together. Insight has been waiting for you to return. It's the perfect place for you, for your skills, your abilities, your unique way of seeing the world. I noticed that about you right from the start. Working with me is what you were always meant to do.'

'The job. I get it now. The second stressor was the job I was offered. They probably came to you to get some background info on me well over a year ago when they were looking for someone. The idea that I would come back to that world and work for someone instead of you must have been intolerable to you. It set you off. You had to do whatever you could to get me back under your control.'

'Have I already said that you were always my favourite?' he replies. Which is as much of a yes as I'm ever going to get from him.

'I hate being your favourite,' I tell him.

He smiles at me with something that approximates genuine affection. 'It's so good to have you back, Kezuma. I hope you come to accept that this is what you were always meant to do.'

'Yeah, the day I take career or vocational advice from a psychopath is the day I know it's time to retire. I'm here for one reason only – let's neither of us forget that.'

I leave before he can say anything else. Before he can fill my mind up with his twisted logic and mangled justifications. I'm going to be with him for the foreseeable, I might as well get used to that, but I also have to believe that I can do some good in this job. I can make a difference here, I know I can.

# Moe

## 18 August, Brighton

He's getting better. Even in this short amount of time he can see that.

He's getting stronger and he can see what is fake and what isn't. He knows the photo was fake. Knows it. He knows Kez is going back to the job she had before because of him. And he knows she loves him.

But . . . But he still can't stop wondering, *What if that photo isn't fake? What if it is real? What if she really did sabotage his family, his life, his mind? What if everything that is happening now really is her fault?*

'Thinking like that, feeling like that is normal,' Matt, the person he talks to every day says. 'Especially this soon after you've got out of that place. It was a bad, intense situation. A lot was done to you psychologically, emotionally. Even physically you were abused because having you live where you were employed meant you were working many, many hours without any real break. That physical stuff helps to wear you down mentally. It takes a while for you to recalibrate and rebuild yourself after being broken down like that. And it will take a while for your feelings to catch up with your thoughts. Right now, Moe, anything you feel is normal. Anything you think is normal.'

That's when Moe accepts he has to keep faking it. He has to keep acting like what Matt says to him is true.

Because whenever Matt says that to him, he's always too scared to ask in return: *'But what if I never stop hating her? What if I get better, what if I get to keep living this wonderful life with Arie and Brandee and my dad and my mum, but I never stop hating Kez? What do I do then?'*

# Kez

## 18 August, Brighton

They're all there, on the beach. A gazebo erected, windbreakers planted into the shingle on three sides, a table groaning with food and drink, a small speaker blasting out tunes. Everyone is there. Hella and Richie, who have brought Moe and Brandee with them, Jeb, Zoey and Jonah, Chris, Ellie, Jasper and Abigail are here, too. As is Remi and her wife and children. Hopefully Karizma is on her way. And I know Brandee's dad is going to try to drop by.

As I approach, Brandee holds up Arie. He grins at me, flings his chubby arms out wide, almost begging me to run into them.

This is what I'm going to focus on for now. This is what matters. Everything fake is far, far away. All that matters is being here, in the now, with all these people I love.

# Credits

*Here are the people who made* Every Smile You Fake *happen:*

**Superstar Editing & All-round Amazingness**
Jennifer Doyle

**Other Editorial**
Jessie Goetzinger-Hall

**Copy editing**
Helen Parham

**Proofreading**
Kate Truman

**Audio**
Ellie Wheeldon

**Cover Design**
Caroline Young

**Production**
Tina Paul

**Marketing**
Jessica Tackie

**Publicity**
Emma Draude

**Sales**
Becky Bader
Frances Doyle
Izzy Smith

**Amazing agenting**
Antony Harwood

**Expert advice**
Graham Bartlett
Lesley McEvoy

# Acknowledgments

*I'm clearing my throat to say thank you . . .*

To my amazing family

To my agent, Ant

To my publishers (who are fully credited at the back)

To my fabulous stair-climbing friends

To my beloved MK2

To my girls J & F

To you, the reader for buying my book.

And, to E & G . . . as always and for eternity.

# Bonus Content

## The Sharenting Trap
by Dorothy Koomson

**It's good to share, but how much is too much
and who pays the true price?**

I don't know about you, but I am endlessly fascinated by people. It's why I studied Psychology at university, why I write books that are character-focused as well as plot-fuelled, and why I regularly fall down rabbit holes of social media beefs as I scrawl through whole threads gobbling up the events, posts and snarkiness that have created the current animosity between two people I don't even know.

My fascination with people is also why I ended up absolutely terrifying myself when writing *Every Smile You Fake*. The information I gained as I researched several parts of the book, was shocking and chilling. I came away a changed person.

The area of research I'm going to talk about here is the one I carried out to create Brandee's backstory.

Brandee's backstory brought me into the ever-intriguing world of family blogging or 'Sharenting' (sharing—parenting) as it's often now called. This is the realm where – mainly mothers when this trend started – share every second of their parenting journey via posts, photos and videos on various social media platforms and blogs. Parents devote hours and hours of time to documenting for a captivated audience, the birth, growth, and development of their offspring; people can tune in to watch as a tiny being goes from bump to baby to toddler to child to teen to young adult.

Family blogging was, initially, a way for parents to give and gain support; women across the globe showed that there was no one perfect way to parent, that everyone makes mistakes, everyone gets it wrong, everyone struggles sometimes. A struggle shared was a worry eased. And the odd picture or video of the child in question was a great way to put a human face on a very human problem.

Then, at some point, sharing became oversharing became an almost compulsive need to document every aspect of children's lives for the outside world. I suspect the change came when money entered the picture and the thought of making a living from just posting a few pictures of your children seemed too easy to dismiss.

## The business of being a child

Sharenting is BIG business across the world. Monetised accounts can pull in thousands of pounds a month from sponsorship deals and ad revenue linked to post or video views as well as follower count. Some American family vlogs can rake in over $180k a year, while others reach the heady heights of $1.3 million and even $4 million a year. That's just for ad revenue and not accounting for products sent, vacations paid for, events invited to. It's no wonder that few parents want it to stop.

With big money rolling in, it can be easy to forget that the child in this situation is the one actually earning the money – without them none of this cash would be possible. But, of course, being young, most of these children don't have bank accounts, let alone know how much they're earning or what their parents are doing with the cash.

Cam Barrett, a child of a former mommy blogger, who has become an advocate for children of social media influencers, said recently in a long Twitter/X thread begging people to stop watching family vlogs: '. . . another child DM'd me and told me their parents said if they chose not to be in the vlogs anymore; they would lose their home, their nice things, and would essentially tear the family apart.'

What Cam is describing isn't an isolated case. During my research, I came across video after video, news story after news story, of children of former blogging and vlogging parents who were forced to keep on making videos, posing for pictures, allowing their private lives to be mined for content so their 'family' could keep making money. Many of them were making content well past the time they wanted to, many of them went no contact with their family as soon as they could. The conclusion I came to was that a lot influencer children were put 'out there' to make parent-controlled content, with very little time off, while their parents decided how to spend the money they earned.

## Who's looking in?

Let's not beat around the bush here: while family vlogging has made sharing parenting burdens easier, it has also made it infinitely easier for predators to find children. According to a statistic presented to the French government recently, fifty percent of all images shared on child-focused pornography forums were originally uploaded to the internet via the child's parents' social media accounts. It's not simply a case of who is watching family influencer content, but why?

Internet safety experts regularly say that seemingly innocuous images and videos of children posted are often gold-standard content for perverts. One TikTok user who posts under the moniker Mom.uncharted has dedicated her platform to calling out parent bloggers and influencers who create content that is lapped up by predators. She repeatedly explains you never know who is watching, what they will get sexually from the children's videos that they watch and how you can avoid it. For example, did you know that videos of a child eating a banana can rack up thousands of views, shares and saves, while the same child eating an apple will barely get out of the hundreds. I'll leave you to work out why. Bathtime videos, swimsuit shots, even nappy changes are gold for a certain demographic. One account that I followed with horrified fascination but no longer posts came under fire because of the 'innocent' things the mother got her three-year-old daughter to do with things like tampons and bananas. Whenever she was criticised, she cried on camera about people being mean to her, how she was a single mother trying to make her way through, how there was nothing wrong about the things her daughter did.

This area of sharenting was a rabbit hole I fell down and felt there would be no end to the fall. Many, many accounts have their very young daughters make GRWM (Get Ready With Me) videos where the children dress up – in clothes bought and sent to them by viewers (very often older men). Other accounts are clearly geared to sexualising children, some accounts have videos where young girls send special messages to older men. This rabbit hole is deep and seemingly bottomless and, as I say, terrifying to see what people are willing to do for clicks.

## What about consent?

The internet is forever. We know that. We're constantly reminded that what we post can follow you into jobs, into public life, into being a catalyst that will lose you your livelihood. But what about the children who don't choose to have their faces and lives and stories out there? What about the youngsters who grow up with a camera in their face and a following they didn't start? Their parents make that choice and they have to live with the consequences.

\*

'I plead [with] you to be the voice of this generation of children because I know first-hand what it's like to not have a choice in which a digital footprint you didn't create follows you around for the rest of your life,' Cam Barrett, mentioned above, testified this year in front of Washington State's congress to try to pass House Bill 1627, a statute that would allow children to opt out of being used by their parents and other caregivers online.

They also told ABC News Live in a separate interview that their mother documented every area of their life from their first bikini to their first period to photographing instead of comforting them when they were in hospital after a car accident. In their testimony, Cam Barrett also said, 'If you Google my name, simply just my first name [their birth name] childhood photos of me in bikinis pop up and I'm terrified to have those weaponised against me again.'

When I was investigating the storyline of Brandee for the book, I found so many instances of parents who did not want to acknowledge or accept that they were harming their children in the present and creating a digital footprint that would blight their child's future. A lot of sharenters didn't want to accept that their vlogging put their children in harm's way for predators, online bullying, abuse, exploitation, inappropriate relationships as a result of having no boundaries and worse.

Sharenters often can't see how they are dehumanising their children by putting their difficult moments, their losses, huge swathes of their life that should be private on the internet. Seeing example after example of this really shook me. I was horrified that so often it seemed the parents who posted this stuff knew what they were doing and did it anyway because they liked the money and, even when there was no money to be made, they craved the attention.

## The rise of AI and Deep Fakes

I think, for me, the most horrifying aspects to so many children being put so completely online, is the intersection it has with the meteoric increase in the use of AI. One of the most nefarious uses of AI comes in the form of deep fakes where people are made to do and say things they haven't. Some recent, well-known victims of this include Sadiq Khan and Martin Lewis. However, there are more and more stories coming out of ordinary women being told by men they know that they've been seen starring in porn videos. Apparently, deep fakes have been created of their faces on other people's bodies and used in adult movies. These films often have the woman's full name with the videos so they come up when anyone does a search for them online.

And there is little these women can do since the videos are everywhere. So imagine what predators are now able to do with the images and videos of children they've saved from all this parenting content out there. Remember that fifty percent of images on porn forums being from parents social media accounts, statistic? This makes it all the more horrific.

## Is there hope?

Not all sharenters behave badly, I want to make that clear. Many of them see that a certain demographic is almost obsessively following their content and take action to stop their children being exposed in this way. Other parents I have seen remove video content at the request of their children. Others still change completely their content so it does not feature their children. It is possible to make money as a family vlogger without doing things that could be seen as exploiting your children.

As mentioned above, there are moves to make it more difficult to exploit children while making sure they are in control of their images and they are properly compensated for the content they make that brings in revenue. In 2020 in France, among other legal changes, a law was passed that created a 'right to be forgotten' for children of influencers, meaning that if a child requests it, social media and other internet platforms have to remove any videos or content of them.

In Illinois, America, a new law has been passed that states that influencers and bloggers must put into trust a percentage of the money made from content including the 'likeness, name, or photograph of the minor'. This percentage is dependent upon how heavily the content relies on the child, even if the child is just talked about and not shown. There's no right to privacy for the child in that law yet, but hopefully that will come.

## What can you do?

So, what can you do to keep your children safe online if you're in the family vlogging world?

1. Avoid, as much as possible, using your children's images, videos and voice for content.
2. If you can't avoid posting pictures of your children, then either blur your child's image or only show the back of them, and change their name for the videos. It goes without saying to NEVER post pictures of them in the bath, without clothes or even in swimwear. Think about where those images could end up.
3. Avoid posting identifying information such as their birthday, school uniforms/crests, the exact location of where you live. In other words, make it difficult for predators to find and follow your children.
4. Keep an eye on who is liking and saving your content – check their accounts to see what other sort of things they're

saving and posting, which other accounts they are following and what they do with that content.

5. Think about only posting content involving your children to a carefully curated audience.

I don't mind admitting that while I loved every second of writing *Every Smile You Fake*, it was an eye-opening experience. I saw some pretty terrible things that I had to distil into a compelling plot with believable characters for the book. My novel is based on the real-life experiences of many, many people. Even if a lot of the time I could hardly believe what I was seeing and knew readers of my book might have a hard time believing it either, I had to keep going. I hope that care and attention I put into the book comes across.

The internet is a wonderful place, but it can also be scary, sinister and damaging. Hopefully reading my book will give you an insight into the sorts of conversations you should be having with your friends, family, children and yourself.

The next time you go to post a picture of yourself or someone else online, do please ask yourself: where could this photo end up? What could be done with it in the wrong hands? And, do I really need to open up my private world to the worst side of the internet in this way?

Dorothy Koomson, 2024

*A version of this article first appeared in Black Ballad in January 2024. For more information visit* www.blackballad.co.uk.